CHICAGO RAILERS HOCKEY

MAKE ME YOURS

USA *Today* Bestselling Author
JENNIFER SUCEVIC

1
LILAH

"Where are you, darling? You're going to miss the start of the game," Aunt Evelyn asks as I rush through the doors of the building where I've worked as a lawyer for the last three years.

"I know, I know." I wrangle my Louis Vuitton bag onto my shoulder while digging around inside for my keycard. "I just need to fax some paperwork to a client for Devon. I found the file lying on the counter. Pretty sure he forgot to grab it this morning. It'll take two minutes, tops. Promise. And then I'll be over."

"That man is lucky to have you," she says lightly. "I certainly hope he realizes it."

Even though she doesn't tack on more, I'm sure she's dying to.

My godmother is not Devon Peterson's number one fan.

"He does," I force out with more confidence than I currently feel. The sound of my voice echoes off the empty corridor as I give Mike, the night guard, a wave while striding to the bank of elevators and taking one to the twenty-fifth floor where our law offices are located. "He's been working on a big case, and all his attention is focused there at the moment."

"Seems like that's how it always is, Lilah," she says gently from the other end of the line. "Maybe, just once, his attention should be on you."

"It is," I reply, a little too quickly. The lie slips out before I can stop it, and I wince.

There's a brief pause. The kind that says she heard everything I wasn't saying. "I hope so, sweetheart. You deserve that. Whoever you're with should make you feel like the most important person in the world."

"He does." Even as the words leave my lips, I realize they're not true.

Devon's life revolves around work. It always has. I knew that before we became a couple. Our families had been pushing us together since I was barely old enough to understand what dating meant. Once I started at his law firm, it just felt inevitable. Like the pieces had been arranged for us, and all we had to do was fall in line.

"Okay," she says, dropping the topic. That's one thing I love about Aunt Evelyn, she always senses when to back off, giving me the time and space to figure something out on my own.

Which is the opposite of my parents.

Even though I'm twenty-eight, they have *a lot* to say about my life. And most of it isn't good.

As soon as that thought pops into my head, I push it aside. It's been a long enough day already. I'm looking forward to unwinding at the game and watching the Chicago Railers demolish the Baltimore Baddies.

"Did you ever mention to Devon that you're not very happy and have been thinking about doing something else?" Evelyn asks, her motherly concern warming my heart despite my rush. "You know I'd give you a job at the arena in a heartbeat. Wouldn't that be fun? The two of us working together?"

"I doubt Hugh would be very happy about that."

While Aunt Evelyn owns forty-eight percent of the Railers,

Hugh Landry holds an equal stake in the team. For over twenty-five years, the two families have been at odds, which is why the remaining four percent, held by a third-party investor, often acts as the tiebreaker when they inevitably disagree. Aunt Evelyn never talks about it, but once upon a time, she and Hugh were engaged.

Until everything fell apart.

"That's just an added bonus to sweeten the deal," she says with a chuckle.

"You're bad, Aunt Evelyn."

"I know. It's part of my charm."

"Is he still trying to buy you out?"

"Of course. Although, that's not about to happen. This is my team and my family's name on the front of the building. I'm not going anywhere. Sooner or later, he'll have to realize it."

"Let's just hope hell doesn't freeze over first."

She grumbles before saying, "Getting back to Devon... You should just tell him you're not happy. If he loves you, he'll want the best for you."

"I haven't made any decisions yet." I chew my bottom lip as the elevator doors slide open and I step into the hallway. "What I need to do is find something I'm passionate about because law just isn't it."

"What about something that involves baking? You love puttering around in the kitchen."

That's more of a hobby, not a job.

"I need something I can make money at." I pause before adding, "And as appreciative as I am of the job offer, I don't think working at the arena is it either. I wish it were. It would make life so much easier."

"Darling, it was just an idea. What I want most for you is to be happy. You'll figure it out. Just give yourself time."

"I'm almost thirty. It feels like I should have my life together by now." My voice dips lower. "I thought by this point,

I'd be married, have a couple of kids, maybe a house in the suburbs."

"Please," Evelyn says with a laugh. "You're still young. Your whole life is stretched out in front of you. We'll brainstorm some ideas when you get here. Speaking of which, I know someone who'll be very upset if you don't show up soon."

Despite the heaviness of our conversation, my lips lift into a smile. "Steele will survive without his lucky charm at the game for five minutes." Even as I say it, I can picture the Railers star center's mock-wounded expression. He's been calling me his good luck charm ever since I started attending his games in college. Although, I'm pretty sure his talent and natural ability have more to do with his skills than my presence in the stands.

"I'll be there as soon as I can," I say, reaching for Devon's office door handle and pushing it open.

The sight that greets me has my entire world screeching to a halt before spinning off its axis. The room might be dimly lit, but there's more than enough light to see everything that's happening inside.

And I do mean *everything*.

Marissa, one of the firm's lawyers, is draped across Devon's desk as he pounds into her from behind. He's got a firm hold on her ponytail as his other hand grips her waist. Every thrust has a moan falling from her lips. His eyes are screwed shut as he continues to fuck her.

"Yeah, baby. That feels so good." He smacks her ass, and the crack of flesh rings throughout the room. "You like that, don't you?"

"God, yes," she groans. "No one's ever fucked me so hard."

My heart does this weird thing where it simultaneously stops and tries to leap out of my chest when he slaps her rounded backside for a second time. The phone in my hand feels more like a brick as it drops to my side.

I blink, unable to believe what I'm seeing.

There's no way this can be real.

I release a choked noise, and Devon's eyes fly open, meeting mine as his body stills. I'm frozen in place as our gazes stay locked from across the room.

"Fuck," he mutters.

"That's right, baby. Fuck me so hard I won't be able to walk in the morning," Marissa demands.

The worst part is the conflict that flashes across his face.

I clear my throat. "By all means, Devon, please finish, and make sure you give it to her hard."

With a gasp, Marissa jerks upright. Though, she doesn't get far with Devon's tight grip on her hair.

As I stare at them in morbid fascination, one thought keeps circling in my mind—

All the times we had sex, he never touched me like that.

Not once.

Maybe things between us would've been different if he had.

"What are you doing here, Lilah? I thought you'd be at the game by now," he asks.

My jaw drops.

The question hits harder than the slap to Marissa's perky ass.

What am I doing here?

The man can't even be bothered with a half-assed *this isn't what it looks like*, which, let's be honest, would have been laughable because it's *exactly* what it looks like.

"Seriously? That's all you have to say when I walk in on you fucking another woman?"

He pulls out of her before stuffing his softening cock back inside his slacks and zipping them. Marissa scrambles up, her hands fluttering over her rumpled skirt, attempting to smooth it back into place. Her silk blouse is hanging open, and there's lipstick smeared across her face. She averts her gaze without so much as an apology.

Instead of rushing for damage control, Devon exhales a slow and deliberate breath.

My heart slams painfully against my rib cage as I wait for an explanation.

"Lilah? Darling? What's going on?"

That's when I realize Aunt Evelyn is still on the phone.

With my gaze pinned to Devon, I raise my cell to my mouth. "Let me call you back."

I cut the connection with a single trembling press of my thumb. The rage that crashes over me is almost blinding as my hands shake with the fury boiling beneath my skin.

Devon clears his throat before straightening his tie. "What would you like me to say?"

My spine stiffens at his lack of contrition. "How about you're sorry for hurting me? That might be a good place to start."

He steps forward. "Would that change anything?"

I shake my head, the truth sinking in. "No. It won't."

"Then what's the point?"

My face scrunches as I parrot the question. "*What's the point?* Are you really asking me that?"

He settles on the edge of the desk. "Look, I'm sorry you walked in and saw what you did. I know that must've hurt."

My mouth drops open. "Is that your half-assed attempt at an apology?"

He drags a hand through his already mussed hair, looking nothing like the man I thought I knew and loved.

"I suppose it is," he says quietly.

A rough laugh breaks from my throat. It's hollow, disbelieving, and edged with more hurt than I care to admit.

I force my gaze from Devon and stare at the other person in the room.

Marissa.

"How long has this been going on for?"

Her eyes slice to Devon in silent panic.

"The very least you can do is give me an honest answer after you've fucked the man I've been living with."

Her tongue darts out to moisten her lips. "Four months."

This has been going on for four months?

The words reverberate through my head.

Then she whispers, "I'm pregnant."

"You're... *pregnant*?"

With a nod, she inches her way closer to Devon. "He was going to tell you this weekend."

Oh my God.

It's like a hatch opens up beneath me and I'm in free fall.

Is this really happening?

I refocus my attention on Devon even as my head continues to spin. "I-is it true?"

For the first time since I stumbled upon them, ruddy color floods his cheeks, and his gaze darts away. "Yeah, it is."

"Four months?" I shake my head as my knees weaken. Any moment now, I'm going to crumble to the floor. "Why didn't you tell me?"

"The situation is complicated," he says with a huff.

"Complicated? You're having a baby with another woman while living with me." When he presses his lips together, I raise my voice. "Were you ever going to tell me? Or were you just going to continue living a double life?"

His hand drifts to the back of his neck, rubbing it like he'd rather be anywhere but here.

That makes two of us.

"I was trying to figure out a way to break things off without hurting you."

A sharp laugh falls from my lips. "Well, congrats. You failed miserably on that front."

"It would seem that I did."

Marissa clears her throat and raises her brows at Devon.

Apparently, there's more.

For fuck's sake, how much worse could this get?

He shifts. "The two of us talked about it, and we feel that, given the situation, it would be best if you put in your notice."

My eyes widen. "You... want me to quit?"

Marissa sidles up to Devon before wrapping her arm around him and leaning into his side. "It would be awkward to have you around when this should be a happy and stress-free time for me." Her hand settles on her abdomen. "And our baby."

"You're absolutely right. I can see how my presence would be an uncomfortable reminder that you've been screwing my boyfriend behind my back for months."

Devon frowns before dropping a kiss against the top of Marissa's dark head. "There's no reason we can't handle this situation like adults."

"You've had months to wrap your brain around what you two have been up to. I, on the other hand, just stumbled across it. So, you'll have to excuse me if I'm still trying to play mental catchup."

The look he gives me is pitying, and I hate it. "Let's be honest, Lilah. Our parents talked us into this relationship, and for a while, it was easy and comfortable."

I nod, the sting replaced by a clarity I didn't have before walking through that door. He's not wrong. Our family connection helped me land the job and then our parents kept throwing us together at every opportunity.

"If you didn't want to be in a relationship, then you should have manned up and said something instead of lying to me, all the while screwing around behind my back with a colleague."

"It's not like we were friends," Marissa interjects.

As if that somehow makes it better.

Or absolves her.

"I guess that's why you had every right to take what was mine."

"He was never yours to begin with," she says quietly.

"Wow. Okay, I guess we're done here." Even though there's so much more I want to say, I keep it trapped inside. Instead, I reach up and tear my work badge from my blouse before tossing it onto his desk.

As I spin on my heel and stride to the door, Devon says, "I'll have all your belongings boxed up from the apartment. Just let me know where to send them."

Un-fucking-believable.

I straighten my spine. "Once I figure it out, you'll be the first to know."

Even though it's tempting to slam the door until it rattles on its hinges, I close it quietly behind me.

Fuck him.

And her.

Oh God… Devon and Marissa are not only having an affair, they're having a baby together. I want to double over with the pain that floods my system.

Is this really the same man who, just six months ago, laughed when I brought up the possibility of having children before letting me know that parenthood wasn't in his five-year plan?

And now he's having a baby with another woman.

My mind continues to spin and my hands tremble as I step inside the elevator. It takes forever as it descends to the lobby.

As I pass by Mike for a second time, he glances at the Chicago Railers jersey I'm wearing beneath my jacket. "Have fun at the game tonight, Ms. Monroe."

"Thanks, I will." I'm barely able to hold back the tears that prick my eyes.

When I finally step onto the street, the cool night air hits me hard, grounding me just enough to realize that my life has changed in the blink of an eye.

I'm jobless.

Homeless.

And the man I thought I'd one day marry is now my ex.

The weight of it all crashes down on me in an instant, leaving me frozen and unable to think about what happens next for me. Emotion bubbles up, threatening to break loose, and that's the last thing I want. I refuse to break down on this street, in front of the strangers rushing by. Or where Devon and Marissa can walk out of his office and see the damage they've inflicted firsthand.

Even though it feels impossible, I square my shoulders and walk down the street a few blocks to a small patch of greenery with a park bench. When my phone rings, I silence it without glancing at the screen.

There's no way I can talk to anyone right now.

Not when I'm feeling so scraped raw inside.

Not to mention, like such an idiot.

The entire time I sit on the bench, staring into space, I can't help but comb over the previous couple months, looking for clues of his infidelity. All the looks and conversations between them that I played off, scolding myself for being jealous. Clearly, I was right to be suspicious, and I should have listened to my instincts. Maybe then I wouldn't have been so blindsided.

I could have better protected myself.

It's only when I'm surrounded by total darkness that I fight my way out of the fog that has descended and glance at my phone.

It's a jolt to realize that three hours have slipped by and I've missed the game.

I need to go.

There's no way I can stay here.

But where to?

Devon's apartment is off the table. They're probably there right now, gleefully packing up my things like it's some kind of celebration.

Even though I'm outside with the chilly fall breeze whipping at my cheeks, it still feels like everything is closing in on me. Any moment, I'm going to have a panic attack.

I squeeze my eyes tightly closed and focus on drawing air into my lungs, holding it for a few beats before gradually releasing it back into the atmosphere. I do that over and over until my heart rate settles and I'm able to think clearly.

Only then do I pull my phone out of my pocket and order a car before noticing a slew of texts and missed calls from Steele.

I wince.

He's probably frantic by now.

For just a second, I consider calling him, but then I shove the phone back into my pocket. The moment I hear his voice, I'll end up breaking down. And that's the last thing I want to happen. This conversation is something that needs to be done in person.

As soon as the vehicle rolls up, I slide into the back seat and rattle off the address.

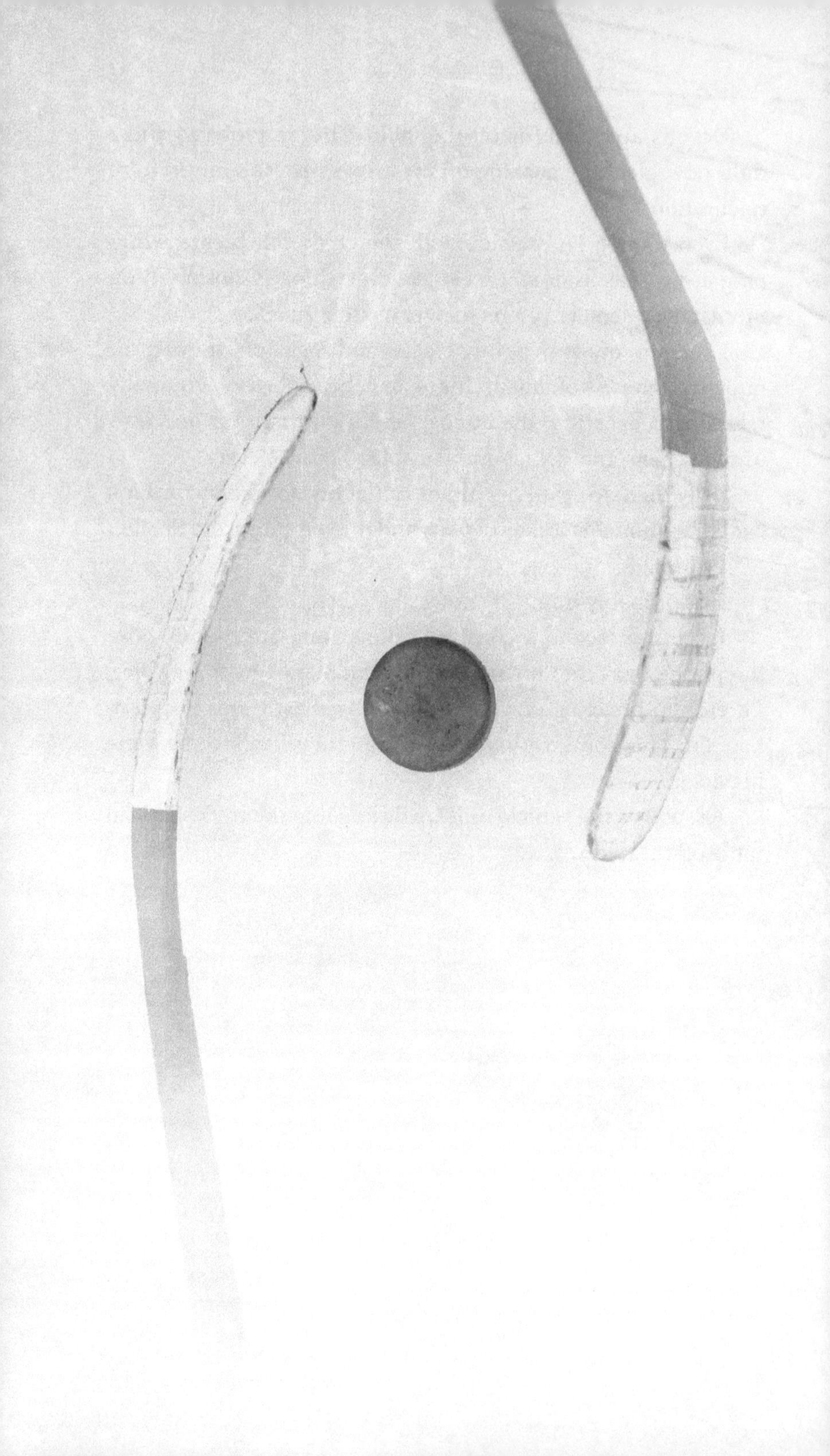

STEELE

I tighten my gloves and roll my shoulders before taking my position at center ice. The energy in the Kingston Landry Arena is electric. It's the kind that usually rushes through my veins and sharpens my focus.

But tonight, something's off.

I can feel it in my bones.

My gaze flicks up to the suite where Lilah always sits, only to find it empty.

I tell myself it's nothing.

That she's just running behind or maybe got stuck at work. Although she never mentioned she'd be late when we touched base earlier this afternoon. I've spent the last six years tracking her presence with the same precision I use to find the back of the net.

Tonight, she's a no show.

She hasn't missed a Railers home game since we both moved to Chicago after college.

"Lock in, Sanderson! You skating or sightseeing today?" Coach barks.

I'm already in motion, my stick connecting with the puck as I send it sailing past Laiken's shoulder into the goal.

Our starting goalie swears.

Normally that would be enough to make me grin.

I glance at the clock. There's eight minutes until the puck drops. Both teams are running through final warm-ups as the crowd files in. My stomach knots in a way that has nothing to do with pre-game jitters.

Knox McNichols, our right wing, skates up beside me. "You're doing it again."

"Doing what?"

"That thing where you pretend you're not looking for Lilah." He taps his stick against my shin guards. "While very obviously looking for her."

"I don't—" The protest dies in my throat as Evelyn Kingston, one of the team's owners and Lilah's godmother, stares down at me from the suite.

Alone.

Oliver Van Doren falls in line beside us, smacking his stick against mine. "It's almost showtime, Sanderson. You ready to wipe the ice with these guys?"

I force a smirk. "Couldn't be more ready."

The lights drop, and the crowd erupts into cheers. Twenty thousand fans rise to their feet as our intro video lights up the jumbotron. It's the same one I've seen a hundred times before, but tonight the highlight reel feels distant. Like I'm staring at it through a tunnel. I can't shake the worry that continues to eat me alive.

The spotlight hits center ice as our announcer's voice booms through the arena. "And now, please welcome the Baltimore Baddies!"

The visiting team skates out one by one as their lineup is announced. The crowd gives the standard mix of polite applause and half-hearted boos, all the while waiting for the real show to start.

The moment the last player takes position, the music shifts, the bass vibrating through my skates. Blue and silver lights sweep across the ice, and the volume inside the arena explodes.

"And now, ladies and gentlemen, please welcome your Chicago Railers!"

I roll my shoulders, shaking out my limbs as my teammates line up. Knox bounces on his skates beside me, a cocky grin plastered across his face.

"Starting in goal, number thirty-five, Laiken Lennox!"

Laiken glides out, lifting his stick to the thundering chants of "Lai-ken, Lai-ken!"

"At right defense, number twenty-three, River Thompson!"

River takes the ice to whistles and cheers.

"At left defense, number four, Jaxon Wilder!"

The spotlight sweeps over our zone, catching Jaxon as he loops around. Six years of these introductions, and my gaze always settled on Lilah. She'd be on her feet with everyone else, but she'd be watching me, not the show.

"At right wing, number eleven, Knox McNichols!"

Knox throws me a look before heading out, like he knows exactly where my head is.

"At left wing, number ninety-one, the big O, Oliver Van Doren!"

The roar builds as Oliver skates forward, fist-bumping Jaxon as he passes.

One more name.

"And your captain, at center, number nineteen, Steele Sanderson!"

I push off, muscle memory taking over as I glide onto the ice. The spotlight follows, the crowd thundering the entire time. As I take my usual lap around our zone, my eyes automatically lift to the suite.

Lilah's not there.

That's all it takes for my calm to fracture.

Where the hell is she?

I settle into position at center ice as my teammates fan out around me.

Knox nudges my shoulder. "Get your head in the game, Cap."

With a nod, I grip my stick tighter and force my expression into something neutral.

Captain's face.

Game face.

The ref skates in, puck in hand.

I bend forward, ready for the drop, but my gaze lifts one last time to the suite.

My lucky charm is still MIA.

The puck drops, and I surge forward, stick colliding with my opponent's. Normally, I'm locked in and focused on what needs to be done. But that's not the case tonight.

Without Lilah's presence, I feel off.

And I fucking hate it.

I take a shot, missing the net by a mile.

"Jesus," River mutters as he skates past. "What the hell was that?"

I grit my teeth, skating harder, trying to push through the frustration making my hands clumsy and my focus scattered.

By the time we hit the locker room between periods, I can feel the guys watching me, silent questions brimming in their eyes.

Oliver tosses me a towel. "Are you playing like shit for the fun of it or what?"

"Fuck off," I grumble, dragging a hand through my sweat-dampened hair.

He snorts. "I'm just saying, man. Maybe pretend like you give a damn about the game."

How can I respond when they're right?

I need to get my head out of my ass. As soon as the game is

over, I can find Lilah and make sure everything's okay. Until then, I need to focus.

I don't play any better during the third period. Thank fuck the guys are there to pick up the slack. The final buzzer sounds, and the crowd roars. My teammates throw their hands in the air as sticks tap against the ice in victory.

Even though it's another win under our belt, there's no pleasure to be found in it. I'd usually be caught up in the rush of the post-game high with them. But tonight, as I skate off the ice, there's only one thing dominating my mind.

Lilah.

I scan the stands one last time, searching for her face in the crowd.

She promised she'd be here.

The empty seat hits harder than I want to admit.

Where the hell is she?

With that jackass boyfriend of hers?

Even the thought of Devon Peterson is enough to make my jaw clench.

She deserves so much better.

Then again, I'm not sure there's a guy out there who's good enough for Lilah Monroe.

She's like the sun rising over the horizon—impossible to ignore and even harder to forget.

When Lilah's near, she's all I see.

All I feel.

All I want.

It's been that way since our freshman year of college, and nothing has changed. If anything, my feelings for her have only deepened, growing stronger with every year, every moment, every look.

The thought of her marrying that smug bastard makes my stomach twist.

Not just because I'd lose her.

But because I know deep in my bones that she doesn't belong with him.

She belongs with me.

To me.

The last time she had "big news" to share, I damn near had a heart attack.

I was convinced he'd proposed.

Instead, she'd gotten a promotion at work.

It was a relief.

But that fear hasn't gone anywhere.

Knox McNichols claps me on the back with a gloved hand. "Cheer up, fucker. We won tonight."

I grunt in response.

There isn't much that comes before hockey.

Lilah's the exception.

The second I step into the locker room, I yank off my gloves and toss them onto the bench as I reach for my cell. My pulse kicks up as my fingers tighten around the slim device and I unlock the home screen.

There's not a single message or missed call from her.

With a frown, I check my inbox.

Still nothing.

"What the fuck?" I mutter before firing off a text.

ME:

Where are you?

I strip off my jersey, grab a towel, and check again.

Nada.

ME:

Everything okay?

No response.

My jaw clenches, and I force myself to breathe through the unease clawing at my ribs.

ME:

Lilah. Call me. You're starting to scare me.

I swear to God, when I finally get my hands on that woman, I'll spank her damn ass. I groan as an image of bending her over my lap and smacking the rounded curve of her bottom shoves its way into my brain. The last place I need to pop wood is in the locker room with a bunch of naked dudes.

I'd never hear the end of it.

Jaxon Wilder watches me with a slow-growing smirk.

"Damn," he drawls, kicking back against his stall. "I didn't realize you were so whipped."

"Shut the fuck up," I snap, stuffing my gear into my locker with more force than necessary.

Jaxon raises his hands in surrender, but the grin remains firmly in place. He's the newest member of the Railers, having just come up from playing for a minor league team. "Relax, man. She probably got held up at work."

Maybe.

Although my gut is telling me there's more to the story.

And the one thing about my gut is that it's never wrong.

By the time we walk into The Rail Yard thirty minutes later, I'm wound so tight I can barely sit still. The place is packed with the usual post-game crowd, buzzing with energy. A flickering neon sign says "Da Bar" in glowing blue letters. Inside, brick walls and dim lighting give it a gritty charm. It's the kind of hole-in-the-wall place you only find if you know what you're looking for. A stuffed bear wearing a Railers jersey stands guard in the corner, and hockey memorabilia—signed pucks, vintage sticks, framed jerseys—fills every inch of wall space. Music hums through the speakers as conversations blend together.

The only thing I'm able to focus on is the weight of my cell in my hand.

I head to our usual booth in the back and drop down onto the seat. The waitress delivers a beer that I barely touch as my knee bounces under the table.

I can't stop checking my phone every two minutes.

"No word yet?" Knox asks, lounging across from me, his arms sprawled over the back of the booth. A few girls vie for his attention. There's never a shortage of them buzzing around, hoping to capture his interest. Much like his older brother, Colby McNichols, Knox is a favorite with the ladies. It's doubtful he'll settle down anytime soon. His career has exploded over the past season, bringing him even more attention, not to mention sponsorship deals, than before. He's on his way to becoming a household name.

With a shake of my head, my gaze combs over the crowd for what feels like the millionth time. "Nope."

"I'm sure she's fine." There's a pause. "She still with that lawyer boyfriend? The pompous one?"

My jaw tics. "Yup."

Unfortunately.

"It's always possible she's with him. It's kind of a normal girlfriend thing to do."

My eyes narrow as I glare at him. "She never misses a home game."

Oliver drops onto the seat next to Knox. "Here's a thought. Maybe it's time to stop pining for her and move the fuck on."

Perfect.

Just what I need.

Another unwanted opinion.

Knox nudges our teammate. "Ouch. That's some tough love right there."

Oliver shrugs. "Look around, Sanderson. There's not a girl in this place who wouldn't drop her panties if you even looked in their direction. All you have to do is wipe the scowl off your ugly mug and give someone the green light to proceed. How long has it been since you got laid? A few weeks?" When I remain silent, his brows rise. "Please don't tell me it's been longer than that."

I press my lips together and refocus my attention on our teammates who are horsing around near the bar. "Don't you have someone else to bother?" I grouse.

A smile spreads across his face. "Come on, Cap. You know you're the only one I want to bother."

Knox, the asshole, decides to jump on the bandwagon and give me shit. "Damn. I didn't realize it had been so long. No wonder you're wound tight."

Before I can tell them both to mind their own damn business, Knox snags a random woman walking past by the wrist. "Hey, sweetheart."

When she glances at him, he flashes a dimpled smile, and she just about swoons on the spot.

I can't help but roll my eyes.

The effect he has on women should come with a warning label. His brother was the same way in college before the future Mrs. McNichols knocked him on his ass.

Knox jerks his head in my direction. "Any idea who the guy over there is?"

She's barely able to take her eyes off Knox long enough to meet my stare. "Sure. I know who all of you are."

"Perfect," Knox says. "How'd you like to—"

And that would be my cue to leave.

I rise from my seat before the question is fully out of his mouth. The last thing I need is pity sex.

Little do these clowns know that it's been way more than a few weeks since I slept with a woman.

Try eighteen months on for size.

I drag a hand down my face, unable to believe it's been that long.

"I'm going to grab another beer from the bar," I mutter,

wanting to get away from this conversation. None of these guys understand the depth of my feelings for Lilah. Once I finally came to terms with it myself, there didn't seem much point in getting tangled up with other women.

Even if it's just to blow off a little steam.

"Come on, Sanderson, don't run away like that," Knox calls after me, humor simmering in his voice.

I flip him the bird and keep on moving.

LILAH

The scent of beer, fried food, and something sweet—maybe caramelized onions from the kitchen—wraps around me as I push open the heavy wooden door of The Rail Yard.

Normally, it's comforting in a way that feels like home.

Tonight, the sights and sounds around me barely register. My legs feel like lead, and my body is running on fumes as my mind replays the moment I walked in on Devon. My hands shake as I bury them in my jacket pockets, not to ward off the chill but to keep my emotions in check.

Any second, I'm going to crumble.

I scan the crowd inside. It's not a surprise to find the place packed. Game nights are always like this. All the diehard fans want to celebrate with the team.

For just a moment, my heart clenches with the fear that he won't be here.

What will I do then?

Even though I've been operating on autopilot, I need to find Steele. When my world is falling apart, he's the only one able to comfort me.

It never crossed my mind that I might not be able to find him.

Or that he might be otherwise engaged. That thought settles at the bottom of my belly like a heavy stone. It's enough to have bile rising in my throat.

I pause as my gaze lands on a few of his teammates. The first is Laiken, the Railers' goalie. He's older, probably around thirty-three or thirty-four. He's handsome in a gruff way, and quiet. I've always found the scruff on his face attractive. He's the kind of guy who likes to keep to himself. It's actually a surprise that he's here since he has a young daughter who's the focus of his life. If that doesn't melt your heart, then you're made of stone.

Then there's River Thompson. He's blond, blue-eyed, and muscular. We didn't attend the same college, but his twin sister is married to Maverick McKinnon, one of Steele's former college teammates from Western University. River's deep in conversation with Knox McNichols as a handful of women vie for their attention.

No surprise there.

I can only imagine that both of their apartments are a revolving door of females.

Oliver—"the big O" as he's known by the Railers fans—Van Doren and Jaxon Wilder have their heads bent together as they laugh. A few groupies hang on their arms.

Just when I consider turning around and walking out of the bar, I catch sight of Steele. There's a frown on his face as he stares down at his phone. Laiken claps him on the shoulder and points in my direction. Steele's head snaps up before swiveling toward me.

As soon as our gazes collide, everything inside me loosens.

Relief flashes across his face before he's moving, cutting a direct path through the crowd. By the time I manage another shuddering breath, he's standing in front of me.

The jumble in my brain melts away as I stare up at him, my heart hammering against my ribs, my throat tight with pent-up emotion.

In silence, Steele scans my face. I can only imagine what a mess I am after crying for hours. There is so much tension in my shoulders that the weight of it presses down on me. It's a wonder I don't buckle under the intense pressure.

Even though a muscle in his jaw twitches, he doesn't ask any questions or push for answers. Instead, he reaches out, his hands landing gently but firmly on my arms. That's all it takes to ground me in the here and now. His warmth seeps through my jacket and into my skin. It's both solid and steady, like an anchor that keeps me from drifting away.

"Lilah."

The sound of my name sliding from his lips is enough to snap the last thread of composure I've been clinging to. My eyes burn and my body quakes, the emotion crashing through me as I press my face into the quiet strength of his chest.

He catches me immediately. One arm bands around my back before tugging me closer as the other slides up to cradle my head like I'm a small child. His body is warm, strong, and steady.

I didn't realize just how much I needed his strength until this moment.

My fingers clutch at the fabric of his shirt as my shoulders shake.

Even now, he doesn't pelt me with questions.

His grip tightens, holding me close.

For the first time since walking in on Devon and Marissa, the storm inside me settles.

I have no idea how long we stand here wrapped up in each other's arms.

When I'm finally able to find my voice, it's scraped raw. "I'm so sorry about missing your game."

"What happened? I couldn't focus without you there. I was worried."

I groan, hating that my drama has affected him. Hockey has always been Steele's number one priority. The last thing I want to do is interfere with his game.

When I fail to respond, he pulls away just enough to search my eyes with narrowed ones. "Are you going to tell me what happened? Or do I have to drag it out of you? Because we both know I will."

Honestly, I'd rather not tell Steele what occurred. I can already predict how he's going to react. He never liked Devon.

Oh, Steele has always been polite, but after all these years, I know him well enough to realize when he's faking it. Not that I ever mentioned it, but Devon constantly complained Steele and I spent too much time together. He'd tell me that men and women could never be just friends. I always disagreed, insisting that Steele was more like a brother than anything else, even though I knew deep down it was a lie.

In all the years I've known Steele, I have never once thought of him as a sibling.

His fingers slip beneath my chin, drawing me back to the present. "Tell me what happened."

His voice dips as a hard edge fills it. The deep baritone is enough to send a shiver racing down my spine before settling in my core. I quickly stomp it out.

As tempting as it is to underplay the situation, the last thing I'm going to do is cover for that cheating sack of shit.

"I walked in on Devon screwing Marissa in his office." A slight tremor runs through me as I add, "On his desk, if you want to get specific."

I still can't believe how he'd been fucking her. The image is burned into my mind, and I can't stop replaying it, no matter how hard I try.

The total abandonment on his face.

Steele stiffens. His grip tightens, and his jaw locks for a beat before he exhales sharply through his nose. "Are you serious?"

"And that's not even the most brutal part," I whisper, desperate to get it all out.

"What could possibly make it worse?"

"She's pregnant."

It's almost comical the way his eyes widen. Any moment now, they're going to fall out and roll around on the floor.

He drags me closer before dropping a kiss on the crown of my head. "I'm so sorry, Lilah. You didn't deserve that. Any of it. I know how much you cared about him."

As soon as the words leave his lips, I realize how wrong they are. It's true, I did care about Devon, but there'd been a lot of cracks in our relationship I hadn't wanted to share.

"Thanks. I'm sure that was painful for you to say."

He snorts as a slight smile lifts his lips. "We both know he was never good enough for you. I've been telling you that from day one."

"True. But you say that about every guy I introduce you to."

"And I stand one hundred percent behind every single instance. None of them have ever been good enough." There's a pause. "So, what happens now? I mean, you're not going to continue working for him, are you?"

I can almost see the way Steele is gearing up for a fight.

"Nope, I quit."

"Thank fuck. There was no damn way I was going to let you go back."

"It would probably be more accurate to say Devon asked that I not return."

"That spineless son of a bitch," he growls.

"Pretty much."

"So, where are you going to stay?"

Emotion wells inside me as I shake my head. I don't think I've ever felt so lost or alone in my life. "I don't know. I haven't gotten that far yet. I'm sure I could stay with Rina or maybe Ev—"

"No way. You'll stay with me," he says, cutting me off. "End of discussion."

I shake my head, already protesting, ready to tell him that I'll figure it out on my own. He doesn't need to swoop in and save me.

"No arguing, lucky charm." His voice is steady and unwavering. "It's already a done deal."

His nickname for me hits me in the feels.

It's the exact balm I need after the past couple hours.

With a tilt of my chin, I search his eyes. "I don't want to get in your way."

He snorts. "Give me a break. My place is huge. You said so yourself when you helped pick it out. It's the perfect spot for you to sort through everything."

There's not a shred of doubt in his expression.

I swallow hard as my stomach twists. My emotions are stretched so tight, I don't know what to do with them anymore.

Even though I should tell him no, my resistance is already crumbling. "Are you sure? I don't know how long it'll take for me to find another job or a place to live."

"There's no pressure. Take as long as you need." He reaches for my hand and laces our fingers together before tugging me in just enough to let me know this isn't an offer.

It's a decision.

One that's already been made.

I hate to admit just how comforting it is to know that, no matter what happens in life, Steele will always be my soft place to land.

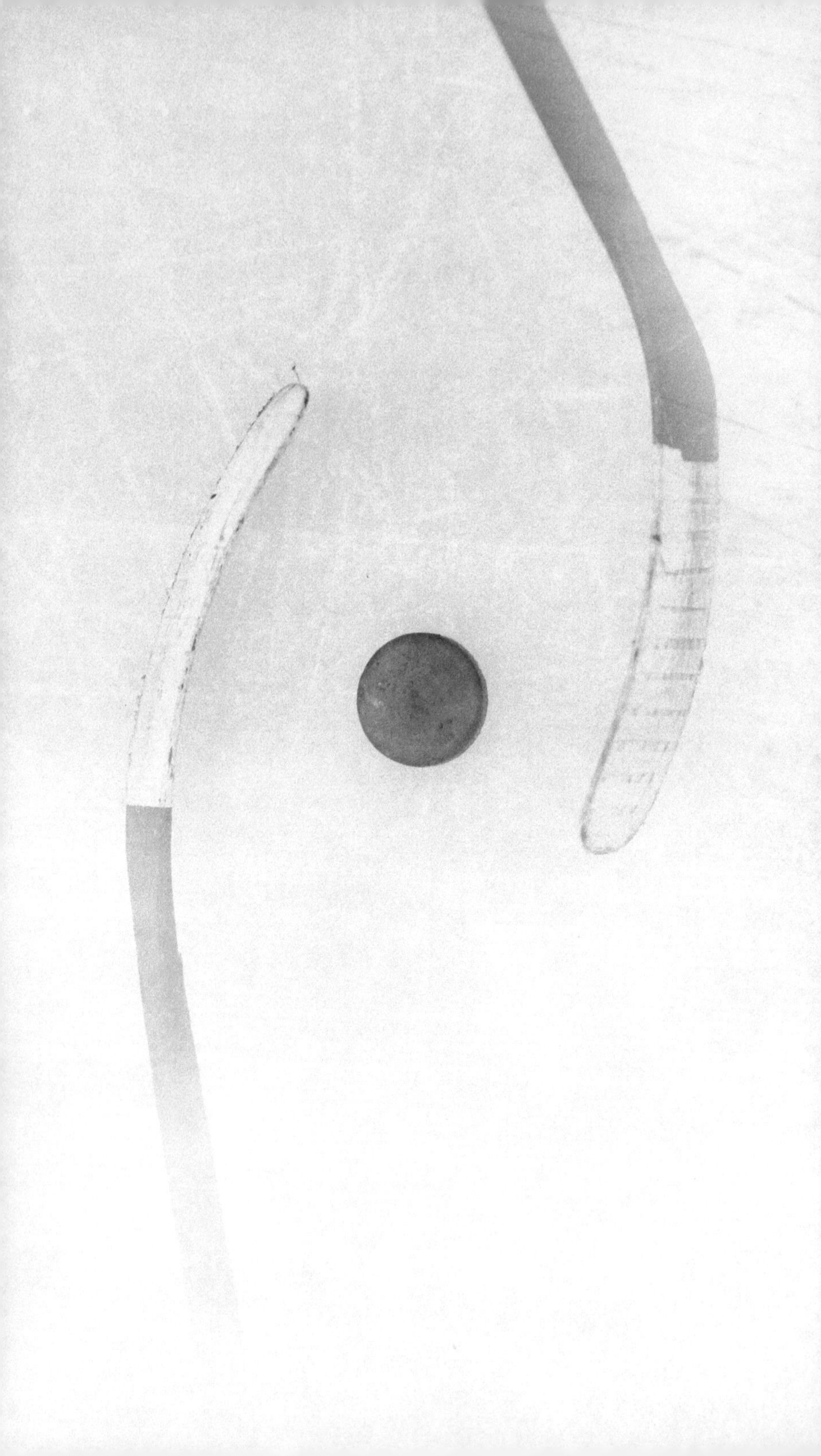

STEELE

The roads glow beneath the streetlights, slick with the remnants of an earlier rain. Chicago is one city that never really sleeps. The hum of traffic in the distance, the faint wail of a siren cutting through the night, the glow of shop signs casting flickering reflections against the wet pavement. It all pulses around me, steady and alive.

Inside the car, there's nothing but silence.

One hand grips the wheel as the other taps against my thigh. The restless energy buzzing through my veins makes it impossible to sit still. Lilah is huddled in the passenger seat, her body turned slightly toward the window, her face illuminated by the neon red of a passing taillight. She hasn't said much since we left The Rail Yard.

I'm sure she's still processing what happened. Overanalyzing everything about their relationship and how it ended.

"Are you okay?" I ask.

Her exhale is barely audible over the smooth glide of the tires against the pavement. "I don't know."

That answer doesn't sit right with me, and my fingers clench around the wheel. "It'll just take time to make your peace with what happened. That's all. Once the shock wears off, you'll be fine."

"You're right." She glances at me. "I know I said it before, but I really want you to know how much I appreciate you letting me stay at your place. You've always been there when I needed you." The corners of her lips tip upward. "You're a good friend."

Even though her words shouldn't be a dagger to my heart, that's exactly what they are. I force a smile in response. Lilah has always been oblivious to my feelings. And I've been too chickenshit to put them out there and rock the boat. I've been afraid to make her feel uncomfortable. There's no way I can lose her.

What the hell would I do if that happened?

Her presence in my life is the one thing I'm unwilling to risk.

"No matter what happens, I'll always be there for you," I say, flicking my turn signal on just before I pull into the private garage beneath my building. The underground parking structure is dimly lit, and the air is thick with the scent of concrete, oil, and rain carried in from the street.

The elevator ride up to my apartment is made in silence. From the corner of my eye, I watch Lilah fidget, shifting from one foot to the other as she chews her bottom lip. It's so damn tempting to pull her into my arms and offer comfort.

A few seconds later, the doors slide open, revealing the sprawling penthouse I bought two years ago when I signed another contract with Chicago. Floor-to-ceiling windows stretch across the length of the wall opposite us, displaying a glittering, uninterrupted view of Lake Michigan. The water in the distance is dark and vast, the city skyline reflecting off its surface. From this height, Chicago looks almost peaceful, the noise from the street muted, the flashing lights just tiny specks against the night.

Lilah hesitates in the cavernous entryway as her fingers tighten around the strap of her purse. "Last chance, Sanderson. Are you absolutely sure about this?" she asks. "Evelyn will let me stay with her until I can get my shit together."

Over my dead body is that happening.

I take her purse and drop it on the credenza near the elevator. "I've already told you that I want you here."

With a sigh, she rubs her arms as her gaze wanders around the space. "I'm serious about not wanting to get in your way."

I roll my eyes before slipping an arm around her waist and steering her into the living room. I'm almost afraid she's going to try and make a run for it. Little does she know, I'm not above tackling her to the floor.

As soon as I make contact, a sizzle of electricity zips through my fingers. How doesn't she feel the energy we always seem to generate?

There's no damn way this is one-sided.

"You won't. Look around. There's plenty of space. Didn't you tell me when I bought the place that it was roomy enough for a family of six?"

Her lips twitch as I sling her words back at her. "It is."

"And you love the views of the lake," I add, trying to throw in any perk I can think of to secure her agreement. "Not to mention the gym on the fifth floor. Did I tell you they added a sauna?"

"Hmm. That does sound nice."

"I used it the other day. It's heaven. Especially after a workout."

"All right. You've convinced me. I'll stay." She points a finger at me. "But only because of the sauna."

And just like that, the tension inside me eases. Instead of giving her time to think—or worse, change her mind—I steer her toward the guest room situated directly across from mine.

Would I prefer for Lilah to share my bed?

Hell yeah.

But that's not going to happen.

What she needs right now is time.

Time to realize that Devon was never the right guy for her.

Time to realize that maybe the right one has been standing in front of her all along.

I nudge open the guest room door and gesture for her to move inside. "Here you are."

She takes a step in, then beelines to the king-sized bed. Her fingers trail along the pillowcase. "I love these sheets."

I lift a shoulder in a half-shrug. "You should. You're the one who picked them out. You told me they were the best. Something like a bazillion thread count."

"One thousand. And they're Egyptian cotton," she corrects before turning toward the dresser where there's a basket of neatly arranged products.

She picks up a small bottle and stares at it as her brows tug together. "Funny. This is the same brand of shampoo and conditioner I use."

I rub a hand along my jaw, embarrassed that she noticed. How can someone be so oblivious in some areas of her life and so detail oriented in others?

It's a real fucking mystery.

"Yeah, I've always liked the scent."

"Huh." She pops open the top and takes a whiff. "Me too. There's just something so comforting about tea tree and mint."

I glance away and try to play it off. "Guess I figured you might need it at some point."

With an exhale, she cocks her head and stares at me, as if only now realizing that I'm a puzzle she might not have all the pieces to.

Her throat works as she swallows. And for a moment, the air turns charged between us.

I look away first, not wanting her to read too much in my

expression. "You can use them while relaxing in a hot bath. Sound good?"

It's exactly what she needs to decompress.

Without waiting for a response, I walk into the adjoining bathroom and twist the knobs, running warm water into the deep soaking tub. It doesn't take long before steam rises in the air, thick with the scent of the orange and ginger bath salts I dumped in.

Another one of her favorites.

"Steele, I can do—"

"You've had a rough day, lucky charm. Just let me take care of you for once." I grab a fluffy towel from the closet and set it on the marble counter.

Lilah leans against the doorframe, watching me in silence. When she finally speaks, her voice is barely above a whisper. "My favorite bath salts too? You're better than a five-star hotel. Maybe I'll never move out."

She has no damn idea how much I'd love that.

I shrug. It takes effort to keep my tone light. "Like the shampoo and conditioner, they smell good."

She blinks before looking down at the swirling water.

I clear my throat and take a step back, jerking my chin toward the tub. "Go have a nice soak. Did you eat dinner?"

"No, the plan was to grab something at the game." Her brows pinch as sadness flickers in her eyes. "But I never made it to the arena."

It feels like someone has wrapped their hand around my heart and is squeezing the life out of it.

I fucking hate seeing her this upset.

Especially over that asshole.

He's not worth it.

The fact that he cheated on Lilah blows my mind.

How could any man even look in another woman's direction if Lilah Monroe belonged to him?

It just proves my point that he was never worthy of her in the first place. He never treated her the way he should have. This girl deserves to be pampered and adored. Before I can think better of it, I swallow up the space between us and reach out, tugging her into my arms. As soon as they're banded around her, she melts against me.

I rest my chin on the top of her head. "Everything will be all right. I promise."

She hesitates for a second before her muscles loosen. "I know. It just…"

"Hurts," I finish for her.

"Yeah. I really didn't expect it. I never thought Devon was the kind of guy who would sneak around behind my back. All it does is make me question my own judgment, you know?"

For just a heartbeat, I pull her even closer. What I really want to do is hunt the bastard down who hurt her and make him feel just a fraction of the pain he caused a woman who deserved so much more.

Even though the last thing I want to do is set her free, I force my arms to drop and take a step in retreat. "Take your bath, and I'll figure out dinner." I pat my belly. "I'm famished."

Some of the sadness fades as she smirks. "What else is new? You're always hungry. How you manage to keep your girlish figure, I'll never know."

I lift a brow and tease, "So you've been checking out my figure, huh?"

A flush creeps into her cheeks as she looks away. "Don't be ridiculous."

The words land sharper than I expect.

And yet, I just smile through it like I always do, even as something constricts inside me. Because no matter how many times I tell myself to move on, it's clear she only sees me as a friend.

Maybe I really am a glutton for punishment. Maybe some

part of me would rather stay close and secretly pine for her than walk away from the only woman I've ever loved.

I clear my throat, needing to pick up the tattered pieces of my ego and get the hell out of here. "Take as much time as you need. When you're ready to eat, the food will be waiting."

"Thanks again, Steele. You're a good friend."

And the hits just keep coming.

After ten years, maybe it's not possible to find my way out of the friend zone.

I disappear into the kitchen to figure out what can be rustled up.

Thirty minutes later, Lilah walks out of the bedroom looking a hell of a lot more relaxed than when she walked into the penthouse. Steam clings to her skin in tiny droplets, and she's wearing the gray Western Wildcats hockey T-shirt I laid out for her since she doesn't have a change of clothes. It's a few sizes too big, hanging off one shoulder as the frayed hem brushes against her thighs.

She tugs at the edge of the worn material. "The sweatpants you left were way too big and kept falling down."

Well, fuck me.

Not wanting to pop wood, I swallow hard before turning back to the kitchen counter. "Should I grab something else for you?"

"Nah." There's a beat of silence before she adds, "As long as you're good with it."

"I don't mind at all," I murmur. "I can crank up the heat if you get cold."

"I'm fine," she says.

"Good." I clear my throat, forcing my gaze away from the long stretch of her bare legs. "I, uh, hope you're hungry."

She walks closer, stopping at the marble island where I've set up two plates with takeout. "Mmm, Chinese. My favorite."

I nod, satisfied with the spread. "I figured you needed some comfort food. Fried rice, sesame chicken, and eggrolls."

Her lips press together, and for a second, it looks like she might burst into tears.

Instead, she takes a moment to collect herself before sliding onto the leather stool and picking up her chopsticks.

A comfortable silence falls over us as I work up the nerve to casually float an idea by her. "Not sure if I mentioned it before, but I've been thinking of hiring a personal assistant."

She pauses mid-bite and cocks her head. "Really? I don't think you did."

"Yeah," I say smoothly, grabbing my beer. "We both know I suck at keeping my schedule straight, and Rina has been up my ass about it." I pause, allowing that to sink in before moving forward with my plan. "I was thinking that maybe you could help me out. Temporarily, of course."

With narrowed eyes, she sets her chopsticks down on her plate. "Did you just make that up?"

I shake my head. "Of course not. A lot of the guys on the team have them."

When she swivels toward me, I keep my eyes pinned to hers instead of allowing them to drop to where the cotton T-shirt rides up her thighs, showcasing even more mouthwatering flesh.

It's not easy.

Especially when an image of dropping to my knees and spreading her legs wide pops into my brain. She can enjoy her sesame chicken and I'll just—

Fuck.

I shove the thought from my head and refocus on securing her agreement.

A frown tugs at her lips. "Seriously, Steele. You don't need to jump in and save me. I'm more than capable of taking care of myself. And I have some money saved up. I'll be all right for a few months."

"Hey, I totally agree. You're more than capable of taking care of yourself. I just figured that since you're in between employment opportunities and I'm looking for someone to help me out, it would be a win-win for both of us. Plus, you're friends with Rina. It would be a seamless transition for all involved. When you think about it like that, it kind of seems like kismet, doesn't it?"

"Or maybe you're just looking for an excuse to keep me around," she mutters.

I clutch my chest in mock offense. "Ouch. I didn't think I needed an excuse to keep you close, lucky charm."

Her fingers toy with the hem of her shirt. "Sorry, that came out wrong. You know I didn't mean it like that."

"I do. Plus, you love bossing me around. What could be better than getting paid for it?"

Even though she rolls her eyes, a small smile simmers around the corners of her lips. "Aren't you going to get sick of having me underfoot all the time? We'll be working and living together. Sounds like a recipe for disaster."

The real problem is that I'm not sure if spending 24/7 with Lilah would be enough to feed the insatiable need I have for her.

Although, it's probably best to keep that thought to myself.

No need to freak her out.

"Nah, not possible." When she stares down at her plate with a furrowed brow, I say, "So, any interest in filling the position? I hear it pays well, and if you do a good job, you'll probably get a fat raise in no time. Also, the boss is a real softie. Sounds like a pretty sweet arrangement, if you ask me."

A sigh slips free from her as she shakes her head. "Steele..."

"Don't even say it."

There's a moment of silence. "Okay."

I lift a brow as my pulse leaps. "Really?"

"Yeah, I'll do it. But, like you said, it's only temporary until I figure out a new plan."

"Sure, sure. Not a problem."

At this point, I'd say just about anything to secure her agreement.

By the time we finish eating, the tension has drained from her body. For the first time since I found her at the bar, Lilah doesn't look afraid of what comes next.

And damn, if that doesn't feel like the first real win of the night.

5
LILAH

I wake up wrapped in the most luxurious sheets imaginable, cocooned in warmth. My body sinks into the mattress like it was made just for me. For one blissful second, I forget about everything that happened yesterday.

The betrayal.

The heartbreak.

The fact that I'm not in the apartment I shared with Devon but alone in Steele's guest room.

The moment I crack open my eyes, it all comes rushing back like a tsunami.

The image of Devon bending Marissa over his desk, fucking her from behind, slapping her ass and yanking her hair while he whispered filthy things that he never once said to me.

Who the hell was that man?

Because it sure wasn't the one I thought I knew.

To top it off, Marissa's expecting Devon's baby, and I was asked to vacate my position so as not to upset the newly pregnant mama. It's tempting to pull the pillow over my face and scream until all the oxygen has been depleted from my body.

How has this shitshow become my reality?

The idea of telling my parents I'm now jobless, homeless,

and single, makes my stomach turn. I'm a grown woman. What they think shouldn't matter.

And yet, it does.

They adore Devon and his family. They used to call us a power couple, convinced we were destined to take over Chicago.

That's a conversation I'm going to put off for as long as humanly possible.

Just thinking of looking for another position as a corporate lawyer depresses the hell out of me. It just feels so soulless.

And, yeah, boring.

For the first time in my life, my path isn't clearly marked. I'm not operating on autopilot.

Instead of panicking, I'm just tired.

Tired of chasing something I'm not even sure I want.

Tired of pretending I don't feel like I've been living someone else's version of success.

Maybe I want something different.

Something my parents or Devon didn't shove me into.

This breakup didn't just crack my relationship.

It shook the entire foundation of everything I thought I wanted.

Now I'm standing in the rubble, trying to figure out if I built any of it for me.

With a groan, I flop onto my side and bury my face in the pillow. Even though this isn't Steele's room, the sheets smell faintly like him. Clean and woodsy, with a hint of cedar. It's a scent so familiar it tugs at something buried within me. I inhale deeply before I can stop myself as my fingers clutch the edge of the pillow like it will somehow anchor me in this moment.

That's when I register that I'm still wearing Steele's old Western Wildcats T-shirt from last night. Maybe that's why his scent surrounds me like a warm blanket. Back in the day, I used to steal it from his dorm room and refuse to give it back. I'd joke that it was my lucky T-shirt, something to wear when I needed comfort.

But this time, I didn't have to steal it.

After my bath last night, I found it neatly folded on the bed.

Somehow, the man always knows what I need. Even when I don't realize it myself.

With a sigh, I push myself up and rub my hands over my face, which is exactly when I spot the steaming cup of coffee sitting on the nightstand.

Right next to a covered breakfast plate that's still warm.

There's a sticky note stuck to the side of the plate with Steele's messy handwriting scrawled across it.

Eat. You'll feel better. I have practice this morning, but I'll be back later. Don't even think about trying to leave. - S

I blink, my throat suddenly too tight.

Devon never did anything thoughtful like make me breakfast in bed or bring me coffee. I pick up the cup and take a sip, the warmth spreading through me. My eyelids feather closed as I savor the delicious cinnamon flavor.

And Devon certainly didn't pay attention to how I like my coffee either.

But Steele has.

I scroll through my phone while eating, catching up on the wreckage that is now my life. There are half a dozen missed calls from Evelyn and a bombardment of texts in the group chat with the girls. There was no way I could keep it all to myself last night.

CALLIE:

Come to the bakery. We'll have coffee, pastries, and a safe space to plot Devon's doom.

RINA:

I second that. No judgment. Only caffeine, carbs, and girl therapy.

SLOANE:

I'll bring the extra whipped cream. And possibly a baseball bat. Just say the word.

CALLIE:

Seriously, Lilah. We've got you. Come hang with us. Please?

A fresh wave of emotion crashes through me. It's different from yesterday. This one feels lighter.

Hopeful.

I type out a reply.

ME:

I'll be there. Thanks.

There's also one unread text from Steele.

STEELE:

You better be eating that breakfast.

Unable to help myself, I huff out a laugh and shake my head.

Of course he'd check.

How did I go from dating a man who never noticed anything, to waking up in the home of someone who knows my favorite breakfast down to the smallest detail?

Aside from Steele being my friend for the last decade, I don't have an answer.

More than that, it's not something I want to dwell on.

Not when I'm feeling so raw.

Damaged.

After breakfast, I take a long shower before pulling on a new T-shirt and a pair of Steele's boxers.

The first thing on the agenda is reaching out to Devon and telling him where to send my belongings. He and Marissa probably boxed them up last night so he could move her right in. Even though I didn't leave my job on my own terms, it's a relief that I won't have to see either one of them again.

Just when I'm trying to figure out what to wear, my phone buzzes with another message from Steele.

STEELE:

Tommy at the front desk is bringing up a
delivery for you. He'll leave it in the entryway.

There's the distant ding of the elevator and another noise before the doors slide shut again. I pad barefoot through the hallway before peeking around the corner to find three large shopping bags from one of my favorite stores.

With pinched brows, I step closer before glancing in the bags. They're filled with jeans, sweaters, T-shirts, panties, bras, socks, and three pairs of shoes. I check the tags, amazed to find everything in my size.

How did he know?

Even more surprising is there isn't anything I don't love or wouldn't wear.

I truly don't understand how some woman hasn't snapped Steele up yet. The man is perfect husband material.

An hour later, I step inside Lakeshore Sweets. The scents of cinnamon, espresso, and vanilla cocoon me in comfort. It's still early enough that the bakery buzzes with a low, cozy energy. Pastries are cooling on wire racks, there's the faint hiss of the espresso machine behind the counter, and Callie, Sloane, and Rina are gathered at a corner table with their coffees in hand.

The three of them are more than just my friends. They're my people. The ones who would show up with baseball bats or bottles of wine, depending on what the situation required.

Callie spots me first, her warm brown eyes flooding with concern. She rises from her chair without a word and then pulls me into a hug so tight it nearly cracks my ribs.

"Oh, honey," she murmurs against my hair. "I'm so sorry."

The dam inside me threatens to break, but I rein it in and pull back with a small smile. "Thanks."

Rina, dressed in a sharp black blazer, leans back in her chair and raises a brow. "Do we need to slash some tires? Because I brought a sharp object, and I'm not afraid to use it."

Sloane, lounging with her coffee cup balanced between two fingers, smirks. "Or we could leave a glitter bomb in his gym bag. Emotional damage and a cleanup nightmare."

I laugh—the first real one in what feels like forever—as I slide into the empty chair they've saved for me. "Thanks for the offers, but no sabotage necessary."

"For now," Rina says darkly, sipping her latte.

Callie nudges a plate across the table. It's got my favorite on it—a warm almond croissant drizzled with just the right amount of glaze. "Eat first. Plot second."

I blink against the sudden sting in my eyes. "I don't know what I'd do without you all."

"Good thing you'll never have to find out," Sloane says, flashing a grin.

I break off a piece of croissant, more to keep my hands busy than because I'm actually hungry. "I'm still in shock."

"No one can blame you for that," Callie says gently. "What you walked in on was awful."

I take in the rich, buttery scent of the pastry, letting it settle something inside me. "I never thought he would betray me like that."

"Bastard," Rina mutters, slamming her cup down harder than necessary.

"Yeah." I let out a hollow laugh. "And the worst part? Turns out I wasn't just cheated on, I was cheated out of better sex too."

Three sets of eyes blink at me before Rina lets out a loud, unfiltered laugh. "Well, damn. Tell us how you really feel."

Callie presses her lips together trying—and failing—not to smile. "I'm guessing that kind of enthusiasm wasn't something you saw from him?"

"Not even close." I take a sip of coffee. "Honestly? Seeing him like that made me realize I never really knew him at all."

Sloane leans forward, her green eyes sharp. "That's not on you. That's on him. It's a choice he made."

Rina nods, her expression fierce. "Exactly. You're incredible. If he couldn't see that, it's his loss. Don't you dare think otherwise."

Callie reaches across the table and squeezes my hand. "And it sounds like it wasn't just about the cheating. It was everything."

"Yeah." I swirl my cup slowly. "I think I was trying to live a life that looked good on paper. Devon. The job. The apartment. It all made sense. But I don't think any of it ever really made me happy."

Sloane's smile softens. "Sometimes it takes everything falling apart to figure out what we actually want."

"And what *do* you want, Lilah?" Callie asks quietly.

I open my mouth before closing it again. "I don't know. *Yet.*" And for the first time in my life, that uncertainty doesn't terrify me. "I'm figuring it out. One croissant at a time."

They all smile at that. It's not a huge moment. It's not a parade or some grand epiphany.

But it's a start.

A step forward.

I glance around the table at these women who have been there for me without hesitation.

No judgment.

No conditions.

Just love.

Maybe that's what I need more of in my life.

People who show up.

People who stay.

Like them.

And Steele.

His face flashes in my mind. His slightly crooked smile, the way he smells like spice and cedar, the quiet strength in his touch. The way he makes me feel like I'm not standing on crumbling ground anymore.

A slow warmth blooms inside me, chasing away some of the heaviness.

Maybe I don't have everything figured out yet.

But then again, maybe I don't need to.

All I have to do is take the next step.

And then another.

One heartbeat.

One choice.

One small leap of faith at a time.

And if I'm lucky, I'll find something better waiting for me on the other side.

STEELE

I take the last gulp of my protein shake and grimace. It's thick, chalky, and tastes vaguely like artificial vanilla.

Behind me, footsteps pad into the kitchen.

"What's in that?" Lilah asks, her voice husky from sleep.

I turn and shake the nearly-empty bottle. "Let's see... protein powder, almond milk, half a banana, creatine, and some other stuff I probably can't pronounce."

She walks over, plucks the container from the counter, and frowns down at the label. "This has more chemicals than a science lab."

I shrug, rinsing the shaker out in the sink. "It gets the job done."

"Barely," she mutters, turning the tub around. "You're a professional athlete. You should be more careful about what you put into your body."

I arch a brow. "Are you offering to be my nutritionist now, lucky charm?"

She glances up, lips twitching. "Well, apparently I'm your new assistant. And it's the least I can do. I'll start making smoothies for you."

I blink. "You know how to make smoothies?"

She shrugs. "I've been playing around with recipes. I like them after workouts. They make me feel more balanced."

I lean against the counter, watching her pull her hair into a messy knot, her eyes scanning the kitchen like she's already cataloging potential ingredients. There's a lightness in her voice that hasn't been there in days, and I'd do just about anything to keep it there.

"You know," I say, "if you keep this up, you're gonna ruin me for my usual post-practice sludge."

She smirks. "You're welcome."

I don't say it out loud, but I like the idea of her making something just for me. I like it even more that she's channeling her energy into something that has nothing to do with her ex.

My phone buzzes on the counter, screen lighting up with the building's front desk number, just as I'm wiping out my shaker.

I swipe to answer. "Sanderson."

"Morning, Mr. Sanderson," Tommy says. "I got a delivery here for Miss Monroe. You want me to bring it up?"

I glance toward the hallway where Lilah disappeared a minute ago. "Yeah, that's fine. Thanks, man."

"No problem. Be there in five."

I hang up just as Lilah walks back into the kitchen, barefoot and holding a small spiral notebook in her hand.

"Who was that?" she asks.

"Tommy. He's bringing something up for you."

She stops short and frowns. "For me?"

I nod. "Yeah. He said something about a delivery under your name."

Her eyes flicker with confusion for a beat before she stills. "Oh. Devon must've sent my stuff."

I open my mouth, unsure what I'm going to say, but the elevator dings before I can get a word out. A second later, the doors slide open and there's Tommy, maneuvering a dolly stacked with boxes.

"Morning," he says, offering a polite nod as he wheels them inside. Two guys follow with their own stacks. "Looks like you got a whole apartment in here."

Lilah folds her arms tightly across her chest, gaze locked on the boxes. Her name is scrawled across the side in thick black marker.

"Thanks, Tommy," I say, giving him a tip of my chin as he backs toward the elevator.

"We've got another load and then we'll be out of your hair. Let me know if you need help getting rid of the cardboard later."

When the elevator doors slide shut, I turn back to Lilah. She hasn't moved an inch.

"I don't know why it's hitting all over again," she whispers. "I mean, we broke up. It's over. But seeing it all boxed up like a return shipment is hard."

Something inside me twists at the expression on her face. Like the delivery is somehow proof of her failure.

"It's just stuff," I say quietly. "Not your life. Not you. Just grab whatever you need, and we'll put the rest in one of the spare rooms until you're ready to tackle it."

She gives a small nod, but her jaw tightens. "It just feels like a lot."

"Hey," I say, stepping in and cupping her face. Her eyes meet mine, shiny and uncertain. "You trusted someone who didn't deserve it. That's on him, not you. Maybe you don't have a plan yet, but you will. You always land on your feet. And in the meantime, you've got me."

Her throat works around a swallow. "You really mean that?"

"Yeah, lucky charm. I've got you. Always."

She steps into me, wrapping her arms around my waist and

pressing her face against me. I hold her tight, one hand sliding into her hair, the other resting over her back.

For a long moment, neither of us moves as the boxes sit untouched a few feet away.

It's only in my arms that Lilah seems to release the weight she's been carrying.

She lets out an exhale, followed by a quiet, self-conscious laugh. "Okay. I need to find my clothes." She untangles herself from me before kneeling next to one of the boxes labeled "closet stuff." Her fingers work at the packing tape.

I grab a box cutter from the drawer and crouch beside her. "Here," I offer, slicing open the top.

Inside are folded jeans, a few blouses, and an old Wildcats hoodie from our college days. She pulls it out, eyes widening.

"I forgot about this," she murmurs, fingers smoothing over the faded fabric.

She pulls out a small jewelry box and sets it aside before digging deeper and freezing.

"Oh my God."

"What is it?"

She lifts out a slightly beat-up photo frame, and my heart skips a beat.

It's a picture of us in our dorm hallway sophomore year of college. I've got an arm slung around her shoulder, and we're both laughing. Our eyes are squinted and heads thrown back. There's a smear of frosting on her cheek and a plastic tiara on my head from a prank someone pulled during my birthday.

We were so damn young.

"I haven't seen this in years," she whispers, running her thumb over the glass. "I used to keep it on my desk when I started law school."

"You kept it all this time?" I ask, trying to play it cool even though my heart is doing somersaults behind my rib cage.

She nods. "You've always been a constant presence in my life. I guess this picture reminded me of that."

Emotion swells inside me.

Without thinking, I take the frame from her and walk over to the console table by the window before carefully setting it down.

Her head tilts as she watches me. "What are you doing?"

"Giving it a new home," I say simply. "Looks pretty good there, don't you think?"

Her eyes warm as her voice dips. "It does."

She moves beside me, and for a long moment, we both stare at the photo. Her shoulder brushes mine, and there's a shift in the air as emotion crackles just beneath the surface.

"You really were always there," she murmurs. "Weren't you?"

I glance at her. "Always."

She gives me a small smile. It's a little sad but stronger than before. After a beat, she bumps her hip against mine.

"Come on," she says. "Let's see what other blasts from the past we can dig up."

I huff out a laugh as we turn back to the mess of cardboard and crumpled tissue paper. She's still sorting through what's hers, what's worth keeping, and what's already in the past.

And me?

I'm just here to make sure she doesn't have to do it alone.

7

LILAH

Steele and I are nestled against each other on the couch as the television casts a warm, flickering glow across the room. We've somehow gotten sucked into a cooking competition, both pretending we don't care while low-key rooting for opposite teams.

His arm is draped over the back of the cushions, fingers idly playing with a strand of my hair.

Over the past week, we've fallen into an easy and comfortable rhythm. For the first time since my life imploded, I feel like I'm going to be okay.

I'm knocked from those thoughts when my phone buzzes on the coffee table.

Mom.

With a groan, I flop back against the cushion. "Ugh. I was really hoping to avoid this convo for a few more days."

Or, ideally, the rest of my life.

Steele glances at the screen and then at me. "You don't have to answer it."

"Yeah, I know," I say, nibbling my lower lip. "But if I don't, she'll just keep calling. And texting. And emailing. If she figures out where I've been hiding, she'll show up downstairs."

Steele snorts. "We can give Tommy her photo and instructions to throw her out if she tries anything."

That mental image has a laugh slipping out before I can stop it.

"We both know she'd file a formal complaint with the building association."

Steele reaches over and gives my hand a squeeze. His thumb runs a slow circle over the back of it that's both steady and grounding. "I'm right here, lucky charm."

Even though the gesture is a simple one, it means everything.

This man is always there for me. Any time things fall apart, he's the one standing by my side, holding the pieces with me. No matter how many times I tell myself it's just who he is, it still makes my heart trip.

After steadying myself, I swipe to answer. "Hi, Mom. How are you?"

"Oh, Lilah," she sighs. "Honestly? It's been an absolute nightmare of a week. The dry cleaner ruined my favorite silk blouse, the neighbors are back at it with their construction, and your father's golf swing—don't even get me started. All those lessons with the country club pro, and he still can't break ninety. Sometimes I have to wonder what we're even doing with our lives."

I bite the inside of my cheek to keep from laughing.

"And we haven't heard from you in weeks. Are you alive, darling? Or did you finally run off to join that cult in Oregon I warned you about?"

Across from me, Steele lifts a brow, clearly amused. I shoot him a glare and silently mouth, "*Stop it.*"

"I'm alive," I say, keeping my voice even. "Just dealing with a few things."

"Oh? What kind of things?"

That's all it takes for my stomach to knot. Steele slides his hand into mine and gives it a gentle squeeze.

Here goes nothing.

"Devon and I broke up."

There's a pause followed by a sharp inhale. "What do you mean you broke up?"

"I mean exactly that. We ended things."

"Lilah Jane," she bites out, her displeasure slicing through the phone. "Fix it."

My jaw drops. No matter what kind of response I was expecting, that wasn't it.

"Excuse me?"

"You heard me, young lady. Call him and apologize. Profusely, if necessary. Whatever it is, I'm sure it's nothing that can't be resolved. Do I need to remind you that Devon Peterson comes from a very respectable family?"

I blink, stunned by her reaction. "Mom, he *cheated* on me."

There's a brief silence and then a huff. "Well, men make mistakes. That doesn't mean you throw away an entire relationship over a minor indiscretion."

I glance at Steele and shake my head, unable to believe the words coming out of her mouth. His jaw is clenched, eyes burning like he's one second away from grabbing the phone and telling Caroline Monroe exactly where she can go.

"Mom," I say carefully, each word deliberate. "He's having a baby with another woman. One of the associates at the firm."

The silence that follows is deafening. It stretches long enough for my heart to start racing and my palms to turn slick. Steele's hand settles on my back, warm and reassuring. It's his silent way of telling me I'm not alone as well as nudging me to rip off the Band-Aid and get the rest out.

"And... I'm no longer working there."

My mother exhales sharply. "Oh my God, you were fired?"

"What? No." I blink. "Not exactly fired."

"You just said you're not working there anymore."

"That's because Devon thought it would be best if I didn't come back," I grit out. "And honestly? He wasn't wrong. After everything that happened, there's no way I could've stayed."

There's a beat.

"Lilah, you can't just throw away your career over something so—"

"He's the one who threw it away," I snap, my voice cracking as emotion claws its way up my throat. "Not me."

Another silence follows, but this one feels different.

Heavier.

Final.

I grip the phone tighter, forcing a calm I don't feel. "I know you liked him and were hoping we'd get married, but it hasn't been right for a while. And I kept holding on, trying to force it, because I didn't want to let anyone down." I blink hard against the sting in my eyes. "But in the end, I was the one left disappointed. I'm sorry if you had this picture in your head of how my life was supposed to look. But that vision? It's not yours to shape. It's mine. And for once, I'm doing what's right for me."

She falls quiet again before asking gently, "Are you okay?"

I glance at Steele and give him a slight smile. "Yeah," I say. "I think so."

She makes a vague noise and mutters something about talking later. And then we say our goodbyes, and I hang up. My shoulders drop as I set the phone down.

Steele wraps an arm around me and gently pulls me against him. "Are you okay?"

"Yeah," I whisper. "Thanks for holding my hand through that."

His lips brush the top of my head. "Haven't you figured out by now that I'll always be here, holding your hand any time you need it?"

I stay tucked into his side as the TV hums in the background, a blur of sound and color I barely register.

For the first time in what feels like forever, I said what needed to be said.

And it felt good. Freeing in a way I hadn't realized I was desperate for.

Like I'm finally starting to find my way back to myself.

STEELE

The scent hits me the second I step off the elevator and into the penthouse. It's something savory and buttery, rich enough to make my stomach grumble after a brutal two-hour practice on the ice.

But it's the humming that really gets me.

It's soft, tuneless, and even more than that, content.

I drop the grocery bag by the bench in the entryway and follow the scent like a bloodhound. The second I round the corner into the kitchen, I freeze.

Lilah's dancing barefoot and wearing a midriff-bearing sweater with the sleeves rolled to her elbows. Her hair is piled on top of her head in a messy knot, and there's flour dusted across her cheek and the counter. One cabinet door is hanging open as a spatula sits against a pan on the stove.

It looks like a bomb went off in here.

And I fucking love it.

This is exactly what Lilah looks like when she's happy.

Really happy.

It's not the kind of quiet composure she used to wear like armor when she was with Devon. This is loose and effortless. She looks like she belongs here, moving around my kitchen.

The last thing I want to do is interrupt.

I just want to soak in the sight for a few minutes.

But then she spins around and her gaze catches mine. A tiny squeak of surprise slips from her as she tugs one of the earbuds from her ear.

"Oh my God, Steele!" She laughs. "You scared me."

I lift a brow and nod toward the apron around her waist. "You're making a mess of my kitchen."

She grins, completely unrepentant. "Kitchens are supposed to be messy."

"Is that so?"

"Mm-hmm." Her gaze drops to my arms, and she does a double take. "Wait. What is that?"

I hold up the tiny gray kitten, who meows. "This?" I say casually. "This is a kitten."

Lilah blinks before moving closer. "Is it a he or she?"

"She," I say, running a gentle hand down the kitten's tiny back, careful not to spook her. "She came from one of the staff members at the arena. Their cat had kittens, and they were looking for homes."

Lilah blinks up at me in confusion. "So why do you have one?"

I smile, brushing a fingertip behind the kitten's ear. "Because I know how much you've always wanted a pet."

Her mouth parts, the words slow to come. "My parents... and then Devon were allergic," she says quietly, like it's a confession.

A realization.

"Right," I murmur. "So now you can have one."

Her gaze drops to the tiny bundle of fur. "But do you want a kitten?" she asks, her voice soft, almost unsure. "What happens when I move out? What if I can't keep her wherever I end up?"

I don't look away. "Then I'll keep her. No questions asked. It gets a little lonely around here sometimes."

A silent war plays out across her face. Joy, surprise, gratitude, and something deeper. Something that looks an awful lot like heartbreak.

She lifts the kitten into her arms, cradling the tiny body against her chest, pressing her cheek to the small, purring head.

"I can't believe you did this," she whispers, her tone thick with emotion.

I step closer. "I knew it would make you happy. That's all I want."

The smile she graces me with is full and wide. It's the kind that takes me apart and stitches me back together in the same heartbeat.

"Thank you."

Drawn to her, I brush my fingers against her flour-covered cheek. "Anytime, lucky charm."

My heart expands. Ever since I met this girl in college, all I've ever wanted to do is make her happy.

After dinner, Lilah settles on the couch with the kitten.

Once the kitchen is cleaned, I drop onto the cushion beside her and turn sideways so I can watch the two of them. Lilah's bare feet are tucked beneath her, and she's stroking the kitten's fur.

"You're good with her," I say after a long beat of comfortable silence.

She glances up at me with a smile. "She's perfect. Thanks again for bringing her home."

"No problem."

Lilah scratches behind the kitten's ears. "What should we name her?"

"What do you mean? Why can't we just keep calling her 'kitten'?"

"She deserves something dignified," Lilah says, with the

kind of serious tone that tells me she's already thinking way too hard about this. "Something elegant. Timeless."

I rub my jaw, pretending to be just as serious. "Like... Duchess Fluffernutter the Third?"

Lilah chokes on a laugh. "Oh my God, stop. Absolutely not."

"You said timeless."

"I meant like Eleanor. Or maybe Margot."

"Mmm. Too regal," I say. "What about... Are you ready for this? Puck?"

She narrows her eyes. "You did *not* just suggest naming her after a rubber disc."

"I absolutely did. It's clever. She's tiny, fast, and changes direction without warning."

"She doesn't belong on the ice."

"That remains to be seen," I say before glancing down at the kitten now stretched across my thigh, purring like an idling engine.

Lilah watches us with a smile. "She likes you."

I meet her gaze. "Hopefully she's not the only one."

Lilah swallows as her hand trails lightly down the kitten's spine. "What about Waffles?" she asks, clearing her throat. "Too ridiculous?"

"Absolutely not," I say with a grin. "Waffles is perfect."

"Okay then, it's settled." She gives a decisive nod and scratches under the kitten's chin. "Welcome home, Waffles."

Waffles purrs louder, as if she's in complete agreement with her newly bestowed name.

Lilah leans her head on my shoulder and, unable to help myself, I press a kiss against her hair. One of my hands rests gently on her thigh as the other strokes the small bundle of fur snuggled between us.

I can honestly say that I've never felt more content.

When she shifts, stretching her legs out toward the coffee

table and flexing her feet with a sigh, I say, "Give them to me. Remember all the foot rubs I gave you in college?"

She hesitates. "You don't have to do that."

"I know," I say, giving her a look. "I want to."

A beat passes before she swings her legs into my lap. My hands wrap around her ankle. Her skin is so soft, it sends a jolt straight through me.

Waffles jumps to the floor, batting around a toy I picked up at the store.

I press my thumbs into the arch of her foot, working steadily. I know exactly where to knead to make her melt, and when she lets out a quiet sound as her head tips back against the couch, my blood spikes white-hot and arousal rushes through my veins.

It takes every ounce of focus not to let my mind spiral to places it shouldn't.

But it does anyway.

Especially when I take in her slightly parted lips or the way her lashes flutter against her cheekbones. She melts into me like I'm the only thing tethering her to the earth.

Doesn't she realize I could put that same look on her face in other ways if she'd just let me? I'd drop to my knees and worship her the way I've been dreaming about for a decade.

As tempting as it is to make a move, there's no way I can do that.

Not now.

Not when she's still nursing a broken heart.

But that doesn't stop me from working my way up her calf. My progress is slow and methodical. I want to drag out this moment indefinitely so I don't have to stop touching her. Her shoulders sink deeper into the cushions, and tension bleeds from her like a deflating balloon.

"You really do have magic hands," she murmurs. Her voice comes out sounding like she's been drugged.

My fingers tighten as my stomach clenches.

This woman has no idea what she's doing to me.

Abso-fucking-lutely none.

Just as I trace along the inside of her knee, Waffles launches herself up onto the couch, her tiny body landing on Lilah's stomach.

Lilah bursts into laughter, one hand going straight to the kitten. "Personal space doesn't exist for you, does it, Waffles?"

I grin, grateful for the interruption and also slightly resentful that the kitten cock-blocked me.

"She's just making sure I behave," I mutter.

Lilah's smile falters just a little. "You've been nothing but kind and sweet."

If she only knew how hard it is to keep my hands to myself, she wouldn't say that.

I clear my throat and gently lower her foot from my lap before I do something we'll both regret.

"You know what? I'm more tired than I thought," I say with a forced yawn, rising to my feet. "I'm gonna take a shower and then hit the sack."

Lilah tilts her head, a small frown tugging between her brows. "Oh. I thought we were going to go over your upcoming schedule."

I nod toward the tablet on the coffee table. "It's all there if you want to take a look. We can dive into it tomorrow."

Before she can say anything else, I make a beeline down the hall like my ass is on fire.

The second I hit the bathroom, I plant my hands on the marble counter. Massaging her, hearing those little sounds she made, feeling her relax under my touch, was too damn much.

I stare at my reflection and know the truth without needing to say it out loud.

I am in so much fucking trouble where this woman is concerned.

9
LILAH

Okay, so maybe Steele wasn't lying when he said he needed help managing his schedule. One thing's for sure—his itinerary is a disaster.

I sit cross-legged on the couch, tablet propped against my knee, trying to make sense of the never-ending stream of commitments. There are PR events, sponsor obligations, and media appearances. Not to mention practices, games, and charity functions.

Does this man ever get a break?

A tiny meow pierces the air, followed by the gentle pitter-patter of paws across the hardwood. Waffles hops up onto the couch beside me, tail flicking before plopping herself down on the tablet. She's only been here for a few hours but already, she's made herself at home.

"Waffles." I sigh, nudging her gently. "I love you. Unfortunately, your fuzzy little butt is not compatible with a touchscreen."

She lets out a purr and tucks herself in more snugly, completely unfazed. I slide the tablet out from under her belly and glance back down at the schedule.

Wait a minute...

"A photo shoot?" I blink. "Steele has a photo shoot tomorrow morning?"

How didn't we talk about this?

He disappeared about fifteen minutes ago to take a shower before going to bed.

Judging from this calendar, I can understand why he felt the need to sack out so early.

I lean against the cushion and stare at the ceiling for a second, wondering how long he's been handling all this by himself. Beside me, Waffles stretches and lets out the tiniest squeaky yawn before curling back into a little ball of fuzz.

"Your dad's gonna run himself into the ground if he's not careful," I murmur. "Good thing he's got us now, huh?"

She blinks up at me like she couldn't agree more.

"All right, you stay here and hold down the fort. I'll be right back."

When she doesn't object, I take that as my cue to move forward with the plan.

With one final look at Waffles stretched out on the couch, I head down the hallway to where the bedrooms are located. My bare feet are silent against the wood floor.

I find Steele's bedroom door cracked open, and rap my knuckles against the wood.

"Steele? Are you still awake? I have a few questions about the schedule tomorrow."

I wait a beat, then two.

For a handful of seconds, I consider turning around and heading back to the living room. But the need for answers regarding his itinerary wins out, and I carefully push open the door before peeking inside. The room is shadowy, the only light coming from the bathroom as steam drifts from the doorway.

As I take a few steps toward it, I spot a pile of discarded

clothing on the floor. It's the same hoodie and sweatpants he wore at dinner. Not to mention a pair of gray boxers.

Oh.

Oh.

The small pile of dirty laundry is my signal to turn around and get the hell out of here.

It's not like we can't discuss the photo shoot in the morning.

The water shuts off until it's nothing more than drips hitting the tile.

I take a hasty step in retreat as Steele moves into view. The sight that fills the space is all it takes for air to clog my lungs.

The man is dripping wet.

And naked.

So very naked.

The first thing I notice is that there isn't an ounce of fat on him. He's all chiseled strength and toned musculature. Every inch is sculpted like a marble statue. His damp hair clings to his forehead as water trails down his pecs and over well-defined abs.

We've been friends for a decade, and I've seen Steele without a shirt hundreds of times before at the lake or pool.

But I've never caught sight of him like *this*.

My greedy gaze slides over his broad shoulders. The sinewy muscles bunch and flex as he dries himself with unhurried strokes. I'm mesmerized by the movement as my attention slips to his tapered waist when he twists around to give me an unobstructed view of his backside.

It's official. Steele is a perfect specimen of a man.

Instead of backing away, my gaze dips lower.

Because how can I *not* look at his ass?

It's so freaking perfect.

A shiver works through me, and I stare so hard, there's no way that every nuance of his backside won't be imprinted upon my memory for the rest of my life.

It's just so muscular.

The urge to reach out and stroke my hands over him is so damn strong. I haven't felt this punch of arousal in...

Maybe never.

My thighs unconsciously clench, and I'm struck with the realization that my panties are soaked.

The last thing I should be doing is standing here and drooling over him.

I'm probably breaking a dozen unspoken friend rules.

His biceps bulge and flex as he dries his hair, turning just enough for me to catch a glimpse of his front. Even though I tell myself not to look, my gaze zeroes in on the thick length of his cock nestled against dark hair. He might not be hard, but he's still impossibly big.

Hung.

Oh my God, did I just think that?

My brain chooses that moment to malfunction.

Maybe it's because I can't seem to rip my gaze away even as I silently scream at myself to do it. Or maybe it's because I'm rooted to the spot, drinking him in like I've been starved for the sight of him.

That's the exact moment Steele meets my gaze in the mirror, and my stomach drops. Heat rushes through me. His expression shifts, and surprise gives way to something darker.

Hungrier.

My face flames so hot, it feels like it's on fire.

It takes effort to jumpstart my brain into action as I stumble back a step. "Oh. Uh. I—"

In one swift movement, Steele fastens the towel around his waist. "Is there something you needed, Lilah?"

How he manages to sound so casual, as if me standing here gawking at him is nothing out of the ordinary, I have no idea. But I still catch the way his eyes burn with an intensity I've never seen in them before.

My mouth opens and then closes like I'm a fish gasping for its last dying breath.

"I... uh... your schedule," I finally blurt, waving the tablet like it has the power to save me from the humiliating moment playing out between us.

"What about it?" He steps toward me, closing the distance with easy, deliberate strides.

My brain short-circuits.

It's completely blank.

And it doesn't help that Steele smells like fresh soap and skin, still damp from the shower, completely unbothered by the fact I just walked in on him.

I need to retreat.

Now.

"Never mind," I mutter. "I'll, uh... just email my questions."

With that, I spin and nearly trip over his gym bag before bolting for the door.

"Lilah," he calls after me.

I wave a frantic hand without looking back. "No worries! We can talk about it tomorrow!"

I barely make it to the living room before scooping up Waffles and hauling ass into my room. Once there, I deposit the kitten on my bed.

She doesn't look pleased by the disruption.

But it's hard to focus on that when my entire body feels overheated.

I'm not just burning up. I'm being burned alive from the inside out.

Holy hell, what was that?

Why did he look at me like that?

Then again, why did *I* look at *him* like that?

With a groan, I realize I'm the one who now needs a shower.

Preferably a cold one.

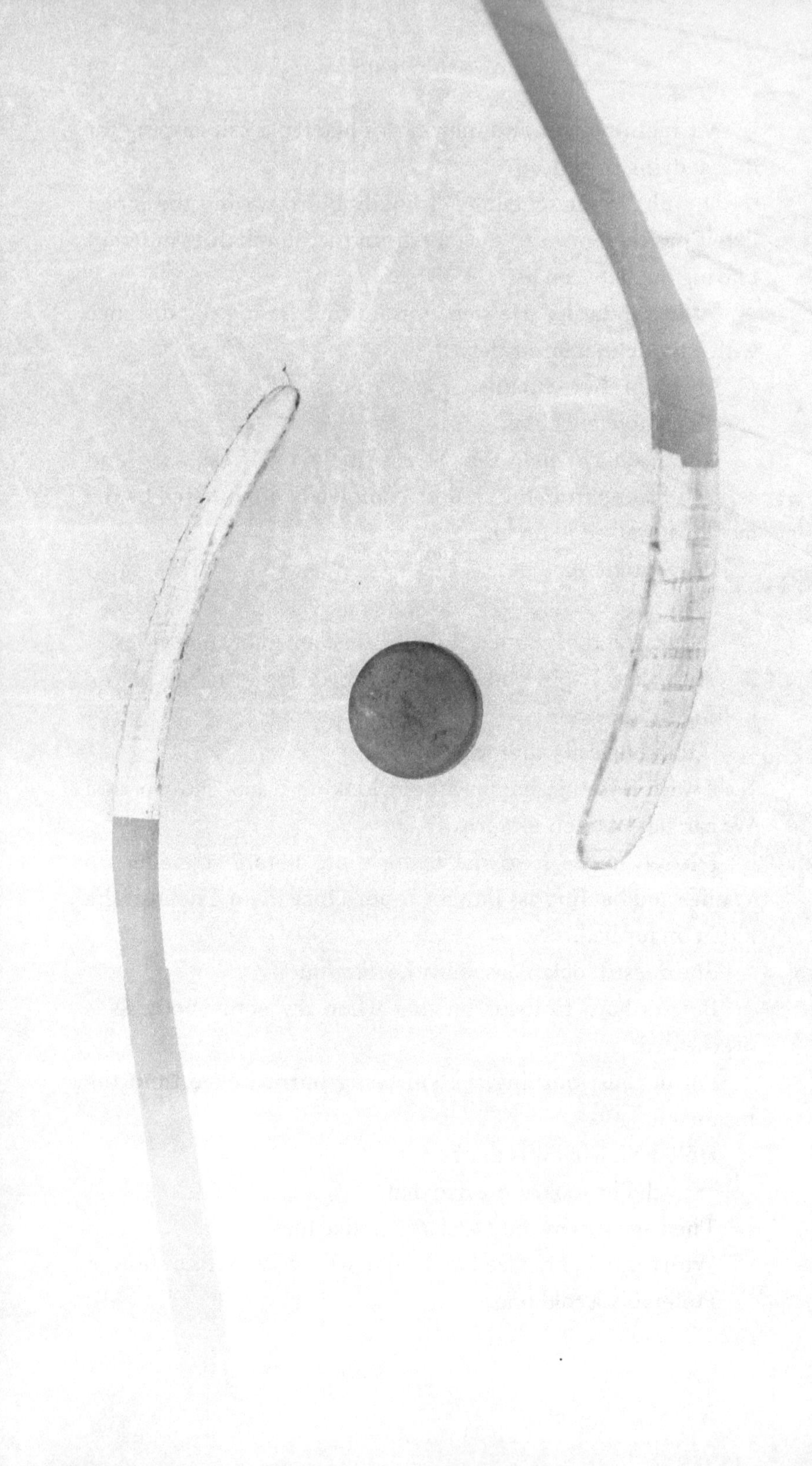

10
STEELE

I roll over for what feels like the hundredth time, the glow of the digital clock taunting me from the nightstand. It's late, and I should be out cold. Practice was brutal. Instead, my body refuses to cooperate and my mind won't shut off.

All I can think about is that Lilah is sleeping just down the hall.

Her reaction to walking in on me after my shower has been on a nonstop loop in my head. The way her gaze slid over me, slow and lingering, felt more like a physical caress, and it's got me in a chokehold.

It's exactly how I always imagined her looking at me.

Like I was more than just Steele, her best friend.

And now she's in my space and under my roof, but the place I want her most is in my bed.

Not for a night.

And certainly not as a distraction.

I want her here for good.

The realization slams into me, and I sit up, staring at the far wall, heart pounding under the weight of it.

For me, it's always been her.

Always.

So why the fuck haven't I manned up and done something about it?

We've been dancing around this for years, orbiting each other, coming close but never colliding.

Maybe it's time.

Maybe I need to stop playing it safe and finally tell her how I feel.

No more holding back or waiting for just the right moment.

Decision made, I throw off the covers before scrubbing a hand over my face and then stalking out of my room.

Her door is cracked open.

Just as I'm about to knock, a sound that's barely audible catches my attention. It barely registers at first, but then it happens again, and my entire body locks up.

Did she just...

My heart slams against my ribs as every muscle coils tight.

No way.

I must have imagined it.

My brain is playing tricks on me.

It's official, I'm losing it.

But then it repeats, and my pulse skyrockets. Heat floods my system, molten and raw, as a dark, possessive surge overtakes me.

Holy fuck.

Is she doing what I think she's doing?

That's all it takes for a war to break out in my head.

If I had an ounce of decency, I'd turn around, crawl back into bed, and pretend I have no idea what's happening behind Lilah's door.

Instead, I push it open just enough to see if I'm right.

The room is bathed in shadows. The silvery glow from the full moon spills through the blinds, illuminating just enough for the image of her to get singed into my brain.

The sheets are tangled around her legs and one hand grips the pillow as the other disappears beneath the fabric of her panties.

My gut twists as heat coils low in my belly.

She's stunning.

And so completely lost in what she's doing that she doesn't realize she's no longer alone.

I can't tear my eyes away from the picture she makes.

I brace a hand against the doorframe and try to get control of myself.

What I'd like to know is who she's thinking about.

It better not be Devon.

Or is there some other asshole who's not even on my radar?

My hand fists at my side at the possibility.

But then I hear my name whispered from her lips. The sound is like a wrecking ball to my fragile restraint, and I still as the world stops spinning.

Every sharp inhale she takes, every small movement, every sigh, is all for me.

Everything inside me splinters apart at that knowledge.

I should leave.

I should definitely stop watching this intensely private moment.

But I don't.

Can't.

I stand here, gripping the doorframe like it's the only thing keeping me upright, and watch as she falls to pieces. Her body shudders as her lips part on a muffled cry.

It takes every ounce of control not to eat up the distance between us and crawl into that bed, pull her into my arms, and finally give us what we both want.

Instead, I force myself to retreat, slipping away from her room.

I drag a hand down my face as my pulse thunders. Every

muscle is wound tight. My heart is racing and my blood roars in my ears.

God, I *want* her so damn much.

But it's more than just want.

More than lust.

It's love.

The kind that settles into your bones and never lets go.

Most guys might panic at that realization.

At just how far gone they are.

But me?

I've known for years.

I've been in love with Lilah Monroe since the first time she leaned over her college notebook, brow furrowed, muttering something about the professor.

I think I've been hers ever since.

And now?

Now I understand there's no coming back from this.

No rewinding.

No pretending that what I feel is anything less than everything.

If I can't have Lilah, I don't want anyone else.

I slip into bed, the sheets cool against my skin, but there's no comfort in them. Not without her. Not when my name, whispered on a moan, is still echoing in my head like a fervent prayer.

I stare up at the ceiling, my body tight with desire, hope, and a little bit of fear.

Because she's always been mine.

I just need to prove it.

And pray she feels the same.

11
LILAH

Someone needs to tell me why the hell I agreed to this.

Oh, that's right.

It's because Steele asked, and I've never been good at saying no to him. Especially when he's always been there for me. If I needed the man to move mountains, he'd do it in a heartbeat.

No questions asked.

It's the only reason I'm standing off to the side on a sleek, upscale photography set, watching him charm an entire room of people. His charisma is effortless. Not something he turns on and off like some pro athletes or celebrities do.

The studio lights highlight every sharp, defined feature of his face from his chiseled jaw, the unfairly perfect cheekbones, to his silvery-gray eyes that have probably sold thousands of jerseys.

And don't even get me started on the suit.

Charcoal gray, perfectly tailored, hugging broad shoulders and a body built for pure destruction on the ice.

He looks expensive.

Powerful.

Untouchable.

He looks exactly like what they're paying for. Power, status, and the kind of allure you can't fake.

If that wasn't enough, his hair is just the right amount of tousled. It's that calculated I-just-woke-up-and-ran-a-hand-through-it kind of perfect that makes women drop their panties without even blinking.

It's ridiculous

Not to mention, unfair.

It's entirely possible I'm staring a bit too hard.

A gorgeous brunette steps into the frame beside him, and my stomach knots.

Here we go.

Krista, or Kayla, or whatever perfect K-name she has, is draped over his arm as her hand rests way too comfortably on his bicep. She tilts her head back and laughs at something he says, flashing a row of perfectly white teeth.

When Steele smirks, something in me ignites. I fold my arms, shifting my weight on my heels. I tell myself I don't care. Steele is free to flirt with whomever he wants. After a few minutes of watching them, it becomes clear that I'm lying to myself, because the longer I stare, the tighter my grip becomes.

It's embarrassing just how unprofessional this woman is.

They're supposed to be doing a sponsorship shoot for a high-end watch brand, and she's over there acting like she's about to climb him like a damn tree.

Her fingers trail down his silk tie. The gesture is both playful and suggestive.

My jaw clenches when Steele doesn't move away.

It's almost a shock when a slow, creeping heat spreads under my skin before knotting low in my gut. It's foreign and sharp, making my stomach churn.

Why am I so mad?

No. I'm not mad. There's absolutely no reason for me to be mad.

I'm just annoyed.

That's all.

Who wouldn't be?

She's acting like a star-struck groupie.

This is business.

A branding thing.

A Railers thing.

Except...

Nobody else seems to care.

I force myself to look away and pretend to check my phone.

This is ridiculous.

I'm being ridiculous.

I really need to chill out.

That's the moment I feel the weight of his stare. I glance up to find Steele watching me. His smirk is gone, only to be replaced with something unreadable. His sharp gray gaze flicks over my face before narrowing slightly.

It's like he knows exactly what's going through my head.

Or he's somehow able to sense it.

I really hope he can't see the jealousy written all over my expression.

A pulse of something jagged ripples through me at the silent acknowledgement of what I'm feeling.

I drop my gaze and refocus my attention on my cell.

It's fine.

I'm fine.

Everything is *fine*.

"Hey, Cam, would you mind if we take a few shots with Lilah?" Steele asks.

My head jerks up so fast, I nearly give myself whiplash.

What?

Me?

No way.

I shake my head, my eyes wide as I glare at Steele.

The corners of his lips lift into that devastatingly cocky grin. It's the one he uses when he's intent on getting his way. "Come on, Lilah. It'll be fun. And it'll give them more photos to choose from."

"But..." I swallow hard, tearing my gaze away from him to look at Cam and his assistants. "I'm not dressed for something like that. I'm not even wearing makeup."

"You don't need any," Steele says firmly.

One of Cam's assistants tilts her head and appraises me. I can't help but squirm under her unrelenting inspection. "You're a natural beauty. A little lipstick, a few strokes of mascara, and you'll be camera-ready."

"See?" Steele beams, as if the decision has been settled.

"There are a few dresses on the rack," Cam adds. "Molly, take her in the back and see what fits."

"No, I really don't—"

There's no time to get the rest of my sentence out as I'm herded toward a smaller room and practically shoved into a chair in front of a mirror. The pushy assistant rifles through the clothing options on the rack while two others attack my hair and face with alarming speed.

It feels more like a pit stop at an Indy race.

Less than ten minutes later, both girls step back, smiling proudly.

I stare at my reflection, barely recognizing myself. "Oh. Wow."

My hair is styled into loose waves that cascade over my shoulders. My skin looks flawless, and my lips are painted a sultry red that somehow makes my eyes seem bigger.

Molly holds out a silver column of fabric that shimmers beneath the fluorescent lights. "Let's get you into this."

Before I can protest, all three of them are teaming up—

stripping off my button-down and skirt and then zipping the dress up my back.

When I turn to the mirror, I exhale slowly, only then realizing how tense I've been.

The gown is absolutely stunning. Sleek and elegant with a high slit that runs up my thigh. Not only does it look expensive, it feels expensive.

"Your boss is going to lose his mind when he sees you."

I blink. "What?"

"Steele Sanderson," one of them says with a knowing grin.

"He's not really my boss," I mutter. "More like a friend."

Molly smirks before grabbing my hand and ushering me back into the studio. "We'll see about that."

As soon as I step foot into the large, sun-filled space, everything changes. Steele is mid-conversation with Cam about the hockey season. The second his gaze lands on me, he stops talking.

And moving.

And breathing.

His gaze rakes over me in an unhurried fashion, as if he's memorizing every inch, before releasing a long, low whistle.

"Damn, lucky charm," he murmurs. "You look like a million bucks. Maybe you're the one who should be wearing the watch."

Even though my stomach is in free fall, I laugh.

"Actually," Cam muses, studying me with an assessing gaze, "that's not a bad idea. I think the company sent over a smaller version."

An assistant appears, draping an elegant timepiece around my wrist. The weight of it feels significant. Steele looks on as the clasp is locked into place, and his jaw tics ever so slightly.

Cam lifts his camera. "All right, Lilah, I want you standing in front of Steele. Close, but not touching yet. This is all about seduction."

I exhale sharply and follow the direction, moving hesitantly into place. Steele stands behind me, radiating warmth and an intensity I'm reluctant to analyze.

How can I when his presence is everywhere, surrounding me?

Especially when I can feel the heat of his gaze burning into the back of my neck.

"Good," Cam calls out. "Steele, rest your hands lightly on her arms, like you're about to pull her in."

My belly clenches as Steele's large hands trail up my bare skin, fingertips brushing over me like a whisper. Even though I try to suppress a shiver, it's no use. There's no way he doesn't realize exactly how he's affecting me.

"Perfect," Cam murmurs. "Lilah, tilt your chin up slightly."

I obey, but the movement brings my profile directly into Steele's line of sight, and something flashes across his face.

Or is that my imagination?

"Now," Cam instructs, "Steele, I want you to pull her closer. Like you're about to whisper something in her ear."

Steele's hands slide down to my waist, gripping just enough to send a ripple of heat through my entire body. He leans in, his lips grazing the shell of my ear.

And then, in a voice so low I barely catch it, he murmurs, "You're killing me, lucky charm."

I close my eyes for half a second and swallow hard.

What the hell is happening?

The camera flashes.

"Beautiful," Cam says. "Now, I want you to turn toward him, Lilah. And Steele—this time, I want you to hold her like she belongs to you."

Everything inside me flips.

I turn, and the second my hands press against Steele's chest, his grip tightens around my waist. It's both firm and possessive.

Something stutters inside me as I glance up, only to find him already watching me.

Gone is the teasing smirk he wears like armor. There's no trace of mischief in his expression, no hint of the charming playboy everyone thinks they know.

What's left is raw.

Focused.

Hungry.

That look alone nearly buckles my knees.

The heat rolling off his body seeps into mine, searing through the flimsy material of my dress. His hands are steady, but there's power simmering beneath the surface, as if he's barely holding himself back.

He shifts beneath my palms, every movement precise and deliberate.

But his heartbeat is hammering just like mine.

I should say something.

Move.

Blink.

But I'm frozen in place by the invisible electric pull that's always been there between us.

Everything else falls away.

The lights.

The studio.

The noise.

Even the people.

It's just me and him.

And this thing between us that I can't name but that feels dangerous in all the best ways.

"Wow," Cam murmurs from somewhere behind the lens. "That's perfect."

Another flash goes off, but I don't flinch.

Don't move.

I'm too caught up in Steele.

In the way his thumb drifts along the curve of my waist.

In the way his attention drops to my mouth.

I remain frozen until the photographer finally lowers his camera, and the moment unravels.

"All right," he announces. "That's a wrap."

But Steele doesn't step back.

And neither do I.

His fingers flex against me. Just once. It's a subtle squeeze, as if he's reluctant to let go. When he finally sets me free, it feels as if a cord has been cut, and I inhale sharply.

My muscles slacken, and I almost stumble from the sudden loss of contact.

I force myself to retreat a single step.

Then another.

I need to put space between us, and hope it'll help to settle the chaos he's unwittingly stoked to life inside me.

"I should get changed," I mutter.

I don't wait for his response.

If I look at him again, I might just do something reckless.

Something I never thought I would.

Instead, I turn and make a beeline for the dressing room, pretending I don't feel the weight of his stare trailing after me. My heels click against the floor, fast and uneven, as if it's possible to outrun the way my pulse is slamming or the way my skin tingles where he touched me.

Inside the dressing room, I shut the door and lean against it.

What the hell was that?

I've known Steele Sanderson for a decade. He's been my constant, the one person I've always trusted.

Not once has he ever made me feel like this.

Until now.

I press my lips together, close my eyes, and try to regain my balance.

But it's no use.

Because deep down, I already know.
This isn't just a moment.
It's a shift.
A spark that's already caught fire.
I don't think I'm prepared for what that means.
But ready or not...
I feel it.

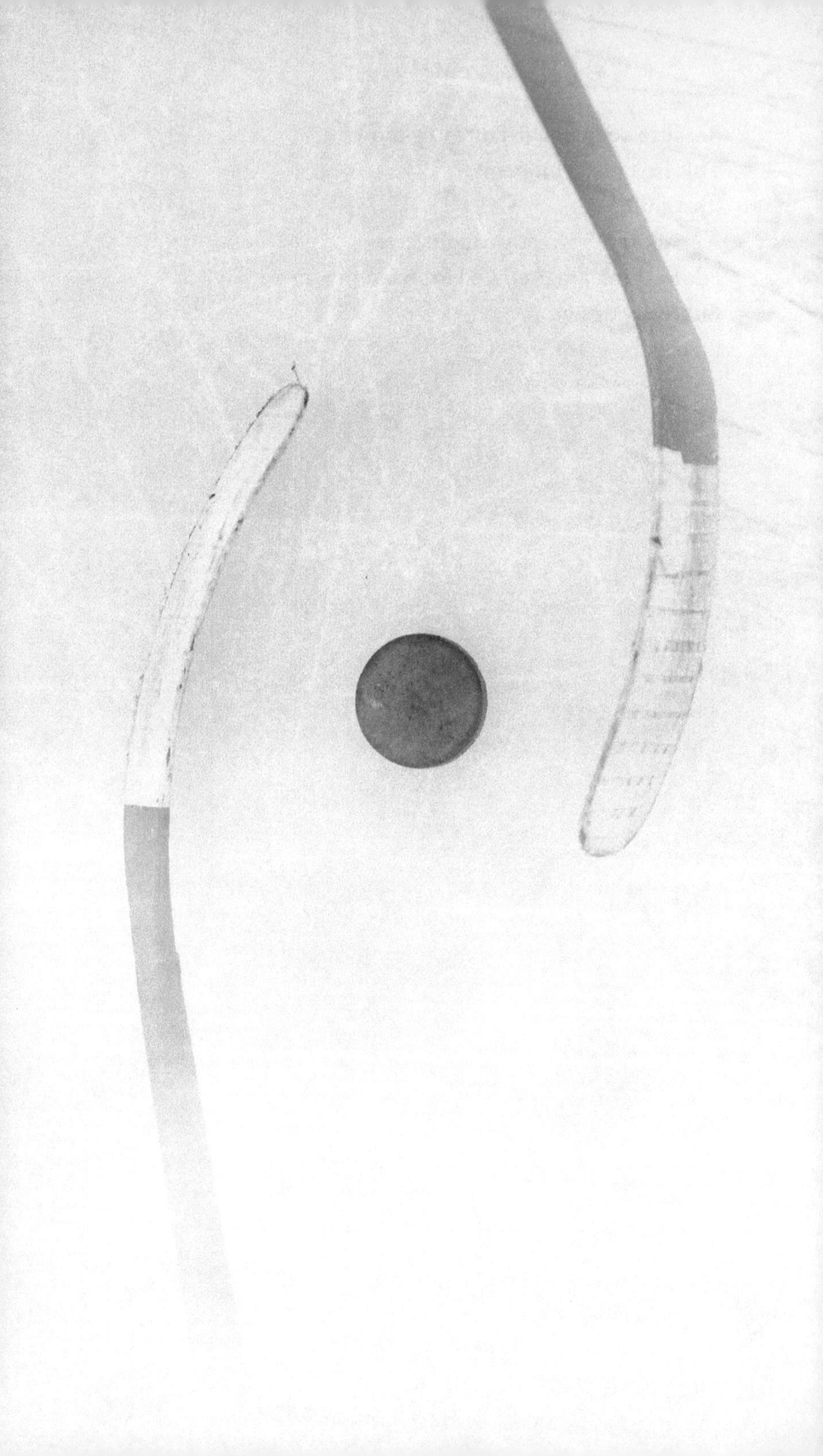

The heavy loft door swings shut behind us with a thud, and the sound echoes through the stairwell as we make our way down to the parking structure. The photography studio is in one of those renovated industrial buildings with exposed brick, high ceilings, and oversized windows that let in just enough light to make everything look effortlessly cool.

But none of it compares to the way Lilah looked in that silver dress. I can't stop thinking about the way her blue eyes locked on mine when I pulled her close for the camera.

For a few stolen moments, she belonged to me.

Even if she didn't realize it.

"You were good in there," I say, glancing at her. "Maybe you should come to more of these shoots. Do a little modeling on the side."

She lets out a dry laugh before shaking her head. "No way. Once was more than enough, thank you very much."

I smirk. "Really? You didn't enjoy it? Not even a little?"

She hesitates, pondering the question.

My guess is that she didn't hate it as much as she wants me to believe. I could see it in the way she relaxed by the end of the shoot and how her body molded itself against mine. Not to mention, the way her eyes softened when she looked at me.

Instead of admitting that, she shrugs. "I mean... it wasn't terrible."

I chuckle, enjoying the way she's trying to play it cool. That doesn't stop me from noticing the way her fingers drift across the bare skin where the watch had been clasped around her wrist, as if she's thinking back to the shoot.

Maybe Lilah isn't ready to acknowledge the way our relationship is changing, but that's fine. I've forced myself to be patient for ten long years. Giving her a little more time won't kill me.

I hope.

The air is cool and crisp with the early afternoon breeze as we reach the parking structure. Without thinking, I slide my hand into hers, threading our fingers together.

For a second or two, she stiffens before relaxing and letting me hold her.

I don't say anything about it.

I just do it like it's the most natural thing in the world.

Like it's something I've been doing for years.

Her hand is delicate against mine, but there's a strength there too. She doesn't pull away as we weave through the cars. Even though I don't want to, I release her to open the passenger door, and watch as she slides inside the vehicle. She moves carefully, adjusting her skirt as it rises up her thighs just enough to make my stomach tighten.

I clear my throat and shut the door before I actually start to drool.

Once I'm inside, I fire up the engine. The low rumble fills the quiet between us as I pull out of the garage and onto the street.

Lilah stares out the window as her fingers brush over her thighs.

"There was nothing to be jealous of," I say casually.

Her head snaps toward me, brows furrowing. "What?"

I keep my eyes on the road. "You heard me."

She lets out a sharp laugh. "You think I was jealous in there?"

"Yup."

"Of what?" she scoffs, clearly trying to brazen this out. "Of that model who was hanging all over you?"

I lift a shoulder. "I don't know. You tell me."

With an exhale, she shakes her head. I don't miss the way her arms fold over her chest.

Totally defensive.

Busted.

She was jealous.

And I fucking love it.

"You're ridiculous," she mutters, but there's no real bite to the words.

"Maybe," I say, taking the next turn a little faster than necessary, adrenaline buzzing through my veins from earlier. "But I'm not wrong."

Even though she huffs, looking back out the window, I catch the way the corner of her lips twitch like she's trying to hide her smile.

"Big game tonight," I say, breaking the tension with a change in topic.

"Against Dallas?"

"Yup." I glance at her. "I missed you last time."

"I know. I'm sorry about that."

"No need to apologize. I like knowing you're out there in the crowd," I admit. "You're my very own lucky charm."

Instead of responding, she watches me, as if seeing something she hadn't noticed before.

When she finally speaks, her voice is quiet. "There's nowhere else I'd rather be."

I nod once as the tension within me tightens for an entirely different reason.

After pulling into the garage and killing the engine, we sit for a second, neither of us moving.

She's so close.

And yet, not nearly close enough.

As much as I want to leave it at that, part of me wants to lean across the console and take our relationship to the next level.

But I don't.

Because the next move is hers to make.

13
LILAH

The energy inside the Kingston Landry Arena is electric. Palpable in that bone-deep, pulse-quickening way only a sold-out hockey game can be. A sea of blue Railers jerseys ripples through the stands, and the crowd roars as the puck is dropped at center ice.

I've been in this building a hundred times, but tonight feels charged in a way I can't explain. Maybe it's because I'm watching Steele with fresh eyes. Or maybe it's because I haven't stopped thinking about the way he looked at me earlier in the car.

Like I'm not just his best friend.

Like I'm something more.

I adjust the sleeves of the oversized Sanderson jersey I'm wearing. The same one he left folded on the back of the couch this afternoon with a note that said—*Wear me tonight. Don't argue.*

The man is bossy.

Thoughtful.

And hard to ignore.

Rina leans in from her seat beside me, holding a glass of wine and smirking like she knows something I don't.

"Soooo," she says, dragging the word out. "Cam sent over a few of the test shots from this morning."

I blink in surprise. "Already? That was fast."

She nods, tossing a piece of popcorn into her mouth. "He was excited. Said the lighting was perfect and your chemistry with Steele was off the charts."

Heat creeps into my cheeks. "We were just following his direction."

"Uh-huh." Rina chews thoughtfully, eyes pinned on me like she can see right through my casual tone. "Well, 'just following direction' is about to sell a whole lot of luxury watches."

Before I can respond, Evelyn, who's seated across from us on one of the sleek leather couches, chimes in, her lips curved around the rim of her wine glass.

"I saw the photographs," she adds, "and they were absolutely stunning."

I flush harder and pretend to focus on the ice. "I doubt the photos were any better than the ones with the model."

Rina snorts. "Please. They were way better. You two looked hot. Like incinerate-your-panties kind of hot." She waves a hand in the air, searching for the right word. "Combustible," she says with a grin. "I've seen smolder before, but whatever you and Steele had going on was full-body heat."

I press my lips together and try not to let her see how those words affect me.

"Well, that's good," I manage lightly. "At least the client will be happy."

"Mm-hmm," Rina makes a low sound of amusement before leaning in as if she's sharing a secret. "Oh, the client's thrilled."

It's a relief when the suite door opens, until I see who it is. Hugh Landry strolls inside like he owns the place.

Which, technically, he does.

The suit he wears is impeccable, and his dark hair, that's threaded with silver, is neatly combed back.

"Evening, ladies," he drawls, giving us a nod before his attention locks on Evelyn.

"You look lovely as ever," he says.

"Thanks," Evelyn replies coolly, not bothering to rise from her seat. She simply lifts her wine glass in a deliberate toast and then takes a sip.

The air between them turns sharp and electric.

Hugh doesn't miss a beat.

"Would you mind if I joined you?" he asks, his gaze skating over her in a way that borders on intimate.

Evelyn's smile is razor-sharp as she flicks a glance toward Rina and me. "We were just discussing some rather private matters," she says lightly, but the dismissal is unmistakable. "Perhaps another time."

Beside me, Rina leans in, whispering behind the rim of her glass, "Five bucks says she throws that wine in his face."

I raise an eyebrow. "That, or they make out right here. Equal odds."

If Hugh hears us, he pretends not to.

Instead, he gestures toward the ice. "Steele's having a hell of a game tonight."

"Of course he is," Evelyn says smoothly, not missing a beat. "He knows exactly what he's playing for."

Something flickers across Hugh's face.

It's not amusement.

Or anger.

It's something heavier.

Something brittle and raw that cracks through the air between them like a thunderclap.

He straightens his cuffs with a flick of his fingers. "I'll let you get back to it, then," he says, tone clipped. "See you tomorrow morning at the meeting."

"Unfortunately," Evelyn mutters into her glass.

For the briefest moment, something that almost looks like

sorrow flashes in Hugh's eyes. But then he's gone, the door swinging shut behind him with a muted click that somehow echoes.

Silence hangs heavy in the air for a beat before Rina releases a low whistle. "Okay," she says, setting her glass down. "Does anyone else feel like we just witnessed the world's frostiest form of foreplay?"

Evelyn's cheeks pinken despite the huff of irritation she lets out. "Don't be absurd."

"Absurd?" Rina grins. "Maybe. But wrong? Not even a little."

I hide my smile behind my wineglass as I glance back toward the ice.

Steele's in the thick of it, locked in a battle along the boards. His body collides with another player, hard, but he stays on his skates, muscling through the hit and keeping the puck alive.

"The man is certainly a force to be reckoned with out there," Rina says.

And he is.

Tonight, he's sharper. Harder. Skating faster, hitting heavier, commanding every inch of the rink like it's personal. Like every shift on the ice means more than just a game.

He's always been good.

Great, even.

But tonight?

Tonight, he's something more.

It's like he's on a personal mission.

Every time he scores, his gaze flicks up toward our suite, and when it finds me, it's like being struck by lightning.

It's direct.

Searing.

And impossible to ignore.

A chill dances down my spine, even though the room is comfortably warm. I tighten my grip on the armrest, trying to steady myself against the thudding beat of my heart.

It feels like Steele isn't playing for the crowd.

Or even for the team.

He's playing for *me*.

Evelyn murmurs from beside me, "That boy is really on fire tonight. It's almost as if something's gotten into him." She tilts her head slightly, cutting me a sideways glance. "Any idea what that could be?"

My throat goes dry. I swallow hard and shake my head, the motion small and helpless.

Rina doesn't bother to hide her smirk. She turns toward me with a raised brow, eyes sparkling with amusement. "Oh, I think I have a very good idea."

When I fail to respond, the three of us fall into silence, each lost in our own thoughts, as the game continues to unfold below. Even as I force my attention back to the ice, I can feel the weight of Steele's gaze and the way it lingers.

Heavy.

Unshakable.

And something inside me understands this moment, this shift between us, is just the beginning.

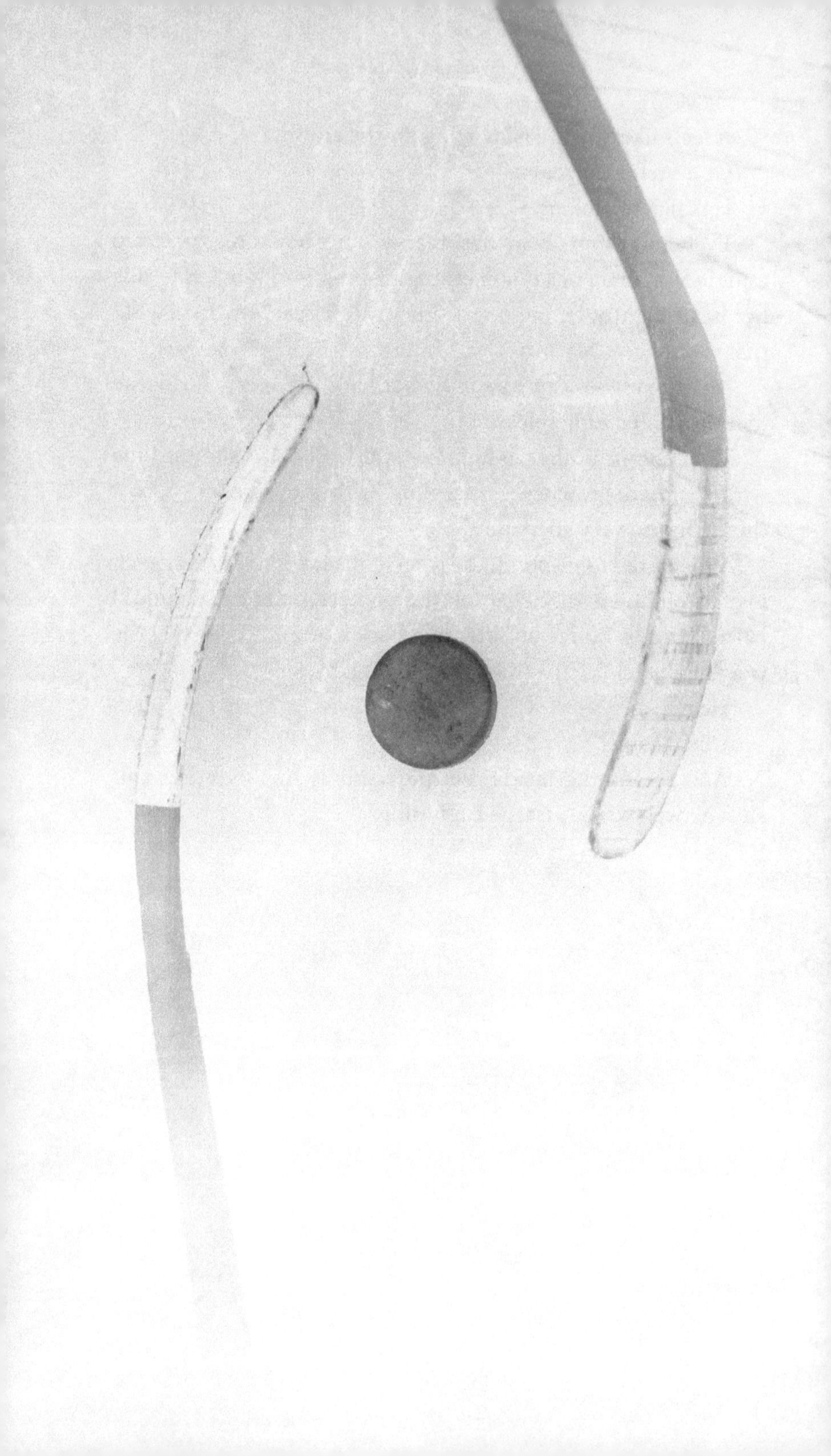

14
STEELE

I skate onto the ice and roll my shoulders in an attempt to shake off the agitation crawling under my skin as the arena roars around me. Lights are flashing, music is pulsing, and the fans are on their feet.

But none of it penetrates.

Not really.

The second my gaze scans the crowd, it finds her. She's in the owner's suite, seated next to Rina, a drink in her hand, wearing the new jersey I bought her. The sight of her wrapped in my name and number sets something primal loose deep inside me.

It's the hottest fucking thing I've ever seen.

All I can think is that the woman is mine.

Lilah might not know it yet, but she belongs to me.

She's always belonged to me.

River skates up beside me before following my line of sight.

"Looks like your woman made it this time," he mutters with a smirk. "Hopefully that means your head will be in the game."

"Shut up," I grumble, gripping my stick tighter.

He just grins. "Admit it, you're gone for that woman."

There's no point in denying it.

Instead, I take that energy and pour it into the game.

Every shift, every pass, every hit, I play the best damn period of my career.

Each time I touch the puck, the crowd roars. Every goal feels like a message, a silent vow.

She's here.

Watching.

And if she doesn't already know she's mine, I'll make damn sure she figures it out soon enough.

Before I know it, we're in the third period and the game is tied. The atmosphere in the arena is thick as the crowd pulses with energy. I dig my skates into the ice and race toward the net, tracking the puck, reading the play before it unfolds. I don't see the defenseman barreling toward me until it's too late.

A bone-crunching collision explodes against my ribs, and the next thing I know, I'm airborne.

The world tilts before impact.

My helmet slams against the boards, and a sharp burst of pain ricochets through my skull. Noise erupts around me. There are shouts and the shrill blast of the ref's whistle along with the scrape of skates cutting across ice. Even so, everything sounds distant and muffled.

I blink, trying to clear the stars clouding my vision as my ears ring. The ceiling of the Kingston Landry Arena looms above me, the bright lights blurring at the edges.

I should get up and shake it off.

Instead, I turn my head and focus on where Lilah is sitting, and squint.

But everything is fuzzy.

I want to tell her not to worry, that I'm okay.

I'll get up in a second.

That's when the world fades to black and it's lights out.

15
LILAH

I wait for Steele to shake off the brutal hit, but he remains still.

My stomach plummets as I grip the hem of my jersey, my knuckles turning white.

On the ice, the medics rush toward him while the crowd shifts from roaring excitement to a low murmur of unease.

When I rise to my feet, Evelyn's hand lands on my arm, steady but firm. "Darling, wait—"

"I can't," I whisper. "I have to get to him."

"Lilah, just—"

I don't wait around to hear the rest. I'm already moving, tearing out of the suite and into the hallway, my heart pounding as loud as the crowd buzzing behind me. I bolt for the stairs, my legs barely keeping up with the surge of adrenaline flooding my system.

By the time I hit the main level, security is everywhere. There's shouting and redirecting as they try to keep things under control. I push forward and weave through the crowd. A few guards recognize me, parting just enough to let me slip past. The echo of my steps follows me down the corridor. It feels like the walls narrow as my pulse thunders.

I just want him to be okay.

Please.

Be.

Okay.

My hands won't stop shaking, and every second that ticks by feels heavier than the last.

When I finally push open the door to the medical room, I'm hit with a wave of concern that stops me cold. Steele is stretched out on the exam table with a bag of ice pressed against his temple. His jersey and pads have been stripped away, leaving his chest bare and much too still.

The sight of him injured and vulnerable nearly brings me to my knees.

His head tilts at the sound of the door, and for a terrifying second, he doesn't say anything. Just blinks up at me with hazy, unfocused eyes.

Somehow, he manages to smirk. It's crooked and tired but unmistakably Steele.

"Hey, lucky charm," he rasps. "Didn't mean to scare you out there."

I exhale sharply and rush to his side. "Well, you did."

"Relax," he mutters, wincing slightly as he adjusts the ice pack. "It's just a little concussion."

I roll my eyes, but it's too shaky to be convincing. "There's no such thing as a *little* concussion. And you should know that by now."

When he doesn't answer, I step in closer. My fingers find his damp hair, and I thread them through gently, like I'm searching for further damage.

He doesn't flinch.

If anything, he leans into my touch.

The doctor continues his exam, rattling off the usual instructions. No screens, no alcohol, no strenuous activity, and plenty of rest. Steele nods along, like he's paying attention, but I know better. I can see in his eyes that he's already fading.

And it only stretches my nerves tighter.

I cross my arms over my chest and force myself to sound calm even though my heart is still in full panic mode. "I'm taking you home."

I half expect him to push back or give me one of those stubborn smirks and say he's fine.

Instead, he just nods his acceptance, allowing me to help him off the table. One of the trainers grabs his personal belongings from the locker room and helps him into a hoodie and sweats. When they're done, I slip an arm around his waist, steadying him. He leans against me as we head for the door and then out of the building to the parking lot.

When he moves to slide behind the wheel of his Lamborghini, I laugh and hold out my hand expectantly. "Absolutely not. You heard what the doctor said."

His forehead creases. "He didn't say anything about driving."

"Give me a break. You have a concussion, Steele. You're not getting behind the wheel of a car that goes zero to sixty in three seconds. Your precious baby will be just fine. I promise."

"I'm not worried about the Lamborghini," he mutters. "And you of all people should know that."

I stare at him for just a second.

"I do," I say, gentler now.

With a quiet sigh, he walks around to the passenger side and then slides into the seat, wincing as he leans back and closes his eyes.

I glance at him, worry twisting low in my stomach. "Are you sure you're okay?"

"I'm fine, Lilah," he says with his eyes still shut. "I just want to go home."

"Your wish is my command," I murmur, settling into the driver's seat and pressing the ignition.

"If only that were true."

My belly dips hard.

I don't respond.

I can't.

Not when the memory of his body against mine during the shoot flashes through my mind.

The drive is quiet, but it's not the kind of silence I can sink into. I keep shooting him worried looks at red lights, watching the way his head leans back against the seat, his features drawn and pale beneath the bruising already blooming at his temple.

By the time I pull into the underground garage, I'm practically leaping from the car. I round the front and open his door, offering my arm without a word. He doesn't fight me, but I can tell it grates on him to lean into me as we walk.

His balance is off and his movements are sluggish. He tries to hide it, but I can feel it in the way he presses more weight into my side with each step we take toward the elevator.

Even with the doctor's reassurance echoing in my mind, I'm still on edge.

That hit was brutal.

Once we make it into his penthouse, I steer him gently down the hall toward his bedroom. Waffles trails behind us like a tiny bodyguard, meowing once before hopping onto the bed and settling at the foot, her big green eyes locked on Steele like she knows something's off.

I ease him onto the edge of the bed and grab a bottle of water from his nightstand, placing it next to the painkillers I find in the bathroom.

"You should rest," I say, brushing my hand lightly against his arm.

He leans forward and braces his hands on his thighs. "I want to take a shower first. I feel gross."

We were in such a rush to leave the arena, he didn't get the chance.

"Okay, I'll help you."

His brows pull together. "I'm fine. I don't need any help."

"You have a concussion, Steele. Your coordination's crap right now. I'd rather not pick your giant ass up off the floor because you slipped."

He frowns and then pouts.

My lips twitch as I fight back a smile. "Come on, big guy. Trust me, you don't have anything I haven't seen before."

The second the words are out of my mouth, a vivid image of when he stepped out of the shower in all his naked glory flashes through my brain. I wince and shove the memory away.

He doesn't respond, just allows me to loop my arm around his waist and steer him toward the bathroom. The second we step inside the luxurious marble space, he grips the doorframe as his balance wobbles.

"See?" I huff. "This is exactly why you need my help."

He arches a brow. "Do you really think you'd be able to stop me from falling?"

I glance at the sheer wall of muscle beside me, and snort. "Not a chance. I'd end up crushed beneath you like a bug."

A smirk tugs at his lips. "That's the last thing I want to happen."

Without a word of warning, he grips the hem of his T-shirt and pulls it over his head before tossing it to the floor. I freeze, my gaze catching on the bruises that bloom across his ribs and the defined lines of his chest.

Before I can process anything else, his sweatpants hit the tile.

Then his boxers.

"Steele!" I choke, whipping around to face the towel rack. "You could've given me a little bit of warning!"

He laughs, completely unfazed. "What? I thought I didn't

have anything you haven't seen before," he teases. "Come to think of it, you have seen the goods."

A strangled sound catches in my throat as my gaze stays glued to the brushed nickel towel rack in front of me. I press my lips together, refusing to touch that comment with a ten-foot pole.

The shower sputters to life behind me, the sound of rushing water filling the space. Within seconds, steam begins to curl through the air, fogging the edges of the mirror and softening the lines of the room.

I ground myself, forcing the emotion to settle.

From the corner of my eye, I catch a glimpse of his reflection before the glass completely clouds over.

Broad shoulders.

Tapered waist.

Muscles that ripple beneath sun-kissed skin.

And that damn V-cut that disappears into a place I am definitely not going to peek at.

Eyes up, Monroe.

Steele is absolutely stunning. The man is built like he was carved from stone, but in this moment, as he braces a hand on the tile, his body unsteady, he looks vulnerable.

Human.

Still infuriatingly sexy, but not untouchable.

"Shit," he mutters. "Okay, maybe I need a little more help than I thought."

I let out a shaky exhale and glance toward the glass enclosure. His head is tilted as his other hand joins the first on the wall for balance and his legs tremble beneath him.

"You're lucky I love you," I mutter, stepping closer before my brain can catch up with my mouth.

His lips curve into a lazy grin. It's the one that's been known to cause minor hysteria across the league. "Yes, I am."

My heart stumbles, then slams back into rhythm.

He's not making this easy.

I inch closer, toeing off my shoes and socks. The tile is cool beneath my feet as the steam rises around me.

"What are you doing?" he asks, voice rough from the hot water and whatever's simmering beneath the surface of this moment.

"Helping you."

His gaze slides down my body and then back up again. "With all your clothes on?"

I blink. "Um... yes?"

He cocks his head. "You'll get soaked. At the very least, take off the jersey and jeans."

I glance down at the oversized shirt and the cling of denim that's already sticking to my legs from the humidity.

I mean, he's not wrong.

But stripping down to my underwear?

In front of Steele?

That feels dangerous.

Then again, is it any different than wearing a swimsuit?

Still...

For some reason, it feels like more.

I hesitate for half a second until he shifts again, unsteady and gripping the tile tighter.

That's all it takes for me to make a decision, and I drag the thick jersey over my head, letting it fall to the marble floor with a dull thud. Then I pop the button of my jeans, pull the zipper down, and shove the denim over my hips until it pools around my ankles.

I kick the jeans aside and straighten.

The air in the room feels hotter now.

Thicker.

My skin prickles as I become painfully aware of the lace bra and matching panties I'm wearing.

When I glance up, Steele's eyes are on me, tracking every

movement. There's nothing teasing about his gaze. It's not cocky or even smug.

Instead, it's reverent.

The look alone sends a shiver skating down my spine. My pulse kicks into overdrive as I move toward the glass door.

With a lift of my chin, I pretend this is a completely normal situation. As if stepping into a shower half-dressed with my best friend, who also happens to be concussed and naked, isn't a big deal at all.

Heat envelops me, caressing my limbs like a physical touch. Part of it is from the steam, but most of it comes from the way Steele is looking at me.

His nostrils flare and his Adam's apple bobs with a hard swallow.

That's all it takes for my pulse to thunder in response.

Not wanting to overthink the situation, I grab the shampoo bottle and squeeze a generous amount into my palm before stepping closer. His height forces me to rise onto my toes as I slide my fingers through his damp hair. The moment my nails gently graze his scalp, he exhales. It's a low, guttural sound that coils in my stomach.

He tilts his head forward, giving me better access, as I carefully massage the shampoo through his thick hair.

My touch is light but deliberate.

"Tell me if I'm hurting you," I whisper, trying to focus on the task at hand.

"You're not," he murmurs. "It feels good."

The tension between us is thick, almost tactile, like steam and desire have blurred into the same thing.

Without warning, Steele leans forward and lowers his head until it rests on my shoulder. My body goes still for a beat as his full weight sinks against me, his broad chest flush with mine, skin slick and burning hot from the water.

And suddenly, I'm holding him.

The sensation is overwhelming. The warmth of his exhale ghosts across my collarbone, and there's a subtle tremor in his muscles as I massage his scalp.

Every part of me is screaming to either back away or pull him closer.

But I can't move.

More than that, I don't want to.

The fabric of my bra and panties is already clinging to me, almost translucent now. I'm not technically naked, but I might as well be. Steele's hands stay carefully at his sides.

Until they don't.

His fingers twitch against my hip. Barely there, but I feel it like a searing, unspoken promise.

He sighs, deeper this time, the sound resonating through him and into me. My fingers falter slightly in his hair before continuing, because if I stop, I don't know what will happen next.

"Lilah," he murmurs.

I swallow hard as arousal flares to life inside me.

Steele's head is still pressed against my shoulder. I'm trapped between the urge to pull away and the terrifying, overwhelming desire to stay right here and keep touching him.

To keep feeling the weight of his hard body against mine.

I should take a step back and create some distance between us before I do something stupid.

When I shift, his arms tighten around my waist. "Stay."

It's not a command.

More of a request.

One I can't seem to refuse.

My fingers continue to move through his hair, massaging his scalp as I rinse away the shampoo. A deep groan vibrates from him as his nose skims my throat.

I swallow hard, willing my hands to stay steady.

Steele is all golden skin and hard muscle, every inch of him powerful even as he leans into me for support. The steam from the shower clings to us, turning everything slick. His shoulders, pecs, along with the sharp lines of his abs. My hands are trembling, but they won't stop touching him.

It's impossible not to notice how good he feels beneath my fingers.

How solid.

"Soap," he murmurs.

It takes me a second to catch his meaning. My brain is working on a five-second delay, and everything inside me feels uncoordinated. As if I've stepped into a dream I have no idea how to wake from.

Right... Soap.

I fumble for the bottle, squeezing a generous amount into my palm before carefully pressing my hands to him. I start at his shoulders, then down his arms, building a lather as I go. My touch is hesitant at first, but it quickly turns into an unhurried exploration.

His muscles flex beneath my hands.

I work the soap over his chest, my fingers gliding along the curve of each muscle and down the ridges of his abdomen. His body is a map I never planned to memorize, but now, I don't think I could forget it if I tried.

I shouldn't be enjoying this.

But, God... how could I not?

The man is spectacular.

Not just because of how he looks, but because this is Steele.

The one who's always been there.

And now he's standing naked in front of me, muscles tight, composure slipping, while I touch him. My heart stutters as my hands drift lower, following the deep cut of his hips, dangerously close to the part of him I absolutely should not be thinking about.

The moment my fingertips graze the edge of that line, reality slams into me.

I jerk my hands back like I've touched a live wire, stumbling a step before catching myself on the slick tile.

Steele's eyes flicker open, his pupils blown wide, jaw clenched like he's barely keeping himself in check.

My heart pounds. I need to get out of here before we cross a line we can't come back from.

I clear my throat, already backing away until my shoulder blades press against the cool glass of the shower door. The contact startles me. It's too cold compared to the heat gathered inside me.

"We should finish up," I blurt. "You need to rest."

For a second, he doesn't respond. He just stares at me like he's trying to read the thoughts circling through my head.

Then his gaze drops for a fraction of a second, and I know he sees everything. The way my soaked bra clings to me. The curve of my hips beneath drenched lace. The fact that I'm barely keeping it together.

He exhales slowly, nostrils flaring, like he's trying to cool the fire between us. "Yeah. That's probably a good idea."

Even as he turns slightly, giving me space, I can still feel the heat of his body.

I can still feel *him.*

Instead of waiting, I step out of the shower and snatch the nearest towel from the rack, wrapping it tightly around myself.

I need the space.

The cool air.

The way I feel right now isn't how I should be feeling about Steele.

I clutch the towel tighter, like it can shield me from the chaos unraveling inside me. My hands tremble as I grab another towel.

Steele steps out of the steam a second later, water dripping from every inch of his perfectly sculpted frame. His hair is wet and messy, his skin flushed from the heat. My gaze flicks upward, only to find him already watching me.

His gray eyes are locked on mine, intense and unreadable. There's something dark in them that crackles between us like static.

Neither of us says a word as the air remains thick.

Almost suffocating.

"Turn around," I whisper, trying and failing to steady my voice.

His eyes spark before he obeys, rotating so his back is to me. The second his gaze disappears, I try to pull myself together.

One second.

Two.

Get it together, Lilah.

I step closer and press the towel to his shoulders.

His muscles jump beneath my touch.

With deliberate movements, I blot away the water clinging to his skin. Everything about Steele is hard and defined. It doesn't take long for me to get lost in the flesh beneath my fingertips. The anxiety filling me gradually ebbs, and I forget about everything except the moment unfolding between us.

Steele remains motionless as the towel glides over his skin. Silence lingers between us as I move from one shoulder blade to the other, sliding along his bulging biceps, and muscular forearms before sweeping across the broad expanse of his back. Every defined muscle and sculpted line are evidence of his unwavering discipline. I've never known anyone who takes better care of their body than Steele.

Need flares to life in my core. It's a steady, thumping beat I can't help but be aware of.

I've seen him shirtless more times than I can count, but this feels different. Like I'm touching him for the first time.

No, not just touching him.

Really *feeling* him.

My hand falters as I trail the towel down the broad plane of his back. My gaze catches on a droplet of water that slides down his spine. Despite the temptation to lean forward and lick it away, I force myself to stay in control. Steele shifts beneath my touch, as if he can sense every heated impulse racing through my mind. I squeeze my eyes shut and push it away.

This is Steele.

My Steele.

And yet, my body doesn't seem to care.

Need pulses through me in a low, steady rhythm that's impossible to ignore. It coils in my belly, a throb of awareness that makes it hard to focus.

Steele shifts again, a flicker of tension rippling through him, as if he feels it too.

He doesn't say a word.

With every pass of the towel, I inch my way downward. It doesn't take long before I'm at his lower back, dangerously close to his ass. I can't imagine what it would feel like to trace over the tight curve of him without the towel between us.

I falter at the base of his spine, unsure if I should continue. Before I can make a conscious decision, the towel dips until I'm swiping over the round firmness of the taut muscles. It's gradually that I slide the material back and forth until not a drop of water lingers. Heat flares in my core, and I have to squeeze my thighs together to stymie the need crashing through me.

Even though I shouldn't do it, I lower myself to the floor and drag the towel over his thighs. They're thick and strong from being on the ice six days a week during the season. I sweep over his calves and feet, which are firmly planted on the gray bath mat. My belly flutters with nerves at the thought of shifting to his front.

You're being ridiculous, Lilah.

This is Steele.

He's hurt and needs your help.

The last thing I want is for him to bend over, get dizzy, and fall.

I keep that thought firmly in mind as I rise to my feet and circle around him until I'm facing the wall of his chest. My breath grows shallow and uneven, betraying the storm brewing inside me.

Even though I refuse to meet his eyes, I'm acutely aware of his heated gaze tracking my every movement. My hands tremble as I sweep wide strokes of the towel over his perfectly defined pecs, captivated by the strength beneath my fingertips. All it would take is dropping the towel, and I could feel him directly against my skin.

The fresh, clean scent of soap clings to him, surrounding me in a dizzying haze and igniting a longing I hadn't known lay dormant beneath the surface of our friendship. I find myself swaying toward him before pulling back and forcing myself to regain control.

"Are you okay?" His hands flex and tighten at his sides, as if he wants to reach out and take hold of me.

Unable to meet his gaze, I keep my eyes focused on his pecs. "Yup, almost done."

A wave of heat crashes over me as I slide the material over one nipple and then the other until both are stiff. When I make one final pass across the sensitive peaks, he lets out a low hiss.

The sound has another burst of need exploding in my core.

I move the towel over his rib cage, tracing the deep grooves of his ripped abdominals. Every ridge is sharply defined, his body carved from discipline and determination. The towel glides lower, and I falter for half a second when I reach the sharp cut of his V-line—a path that arrows straight down to the coarse, dark hair at his groin.

A flutter of nerves takes root in my belly, blooming into something deeper, more dangerous, as my gaze dips lower. He's thick and swollen, his arousal impossible to ignore. Heat pulses through me, a molten ache that settles low in my abdomen as my thighs press together.

My fingers twitch with the need to touch him, but I settle for a few brisk pats, clinging to what little restraint I have left. Steele groans, the sound low and guttural, as his hips jerk forward in response. The movement is raw and instinctive. It only intensifies the ache thundering through me. I shift lower, forcing myself to focus, pretending my hands aren't still trembling as I bring the towel to his shins.

The moment I settle in front of him, it hits me like a jolt.

This position puts me eye level with his cock.

My lips part as his thick, glistening length bobs just inches from my face.

A wave of desire crashes over me. It's both fierce and consuming. I want to taste him. To feel the weight of him on my tongue. Does he taste as clean and fresh as he smells? The question strikes like lightning and lingers, sparking need in every cell of my body.

I take a shaky inhale and tilt my head back, unable to resist seeking out his gaze. When our eyes meet, a tingling sensation skitters along my skin.

Desire flares in his expression, hot and hungry, before it slams into me with the force of an avalanche. No man has ever looked at me the way Steele does now. As if I'm everything he's ever wanted.

One large hand lifts to cup my cheek with a tenderness that unravels something deep inside me. His thumb strums lightly over my parted lips, and it's that small, affectionate touch that undoes me. He groans again, and it vibrates through me like a caress.

Our eyes stay locked as the rest of the world fades.

"Lilah…"

I blink as shock spirals through me.

Am I really crouched before him?

"I-I think you're dry," I stammer.

His hand falls away as I scramble to my feet, unsure where to look or what to do.

"Want to give me the towel?"

"Oh. Of course." I thrust it out to him.

He takes it from my hand before securing it around his waist.

"Look at me, Lilah," he murmurs, the words coming out rough and strained.

It's so tempting to bolt. Instead, I force my gaze to his.

We stand still, towels clinging to damp skin, tension thick and electric like the air before a storm.

I don't know who moves first.

Maybe we both do.

Maybe neither of us do.

But suddenly, his forehead is brushing against mine, his breath fanning across my parted lips.

"Steele," I whisper, barely able to get his name out.

His fingers find my waist before flexing around it.

With a sharp exhale, he steps back. His jaw is tight and his expression is unreadable as he plucks another towel from the rack and dries his hair. "Would you grab me a pair of boxers and then help me to bed?"

My fingers twitch at my sides as I nod and then spin toward the door, escaping to the safety of his bedroom where I can finally clear my head.

The longing I feel for him is frightening. I've never felt this kind of need thrum through me.

Certainly never for Devon.

Or any of the other boyfriends I've had.

I pull open the dresser drawer and grab the first pair of boxers my fingers come in contact with. When I step back into the bathroom, Steele is slouched against the marble counter, eyelids half-closed, swaying slightly, like he's seconds away from face-planting.

When he reaches out to take the underwear, I gently brush his hand aside.

"Let me," I murmur. "It'll be quicker, then you can get to bed. You look like you're about to collapse."

A tired half-smile tugs at his lips. "Funny, because that's exactly how I feel. Like I got hit by a truck."

"You pretty much did," I say, crouching in front of him. "And that truck's name was Henrik Sundström."

"Remind me to return the favor next time we play Dallas."

For a second time, I drop to my knees in front of him, then help as he steps into the boxers. He lifts one leg, then the other, silent except for the occasional sharp inhale. I guide the fabric carefully up his legs, over his muscular thighs, until it settles at his hips. He clutches the towel at his waist, holding it in place while I finish.

Then I rise, wrapping an arm around him. "Come on, big guy. Let's get you to bed."

With a snort, he leans into me as I guide him into the other room. His steps are heavy, sluggish, but he doesn't fight me. I pull back the covers and help him slide between the sheets, then tuck the blanket around him.

Waffles hops onto the bed and settles against his side.

I run my fingers gently through his damp hair. "I'm glad you're okay," I whisper. "You scared the hell out of me."

His eyes stay locked on mine. "I'm sorry, Lilah. That's the last thing I'd ever want to do."

I lean down and brush a kiss across his forehead. The caress lingers before I finally pull away. His fingers find mine, tightening around them, making it impossible to retreat.

"Stay," he murmurs.

I freeze.

His request is quiet and laced with exhaustion.

I'm torn. With the way I'm feeling, staying feels dangerous.

"Please?" he adds.

And just like that, leaving doesn't feel like an option.

"I need pajamas," I say, weak with the fight I've already lost.

"Just grab my robe."

After a moment's pause, I nod and walk away. In the bathroom, I drop the towel, peel off my damp underwear and bra, and reach for the oversized plaid robe hanging on the back of the door. It smells like him. Clean soap, mint shampoo, and something undeniably Steele. I wrap it around me and tighten the belt at my waist.

When I return to the bedroom, the only light illuminating the space spills in from the hallway. I flick it off, crawl into bed beside him, and settle against the pillow.

Steele shifts toward me until we're only inches apart. The weight of him beside me settles something deep inside my chest.

"You know I love you, right?" he whispers into the darkness.

My heart skips a beat. "Steele—"

"I always have."

I shudder as every wall inside me crumbles. I want to tell him it's the concussion talking, and that he won't remember this in the morning.

But I don't.

Because I know he means it.

"I love you too," I whisper.

A quiet, contented sigh escapes him, and within seconds, he's out.

I lie there in the dark and watch him before reaching out and brushing a stray curl from his forehead.

I've never cared for anyone the way I do this man.

And I don't think I ever will again.

I wake slowly, surfacing from sleep like I'm swimming through fog. My head still aches, but it's dull now. Less of a pounding and more of a persistent throb.

Manageable.

But something feels off.

Not wrong, just different.

There's something warm and delicate pressed against me.

The faint scent of honey and vanilla wraps around me. It's both comforting and familiar.

Even before I open my eyes, my pulse kicks. My body knows. Maybe my brain hasn't fully caught up, but everything else has.

When I finally blink into the early morning light, the view stuns me into stillness.

Lilah is tucked against me, her legs tangled with mine, her cheek resting over my heart like she was always meant to be there. The tie of the robe she's wearing has loosened during the night, and the plaid fabric has slipped so that it barely clings to her curves.

There's smooth, creamy skin everywhere.

Her bare thigh is draped across me, and the dip of her waist is exposed beneath the open material, along with the gentle swell of her hip that peeks out just below the edge of the covers.

Jesus.

I don't move as every muscle in my body goes rigid and my brain scrambles to process what the hell is happening.

Because this isn't a dream or even one of those half-awake fantasies I've been torturing myself with since the night she moved in.

This is real.

Lilah Monroe is in my bed, wrapped around me, her exhalations steady as they fan across my collarbone. Her lips are parted slightly, and her face is peaceful in sleep.

All I can think about is how close we are and how damn right it feels.

How completely bowled over I am by her without her even trying.

She shifts, and her lips brush the skin just above my heart.

Fuck.

My control, already fragile, splinters completely apart.

I clench the sheets, as if that will somehow anchor me to reality, giving me the necessary restraint.

Because there's no way I can touch her.

Even though all I want to do is run my hands over her.

Her lashes flutter, and for a second, she doesn't move. She doesn't seem to realize where she is. She simply nestles closer, releasing a contented sigh that undoes me in ways I don't have words for.

We stay like that, suspended in quiet, for just a moment as her eyelashes feather shut again and our bodies remain tangled.

When her eyes blink open for a second time, she freezes. Her body stiffens against mine as the realization of where she is and who she's lying against sinks in. Her gaze flicks to mine, and for a moment, our eyes lock.

"Oh my God," she chokes out, bolting upright so fast she nearly tumbles off the bed. She grabs the sheets and yanks them up to her collarbone like I haven't already seen more than that robe was ever meant to hide.

I can't help the smirk that tugs at my lips as I prop myself up on one elbow and watch her unravel. "Morning, lucky charm."

Her cheeks flush a deep, gorgeous shade of red as she clutches the blankets tighter. "Steele, we... um... we didn't..."

She trails off, clearly struggling to make her mouth cooperate with her brain.

Is it terrible that all I can think about is how damn adorable she is when she's flustered?

"Nope," I say, dragging out the word with a lazy grin. "But if we had? Trust me. You'd remember it. There'd be zero confusion."

Her mouth opens and then closes. The blush heating her cheeks creeps down her neck like wildfire, and with a groan of embarrassment, she drags the blanket over her head.

I chuckle, but under the teasing, my heart is pounding. Because waking up with her in my bed and tangled up in my sheets is everything I've ever wanted.

And I meant every word I said last night.

I love her.

Lilah peeks out from beneath the covers, obviously weighing her chances of a quick escape. After a beat, she lets out a small, awkward cough and sits up, still clutching the sheets like they're her last line of defense.

"I should probably go make breakfast," she mutters, gaze darting everywhere but at me.

Decision made, she swings her legs over the edge of the bed and rises to her feet before fumbling with the robe, retying the belt. Then she's on the move, heading for the hallway.

Just as she reaches the door, I say, "Lilah."

She stutters to a stop but doesn't turn.

"You don't have to run," I say quietly. "Not from me."

Her spine stiffens slightly, and when she finally looks over her shoulder, uncertainty flickers in her eyes. "I'm not running."

I think we both know that's not true.

My voice gentles. "Yeah, you are."

"I'm making breakfast," she says before disappearing around the corner.

Even though every instinct screams at me to follow her, I don't move.

As much as I want to chase her, what Lilah needs right now isn't pressure.

She needs space.

Time to process.

Time to figure out what she wants.

And I hope when she does...

She realizes that what she wants is me.

17

LILAH

I grip the kitchen counter, hoping it will ground me in the here and now, as my heart continues to slam from waking up entwined with Steele. There's no way to forget how his body heat soaked into me. Or the low raspiness of his voice as it wrapped around me like a blanket, cocooning me in comfort.

Above all else, Steele has always made me feel safe.

But that's not necessarily the case right now.

Something else besides friendship is brewing beneath the surface.

Something bigger.

Something I'm not sure I'm ready for.

Because once we cross that line, there's no going back.

Unfortunately, my body doesn't care one bit what my brain is screaming.

I'm flushed and restless. My skin feels too tight, too sensitive, like I'm barely holding myself together. My thighs are clenched, as if that will be enough to chase away the heat that's coiling low in the pit of my belly.

What I need more than anything is a distraction.

Breakfast.

Right.

I need to make breakfast. If I can just focus on that, maybe I'll feel normal again by the time I have to face Steele.

I open the fridge and pull out the eggs, setting them on the counter with hands that won't stop shaking. After sucking in a deep breath, I exhale, trying to talk myself down from the ledge.

This is Steele we're talking about.

The one constant in a life that's been unraveling since the day I caught my boyfriend fucking another woman.

I need him to stay *Steele.*

Uncomplicated.

Solid.

Steady.

"You okay, lucky charm?"

His voice from behind me has everything tilting sideways again. It's low and raspy. Even though it's still thick with sleep, it's edged with concern.

And just like that, my composure fractures. I close my eyes for half a second before forcing myself to turn around.

That's a big mistake.

Huge.

He's leaning in the doorway, arms crossed over his bare chest, skin still flushed from sleep. His sweatpants hang loosely around his hips, and his dark hair is a tousled mess I want to sink my fingers into.

No.

No.

No.

Don't think like that.

My mouth goes dry as my brain short-circuits.

He looks unfairly good.

Even worse than that?

I see it now.

The sharp jawline.

The carved lines of his body.

The way his gaze tracks me, as if I'm something he wants to unwrap.

When did Steele become *that* guy?

His eyes search mine as he steps into the kitchen. "You ran out of the bedroom like your ass was on fire. You sure you're good?"

Unable to continue staring at him, I spin back toward the stove. I need something—*anything*—to focus on besides the six-foot-three problem that just walked into the kitchen. He's not even crowding my personal space and I feel knocked off balance.

"I'm fine," I mutter, cracking an egg against the side of the pan a little too aggressively.

It splatters everywhere.

With shaking hands, I grab a spatula and try not to think about how I helped him shower last night or dried him off. Or how I watched water slide down every inch of that ridiculously sculpted body like it was the most fascinating thing I'd ever witnessed.

If I'm being honest, it just might have been.

God, I need help.

The professional kind.

I move around the kitchen like a hummingbird, grabbing things I don't need and opening drawers I'm not even thinking about. I'm flustered and uncoordinated, and the worst part is, he's not saying a damn thing.

Just watching.

Calm and still.

Like he knows the reason I'm unraveling and he's willing to patiently wait me out.

He's always been steady and loyal. The one person who's never let me down.

What I need most right now is for him to stay that way. Especially when everything around me has imploded.

My job.

My living situation.

My entire future is now riddled with uncertainty.

And my parents have never been the supportive type.

But Steele?

He's always been my anchor. I'm afraid of what will happen if we rock the boat and venture into something more. Especially if it doesn't work out.

Would I lose him too?

I don't think I could deal with that.

I'm jerked from the turmoil of my thoughts when his hand brushes across mine.

"Let me help," he says, voice low and easy, like we're not standing on the edge of something that might break us wide open. "You're going to massacre those eggs."

"No, I'm not," I lie.

He arches a brow. "Lilah. That egg has already died twice."

Despite everything, a laugh slips free from me. It's half-mortified and half-relieved. I step aside, giving him room to maneuver. He grabs a fork and starts whisking the rest of the eggs with practiced ease, completely unfazed by his lack of clothing.

I try not to stare, and fail spectacularly.

When he turns his back to me, I let my gaze wander for just a few greedy seconds. I'm struck by the wide spread of his shoulders and the subtle flex of his forearms as he moves. And don't even get me started on the way his hair curls slightly at the nape of his neck.

These aren't things I've ever noticed before.

Or maybe I have and I just didn't allow myself to see them.

"I didn't realize you had skills outside of hockey," I murmur, the words slipping out before I can stop them.

He glances at me from over his shoulder as a lazy, knowing smile tugs at his lips. "Don't fool yourself, lucky charm. I've got lots of hidden skill sets. And I'm more than happy to show them off. All you have to do is say the word."

My eyes widen as heat creeps up the back of my neck, and I get the distinct feeling we're *not* talking about scrambled eggs anymore.

"I believe you," I say, hoping it comes off playful, and not like I'm barely holding it together.

This conversation feels all sorts of dangerous. And yet, some reckless, curious part of me is tempted to push it further.

But I don't.

Are you kidding?

Of course I don't.

Because even with the air thick between us, crackling with things neither of us are saying, I'm still afraid of what it could mean if we cross that line.

So instead, I pivot, pointing to the eggs in the pan. "Better watch those, or they'll burn."

"We wouldn't want that," he says, refocusing his attention.

We move around each other, falling into an easy rhythm that's comfortably domestic.

It shouldn't feel like this.

Like home.

All I can think about is how different this is from what I had with Devon, who never once stood beside me while I cooked or asked how I liked my eggs or teased me just to see me smile.

With Steele, it feels like he sees all of me.

Even the parts I'm careful to keep hidden away.

The tension between us is still there, coiled and pulsing, but it's gentler now. Like it's shifted from wildfire to something that's more of a slow burn.

He pours the eggs into the pan and then starts stirring. I grab plates, trying to distract myself with tasks that don't involve ogling him or confessing things I'm not ready to reveal.

"Thanks for helping," I say after a moment.

His shoulder bumps mine. "Always."

That one word lands deep. It echoes in the part of me that's still trying to figure out what steady looks like.

Because Steele, standing here in the kitchen, making breakfast like we've done this a hundred times before, feels precariously close to something permanent.

That's when I realize I never asked how he's doing.

Oh my God.

How could I forget about the hit he took last night?

He's throwing me off so much, I'm not thinking straight.

And that's never happened to me before.

I search his face. "How are you feeling?"

He takes a moment before answering. "I've got a slight headache and some soreness. Nothing a little time won't fix."

"Good. I'm glad." I pause, then admit, "You really scared me."

"I'm sorry about that."

I nod. "I know. Guess it's an occupational hazard, huh?"

He smirks.

When the eggs are done, we move around each other with quiet familiarity, piling plates and refilling coffee. It's almost easy to forget that I woke up in his bed, practically naked, our bodies tangled up in the sheets. Or how scared I am that our relationship might be changing.

But then he offers me a mug, and our fingers brush. That's all it takes for everything to slam back into me. It would be impossible not to notice the way Steele looks at me now is different. Like he sees more than his friend standing before him.

I take a sip of coffee, trying to hide the fact that I'm unraveling all over again.

"Sure you're okay?" he asks.

I nod, even though the answer is more complicated than that. "Yeah. Just tired."

His eyes remain on me for a beat longer than necessary. "Really? I slept the best I have in years."

The truth is that I did too.

Pressed next to Steele's strong body?

How could I not?

Although, there's no way I'm about to admit that.

Instead of responding, I lower myself onto the stool beside him and push a bite of eggs around my plate. The silence between us stretches, strangely comfortable, until his phone buzzes on the counter.

He picks it up, brows pulling together as he scans the screen. "It's Coach. He wants me to swing by the arena and check in with the team doc this morning."

I glance up, concern flickering through me. "Should I drive you?"

His gaze lifts to mine and lingers before he smiles. "Nah. Stay here. I'll grab a ride."

The words are simple. Easy. But the way he says them is like he's not just thinking about himself. He's thinking about me. As if he somehow understands that I might need the quiet more than he needs the company.

A part of me wants to go with and make sure he's okay. To be near him in a way that doesn't feel purely platonic anymore.

But another part, the one still rattled from everything that's shifted between us, knows a little space might be exactly what I need to figure out what the hell is happening before it all spirals out of control.

"Okay."

After a few more bites of breakfast, he stands and carries his plate to the sink. "I'm gonna shower and head out."

I nod. "Sounds good."

He pauses at the threshold of the kitchen as a grin tugs at the corners of his mouth. "Unless you'd like to offer your assistance again?"

That's all it takes for the memories to crash over me. The way his slick skin felt beneath my palms, how his muscles flexed under my touch, the heavy steam swirling in the air around us, and the quiet that settled deep inside me the moment I laid my hands on him.

Heat surges through me, threatening to pull me under.

"Lilah?"

I blink. "No. I think you can handle it on your own."

He smirks. "Probably. But it'd be a hell of a lot more fun with you."

I clear my throat, along with those lingering images. "I'm going to take my own shower and get dressed. I'll see you when you get back."

"Suit yourself." With a chuckle, he saunters out of the kitchen like he didn't just set my internal temperature on fire.

I can't stop from watching the way his muscles shift and flex with every effortless move as he walks down the hall.

Yup... a little space is exactly what I need to get my head on straight again.

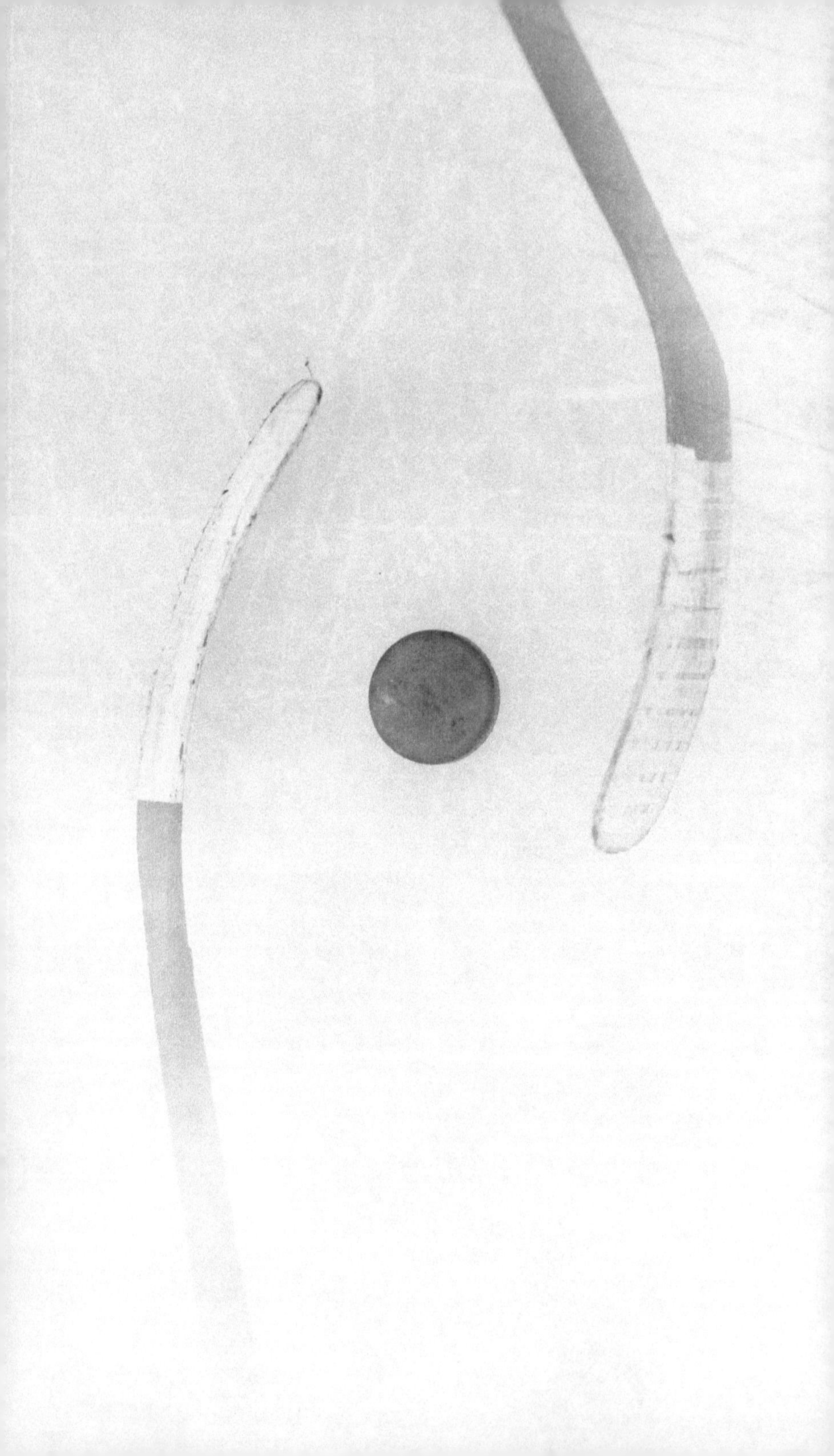

The doc clears me to return to light practice tomorrow, but not before shining a penlight in my eyes one last time. I'm still a little foggy, but the throbbing in my skull has dulled from the relentless jackhammer it was last night.

Once out of the medical suite, I stretch my shoulders, trying to roll out the tension still coiled tight in my muscles. The scent of floor wax and fresh sweat hangs in the air. It's comforting in a weird, twisted way.

Kind of like home.

"Hey," a familiar voice calls out.

I glance up and spot River walking down the corridor, dressed in a Railers tee and mesh shorts, a water bottle tucked casually under one arm. His hair's a little damp, like he just worked out.

"How're you feeling after that hit last night?"

"Better," I say with a crooked grin. "Doc says I can skate again tomorrow if I take it easy."

He gives me a once-over. "You actually gonna listen?"

"Absolutely not."

River snorts. "Yeah, I didn't think so."

We fall into step, heading toward the locker room, our conversation easy and light. River's one of the few guys on the team I've always clicked with. Low drama, sharp wit, and lately, a lot more focused on what's important. He's dialed in now in a way he wasn't a couple seasons ago. He used to be more of a wildcard.

It's nice to see.

We're halfway down the corridor when someone calls out, "Yo, Thompson!"

We both glance over our shoulders to find Zane Holloway jogging to catch up, all swagger and designer everything. His oversized Versace sunglasses are perched on top of his head, and a Gucci duffel bag swings from one shoulder, completing the look.

"Jesus," River mutters. "Could the dude be any more flamboyant?"

"Doubtful."

Zane catches up and claps a hand against River's back. "I've been trying to get ahold of you. What's going on? You ignoring my calls now?"

River shrugs him off. "Sorry, I was working out. You should try it sometime."

Zane chuckles. "Please. Who has time for that when Gigi's in the middle of filming? I'm gonna be all over the new season. She's talking to her agent about a spin-off. A whole show built around us. You know how dope that'll be?"

River shoots me a look like he's begging me to drag him out of this conversation.

"Sounds like you've got it all figured out," he says flatly.

"Damn right, I do." Zane taps the side of his head. "Gotta stay three steps ahead, baby."

He finally acknowledges me with a chin lift. "Hey, Cap. Feeling better? Couldn't believe they had to carry you out on a stretcher. That was rough, man. Low-key embarrassing."

I keep my tone neutral, even though my knuckles twitch. "I'm fine, thanks for asking."

Zane turns his attention back to River. "You still dragging ass, or are you finally coming out with us next weekend? Gigi's got a friend. She's a model, twenty-two, barely speaks English. You don't need conversation, right?"

"Hard pass," River says without blinking.

"Man, when did you get so boring? You used to be a good time."

"I don't know," River says dryly. "Maybe when I started giving a shit about the right things."

Zane barks out a laugh. "I *am* focused on the right things. Money, exposure, and banging ten-out-of-tens. Tell me, what's more important than that?"

River's jaw tightens. "Have you checked in on Callie lately? Or seen Nora?"

Zane waves him off like he's being asked about the weather. "Callie's good. She's solid. Honestly, if I had to knock someone up, I picked the right girl. She can handle it. The last thing she needs is for me to hover." He shrugs like it's no big deal. Like fatherhood is something that happened *to* him, not something he should take responsibility for. "And she'll be working that charity thing on Thursday," he adds with a straight face. "I'll check in then. She can meet Gigi in person."

River's jaw tics. "Yeah, I'm sure Callie will love that."

Either Zane doesn't catch the sarcasm or he just doesn't care. "Probably. Maybe Gigi'll give her an autograph or something."

My gaze shifts to River. His whole posture has changed. His shoulders are drawn and his arms are crossed as tension rolls off him in heavy waves.

"You're a real dick," River says, voice calm but cutting.

Zane just grins like it's a compliment. "Come on, man. Don't be so fucking serious."

When his phone buzzes, he glances at the screen before answering with a grin. "Hey, babe. Yeah, I'm on my way. They're filming already? Perfect."

He ends the call and slips his phone into his back pocket before slapping River on the shoulder like they're still bros. "Catch you losers later."

We watch him stroll off like he didn't just insult the mother of his child and brag about his airtime without missing a beat.

River's jaw clenches again. "Was he always that big of a douche?"

"Yup," I say on an exhale. "Although, it used to be less obvious."

River doesn't say anything for a moment. Just stares down the hallway where Zane disappeared, like he's fighting the urge to go after him and unload everything he's been holding back.

"I really fucking hate how he treats Callie," he mutters.

I nod. "I know. She deserves better."

He doesn't respond, but then again, he doesn't need to.

Both his thoughts and feelings are written clearly across his face.

It's only a matter of time before he acts on them.

19
LILAH

I stand at the kitchen counter, surrounded by open jars, produce scraps, and a half-written list of smoothie combos I've been tinkering with. The blender whirls as I pulse together a new mix. This one has mango, spinach, protein powder, almond butter, and a touch of cinnamon.

The second I pour it into a glass, I slide it across the island to Steele. "Okay, taste test time."

He grabs it without hesitation and takes a long sip before staring at the half empty glass. "That's actually good. What's in it?"

I arch a brow. "If I told you, then I'd have to kill you. Top secret recipe and all."

He grins, but before he can say anything else, his phone buzzes on the counter. He glances at the screen and then answers with an easy, "Sanderson."

There's a pause. "Yup. Bring it up."

His gaze remains locked on me as he ends the call.

"What was that about?" I ask, wiping my hands on a dish towel.

The smirk he shoots my way is full of secrets. "You'll see."

Before I can question him any further, the elevator dings

down the hall. A second later, the doors glide open before closing again.

Steele tips his head toward the entryway. "Maybe you should go check it out."

Cold dread trickles down my spine. The last time something arrived at Steele's door under my name, it was a stack of cardboard boxes. My entire life packed up and dumped at his feet.

I hesitate for just a beat, then exhale and pad toward the front entrance, wiping my hands once more for good measure. Steele trails behind me, close enough that I can feel his presence but quiet enough not to be in my personal space.

Even though I've been trying to forget the feel of his body in the shower or the sight of him asleep beside me in bed, the truth is, it's always there, simmering beneath the surface. Now that I've seen him that way, I can't unsee it. There's no way to shove it down and forget it happened.

A black shopping bag rests just outside the elevator. I glance at him with a raised brow.

Instead of giving me an explanation, he nods. "Go on, open it."

Curiosity pricks at me as I reach inside and pull out a box. As soon as I lift the lid away, I gasp.

Inside is the silver dress I wore for the photo shoot. The one that hugged every curve and made me feel like a sexy goddess.

"Cam said you could keep it. I thought you'd like to wear it tonight for the charity dinner."

There's a smaller box tucked beneath it. Shoes. Delicate, strappy silver heels with a soft shimmer.

I blink at him and shake my head. "I can't believe you did this."

Devon certainly never would have.

That thought sneaks in uninvited, and once it takes root, it's unshakable.

My ex never thought about things like this. Never tried to make me feel special. Not that I expected to be lavished with gifts, but the gesture alone, knowing Steele was thinking about me enough to plan this, settles deep within.

"Lucky charm? You okay?" Steele asks quietly.

I blink again, and realize my vision's blurred with tears.

"I—" My voice cracks, and I try to laugh, brushing them away before they can fall. "It's nothing. I'm fine. Just... thank you. I love it."

His brows draw together as he steps closer. "Hey," he says, cupping my cheek. His thumb swipes gently under my eye, chasing away the moisture. "Talk to me. What's wrong?"

"Nothing's wrong," I whisper, even though that's not exactly true.

The way he looks at me with this kind of quiet, focused intensity makes me feel like I'm seconds away from coming undone.

"I just wasn't expecting it," I say finally. "No one's ever thought about me like this."

"I do," he says simply. "All the time."

His tone is tender, but the words land like thunder.

I can't move.

I can't speak.

I just stand there with a dress in my arms and his gaze burning into mine.

And God help me, I don't know what scares me more. That I feel something I've never felt before...

Or that I don't want it to stop.

I'm adjusting my cuff links when the sharp click of heels striking the wood floor catches my attention. I turn, ready to throw out some smart-ass comment about how she always takes too damn long to get ready, when I catch my first glimpse.

That's the exact moment everything inside me goes silent.

Lilah stands in the doorway, wrapped in the silver dress that was delivered earlier this afternoon. It's sleek, hugging every curve like it was made for her. The fabric dips low in the front, showing just enough cleavage to make my fingers twitch with the need to touch.

Her hair is pinned up with a few loose tendrils left to frame her face, and her makeup is subtle yet flawless, her lips painted a pale pink.

The woman is a fucking knockout.

Something tightens inside me, making it hard to speak. "Jesus, lucky charm."

With a tilt of her head, her lips curve into a smirk. "Does it look as good as you remembered?"

My feet are on the move before my brain can catch up.

Once I've closed the space between us, my hand finds the small of her back.

"Even better."

She stills, her gaze dropping to my lips.

It's so damn tempting to lean in and kiss her. But I'm trying to give her time to figure out what she wants.

I close the distance between us just enough for my lips to brush against the shell of her ear. "You have to be the most beautiful woman I've ever seen." My voice drops, turning rougher. "I'm proud to have you on my arm tonight."

I'm standing close enough to feel the shiver slide through her body.

"Thank you," she says.

"Ready to go?"

"Yes." There's a pause before she adds, "Thanks again for the dress. You didn't need to have it sent over."

I pop a brow. "After seeing you in it at the photo shoot? Like hell I didn't. It was made for you."

"I appreciate it."

Even though her voice is steady, her fingers tighten around her clutch.

Good.

I want her to be just as affected as I am.

The way I've always been where she's concerned.

I grab my jacket from the hook near the door before placing a hand on her lower back as we walk to the private elevator. Every step we take, the slit in her dress parts just enough to catch a glimpse of her thigh.

The elevator doors glide open and she steps in first before I follow, hitting the button for the underground garage. The second they slide shut, the small space amplifies the crackling tension between us. The scent of her perfume hits me. It's citrusy with a hint of vanilla. I swear it's something that's been burned into my memory.

She doesn't look at me, but her body is angled just enough that her bare shoulder brushes against my arm. The contact is light, barely there, but it short-circuits something in me.

It's taking everything I have not to pull her into my arms and kiss her the way I've imagined for years.

But I don't.

Because she's not ready.

And once I lay my hands on her, there's no going back.

"Steele?"

"Yeah?" I say, keeping my tone steady even as my pulse kicks up a notch.

She finally glances at me, and the tenderness in her eyes catches me off guard.

"Thank you," she says. "For everything. Not just the dress, but for letting me stay with you and giving me a job. You're always there when I need someone."

I reach for her without thinking, wrapping an arm around her waist and pulling her gently into my side before dropping a kiss on the top of her head.

"I'll always be there for you, Lilah. Always."

She leans into me for just a second, and it sends a crack right through my resolve.

The elevator chimes, and the doors slide open with a quiet whoosh, spilling us into the cool, echoing space of the underground parking garage.

I click the fob for the Lamborghini, and the headlights blink. We walk side by side, our steps echoing on the concrete. Once we reach the car, I open the passenger door.

"Chivalry?" she teases, sliding onto the seat, her dress riding higher on her thigh as she settles on the buttery leather.

With my gaze locked on hers, I lean in. "You're damn right. Only the best for my lucky charm."

Even though she rolls her eyes, her smile lingers as I close the door and walk around to the driver's side. The second I slide in, the scent of her perfume wraps around me again.

The engine purrs to life, and we ease out of the garage, merging onto Lake Shore Drive with the skyline glittering beside us. The lake reflects the lights of the city in fractured, shimmering ribbons.

The radio hums in the background, filling the space.

"We don't have to stay for more than an hour or so," I say, my hand resting on the gearshift close to her thigh.

She glances at me. "I'm sure there'll be lots of people who want to meet you."

"Maybe. Doesn't change the fact that you're the only one I want to talk to."

Her lips curve as she rests her head against the cushion. "Rina isn't about to let that happen."

"You're probably right about that." I flick a glance her way. "Guess we'll just have to avoid her for the night."

We're less than five minutes away from arriving at a charity event full of cameras, reporters, and half of the city's most influential movers and shakers. Right now, all I want is more time with Lilah in this car to pretend the rest of the world doesn't exist. She looks so damn good, I just want to keep her all to myself.

As soon as I pull up to the front entrance of the building, a valet rushes around to open my door as another one helps Lilah out of the vehicle. The second we step onto the red carpet, cameras go off like fireworks.

Reporters shout my name, tossing out questions, trying to pull my attention to them, but I don't give a damn about the press. My focus is entirely centered on Lilah. It's on the way her fingers tighten around my arm and the way she stays close as the crowd surges forward.

Even though she's been to a few events with me when she's

in between boyfriends, she's not used to this kind of rabid attention.

I lean down, my lips brushing against her ear. "You okay?"

She nods, but I feel the tension in her body, in the way she grips my sleeve just a little too tightly. I do the only thing I can and make sure she knows she's not alone. My hand slides from her waist to the small of her back, pulling her in closer.

The cameras eat it up as reporters ask if we're together.

It's tempting to tell them we are, but I keep my mouth closed. The last thing I want to do is scare Lilah away.

Let them talk and speculate.

I don't give a shit.

Just as we're finishing up, Zane and his reality star girlfriend arrive in a sleek black limo. The press surges toward them, screaming both of their names, hurtling too many questions for them to possibly answer.

Zane struts in wearing a fur coat and oversized, blinged-out sunglasses. Thick gold chains glint around his neck under the burst of camera flashes. Beside him, his girlfriend wears a sheer dress that leaves absolutely nothing to the imagination.

If their intention was to make a spectacle of themselves, they've succeeded. With a shake of my head, I steer Lilah inside the building.

The venue is all crystal chandeliers and flickering candlelight, a live band playing something slow and smooth in the background.

I scan the room, and spot Rina at the far end talking with Oliver. Although, it looks more like she's reading him the riot act. No surprise there. I'm pretty sure my teammate exists solely to drive our PR manager insane. You'd think by now Oliver would've figured out that life would be a hell of a lot easier if he just did what she wanted.

"I don't think we'll have to worry about Rina tonight." I

point to where they're standing. "Looks like she already has her hands full."

"Actually, she looks ready to strangle him."

"What else is new?"

A smile quirks Lilah's lips as her blue eyes settle on me. "It's okay if you need to circulate. There are a lot of important people here."

"Nah."

Maybe.

All right, fine. I should probably say hello to Hugh, and network with a few of the high-profile sponsors. Otherwise, I'll be the one who gets an earful from Rina in the morning.

And that's never a fun experience.

Been there.

Done that.

I'm about to suggest Lilah come with me, when I catch sight of the dance floor and a different idea takes form.

I lean down, my voice low against her ear. "Come dance with me."

She pulls back in surprise. "I'm sorry, since when do you do that?"

"Since I have a beautiful woman on my arm." Already, I'm leading her toward the space set aside for music and movement.

Lilah's hand fits perfectly in mine as I guide her toward the edge of the floor. The low thrum of music pulses through the ballroom, softened by the ambient lighting and the warm glow from the crystal chandeliers overhead. The hum of laughter and conversation surrounds us.

Once I carve out a space, I pull her into my arms until her body fits perfectly against mine. One hand finds her waist while the other threads through her fingers.

A faint exhale escapes her as she rests her cheek against my chest.

Her silver dress clings to every curve, the fabric brushing lightly against my suit with each sway. But it's not just the way she feels pressed against me that unravels me. It's the way she tilts her head back, eyes locking on mine like I'm the only person in the room. Like I'm the only one who's ever mattered.

My movements are smooth and easy. I might not like to dance, but my mother made sure I learned when I was in high school.

Don't think I didn't hear a lot of shit talk from my teammates when they found out.

There's something about holding her in my arms that feels different tonight.

Like maybe, for the first time, she could really be mine.

All the patience, all the years of waiting, has finally led here.

To *her*.

Right where I always hoped we'd be.

I tighten my grip as my thumb brushes over her hip.

"Did I mention earlier that you look pretty handsome?" she murmurs with a half-smile.

"I think we both know I'm not a fan of tuxes," I say, pulling her a little closer. "But for you? In that dress? Totally worth it."

She laughs. The sound is delicate and unsure, but it dies on her lips as my gaze drops to her mouth, and for a beat, everything else falls away. The air thickens as her expression shifts. A flicker of something raw flashes across her face.

As if she's finally starting to feel the pull between us too.

The gravity that's been dragging us closer with every heartbeat.

My hand tightens at the small of her back as I lean in. That's all it takes for her to falter, her lips to part, and—

"Steele."

I blink as Rina's voice cuts through the moment like a burst of cold air. I turn to find her standing at the edge of the floor, tablet in hand, her expression apologetic.

"Hugh is looking for you." Her red lips curve as she glances between me and Lilah. "There are a few donors he wants you to meet."

My hand stays anchored to the small of Lilah's back, my body angled toward hers. "Does it have to be right now?"

Rina lifts a brow in amusement. "Unless you want to field a strongly worded text from Evelyn in shouty caps... yeah. Now."

I glance down at Lilah to find her gaze fixed on my chest, as if she can't quite bring herself to meet my eyes. When she finally does, her smile is cautious.

"I'll grab a drink," she murmurs. "You go charm the big shots."

The casual tone doesn't fool me. Not when there are questions written in her eyes that she's not quite ready to ask out loud.

I lean down, brushing a kiss against her cheek, my lips lingering for just a second longer than appropriate. "I'll find you as soon as I'm done."

She nods, eyes darting away. "Okay."

I hate that I have to let her go, even for a second.

Before I can say anything more, Rina links her arm through Lilah's and guides her away. "Come on. You owe me a few answers."

Lilah groans. "Rina."

As they disappear into the crowd, Lilah tosses an unsteady look at me over her shoulder, as if she's feeling the shift too, and isn't sure what to do about it.

But that's okay.

Because I am.

And I'll make damn sure she never has to doubt it.

21
LILAH

The second Rina hooks her arm through mine and steers me toward the buffet, I know I'm about to get interrogated.

"Okay, spill," she hisses. "Has anything happened between you and Steele?"

I choke on a laugh, trying to play it off even as my heart does this weird little stutter.

"Of course not," I say, giving a breezy wave of my hand. "It's not like that between us."

Only, the words ring a little hollow even to my own ears.

Because lately, everything feels like it's shifting under my feet.

The way he looks at me.

And the way I catch myself looking back.

Or how being close to him no longer feels safe the way it used to.

Instead, it feels electric.

Dangerous.

Rina arches a brow, clearly not buying a single word.

Before she can press me further, we spot Callie setting out fresh platters of desserts on one of the banquet tables. She's in motion, rearranging trays with the kind of graceful focus I envy, her hair pulled back in a loose braid that keeps slipping over her shoulder.

"Hey, girl!" Rina chirps, dragging me along.

Callie looks up, her face brightening when she sees us. "Hey! You both look absolutely gorgeous!"

We lean over to check out the spread. There are mini cheesecakes, chocolate tarts, and delicate sugar cookies iced to perfection.

"Everything looks *incredible*," I tell her, meaning it.

Rina nods. "Seriously. You killed it."

Callie smiles, but there's a flicker of nerves in her expression as she tucks a strand of hair behind her ear and offers a small shrug. "Honestly, I almost didn't take the job," she admits. "I wasn't sure about working an event where Zane would be. But the money was too good to pass up, and I need it now more than ever."

"Well, I'm glad you did," Rina says. "It's an amazing opportunity for people to sample the kind of desserts you make. Who knows where it might lead?"

"I'm so proud of you," I add. "I know it's not easy to be around him and..." I trail off as the person we've been discussing walks toward us. "Incoming."

"Hey, Callie," Zane says as he strolls up, his arm slung around a petite blonde woman whose dress is almost nonexistent. It takes effort not to stare at her nipples, which are clearly visible through the sheer material. She's all perfect makeup, designer shoes, and an air of practiced disinterest.

"Hello, ladies." He nods at us, like we're fans he's generously acknowledging.

We murmur stiff hellos, neither of us making an effort to hide our frostiness.

Zane either doesn't notice or doesn't care. Probably a mixture of both. He's always been all about himself.

He turns to the blonde at his side and says, "This is Callie, my kid's mother."

Callie's eyes widen, her body going rigid for a split second before she pastes on a polite, detached smile.

I honestly don't know how she does it.

The blonde gives Callie a once-over, the kind of up-and-down scan that makes my hackles rise.

"I'm Gigi. It's so great we could meet," she says with a fake little smile, like she's already mentally scrubbing Callie from her mind.

Zane chuckles and adds, like he's tossing her a bone, "Callie runs a little bakery around the corner from the arena."

"That is so adorable." Gigi glances at the table. "I'd try one, but I don't eat refined sugar or gluten."

Callie's brows draw together. "Oh."

Gigi pulls out her phone and starts snapping selfies with Zane. She's all staged smiles and sultry angles, as if she's starring in her own personal photo shoot instead of attending a charity gala.

Zane turns to Callie and shoves his phone at her. "Hey, can you take a picture of us real quick?"

Callie hesitates before forcing a smile and taking the phone from him. Zane yanks Gigi against him and plants a kiss on her that's so over-the-top it's almost embarrassing.

"Ewww," Rina mutters from beside me, scrunching her face in disgust.

Callie bites her lip, clearly mortified, but she snaps the photos anyway before handing the phone back.

Zane doesn't bother thanking her.

"C'mon, babe," he says to Gigi, sliding his arm around her waist. "Let's mingle."

And just like that, they disappear into the crowd, leaving the scent of expensive cologne and perfume behind in their wake.

Callie stands there for a second, staring after them with a strange look on her face.

"I really don't know what I ever saw in him," she says, her tone disbelieving.

Rina slips an arm around her shoulders. "Girl, as far as I'm concerned, you dodged a major bullet."

I nod, offering her a small, supportive smile. "Seriously. He doesn't deserve to be in the same zip code as you or Nora."

Callie releases a shaky laugh, her shoulders relaxing just a bit.

As she turns back toward the table to adjust a tray, I catch a glimpse of someone watching her from across the room.

River.

He's standing near the edge of the crowd with a frown etched on his face as his gaze tracks Callie with an intensity that makes my pulse skitter.

I nudge Rina lightly, and nod in his direction.

She follows my gaze and grins. "Now *that* would be an interesting turn of events," she murmurs.

And for some reason, that makes me smile more than anything else.

22
STEELE

The second we walk through the penthouse door, Waffles comes bounding toward us, her tiny paws skidding across the hardwood floors. With a laugh, Lilah kicks off her heels before crouching down to greet her. The hem of her silver dress pools around her, and for a second, I just stand and watch.

I haven't been able to stop staring at her all night.

And seeing her barefoot, smiling, her arms wrapped around the tiny ball of fur I brought home for her, just about knocks the wind from me.

She glances up with a gentle expression. "Thank you again for her," she says, cuddling Waffles closer and pressing a kiss to the kitten's head.

I struggle against a swell of emotion. "I'd do just about anything to put that look on your face." The words are out of my mouth before I can stop them.

Lilah rises to her feet, with Waffles in her arms, before closing the distance between us. When her gaze dips from my eyes to my mouth, the air around us turns thick and heavy, pressing in on all sides. For just a moment or two, I swear she's about to kiss me.

My heart stutters. I don't think I've ever wanted anything more in my life.

At the last second, she leans in and presses her lips against my cheek.

It's innocent.

Sweet.

And my complete undoing.

It takes every shred of self-control I have not to haul her against me and kiss her the way I've been dying to for years.

Waffles meows, and the moment dissolves. Lilah gives a light chuckle as she steps back with the kitten still cradled in her arms.

I'm nowhere near ready for this night to be over.

"Would you like a glass of wine?"

She smiles. "Sure."

I shrug off my jacket and loosen my tie before popping open the top buttons of my dress shirt as I move toward the kitchen. Her attention stays on me as the silence stretches between us. I pour her a glass of wine and then grab a bourbon for myself before heading back to the living room. I find her tucked into the corner of the couch with Waffles pressed against her side.

After settling beside her, I pass her the wine.

"Did you have a good time tonight?" I ask, taking a sip of my drink.

She nods, a small smile tugging at her mouth. "Yeah, it was nice." Then she rolls her eyes and her expression turns wry. "Zane, however, is a total jerk. I can't believe he brought his new girlfriend over and introduced her to Callie like that."

"Zane's an asshole who never deserved her in the first place," I say with a grunt.

Lilah's head tilts, a grateful look crossing her face. "Thank you for saying that."

I frown. "Why wouldn't I? It's the truth."

With a shrug, she runs her fingers along the stem of her glass. "I don't know. He's your teammate. Bro code, I guess?"

I level her with a look, one that leaves her fidgeting beneath my steady gaze. "Come on, Lilah," I say. "You know me better than that."

"You're right, I do. That's not the way you operate."

She sips her wine before rising and padding across the room toward the floor-to-ceiling windows.

Something shifts inside me as I watch her.

"This view has to be one of the best in the city," she says, gazing out at the glittering skyline. "I never get tired of it."

Unable to resist the lure of her, I set my glass down and cross the room to stand behind her. I'm close enough to feel the warmth of her body as the scent of her perfume dances in the air.

"You're wrong," I murmur. "The view's got nothing on you standing there in that dress."

"Thank you. You're always so good to me."

A comfortable silence settles between us as a faraway look enters her eyes.

It doesn't take long before a frown mars her expression.

"Penny for your thoughts," I say softly.

A weak laugh tumbles from her lips as she takes a sip of her wine like she's trying to buy time.

My mouth curves into a grin as I catch the slight color that blooms in her cheeks. "Wait just a second. Are you actually blushing?"

She raises a hand to her face as it floods with more color.

"Okay, now you *gotta* tell me what you're thinking about," I say with a low laugh, nudging her gently.

She groans. "No, I can't."

That's all it takes for my brows to rise.

In all the years I've known Lilah, she's never shied away

from talking to me. So whatever this is, it matters. And there's no way in hell I'm walking away until I get to the bottom of it.

23
LILAH

Unsure how to respond, I take a deep gulp of my wine.

"Holy shit," he says with even more amusement. "Does this conversation really call for liquid courage?"

"Maybe," I mutter, lowering the glass. "This is so embarrassing. I don't want to tell you, okay? Can we just drop it? Please?"

He shakes his head. "No way. Spill."

I glance at the wine, watching the deep red swirl in the glass. "Ugh." It takes several seconds to work up the nerve to speak again.

"So, I told you I walked in on Devon and Marissa while they were..."

"Fucking," he supplies, the humor in his voice vanishing like smoke.

I swallow hard and take another drink, finishing it off. "Yeah. That."

The memory presses in, hot and sharp. "He had her bent over his desk and his hand was in her hair, gripping her ponytail. He slapped her ass a few times, all the while talking dirty."

I finally dare a glance at him from beneath my lashes. His

face gives nothing away, but the intensity in his eyes is palpable, as if he's absorbing every single word.

"It felt like I was staring at someone I didn't even recognize," I whisper. "Like she was able to unlock a part of him that I couldn't." I glance down at my empty glass. "I need a refill."

He takes it gently from my hand and sets it on the console table. "No, you don't."

The way he looks at me sends a jolt straight through my body. His gaze flickers to my mouth and then back to my eyes.

I blurt out the one thought I haven't been able to make sense of. "He was never like that with me."

A taut silence stretches between us until it's on the verge of snapping.

"Is that what you wanted from him?" he asks.

I freeze as he moves closer, invading my personal space.

Unable to hold his gaze, I look away.

His fingers slip beneath my chin, coaxing my attention back to him. "Is that what you wanted from him?" he repeats, gentler this time.

My tongue darts out to moisten my lips as I force myself to answer the question. Talking to Steele about this is so much more embarrassing than I imagined. "I don't know. I mean... maybe? I guess I just..." I trail off, unsure how to express the tangled thoughts running rampant through my head.

"Hey, it's me, Lilah," he says. "We can talk about anything."

I exhale.

He's right.

We can.

"Yes. I think... I wanted something *more*. But Devon never saw me that way."

Steele's jaw flexes.

"I guess I don't understand why," I add, eyes falling shut. "Why her and not me? What was it about her that made him so uninhibited?"

Steele swears, and when my lashes flutter open, I find his hands balled at his sides.

"Don't do that. Don't compare yourself to her. You're... Jesus, Lilah. You have no idea." He drags a hand through his hair. "The way you're wired, the things you want, they're not wrong. Wanting to feel that kind of passion, that connection? It's not something you should be ashamed of."

I don't realize I'm trembling until he reaches out and places a hand on my waist to steady me. His eyes search mine, like he's trying to read everything I'm holding back. All the things I'm unwilling to put into words.

Steele exhales slowly, like he's barely holding himself together. "You think you weren't enough for him. But that asshole couldn't even begin to understand what he had. Or what you needed and deserved." His voice is a husky whisper when he speaks again. "If I were him, I never would've left your bed. I'd have worshipped every damn inch of you. I would have touched you in all the ways you craved until I learned how to read your body like it was the only language I understood."

Heat blooms beneath my skin.

It's hard to make sense of what's shifting between us.

Or maybe I already know exactly what it is.

And that's the part that terrifies me most.

"Steele..."

He lifts a hand, brushing a strand of hair away from my cheek. "Is that what you want, Lilah? To experience that kind of passion? To have someone take you like an animal, to make you feel like your brain can finally click off and you can stop thinking for a change?"

The arousal that slams into me at those words is almost enough to knock me off my feet.

Because the answer is there.

On the tip of my tongue.

Fighting to break free.

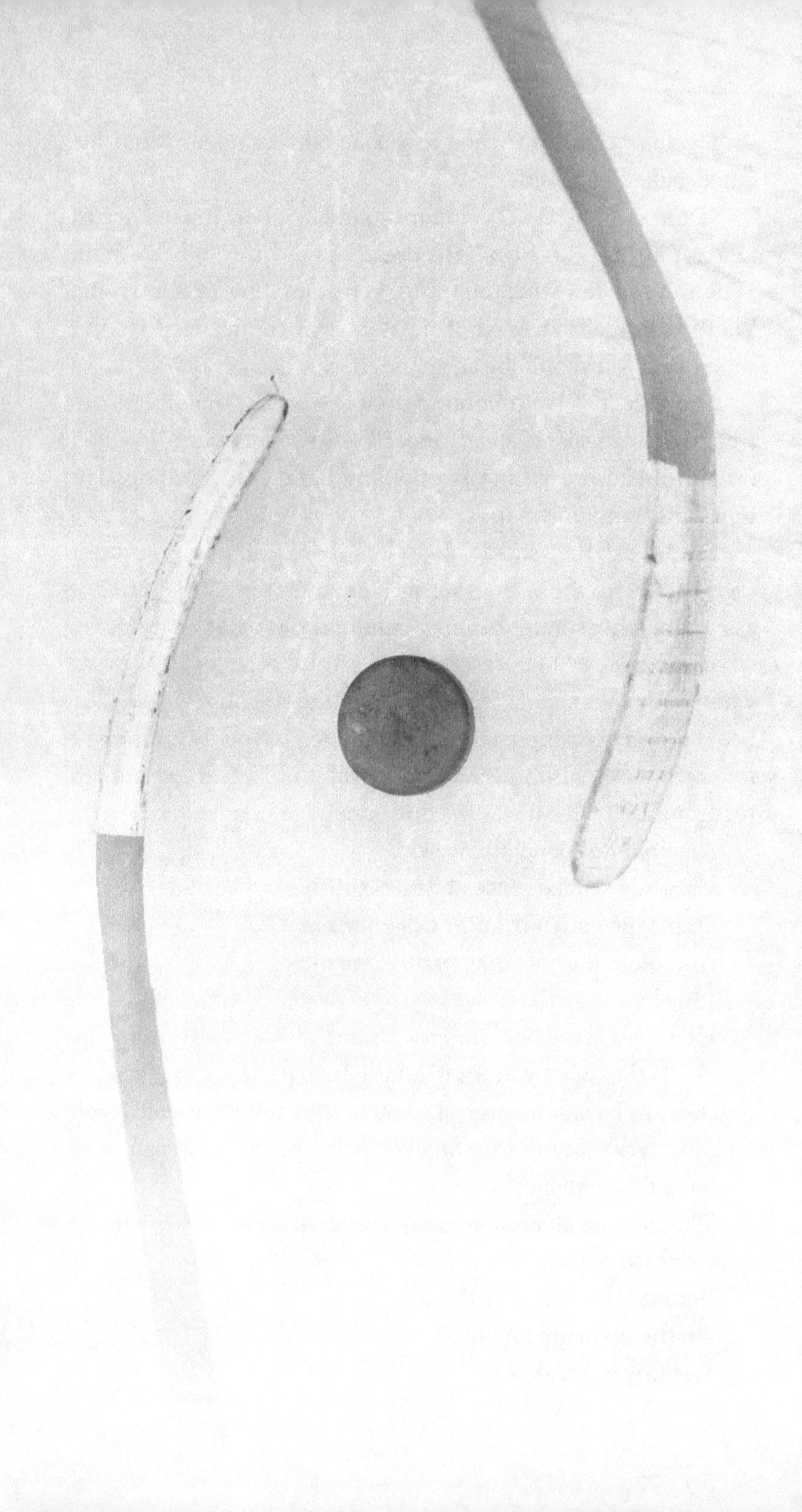

24
STEELE

She doesn't respond right away.

Not with words.

But it's there in the way her lips part and her chest rises and falls with each shaky inhalation. Or how the air between us turns charged until it's almost crackling.

She's right there on the edge with me.

But then, she takes a single step back.

That's all it takes to knock the air from my lungs.

"I'm afraid to ruin what we have," she whispers. "You've been my friend for so long. I can't lose you. I just... I need to think."

My heart is beating so loud it drowns out everything else. The last thing I'm going to do is push her into something she doesn't want or isn't ready for.

"That's fine. Take all the time you need. Whatever you decide won't change anything between us." My fingers slip beneath her chin again so she has no choice but to meet my eyes. "You understand that, right?"

Her gaze reluctantly finds mine before searching it for the truth. "Yes. I don't want to make another mistake. I can't afford to."

It kills me that she sees this—*us*—as a potential mistake.

Because to me, it's the only thing that's ever felt right.

The only thing that's ever made sense.

I force a smile and gentle my tone. "Then don't think of it as some big decision about the future."

Her brows pinch. "What do you mean?"

I take a step forward, watching her carefully. "I'm not asking for forever, Lilah. I'm not even asking for a relationship."

Her eyes widen slightly, but she doesn't interrupt.

"While you're here," I say, "we could just be..." I drag a hand through my hair. "Call it whatever you want. A break. A distraction. Friends with benefits."

I hate the words as soon as they leave my mouth. But if they get me even a piece of her, I'll choke them down.

Her brows lift as her expression turns amused. "Friends with benefits?"

I lift one shoulder in a casual shrug and force a crooked smile. "Sure. No pressure. No strings. You set the pace, and I'll follow your lead."

She crosses her arms like a shield across her chest, but I see the way her eyes darken with the idea. The hesitation that battles her curiosity. "I don't know."

The last thing I want to do is spook her.

It's slowly that I lift my hand to her face until my fingers can graze her cheek. She doesn't even realize it when she leans into my touch.

But I do.

I see it.

I feel it.

And it gives me the tiniest sliver of hope.

"Take some time," I murmur, "and think about it. It's your choice, Lilah. It always has been."

Her lips part to say something, but I don't give her the chance.

I lean in, brushing my mouth over hers just once. It's barely a kiss. Just enough to taste her. Just enough to destroy every bit of control I have left.

I keep my eyes locked on hers. "If you want this," I whisper, "I can give it to you. I'll give you all the pleasure you can stand."

She goes still.

And so do I.

It feels like we're suspended in a moment.

My thumb traces the corner of her mouth. "And then I'll give you even more."

Her pulse flutters beneath her skin.

Instead of pressing for an answer the way every instinct demands, I force myself to take a step back and let her go.

The next move needs to be hers.

And if she says yes?

She'll never want anyone else again.

Not after me.

Not after this.

I'll make damn sure of it.

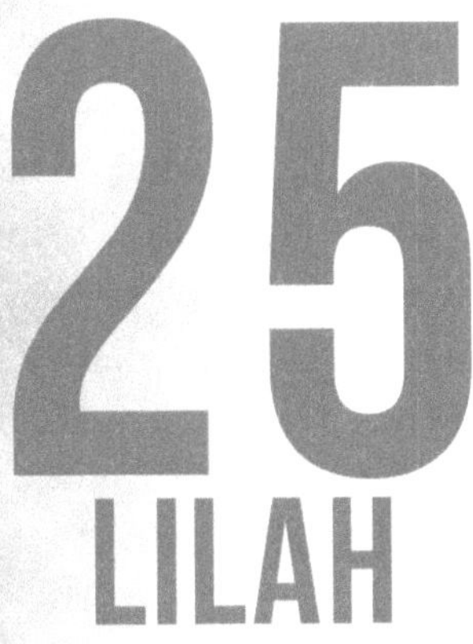

25

LILAH

I wake to the faint scent of coffee.

Not the rich, earthy aroma from the kitchen kind of coffee, but the close, immediate kind. The kind that means someone set a fresh cup beside my bed.

Sure enough, I roll over and find a steaming mug on the nightstand. My favorite blend, the one Steele hunted down last week after I casually mentioned it.

I melt.

God, that man.

How am I supposed to make a decision when *this* is the baseline?

I sit up and then wrap my hands around the warm mug. I'm bombarded with a thousand emotions I can't even begin to untangle. Because Steele Sanderson isn't just the guy I'm staying with. He's become an important presence in my life.

And now he's offered me something that's threatening to change everything.

Friends with benefits.

That's what he called it.

But let's be honest, I've known Steele too long. I'm afraid that if we enter into a casual arrangement, it'll end badly.

Why would I want to jeopardize our friendship over a meaningless fling?

And yet, I'd be lying if I didn't admit to being tempted.

I barely slept last night, my mind refusing to shut off. Every time I closed my eyes, I remembered the way he sounded when he whispered that he could give me what I wanted.

That he'd worship me.

That he'd know exactly how to touch me.

I'd nearly combusted on the spot.

With a sigh, I clutch the mug tighter.

What I need is help.

Backup.

I grab my phone and tap into the group chat with Callie, Rina, and Sloane.

ME:

Emergency girl huddle. Can we meet at Lakeshore Sweets? I need advice. 10 a.m.?

Rina replies instantly.

RINA:

Count me in. Unfortunately, I gotta deal with my problem child first and then I'll be there.

Callie follows seconds later.

CALLIE:

Been at the bakery since 5. Come on by.

SLOANE:

We'll have a table and sugar waiting.

I drag myself out of bed, toss on leggings and an oversized sweater, and try to make my hair look less like a tornado. After swiping on a little mascara and lip balm, I slip on my sneakers, grab my bag, and head to the bakery.

Lakeshore Sweets is bustling with activity when I walk in. Delicious scents wrap around me like a hug. It's cozy and warm. A welcome change from the storm raging inside me.

Callie is behind the counter, helping a customer, while Sloane wipes down a nearby table. I wave, and they both grin before nodding toward the corner table where a giant carafe of coffee and a plate of cinnamon rolls already waits.

Moments later, the bell above the door jingles again. Rina blows in like a hurricane in heels, with oversized sunglasses covering half her face. She yanks them off with a dramatic sigh as she slumps onto the chair beside me.

Callie eyes her. "You look like you could use a large Dirty Cinnamon Hustler."

Rina moans. "Yes. Immediately. And make it extra dirty, please."

Sloane snorts. "Let me guess. Oliver?"

"When isn't it Oliver?" Rina mutters. "That man has zero boundaries and even less common sense. I swear, one more stunt and I'm going to strangle him with his own jockstrap."

She takes the offered coffee from Callie and sips before letting out a blissful sigh. "Okay, I think I seriously just orgasmed. What did you put in it? Crack?"

Callie laughs. "You're welcome."

Rina turns to me with narrowed eyes. "All right. Spill. What's the emergency?"

I hesitate, toying with the edge of a napkin. "It's Steele."

Three heads snap toward me like I just announced I joined the Oregon cult my mother warned me about.

Rina leans in. "Please tell me you two finally did the deed."

I nearly choke on my coffee. "What? No!" There's a pause before I amend that statement. "Well, not yet."

"Oh my God," Rina exclaims. "You're actually *thinking* about it."

Callie's brows lift. "Wait, are you saying—"

"He offered... something," I cut in. "And now I can't stop thinking about it."

Rina's eyes light up. "What kind of something are we talking about?"

"Friends with benefits," I murmur with a cringe. "Even saying that out loud feels weird."

Sloane lifts her mug. "I was not expecting that."

Rina throws her hands up. "I can't even believe you're on the fence. It's Steele. The guy practically breathes swoon. Have you seen him lately? I'd climb him like a tree."

Callie rolls her eyes. "Ignore her. I understand, Lilah. You two have been friends for years. That's a lot to risk."

They both turn to Sloane, the official tiebreaker.

The dark-haired woman leans back in her chair with her arms crossed, and studies me carefully. "What is it that *you* want?"

I open my mouth before slamming it closed again.

The answer terrifies me.

Finally, I whisper, "I think I want to say yes."

Sloane nods. "Then do it."

Rina raises her cup. "To bad decisions and hot sex."

"To friendship," Callie says with a laugh. "And figuring it out as we go."

We all clink our mugs together, and for the first time since Steele made his offer, the weight pressing down on me eases just a bit.

Because no matter what happens, I have these women to help me get through it.

We pull up to Gold Coast Table, the rooftop restaurant where we're meeting my cousin and his wife. It's one of Lilah's favorite spots with one of the best views in all of Chicago. I booked it on purpose, hoping the setting would ease some of the strain still lingering between us.

The valet takes the car, and I round to her side, holding out my hand.

As soon as we touch, a spark zips through my fingertips.

We ride the elevator up in silence, the ambient music doing little to drown out my worries. Her perfume lingers in the air, subtle and warm, and I have to stop myself from leaning closer and inhaling a big breath of her.

When the metal doors slide open, we're greeted by a wash of golden light and the low buzz of conversations. It's the kind of place that slows time and makes the world feel smaller. More intimate.

I keep my hand at the small of her back as we walk, guiding her through the maze of white tablecloths and flickering candles. I probably shouldn't touch her like this until she gives me her answer.

But I can't seem to help myself.

I've waited too damn long for her.

And I really hope tonight changes everything.

The hostess leads us to a table near the railing where Bridger and Holland are already waiting, tucked into one of the best spots on the patio. Fairy lights twinkle overhead, casting a subtle glow across the table. Portable heaters hum, warming the crisp evening air.

Bridger rises with a grin and pulls me into a quick hug. "Good to see you, man. It's been way too long."

"We've missed you two." I clap him on the back before leaning down to kiss Holland's cheek. "You look amazing. Everything good with the baby?"

Beaming, the redhead rests her hand over her bump. "She's doing great."

"She?" Lilah asks, her voice touched with surprise.

Bridger nods, pride written in every line of his face. "Yup, found out last week. It's official, we're having a girl."

I glance at Lilah. Her smile is tender, but there's something behind it.

Something quiet and aching.

Longing, maybe.

Or maybe not, and I'm totally misreading it.

But it settles in my chest anyway as I imagine her swollen with our child.

Fuck.

My hands linger a beat too long on her shoulders before I pull out her chair. When she sits, I drop down on the one beside her, and my thigh brushes lightly against hers under the table.

"I'm glad you were able to make it into town," I say to my cousin. "Will you be here long enough to catch a game?"

Bridger shakes his head. "Wish I could, but we've got an investors' meeting Friday morning. Maybe next time, when you're playing Mav or Hayes. I wouldn't mind watching you hand them a good beating."

"Yeah, we don't get together like we used to," I say with a chuckle.

Holland sighs. "Everyone's scattered now. Careers. Families. It's harder to keep up."

The waiter arrives, and I order for both of us out of habit.

Espresso martini for Lilah and a beer for me.

She doesn't question it. Just smiles like she's still not used to being taken care of. Like it surprises her that someone remembers what she likes.

Conversation flows easily as we trade memories and laugh over ridiculous moments from college, slipping into a rhythm that feels effortless.

Familiar.

My hand finds the back of Lilah's chair, and when my fingers brush her shoulder, she doesn't flinch or pull away.

That simple touch anchors me.

It always has.

And I'm pretty sure it does the same for her.

She laughs at one of Bridger's stories, the sound carefree as her eyes crinkle with humor. That's all it takes for something inside me to twist. I want to be the reason she smiles like that.

Every damn day.

More than that, I want to erase every memory of Devon fucking Peterson for making her feel like she wasn't enough.

Because the truth?

She was always way too good for him.

And the fact that she questions her own worth because that asshole couldn't keep his dick in his pants?

I'd like to find him and make sure he knows exactly what he lost.

For now, I'm content to just sit beside her, our shoulders brushing, my fingers tracing circles across her skin as I watch her come back to life. I hope like hell I'm the one she chooses when she's ready to let someone in.

I'm not sure she even realizes the way she leans into my touch as the four of us continue talking.

But I sure as hell do.

When it comes to her, I notice every little detail.

"I need to use the restroom," Holland says, rising from her chair with a mischievous smile. Her gaze slides to Lilah. "Want to join me? That way I can grill you in private about your current living situation."

The corners of Lilah's lips lift. "Is that really necessary?"

Holland's already turning toward the restaurant. "Oh, you bet it is."

Lilah groans before standing and smoothing her dress as she follows. I don't realize how long I've been staring until Bridger lets out a low, amused chuckle.

"Good to know nothing's changed on that front," he says, swirling his whiskey like the smug bastard he is.

I drag my gaze away from the door. "What front?"

He snorts. "When are you finally going to man up and tell Lilah how you feel?"

My fingers tighten around my bottle. "I'm working on it."

"Working on it?" He laughs. "Dude, this has been going on since college. At the rate you're moving, you'll be in a retirement home by the time she figures it out."

I take a pull from my beer, ignoring the heat that creeps up my neck.

Bridger leans back in his chair, still grinning. "Look, I get it. She's gorgeous, smart, and funny. Way too good for you, obviously."

I huff out a laugh. "Obviously."

"If you don't do something soon, someone else is going to. You remember what happened a few years back? She was single, you hesitated, and some other guy swooped in before you could make a move."

The memory hits like a punch to the ribs.

I haven't forgotten.

Not even for a second.

The thought of her with someone else now?

It makes my stomach churn.

"That's not going to happen this time," I say, tone hard.

Bridger watches me for a beat before nodding. "Good. I love you, man. I just want to see you happy. And you and I both know... for you, that's Lilah."

He's not wrong.

It's always been her.

Before I can respond, the restaurant doors swing open again, and Lilah steps back into the light. Holland is beside her, still chatting, but she's the only thing I'm cognizant of.

The breeze lifts her hair, and in that short black dress, with the muted glow of candlelight catching in her eyes, she's a fucking vision.

Enough to bring any man to their knees.

I don't even try to hide the way I look at her.

She slides back into the seat beside me, and my hand instinctively finds her knee under the table. She tenses for the briefest moment but doesn't pull away.

That's all the encouragement I need.

My fingers flex against her warm skin, and even through the noise of conversation and clinking glasses, my focus narrows to just this.

Her.

My cousin, of course, can't resist the opportunity to needle me.

"So," he says casually, "how long do you think you'll play house with this guy?"

Lilah raises her glass, taking a sip of her espresso martini.

"I'm not sure. Hopefully not too long. I've been checking out apartments online."

Excuse me?

She glances over at me when my hand tightens on her knee.

"He's been great," she adds. "But I don't want to keep cramping his style."

A growl builds in my chest. "You're not cramping anything. You can stay as long as you want. Hell, you can stay forever."

Her lips part as her eyes widen.

It's almost a surprise when she doesn't argue.

Bridger leans forward, clearly loving this. "Oh, I wouldn't worry about cramping his style. Steele hasn't had a girlfriend in —what is it now? Three years?"

I shoot him a glare. "It's been a while."

My cousin laughs.

Fucker.

He knows exactly how long it's been.

And the reason for it.

Holland rolls her eyes. "Behave, Bridger. Or next time, the kids are babysitting you."

I take a moment to steady myself, trying to rein all the emotion back in. "Besides, how can Lilah move out when Waffles is just getting comfortable?"

Bridger frowns. "Who's Waffles?"

"Our kitten," Lilah says with a small smile. "Steele brought her home a few weeks ago."

Bridger looks between us with interest. "You two have a cat? How's that going to work down the road?"

"Shared custody," I say smoothly. "Weekends and holidays are negotiable."

Bridger whistles. "Wow. You two really are doing this whole thing backward."

The table bursts into laughter, and the conversation veers

off into lighter territory, but the tension between me and Lilah doesn't fade.

It continues to simmer, low and steady, thickening in the air with every glance, every touch.

And it's getting harder to hold back.

After dessert, Bridger's phone buzzes. One glance at the screen has him muttering an apology before answering. A moment later, he slips the cell into his pocket with a faint smile.

"Sitter's checking in," he says, rising to his feet. "Looks like it's time for us to head home."

Holland stands as well. "Thank you for dinner. We needed a night like this."

There's a round of hugs and goodbyes, easy laughter, and promises to get together again soon. Then Bridger slings an arm around Holland's waist, and the two disappear into the night, leaving behind the echo of a perfect evening.

Lilah moves to the railing and gazes out over the skyline, her hands resting lightly on the iron bar. The breeze toys with the hem of her dress as her long blonde hair slips over her shoulders.

She looks so fucking gorgeous it hurts. An ache coils low in my gut. All I want to do is slide my arms around her from behind and press my lips to the gentle curve of her neck, finally confessing everything I've kept buried for years.

I keep telling myself she needs time.

That I have to be patient.

But I don't know how much longer I can do that.

Because I'm scared my cousin's right. That if I don't step up soon, someone else will. Some other guy will see the amazing qualities I do, and he'll say what I haven't, and take her before I ever get the chance.

I can't let that happen.

Not again.

I'm being pulled in two directions.

Because I know the truth deep in my bones. Once I have her, I'll never let go. There's no pulling back. No pretending we're just friends.

I want Lilah Monroe.

Not just for tonight.

Not just for tomorrow.

But for every damn day after.

27

LILAH

The hushed sounds of the rooftop fade behind me as I step toward the railing, drawn to the glow of city lights dancing across the water. Lake Michigan stretches out before me like a black mirror. The cool wind kisses my skin, wafting over my arms and sneaking down the open back of my dress, making me shiver.

I don't hear his footsteps.

It's more that I feel him.

That unmistakable presence that's steady, solid, all heat and quiet power coming up behind me. My body reacts before he even lays a hand on me.

When his arms wrap around my waist, I let myself melt into his embrace.

Into *him*.

He's so much bigger than me. All hard lines and muscle. He's a fortress at my back, a shield that blocks out the world.

Devon never felt like this. He was leaner, sharper in his movements. Always careful. Controlled. Measured.

But Steele?

Steele doesn't *ask* for space.

He simply *takes* it.

Every gesture, every touch, every unspoken word says *mine*. And I love it.

I love the way I feel when he's touching me, as if I'm something worth holding on to.

My fingers drift to his forearms, tracing the thick cords of muscle below his rolled-up sleeves. I'm hyperaware of every inch of him. The scent of his cologne, the heat of his body, the steady thrum of energy rolling off him like a storm about to break.

I feel safe and protected.

He dips his head and brushes a kiss across my neck. The touch is worshipful. That's all it takes for a wave of heat to ripple through me, starting low in my belly before spreading outward.

"Have you come to a decision?" he asks.

My pulse throbs in my wrists and between my legs.

I close my eyes for a second, trying to steady the rush of thoughts. I've been wrestling with this answer for days. Second-guessing myself. Worrying about what would happen when it inevitably ended.

But right now, in this moment?

There's no question as to what I want.

"Yes," I whisper.

He stills behind me. The breath he draws into his lungs is sharp and audible, full of disbelief and something else entirely.

Relief, maybe?

His body tenses, wound tight like a spring on the verge of release. I feel the barely-contained hunger and emotion.

One of his hands slides up, slow and deliberate. His palm curves over my breast, the heat of it burning through the thin fabric of my dress. When his thumb brushes across my nipple, my body arches into the touch before I can stop it. His hand rises higher. Skimming the length of my neck before wrapping gently around the base of my throat.

The pressure is light yet possessive.

My knees nearly buckle. The frantic rhythm beneath my skin betrays just how undone I am.

And God help me, I love it.

I let out a whimper before I can stop it, and his fingers flex against me. He tips my chin back, guiding me until my head rests against his shoulder. And then his mouth is on mine.

Hot, insistent, and hungry.

He kisses me as if he's been waiting his whole life for this moment. Like he's held himself back for years and I've finally given him permission to let go.

I feel every stroke of his tongue.

Every brush of his lips.

Every beat of his heart against my back.

No one's ever kissed me like this.

When he finally eases back, his forehead presses to mine. We're both unsteady and panting. His hand stays locked around me as I tremble against him.

Any lingering doubts have been shattered by the weight of what I feel right now.

Desire.

Need.

And something far deeper, far more terrifying.

Steele's fingers slide beneath my chin again, tilting my face toward his.

"There won't be regret," he says, voice thick and raw. "Not from me. Not ever."

And I believe him.

With every beat of my heart, I believe him.

I hope I never forget how this moment feels.

How *he* makes me feel.

Like I'm his.

Like I've always been his.

I just didn't know it.

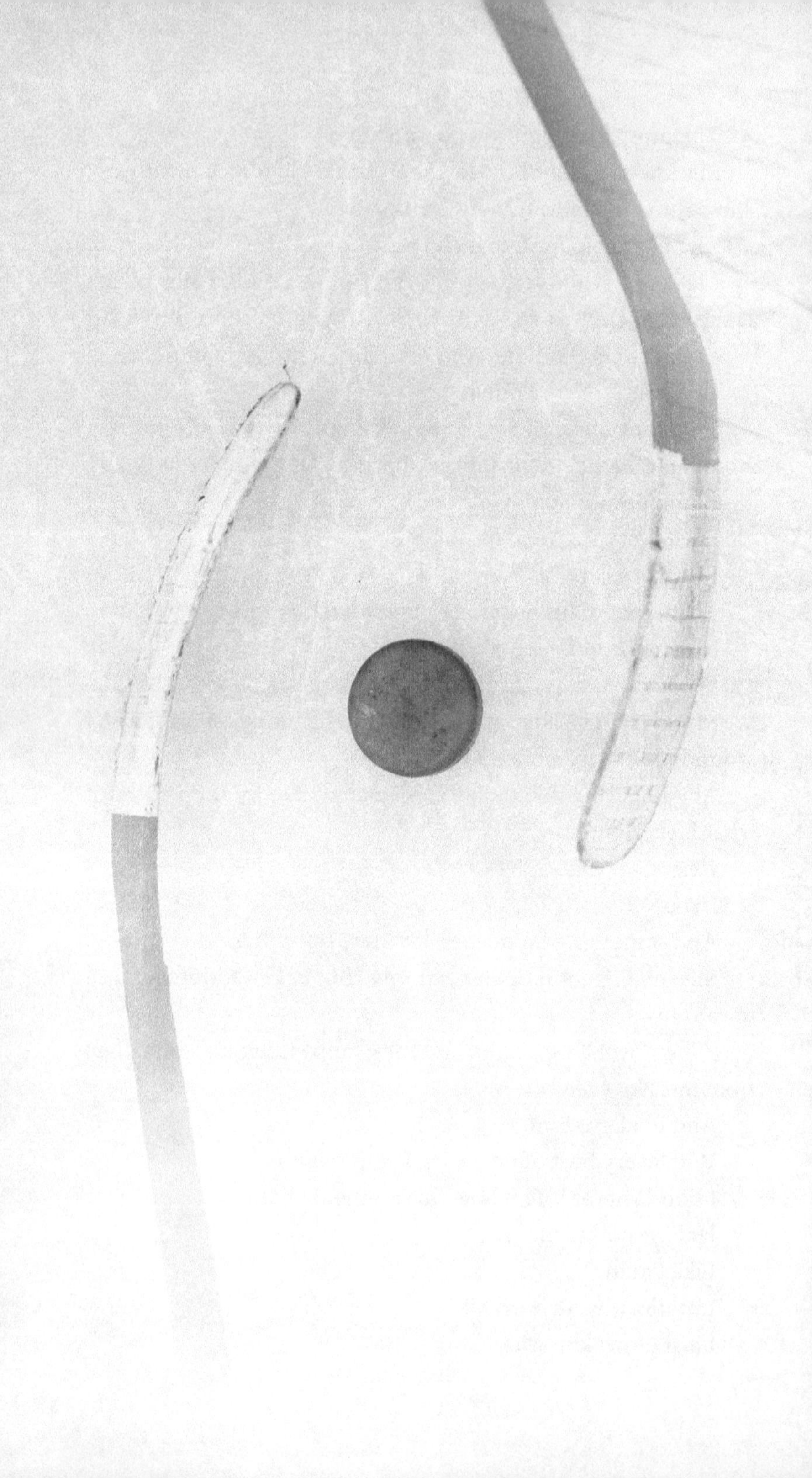

28
STEELE

By the time we step out of the restaurant, I'm barely hanging on by a thread.

The night air is cool and crisp against my skin, but it does nothing to dull the heat simmering just below the surface. Lilah's hand rests lightly in mine, her touch grounding, even as everything inside me spirals.

The valet pulls up quickly, the engine of my Lamborghini purring. I slip a bill into the kid's hand and then round the car to open the door for Lilah. She slides in with a quiet murmur of thanks, the black dress riding up her thighs as she settles into the passenger seat.

I circle the hood and slip behind the wheel, gripping the leather as the engine growls beneath us. The low, luxurious sound has nothing on the rush roaring through my veins.

Lilah shifts beside me, tugging at the hem of her dress, her perfume lingering in the cabin. As familiar as the subtle scent is, it's no less potent. A mix of honey, vanilla, and something entirely her. It coils low in my gut, fraying every last thread of control with it.

I tighten my grip on the steering wheel and focus on the

ribbon of road stretched out in front of me, silently counting the miles between us and home.

All I want is to get her there.

Alone.

She's been driving me out of my mind all damn night. The way she sat next to me at dinner, smiling and laughing, completely unaware that with every glance, every brush of her fingers, every shift in her seat, I was unraveling.

The little black dress hugs her curves in ways I want to memorize with my hands and my mouth. Her legs are bare and crossed, her skin glowing in the reflection of the city lights. The gloss on her lips is still faintly smudged from when I kissed her on the rooftop.

I want to taste it again.

And then again.

She glances at me, and even in the dim cabin, I can see it.

Excitement.

Nerves.

And questions.

She said yes.

And now she's wondering exactly what that means.

Only wanting to put her at ease, I reach across the center console and find her hand before threading our fingers together and bringing them to my lips to press a kiss against her knuckles. Her skin is smooth beneath my mouth, and I linger there, letting the moment settle between us like smoke.

She stills for a heartbeat.

When I glance over, her cheeks are flushed, her chest rising and falling just a little too fast.

Good.

I want her flustered.

Unsteady.

Undone.

Because that's what she does to me just by existing.

I flick on the turn signal and merge onto the road that winds back toward my penthouse. The city blurs outside the windows with neon signs, headlights, and glittering high-rises. Inside the car, it's quiet. Thick with anticipation.

Lilah shifts again.

She uncrosses and then recrosses her legs, thighs pressing together, as if she's trying to stifle the ache building between them.

My lips lift into a knowing smirk.

She's squirming.

And I fucking love it.

I want her need to rise like a tide until there's no holding it back. Until the only thing she can think about is me. My hands. My mouth. The things I plan to do to her once we're alone.

The things she doesn't even realize she's been craving for years.

"Take off your panties," I say, eyes pinned to the road.

Her head snaps toward me. "Wh-what?"

"You heard me," I say, calm and steady. A low thread of command woven into every word. "I want them off."

The silence that stretches between us is taut and electric. She doesn't move at first. Doesn't speak. I can feel her watching me, weighing her response.

Weighing what she wants.

She shifts, and everything inside me tightens.

When her hands disappear beneath the hem of her dress, I grip the wheel as she slides the black lace down her hips and thighs, inch by torturous inch. My peripheral vision catches every subtle movement as her fingers work. There's the graceful flex of muscle under satin skin and the teasing flash of bare thighs as the panties slip past her knees.

She hesitates before lifting the scrap of fabric.

"Give them to me," I murmur, extending my hand.

Without a word, she places them in my palm. The lace is warm from her skin, damp with arousal.

I bring it to my nose and inhale deeply.

The scent of her hits me like a drug. It's both intoxicating and addictive.

"Fuck," I bite out. "I've spent years wondering what you'd smell like."

And now that I know?

I don't think I'll ever recover.

When she gasps, I glance over to find her flushed and trembling, her hands fisted tightly together like she's trying to contain what's already spilling over.

And we haven't even started yet.

I tuck the lace into my jacket pocket and then slide my hand onto her thigh. Her skin is silken, warm, already quivering beneath my touch. I squeeze gently, then start to inch upward. My movements are measured. I want her panting by the time we reach the building.

I want her desperate.

Consumed with need.

She exhales as my fingers trail higher.

"Widen your legs for me."

She obeys instantly.

There's no hesitation.

Or shame.

Just need.

She parts her thighs with a whimper, the vulnerability of the gesture nearly knocking the air out of me. My fingers stroke the slick seam of her with a featherlight touch. No pressure. No intrusion. Just a steady, teasing glide across the surface of her pussy. She twitches beneath my hand and her hips shift.

And still, I don't give her more.

Not yet.

She's drenched. Hot and pulsing beneath my fingertips. Her

slickness coats my fingers with every pass, and it takes all of my self-control not to abandon the wheel and bury myself in her right here, right now.

But I won't rush this.

Not tonight.

I want her riding that edge so long she forgets her own name.

Her hips begin to roll subtly, seeking friction. Her hands grip the seat as her breathing turns ragged.

I keep the pressure light.

She moans as her head tips back against the leather, her body restless with want. "Please."

I glance over, needing to see her face. "Please what, baby? What do you want?"

Her eyes are half-lidded and heavy with arousal as a deep flush stains her cheeks. "I want you to touch me."

"Where?"

With a groan, she shifts closer.

Seeking more.

I pull back just enough to tap her inner thigh. "That's not an answer. If you want me to play with your body, you need to be specific. Try again."

Her bottom lip catches between her teeth. "My pussy."

Those two words nearly undo me.

"That's my good girl," I rasp, sliding one finger inside her heat.

When she cries out, my jaw clenches. Her inner walls tighten around me, hot and wet and pulsing. I curl my finger, slow and deep. Her thighs tremble. She's unraveling beneath my touch, shaking apart in the passenger seat of my car.

I keep driving the entire time I touch her.

My foot presses harder on the gas. We're going twenty over the speed limit now, but I don't give a shit. All I care about is the way she whimpers beside me. The way she holds my wrist like it's the only thing anchoring her to earth.

"Steele..." Her voice is rough. Desperate. "Please... just... fuck me."

God.

Her need is so raw and real.

I glance over at her. She's panting, her head tilted back, her chest rising and falling in sharp little bursts. Her legs are spread open, and her body is begging for release.

And she's so fucking beautiful like this.

I work her faster, then slower, fingers dragging her to the brink again and again, only to back off at the last second.

She curses.

Pleads.

Whines.

It's exactly how I want her.

The way I've always imagined her.

By the time we pull into the parking garage, she's incoherent. Her thighs are damp and her lips swollen from being played with.

And the best part?

We haven't even gone upstairs yet.

Because once we're through that door, Lilah Monroe belongs to me.

Every inch.

Every moan.

Every heartbeat.

Forever.

29
LILAH

My legs tremble as Steele steers me into the elevator, his hand firm at the small of my back.

At this point, I'm barely holding it together.

Every nerve ending is on fire, my body flooding with sensations. The heat between my thighs is unbearable, and the slickness coating my skin has me squirming with desperate need. I've never felt anything like this edge-of-insanity, can't-think-straight kind of arousal that pulses through me like a second heartbeat.

And the person who did this to me?

Steele.

The same guy who used to pass me tissues during rom-coms, and eat half my fries when he thought I wasn't looking. Now he's the man who just had his fingers buried inside me with expert control before leaving me hanging on the edge of oblivion like it was nothing.

I glance at him out of the corner of my eye, needing to see him.

Really see him.

And I do.

For the first time, I'm aware of everything that's been simmering beneath the surface of our friendship.

He looks calm. Composed. His hands are shoved in his pockets as he watches the elevator numbers crawl toward the penthouse, like he didn't just turn my world upside down in the front seat of his car.

I want to scream.

Why isn't he slamming me against the elevator wall?

Or kissing me?

Or finishing what he started?

I'm seconds away from begging when the elevator dings and the doors slide open. Relief floods through me as I bolt into the penthouse.

But Steele takes his sweet damn time.

The man is unhurried.

Unbothered.

Completely in control.

I turn just in time to see him waltz into the living room, calm as ever, unlike me, whose body is still trembling and soaked from the ride over.

He pours himself a bourbon before pulling a cigar from the humidor and clipping the end.

"What are you doing?" I blurt, nearly dancing in place.

He glances over his shoulder, then strikes a match and lights the cigar with the same precise control he seems to use with everything else in his life. He takes a pull, and the ember glows to life before he exhales a stream of smoke that unfurls in the air between us.

"Enjoying a bourbon," he says, "and a cigar."

He lifts the glinting crystal glass in his hand again before taking a sip and letting the silence settle for a beat. "Do you want one?"

"No." I lick my lips and shift again. "I thought..."

My words trail off. I have no idea how to finish them. I'm

still standing here, flushed and aching, while he's cool and unhurried, puffing on a cigar like we've got all night.

"What, Lilah?" he asks, his tone razor-sharp but patient as he settles on the sleek sectional. "What did you think?"

I press my thighs together as the ache continues to pulse low in my belly. "That we would..." I trail off again, heat flooding my face.

He tips his head, eyes hooded behind a curtain of smoke. "I think we should talk about the rules first."

Rules?

The word slams into me with more force than I expect.

"Rules?" I echo, blinking.

"Yes."

"What rules?"

He sets his bourbon on the side table, the crystal clinking against the glass. Then he leans forward, bracing his forearms on his thighs, cigar balanced between two fingers. Smoke spirals lazily upward, drifting between us.

The moment stills, and it's just the two of us, suspended in the tension.

"Whatever I tell you to do... you do," he says, voice low, firm, and edged with something darker. A command disguised as an offer.

My mouth opens, then closes again as I falter. The room suddenly feels warmer, the air heavier. The ache between my legs reignites like a spark catching on dry leaves.

But still, I hesitate.

"Do you trust me?" he asks.

That question lands with quiet impact but carries weight.

My answer is instant. "Of course I do."

Something in his gaze gentles, but only for a second. There's still steel beneath it. He leans back again, smoke trailing from his mouth in a cloud that rises toward the ceiling. The rich, heady scent of it mixes with the bourbon and the heat gathering between us until anticipation thrums in every nerve.

"Then it shouldn't be an issue," he murmurs. "Whatever I do, or tell you to do, is with your pleasure in mind. I'll never take anything you're not willing to give. But if we're doing this, I want you open to everything I have to offer. Do you understand?"

My pulse pounds so hard I'm afraid he can hear it.

"Yes," I breathe, my voice nearly swallowed by the moment.

He nods once, a slow, deliberate dip of his head. "Good."

There's a beat of silence as he lifts the glass again, sipping before adding, "And after this—whatever this becomes—we remain friends. We go back to what we were, if that's what you want. No pressure. No guilt. No fallout."

It takes effort to get the question out. "What if you change your mind?"

His eyes cut to mine, sharp and steady. "That's not going to happen."

The conviction in his answer cuts through the remaining fog of doubt.

"Are we in agreement, then?"

I hesitate only for a second. "Yes."

He nods again, setting the cigar in the ashtray. The shift in energy is palpable, like something electric has been switched on in the room.

"Are you taking birth control?"

I blink at the sudden shift, then nod. "Yes. The shot."

He watches me closely and then gives a small, satisfied nod. "Good. Then there's no need for a condom. When I take you, I want you bare."

The words loosen something inside me, but he's not finished.

"I'm clean," he adds. "I haven't been with anyone in eighteen months."

That casually thrown out comment knocks me off guard, and my brows draw together. "What? Why?"

His gaze burns into mine. There's no smile or hesitation on his part.

Just the truth.

"Because there wasn't anyone I wanted."

My lips part. "But women throw themselves at you all the time."

He shrugs. "Does it really matter if I'm not interested?"

There's something in the way he says it that quiets every part of me.

I open my mouth to respond, but nothing comes out at first.

Then, I ask the only question that truly matters. "But you want *me*?"

His gaze never leaves mine as he takes another puff of his cigar. The smoke slips from his lips like a secret. "More than you'll ever know."

The finality in his statement pins me in place.

"Are we in agreement then?"

My heart hammers. "Yes. And just so you know, I got tested after everything with Devon. I'm clean."

His body relaxes slightly, but there's nothing easy about the way he looks at me. Nothing subtle about the need in his eyes.

"Good. Now that it's settled, I want you to take off your dress."

Even though a shiver skitters through me, I don't hesitate. My hands tremble as I reach behind me and find the zipper. The fabric slides down my body and falls to the floor with a whisper until I'm standing before him in nothing but my strapless bra.

"Take that off as well."

I unclasp it slowly. The lace falls away before dropping to the floor and I'm totally bare. Every inch of my skin prickles under the weight of his stare. I fight every instinct to cover myself, my hands twitching at my sides.

Before I can act on the impulse, his voice cuts into my thoughts. "Don't ever hide yourself from me. Understand?"

I nod as heat crawls down my neck.

When I take a step toward him, he raises a hand.

"Stay right there," he says. "In the middle of the room."

I freeze.

"The moon's hitting you just right," he murmurs, puffing on the cigar again. "Let me enjoy the sight."

His gaze drags over me like a caress. It doesn't feel like he's just looking. It feels like he's soaking me in.

I've never felt so exposed. So desired. So undeniably wanted.

The cherry of the cigar glows bright as he inhales again and then exhales. He continues watching me.

Studying me in silence.

The smoke floats between us, and the way he looks right now—relaxed, hungry, dangerous—does something wild to my insides.

"Do you have any idea," he says quietly, "how long I've waited for this moment?"

I shake my head.

He lifts the cigar again. The motion is smooth and deliberate. He holds it between two fingers as his wrist rests casually on the arm of the couch.

"Since freshman year, Lilah." There's a pause. "That's a long time to want someone."

And just like that, I know this night will change everything between us.

It's just as frightening as it is thrilling.

He leans back into the couch cushions and lifts his glass to his mouth again. It's with practiced ease that he brings the cigar to his lips and takes a drag. The ember glows, and when he exhales, the smoke rolls from his mouth in a thick, languid cloud that fills the space between us.

"So, if you don't mind," he says, voice wrapped in velvet and fire, "I'm going to take my time with this."

My skin prickles, heat rising in a slow, consuming wave. I'm standing in the middle of his living room, completely bare under the silver spill of moonlight. Every inch of me is exposed, trembling, strung tight with want. I shift on my feet and press my thighs together, desperate to stifle the throb between them.

His eyes flicker, sharp and observant.

Nothing escapes his notice.

His head tilts slightly, a wisp of smoke trailing lazily from his lips. "Is your pussy wet?"

The casual way he asks the question leaves me momentarily speechless.

Like he's asking if I'd like a drink.

Or if I've seen the weather report.

But we're not talking about either of those.

We're talking about the slick heat between my thighs. The ache he's coaxed into an inferno. And the fact that he hasn't laid a single hand on me since we stepped out of the car.

Somehow, that cool and easy tone only makes it worse.

"Lilah," he prompts, raising a brow and taking another puff of his cigar. "Answer me."

"I... ah..." The words die on my tongue.

He lifts his glass again, utterly composed. "Perhaps you should check?"

My eyes widen. "You want me to *check*?"

"Yes."

"I—" I swallow. "You want me to touch myself?"

He exhales a stream of smoke, his gaze never wavering. "Just like you did the other night."

My mouth goes dry as heat floods my face.

"You heard me?" I whisper.

He nods, calm and utterly unapologetic. "Not only did I hear you, I watched."

There's a flicker of mortification, but it's instantly eclipsed by something darker as arousal curls through me.

"You did?"

He takes another sip of bourbon. "Yes. So, I know you understand exactly how to touch your pussy."

The crudeness of his words doesn't shock me anymore. It makes my thighs clench even tighter. And this time, I don't even try to stop it.

"Sit," he says, motioning to the thick glass coffee table in front of him.

I blink. "On the table?"

"Lilah."

It's just my name.

But the way he says it?

Low. Patient. Full of authority.

It's impossible to resist.

I cross the room, my bare feet whispering over the floor before lowering myself carefully onto the glass. It's cool against my skin, hard and unyielding, which only sharpens everything I'm feeling.

I spread my legs a little, feeling both unsure and self-conscious.

He exhales, smoke unfurling from the corner of his mouth as his gaze sweeps over me.

"No," he says slowly. "That won't do. Lie back, sweetheart. And spread your legs wide."

My pulse pounds in my ears as I ease onto my back. The sharp edge of the table bites into my spine. Even though I'm quivering with nerves, I do exactly as he instructs and part my legs wider until I feel the air brush over the slick heat of my center.

I'm completely open to him.

Exposed.

Bare.

And somehow, it only amplifies my arousal.

"More," he murmurs, swirling the bourbon in his glass. "I want to see all of you. Every pink inch."

I shift again, spreading my legs farther apart until I feel vulnerable and filthy and powerful.

He still doesn't move.

He just watches.

And somehow that's worse.

Better.

All of it.

His gaze skates over me like a caress as he takes another puff of his cigar. The glow brightens in the shadows before he releases the smoke in a lazy stream.

I've never been studied in this manner before.

"I'm waiting."

My hand trembles as I slide it down my stomach. When my fingers find the slick ache between them, my eyelids feather shut on instinct.

"Eyes on me," he growls.

My lashes snap open and my gaze locks back on him.

And when I touch myself in front of him, it's like something inside me unravels.

"Good girl," he murmurs, voice rough and low, edged with bourbon and smoke.

The praise, paired with the warm scent of tobacco and the intensity of his expression, sends a fresh wave of heat spiraling through me. I moan, fingers circling my clit in slow, shaky strokes.

Just like I did the other night.

Only this time, I'm not alone.

Steele is here.

Watching.

Guiding.

Owning every sound that spills from my lips.

"So tell me," he rasps, "are you wet?"

"Very."

"I can see it," he says, gaze locked between my legs. "Glistening on your skin. Absolutely stunning."

My spine bows against the cool surface, a shiver rolling through me. Still, he doesn't move. He just watches, completely in control, his bourbon clutched in one hand, his cigar burning low between the fingers of his other.

And I've never felt more wanted.

More seen.

More his.

I grow more desperate with every caress, but it's not enough.

No matter what I do, it's not him.

I need his mouth.

His hands.

His control.

I've never felt anything like this before.

Not even close.

I'm buzzing, every inch of me hypersensitive. Strung impossibly tight, electric and sparking with need. Every flick of my fingers pushes me toward something that feels dangerously close to unraveling.

From the couch, Steele's gaze pins me in place. The cigar between his fingers glows as he lifts it to his lips again, smoke escaping from his mouth, as if he's unaffected.

But when he speaks, his voice is rougher.

"Goddamn, Lilah," he rasps. "You have no idea how gorgeous you are stretched out and shaking for me."

My lips part as a small whimper breaks free, and my fingers falter.

Steele sets down the glass and leans forward slowly, like

he's in no rush, like he's savoring every second of this. I brace for the touch of his hand.

I need it.

Crave it.

Instead, something else brushes between my thighs.

A foreign, unexpected sensation.

Something that's both warm and solid.

The blunt end of the cigar.

My eyes widen and a startled sound slips from me.

He drags it along the seam of my body, featherlight and maddeningly slow, never pushing in. His lips lift into the faintest smile, as if he's reading every thought that flickers through my head.

"Do you feel that?" he murmurs, dragging the smooth end over my most sensitive flesh.

I nod, unable to speak.

When my hips shift helplessly toward the sensation, the cigar disappears.

My breath catches as he lifts it to his mouth and takes a puff.

"Fuck," he says hoarsely. "You taste like honey."

I shake.

And when the cigar returns to my skin, I nearly sob.

He strokes it along my lower lips again, teasing and coaxing. Circling. Painting my arousal across my own flesh. It's too much and not enough.

And then he eases it inside me just a couple of inches. Just enough to make my entire body jerk.

But only for a moment.

Then he pulls back and circles my clit with maddening precision, driving me higher with every pass.

I can't think.

Can't breathe.

My hips lift and my back arches as my body silently asks for more.

And when I whisper his name again, my tone pleading and begging, he groans.

"Look at you," he rasps. "Completely undone. Just for me."

I whimper in response.

"You know how hard I am right now?" he asks roughly. "All because of you. The way you look. The way you taste. The way you beg for my touch."

Tears prick the corners of my eyes as I moan, desperate and aching.

"Tell me," he says, circling my clit again. "How badly do you want to come?"

"More than anything," I whisper, my voice breaking. "Please, Steele."

He dips the cigar inside me again, once and then twice.

My body rises off the glass in desperation. "Please," I sob. "I need… please—"

"Good girl," he whispers, and that's all it takes for the world to shatter.

Pleasure slams into me like a tidal wave, knocking the air from my lungs. My thighs quake, and I cry out, unable to stop the onslaught of sensation. Never once does he move or let up. He strokes me gently with the cigar, dragging every last tremor from my body until I'm a shaking, wrung-out mess.

My chest heaves.

"Come here, Lilah."

On legs that barely hold me, I rise from the table and wobble toward him. The room tilts, and I grab the couch for balance.

He remains seated with his legs spread. When I stop between them, he looks up at me with eyes that are heavy-lidded, dark, and full of hunger.

"Kneel," he says.

My knees hit the floor with a dull thud.

He doesn't need to guide me. I reach for him, fingers shaking as I find the thick belt, loosening the leather before unzipping the fly of his pants and slipping my fingers inside the damp cotton of his boxers. Even though I just came, more arousal gathers on my sensitive flesh.

"Take my cock out," he orders. "And then stroke me. Show me exactly what you want."

His head tips back as I wrap my hand around his hard length. The low sound he makes sends another ripple of heat through my core. His fingers curl around the tumbler again as he takes a sip and then another drag from the cigar.

"Eyes on me," he says, the words striking something deep inside my core.

My gaze remains locked on his as I take him into my mouth, savoring the salty taste of him as my tongue swirls around the tip. I've been thinking about him ever since the night I helped him in the shower, the memory seared into my mind like a brand.

Now, with him trembling beneath my touch, I can't hold back. I slide down the length of his erection, my lips gliding with practiced ease, then back up again, bobbing with a rhythm that has his breath catching.

His fingers slip into my hair, not to force, just to guide. It's as if he needs the anchor just as much as I do.

"That feels so good, baby. Can you take just a bit more? Can you take every inch?"

I've never in my life wanted to please a man more than I do Steele. What we're sharing feels unbearably intimate. And I want him to fall apart with the same intensity that I unraveled with minutes ago.

He groans when his cock hits the back of my throat.

Tears sting my eyes as I take even more of his hard length until I'm almost gagging.

He thumbs them away before bringing his hand to his mouth and licking the moisture.

I might be the one giving him pleasure, but I'm more turned on than I ever have been in my life. I don't understand how that's possible when I'm the one on my knees.

"Mmm, that's it, baby. Just like that. It's so good when your muscles tighten around me. Fuck. Are you going to swallow down all my cum like a good girl, Lilah?"

I moan around him, wanting to give him this so badly.

His release crashes through him with a raw, broken groan and his cum splashes against the back of my throat as I greedily drink it down just like he asked. I feel the impact of his orgasm everywhere.

In my bones.

In my blood.

In the space between us that will never be the same again.

He doesn't say a word as he sets down the cigar, then scoops me into his arms and carries me down the hall to his room.

The mattress dips beneath me as he leans in and says, "From now on, you sleep here with me. No clothes. I don't want anything coming between us while we're together."

I don't argue.

Because I already know there's no going back from this.

Not now.

Maybe not ever.

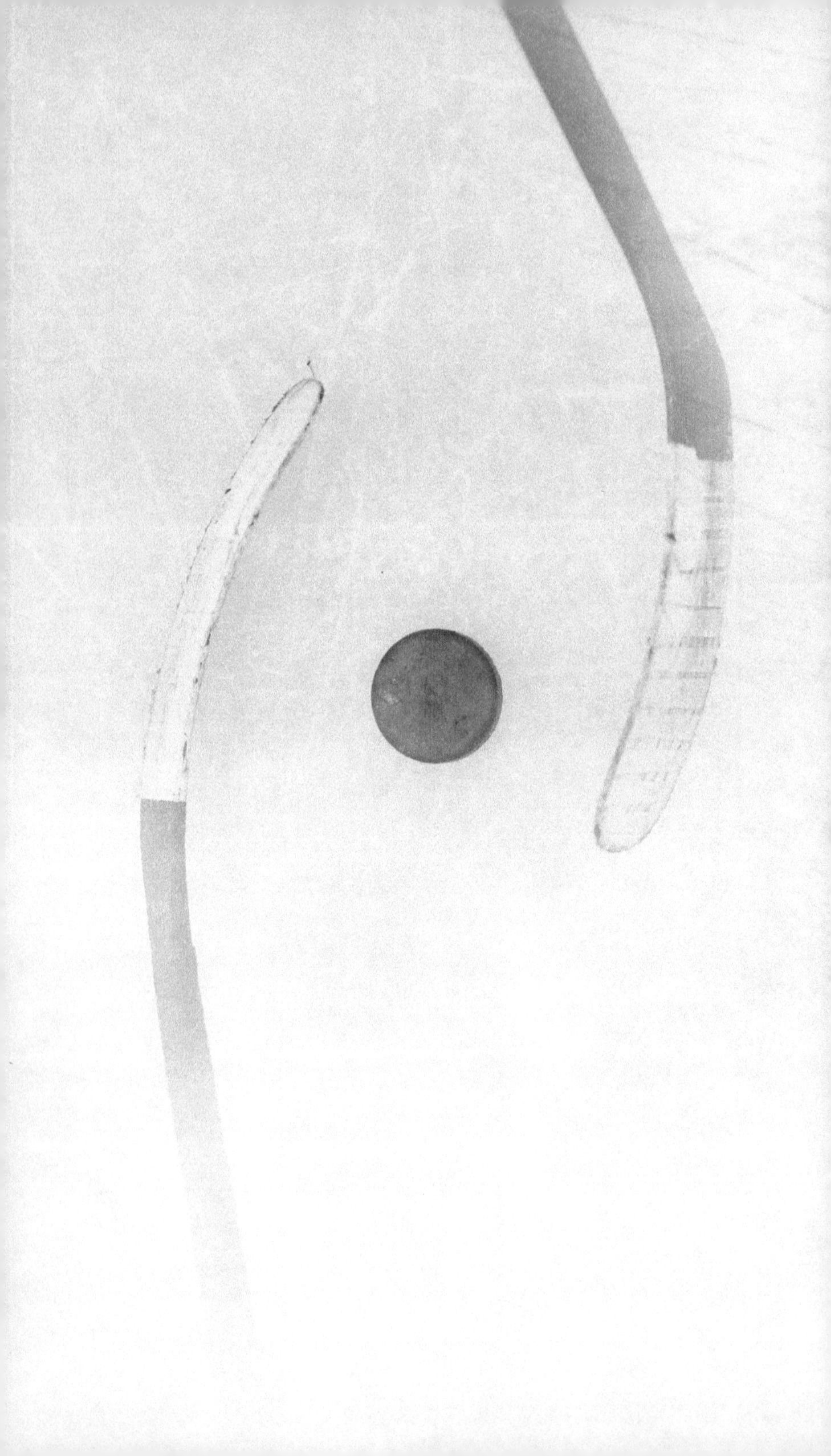

STEELE

he golden morning light spills in through the floor-to-ceiling windows, casting long, drowsy shadows across the bedroom.

And her.

Lilah's lying beside me, still tangled in the sheets, the sunlight bathing her bare skin. Her hair is a mess around her face, her cheeks flushed from sleep, her lashes resting against them like crescents.

She's the most beautiful thing I've ever seen.

I lie here, unmoving, afraid the slightest shift might wake her.

Not yet.

Because in this quiet, unguarded sliver of time, everything feels damn near perfect.

She's here in my bed.

Wrapped in my sheets.

Just like I've always dreamed.

And for as long as she's here, this is exactly the way I want her.

Every morning.

I drag in a breath and let those thoughts settle deep in my

chest. It doesn't do anything to steady the ache I've been carrying around for years. Even though she said yes last night, I know she sees this as temporary.

A placeholder for something else.

Someone else.

But that's not what I am.

I want to be her everything.

All right, so maybe that's exactly what I told her. That we could keep this casual. That we could draw lines and stay on the right side of them.

But I lied.

After what happened between us, there's no way I can ever go back to being just her friend.

Not after tasting her skin and hearing the way she moaned my name.

We didn't have sex last night, even though I'd wanted to.

So fucking badly.

But I didn't.

Because I want to draw this out.

I want to take my time and make her fall in love with me in ways that leave no room for doubt. I want to show her how it can feel when someone touches her with reverence.

Worships her.

Loves her.

And I do.

So much it hurts.

I shift closer, careful not to wake her as I drag the sheet down just enough to bare her breasts. My gaze sweeps over the curves of her body, the way her chest rises and falls with each steady breath.

My mouth waters.

I lean down and brush my lips over the swell, savoring the softness of her skin. When she shifts beneath me, I take her nipple into my mouth and suck gently. Her body arches in response, and a moan tumbles from her lips. The sound is sweet music to my ears.

I swirl my tongue around the sensitive peak as her fingers thread through my hair.

"Steele…"

I lift my head just enough to look at her. "Morning, lucky charm."

Her eyes flutter open. "That's certainly one way to wake up."

With a grin, I brush my knuckles down her side. "Just trying to set the tone for the day."

Still smiling, she stretches, her body pressing against mine in a way that has every part of me straining toward her.

"I think I'm gonna like this arrangement," she murmurs.

I press a kiss to her collarbone, my lips lingering, allowing the moment to draw out.

"You're not the only one."

If I have it my way, she'll be waking up like this every morning with my mouth on her skin and my heart in her hands.

She stretches again, and her palm drifts between us, brushing against my abs before slipping lower.

When her fingers wrap around me, I groan. She strokes me once, the movement slow and sweet. My hips jerk at her touch.

"Are you trying to kill me?" I rasp, smacking a kiss to her lips before rolling out of bed, leaving her blinking.

"Wait. What are you doing?" she asks, pushing up onto her elbows, her hair wild and her voice still husky with sleep. "I thought…" Her cheeks flush as the sentence trails off.

That we'd have sex.

It's written all over her face.

And damn, if that doesn't make me smile.

"I was gonna make us breakfast," I say, tugging on a pair of gray sweatpants.

"Now?" she huffs, clearly annoyed to be left high and dry.

I hide my grin and head for the door. "What's wrong? You said you liked this arrangement. Is there a better way to wake up than having your titties sucked? Plus, I'm going to feed you. I think you're really making out here."

"Steele."

"Join me in the kitchen when you're ready."

She groans into the pillows as I leave, and I can't stop the quiet laugh that breaks loose from me.

Such an impatient little thing.

She has no idea how difficult it was to walk away.

I adjust my hard-on and make my way to the kitchen before pulling out all the necessary ingredients for blueberry pancakes. They're her favorite. The kind she used to make after late study nights in college when she needed comfort food. Back then, she'd dance around her tiny apartment barefoot, hair in a knot on her head, singing off-key to old Taylor Swift songs.

I was in love with her even then.

The batter's just about done when footsteps pad across the hardwood.

When I glance up, the whisk in my hand stalls.

She's wearing one of my old, faded T-shirts—the hem barely brushing the tops of her thighs—and pink fuzzy socks are pulled halfway up her calves. Her hair is still a mess, and her lips are still pink from sleep.

She looks...

Downright edible.

Something catches inside me as she pushes onto the counter and settles there. Her legs part just enough for me to catch a glimpse of her bare pussy.

There are no panties in sight.

Jesus.

I grit my teeth and flip the first pancake as steam rises from the griddle.

"It smells good," she says, swinging her legs lazily.

It takes all of my self-control to focus on the task at hand. I slide a finished stack onto a plate and bring it to her, setting it beside her hip before picking up the fork.

She raises a brow. "You're feeding me now?"

"Uh-huh." I spear a bite and hold it to her mouth. "Open up."

With her gaze locked on mine, she does exactly as I ask, and her lips close around the fork with a satisfied hum.

"Damn," she murmurs. "That's good."

I feed her another bite, watching her chew as my gaze drops back to her bare thighs. Her shirt rides higher when she shifts, spreading her legs a little wider.

Heat sears through my bloodstream.

I don't know how much longer I can take this.

"Not hungry?" she asks, licking a drop of syrup from her thumb.

I set the fork down. "I'll eat as soon as I'm done feeding you."

The moment she finishes the last bite, I slide the plate into the sink and turn back.

Her eyes are wide as I step between her thighs.

"Now I'm ready to eat breakfast," I murmur. My hands wrap around the backs of her knees as I drag her closer to the edge of the counter.

She breathes my name, hands bracing behind her, knuckles white against the marble.

"Now, be a good girl for me and take off your shirt."

Without hesitation, she lifts the fabric over her head, revealing inch after inch of creamy skin until she's bare again, glowing in the morning light like a fantasy I've conjured into reality.

I trace my fingers down her sides until they settle at her

hips. Then I reach around her to grab the bottle of maple syrup from the counter.

Her brows lift slightly. "Steele..."

"Pretty sure everything tastes better with syrup," I say with a smirk.

Her breath catches as I drizzle a line over the swell of one breast. It glistens as it trails down her skin. I dip my head and kiss her lips once before moving lower to chase the sticky sweetness with my tongue.

I lap at her, savoring the way her body trembles beneath my mouth. Then I suck her nipple between my lips. With a whimper, she arches into me.

Her fingers twist in my hair as I dust kisses across her chest, worshipping every curve. "Makes me wonder what else I could lick off your body," I whisper against her skin.

That question earns me another thick shiver.

I spread her thighs wider as I drop to my knees like a man devoted, my gaze locked on hers the entire time. "Now this," I murmur, pressing my lips to her inner thigh, "is exactly what I woke up craving."

I kiss her again, this time lower, tasting her sweet heat. Her gasp echoes in the kitchen as my tongue flicks her clit before sweeping along her center, collecting every drop of honey.

I take my time, stroking her with slow, teasing licks, sliding my tongue inside her softness and groaning when she spreads her legs even wider, giving me more room to maneuver. Her thighs tremble, her breath comes in ragged bursts, and all I want is to keep her on this edge, floating and open and mine.

Touching her like this, playing with her like this, is everything I've ever wanted.

If I keeled over tomorrow, I would die a happy man now that I've had my face pressed against her pussy, tonguing her sweetness, slipping inside her core.

It doesn't take long before her body tightens, her fingers tunneling in my hair as she grinds against my mouth.

"Steele," she groans, my name sounding like a broken prayer.

"That's it, baby," I whisper between strokes. "I want to watch you fall apart on my tongue."

When she comes, it's with a cry that echoes off the walls. Her whole body trembles, and I hold her through it, hands firm on her thighs, mouth claiming every single shiver.

It's only after the last shudder rolls through her that I rise and brush a kiss against her swollen lips before scooping her into my arms and carrying her back to the bedroom.

31
LILAH

The elevator doors glide open with a ding, and I step out, smoothing my hands down the sides of my coat. I can't stop thinking about how good it's felt to wake up in Steele's arms these past few mornings. Each night he pushes my body to the brink, giving me orgasm after orgasm, but he has yet to slide deep inside me. If the man is trying to drive me insane, he's doing a damn good job of it.

My heels echo across the polished floors of the Kingston Landry Arena as I head down the corridor to meet Rina and go over Steele's social media engagement schedule for the rest of the month. I've walked these halls a hundred times, and I still love the sight of the framed team photos and banners that stretch toward the ceiling. It always fills me with pride to see Steele's picture and name up there.

"Lilah! Over here!"

I glance up and spot Evelyn and Callie standing near one of the massive windows.

Nora, Callie's two-year-old daughter, is perched on her hip, her wild curls bouncing as she turns to look at me.

My heart melts instantly. As soon as I'm close enough, I lean in and blow a raspberry against her cheek. She's the absolute sweetest. With a squeal, Nora buries her face against Callie's shoulder, making us laugh.

"Hey, girl!" The pretty blonde grins, pulling me into a quick one-armed hug. "How's everything going?"

There's a playful yet pointed edge to her tone. It's obvious she hasn't forgotten our conversation at Lakeshore Sweets and is fishing for an update.

Heat floods my cheeks, and with a laugh, I hedge, "It's good."

"Is it now?" She smirks. "Exactly *how* good?"

"We'll talk soon," I promise. "There's a lot to tell you."

Evelyn's eyes sparkle with mischief. "Is this the part where you confess something scandalous?"

"Nope, not at all," I lie breezily. At least, nothing I'm ready to share with my godmother. I decide it's best to pivot. "Actually, what do you think about a girls' night this Friday?"

Evelyn shakes her head. "I'd love to, but I've got a date."

My brows rise with that information. "Anyone we know?"

A secretive smile simmers on her lips. "Nope."

"That sounds great," Callie chimes in, adjusting Nora on her hip. "Let me check with my parents to see if they can watch this little bundle of energy. Are we staying in or going out?"

"I was thinking Steele's place. We'll keep it low-key."

"I'm in. I'll bring dessert, Rina can grab wine, and Sloane can pick up takeout. And you?" She grins. "You can bring all the juicy details. Just know I'm living vicariously through you right now."

"I'll text Rina, and you can check with Sloane to see if she's free."

"She probably needs a night off," Callie says, bouncing Nora gently. "If she's not working at the bakery, she's juggling her siblings or cramming for school. The girl's got a full plate."

I smile at Nora. "Hmm, kind of sounds like someone else I know."

Callie nuzzles her daughter's cheek. "It's totally worth it. She's the best thing that's ever happened to me."

"Yes, she is," Evelyn says, brushing a hand over Nora's curls. "We were just talking about how much everyone loved Callie's desserts at the event. She's officially our go-to for all Railers gatherings."

"That's amazing!" I beam at Callie.

"It is," she says, though her smile flickers briefly.

I don't need to ask to know her thoughts have drifted to Zane and the woman he paraded around the other night.

Before I can say anything, she squares her shoulders. "Don't worry," she says. "I'm not letting him mess with what I'm building."

"I'm glad to hear it," Evelyn says firmly. "You need to do what's best for you and Nora. That's what matters."

"Exactly."

I squeeze Callie's arm. "Everything you made was incredible. You should be really proud of yourself."

She shrugs off the praise, but this time her smile is more genuine.

And because Evelyn can't help from playing matchmaker, she shifts gears with a wicked gleam in her eyes. "You know, I think it's high time you got back out there. I'm certainly not saying you need a man, but sharing your life with the right person can be amazing."

Callie groans. "Do not even think about setting me up."

"Too late. I already have someone in mind for you," Evelyn teases. "Beau Masterson, the restauranter. He was blown away by your desserts and even more so when he saw you. I would've introduced you if you hadn't been so busy."

With a blush, Callie shakes her head and laughs under her breath.

Before she can reply, a deep voice cuts in. "The last thing Callie needs is a rich playboy in her life."

We all turn to find River approaching, a frown tugging at his mouth. His gaze sweeps over Evelyn, then me, before locking on Callie and then growing tender when it lands on Nora.

"Hey there, sweetheart," he murmurs, reaching out to brush Nora's curls.

Callie immediately takes a small step in retreat, and his hand drops awkwardly back to his side.

Evelyn waves toward the petite blonde. "You don't think it's time Callie moved on? She's young, beautiful, and has a lot of life to live."

River's eyes find Callie again. His voice is quiet but certain. "Of course she does, but another womanizer isn't the answer."

Callie's chin lifts. "That's not your call to make," she says, cool and steady.

"I never said it was—"

She cuts him off, turning back to Evelyn with an overly bright smile. "Actually, you're right. If Beau's interested, give him my number."

Evelyn claps her hands together. "Wonderful! He mentioned the possibility of featuring your desserts at his restaurants. This could be a huge opportunity for Lakeshore Sweets."

"Thank you," Callie says, voice steady even though her arms tighten around Nora. "I appreciate you always looking out for me."

"Of course. You're like family."

River shifts his weight before running a hand through his blond hair. "Callie, can we talk?"

She takes another step in retreat. "Sorry, I need to get back to the bakery. Sloane's probably swamped with customers by now."

Without waiting for a response, she turns and heads toward the elevators with Nora still clutched tightly against her.

River watches her go, frustration radiating off him in suffocating waves, but he doesn't follow. Instead, he forces a smile. "Guess I should get going. I'll see you both later."

And then he's gone, disappearing down the hall.

Evelyn watches him retreat with a speculative look. "Seems River's got his heart set on someone."

"Yeah," I say. "Not that she's going to make it easy on him."

Evelyn's smile is slow and knowing. "Maybe she just needs a little nudge in the right direction."

I narrow my eyes. "If you're plotting something, you might want to rethink it."

"Oh, but meddling is half the fun," she says with a mischievous grin.

A laugh bursts from me before I can stop it. "Which brings us back to your date on Friday. Come on, I need details."

She waves a dismissive hand. "If he earns a second one, we'll talk."

Before I can dig for more, she changes the subject. "Are you here for Steele?"

"Actually, I wanted to run his calendar by Rina in person."

"Oh, you just missed her. She had to clean up one of Oliver's messes. I believe she said something about being five seconds away from strangling the man."

I laugh. "Yeah, that sounds about right. Steele and I went to college with his brother, Hayes. He was the same way until a feisty ice skater straightened him out."

"Isn't it amazing how the love of a good woman can work miracles?"

"We'll see about that," I tease. "If Oliver ever finds one who can keep him in line."

Evelyn's eyes twinkle like she knows a secret. "Yes. We will definitely see."

I glance at my watch. "Hmm. Maybe I'll wait around for Steele to finish up."

I take a step back and immediately slam into a solid chest. Strong hands catch my shoulders, steadying me. For a second, my heart leaps, thinking it's Steele, but then the unfamiliar scent of expensive cologne hits me, and I turn to find Knox McNichols flashing a sheepish grin.

"Sorry about that," he says. "I didn't mean to startle you."

"It's fine." I adjust my footing, noting how close he still is.

The man is attractive, for sure. But his brand of handsome doesn't stir anything inside me.

He shifts. "Actually, this is perfect. I was hoping we might run into each other."

I lift a brow. "Oh?"

"If you're free, do you want to grab lunch?"

Before I can answer, Evelyn jumps in. "Why, Knox, what a fabulous idea. Lilah would absolutely love that."

I blink. "I would?"

"Absolutely." The older woman beams before turning to Knox. "Didn't you mention the other day that you needed a new assistant?"

Knox's smile fades slightly. "Yeah. I had to fire the last one after I found out she was selling stories to that Railers gossip site."

"Well," Evelyn says breezily, "you couldn't find someone more trustworthy than Lilah."

I glance between them. "I'm not sure I can juggle two players' schedules."

"Well, there's only one way to find out," Evelyn says, already dismissing my concerns.

Knox grins. "We can talk about it over lunch. I know a great spot nearby."

I open my mouth to argue, but Evelyn's already glancing at her watch. "Perfect! There's no time like the present."

As soon as her sparkling eyes meet mine, I realize I've been Evelyn'd.

Knox gestures to the elevator, oblivious to the older woman's machinations. "Come on, I'll fill you in on the way."

As I fall into step beside him, I glance back at my godmother.

"Have fun, you two!" she says with a wink. "And don't worry about Steele. I'll fill him in."

I tap my fingers against the locker room bench, my phone resting in my palm, the screen glowing with an unread message count of zero.

Lilah hasn't texted me back.

She always responds.

Even if it's just a thumbs-up emoji or a sarcastic *I'll be there, stop being needy, Sanderson.*

But today?

Nothing.

With a scowl, I fire off another message before I can stop myself.

ME:

Hey, did you want me to pick you up and we can grab something to eat?

Still nothing.

ME:

Or should I just bring something home?

An uneasy feeling gnaws at me, clawing at my ribs. What if I pushed her too far and she changed her mind about our arrangement? Or what if she decided that we really are better off as friends?

If I thought she was in my blood before, it's nothing compared to what it feels like now that I've touched and tasted her.

"Dude, what the hell did your phone do to you?" Oliver snickers from across the room, chucking a towel at me.

I catch it midair and throw it back, harder. "Fuck off."

He grins but doesn't press his luck before disappearing toward the showers.

Unable to help myself, I check my phone for the umpteenth time.

Still no response.

Where the hell is Lilah, and why isn't she answering my texts?

The click of heels on tile makes me glance up, and I find Evelyn Kingston standing in the locker room, her sharp green gaze already locked on me as a smile lifts the edges of her lips.

"Ah, Steele. Just the man I wanted to see."

I stand, shoving my phone in my pocket. "Hey, Ms. K."

She glances at Jax, who's a few lockers down, tugging on his hoodie. "Jaxon. It's good to see that you're settling in with the team."

He flashes a cocky grin. "I love Chicago and am stoked to be here."

Evelyn cocks her head and purses her lips. "Are you married?"

His grin falters. "God, no. Why the hell—"

He catches my glare and immediately shifts gears. "I mean, no, ma'am. I'm not."

"Good to know." She gives him a bright smile before shifting her attention back to me.

"What's up?" I ask, only half-listening as I pull out my phone again.

Evelyn crosses her arms as her gaze sharpens on me. "Are you waiting for something? Or, perhaps, some*one*?"

My jaw tightens as I debate whether to admit the truth. That struggle lasts all of five seconds before I blurt, "I was trying to get ahold of Lilah, but she's not responding."

She hums like this is fascinating information. "Huh, that's odd. I just saw her in the hallway a little while ago."

I had no idea she'd be at the arena today. "Oh?"

She smiles sweetly in response. "Yes. In fact, she and Knox just left for lunch."

Everything inside me goes still.

Lilah's with Knox?

My fingers dig into my palms as heat rises in my chest that has absolutely nothing to do with the lingering adrenaline from practice.

"I'm sorry, she's with who?"

"Knox," Evelyn says, her smile turning smug as a glint sparks in her eyes. "They went out to lunch. I might have suggested Lilah offer her personal assistant services to him, and he seemed very enthusiastic about the idea."

The hell she's going to be a personal assistant for Knox. He's ten times worse than his older brother, Colby, ever was. And I didn't think that was possible.

A muscle tics in my jaw. "Where'd they go?"

She tilts her head and taps a perfectly manicured finger against her lips. "Oh, I don't know if I should say. After all, Lilah is a grown woman. If she wants to go on a date…"

Date.

That single word detonates inside my head.

"Evelyn."

Thankfully, she takes pity on me. Or maybe she doesn't want to watch me unravel in real time. Either way, she rattles off the name of the restaurant.

Then, as if she hasn't just thrown gasoline on an open

flame, she adds casually, "I actually think Lilah and Knox would make a rather handsome couple, don't you? He could use someone sweet and caring in his life."

Instead of responding, I storm out of the locker room, hell-bent on finding out exactly what the fuck is going on. In less than five minutes, I'm sliding behind the wheel of my car, pulling out of the parking lot with my hands clenched so tightly around the steering wheel my knuckles turn white.

The drive to the restaurant should be easy, but traffic is a nightmare. The streets are packed with businesspeople, tourists, and locals, all moving at their own pace. Horns blare, cab drivers weave aggressively through lanes, and pedestrians jaywalk.

I barely notice any of it.

My mind is locked on one thing.

Lilah.

Who's probably sitting across from Knox and laughing at something he said. The guy thinks he's a real funny fucker. He's able to turn on the charm any damn time he wants. It's exactly how he smooth-talks women into his bed. I've seen it play out more times than I care to count, and I don't want that to happen with Lilah. I'll kill him with my bare hands if he touches one blonde hair on her head.

Maybe I shouldn't have been so quick to slap a friends-with-benefits label on what we have.

Maybe I should have been honest about how I really feel.

But I was afraid of pushing her away.

In that moment, I would've said or done just about anything to secure her agreement.

Although, one of the damn rules I should have laid down is that there's no going out to lunch with any of my teammates.

Hell, no going out with anyone.

Period.

And she sure as shit isn't going to become a personal assistant to any other man but me.

I grind my teeth, shifting lanes and catching a glimpse of the Chicago River to my right. The midday sun reflects off the water, shimmering against the backdrop of towering steel and glass skyscrapers.

I can't stop thinking about how much I've loved having Lilah in my space these past few weeks. The way she relaxes on my couch with Waffles, hums to herself while puttering around my kitchen, or wanders through the penthouse in one of my T-shirts. It never fails to tug at something deep in my chest.

She's turned my place into something it never was before.

A home.

My mind tumbles back to the way she bites her lip when she's deep in thought, or how her perfume lingers in the air long after she's gone.

This isn't just jealousy.

It's a gut-deep, possessive kind of frustration. The kind that tells me I'm running out of time to figure this out before someone else steps in. I hit the gas a little harder as I take the next turn before pulling onto the street where the restaurant is located and cutting into a parking space the second one opens up.

Of course he'd take her to one of those trendy Chicago spots with exposed brick walls and floor-to-ceiling windows. It's the kind of place that caters to lunch meetings, startup tech bros, and the weekend brunch crowd.

I push open the door, the bell above chiming with my entrance, and scan the dining area.

It doesn't take long to find her.

She's near the back, sitting at a small corner table, legs crossed, laughing at something Knox just said. Her smile is infectious. It's the kind that hits low in my gut and squeezes.

And I hate how good they look together.

Not because they're a thing but because they *could* be. That's all it takes for my jealousy to spike like a fever.

My jaw tightens as I cross the restaurant.

Knox spots me first. The smug bastard gives me a chin lift. "Hey, Cap. Didn't know you'd be joining us. Grab a chair, we were just about to order."

Lilah's eyes widen. "Steele?"

I don't bother to hide my irritation as I drop into the empty chair across from her, my stare fixed on her face.

"I didn't realize you'd be going out to lunch with Knox," I say, barely able to keep my voice level.

She shifts on her seat. "It was kind of a spur-of-the-moment thing."

Knox jumps in, humor simmering in every word. "I'm on the hunt for a new PA and thought we could *share* yours. What do you think?"

My mouth flattens. "That you have a death wish."

He grins. "Yeah, I figured that might be your response."

"And yet, you still took her out and asked her to work for you."

Knox shrugs, the picture of innocence. "I need someone I can trust. Someone who won't sell my secrets to that gossip site. Lilah fits the bill."

I shoot him a sharp look. "Find someone else. Lilah's not interested."

He leans back in his chair, fingers tapping thoughtfully on the table. "Maybe you should let her answer for herself. For all we know, she might *enjoy* handling two hockey players at the same time."

Any second now, I'm going to lunge across this table and wring his damn neck. The guy is purposely pushing my buttons.

"Don't you have somewhere else to be?" I grit out, muscles coiled tight.

"Nope. Once Lilah agreed to go out with me, I cleared the entire afternoon." He flashes her a wink. "But, hey, no pressure."

"This isn't a date," I snap. I'm dangerously close to dragging him out of here by his collar. I've always held a tight leash on my temper. On the ice, in the locker room, and in life. But that leash has now reached its snapping point. "It's not happening," I state. "She's busy."

Lilah exhales. "Steele, you're being ridiculous."

I glance at her. "Am I?"

Knox bites back a laugh. "You seem a little territorial for someone who claims she's just a friend."

"I swear to God, Knox, you're about two seconds away from finding out exactly how territorial I can be."

With a grin, he holds up both hands in surrender. "All right, all right. I can take a hint." Standing, he straightens his jacket and flashes a wink at Lilah. "If you change your mind, give me a call. I'd be more than happy to have you on the Knox McNichols team."

The guy has no idea how close he is to needing dental reconstruction.

Once he's gone, the silence stretches tightly between us.

I don't speak.

I just stare at her.

Lilah fidgets before finally breaking. "I wasn't seriously considering it, if that's what you're worried about."

"It kind of looked like you were," I say, arms crossing over my chest. "You were laughing and smiling. Giving him your attention."

"It was Evelyn's idea, and I thought I'd hear him out. That's all."

I let out a humorless laugh. "That's never all when it comes to Knox, and you know that."

She rolls her eyes. "Knox doesn't have an effect on me."

"He should have known better than to ask you to work for him."

Her chin lifts and her eyes sharpen. "Oh? And why is that?"

"Because he knows you belong to me."

The words land between us with the weight of a confession.

Lilah's lips part and her brows lift as her eyes search mine, like she's trying to read between every line.

"I thought," she begins, "this was just a friends-with-benefits thing."

I lean in, lowering my voice so it's just for her. "It is." There's a beat of silence, thick enough to choke on. "Which is exactly why," I add, gaze locked on hers, "we should've established another rule. No one else touches that pussy but me."

It's satisfying to watch the way her breath catches as color rushes to her cheeks.

"You may have touched me..." She licks her lips. "But you haven't fucked me."

The words hit me like a punch to the gut. My pulse spikes and my cock stirs to life, and it takes everything I have not to flinch.

Instead, I hold her gaze, pretending like I'm not being burned alive inside.

"Is that what you want, lucky charm?" My voice dips, turning low and dangerous. "To be fucked?"

She gives me a small and hesitant nod.

Before I can respond, the waiter appears. "Are you ready to order?"

Lilah jolts like she forgot we were in public. "We're not staying—"

"Actually," I cut in, "we are. And we'd like to order lunch."

She snaps her head toward me. "We would?"

I smirk. "Absolutely. You came here with Knox because you were hungry. And now I'm going to feed you."

She pouts. It's an honest-to-God, full-lipped, bratty little pout. And my restraint nearly shatters. I want to lean across the table and kiss her senseless. I want to pull her into my lap and make her squirm until she begs me to take her home.

Instead, I lift my gaze to the waiter. "Two steaks. Both medium rare. She'll have an espresso martini and I'll take a lager."

He jots it down and leaves. The moment he's gone, Lilah leans forward, eyes wide, voice low. "I thought you were going to... you know."

I raise a brow. "Fuck you?"

Her cheeks flame as she nods. It makes her look so damn sweet. And completely fuckable.

I lean in again. "Oh, I have every intention of fucking you, Lilah."

Her breath stutters.

"But first," I say, fingers trailing along the edge of the table, "I'm going to bend you over my lap and spank that perfect ass until it's cherry red."

She gasps as her brows rise. Her reaction is everything. The need in her eyes is written in bold neon.

"I think we both know there are things I don't mind sharing with my teammates," I continue in a warning growl. "But you're not one of them. You're mine. Remember that next time another man asks you out to lunch. No matter what the reason is."

She shifts in her seat, probably wondering whether I'm making a threat or a promise.

Spoiler alert. It's both.

"And after I've reminded you exactly who you belong to," I say, letting every word sink in, "I'm going to fuck you so hard, you won't remember the name of any guy who's ever looked at you."

Lilah's lips part on a shaky exhale. Her pupils are blown

and her expression dazed. She's spiraling, and I'm right there with her.

"Is there anything you'd like to say about that?" I ask.

She swallows hard. "No."

"Good."

I lean back in satisfaction before flashing her a cocky grin. "Now, I want you to make sure you eat all your lunch, lucky charm."

"Why?"

I smirk. "Because you're going to need every ounce of energy you've got for this afternoon."

And by the time I'm done with her, there won't be a question in her mind as to who she belongs to.

33

LILAH

I can't stop shifting in my seat as we drive back to the penthouse. The leather is cool beneath me, but I'm burning from the inside out. And not just from the unseasonable heat beating through the windshield. This is something else. A pressure. A buzz. A low, coiling thrum of need I've never experienced before.

Steele's hand rests on my knee.

Simple.

Still.

And yet it's the most distracting thing in the world.

Every part of me is focused on the spot where his fingers grip my leg through the denim. His thumb strokes tiny, absent circles, each one sending a tremor through my core. I find myself inching closer to the center console, silently encouraging his hand to slide higher.

Just a little.

I want more.

A lot more.

I want him to stroke me through the fabric and show me exactly how serious he was back at the restaurant.

Because right now?

I'm wound so tight I feel like I could snap.

I glance at him out of the corner of my eye, and something constricts low in my belly. His jaw is locked, his profile cut from granite as he focuses on the road stretched out in front of him. He hasn't said a word since we left the restaurant, but his silence speaks volumes. His dominance hangs in the air, heavy as the tension between us.

It's not something I expected from him.

Steele has always been the easy one. The quiet refuge when everything else felt like chaos.

Always kind and steady.

But now?

Now he's something else entirely.

This man has an edge.

He's decisive.

Possessive.

Commanding in a way that makes my thighs clench and my breath come in short little huffs.

He threatened to spank me.

Spank me!

My brain stumbles over it, and a shiver of need dances down my spine as I try to process the words and what they mean. What it would feel like. The idea that his hand would be on me like that, demanding and claiming, makes my insides twist and flutter.

No one's ever laid a hand on me like that before.

Not in anger or in dominance.

Not in anything close to the way Steele means it.

But my panties are soaked at the idea. Completely drenched, clinging to me in a way that makes every shift in the seat an exercise in restraint. My body already knows the answer, even if my mind is scrambling to catch up.

Once we pull into the private garage beneath the building, Steele kills the engine with a flick of his wrist. The hum of the car dies, only to be replaced by silence and the thudding of my own heartbeat in my ears.

He's out of the driver's seat and at my door before I can gather my thoughts.

"Come on, lucky charm," he says, holding the door open, his voice quiet and controlled. It turns me on more than I could have ever thought.

I can't help but see the man before me with fresh eyes.

His hand slides to the small of my back as I step out. That one touch sears through me, warm and grounding. It stays there as we move through the building to the private elevator.

I stand beside him, holding myself perfectly still. I can feel him watching me. Not just looking but really seeing. It's like he knows exactly what I need and how much I'm falling apart inside.

The elevator dings, and the doors slide open to reveal the interior of the penthouse. His hand never strays from my back as we step inside. I pause in the living room as images from the other night tumble through my head. My heart hammers behind my ribs when he stops too.

"Are you really going to spank me?" I ask.

He turns toward me before stepping into my space and erasing the distance between us until it becomes necessary to tilt my chin to maintain eye contact. Both of his hands slide into my hair, cradling the back of my head. His eyes search mine with a seriousness that makes my knees wobble.

"Yes, Lilah," he murmurs. "I am."

His lips tease my mouth as they brush over mine. Just when I sink into the caress, he pulls back.

"I promise that you're going to enjoy every moment because I would never do anything that didn't ultimately give you plea-sure. Do you understand?"

I nod as heat explodes through me.

His fingers tighten slightly in my hair. "Words, lucky charm. I want you to use them."

"Yes," I whisper, my entire body trembling and on fire. "I understand."

His mouth dips toward mine, and his lips graze my cheek. "Tell me, is that sweet little pussy sobbing for me right now?"

There's no use pretending.

I chew on my bottom lip, cheeks blazing. "Yes."

A low groan vibrates in his chest, and his eyes turn molten.

"Good," he murmurs, releasing me slowly, letting his hands drop to his sides. "Now, go into the dining room and pull out one of the chairs for me."

My knees feel weak as I turn on shaky legs. Each step feels deliberate as I make my way to the table and pull out one of the high back chairs before standing behind it. My fingers twist nervously as I face the window.

Waiting.

Wanting.

Trying not to fall apart from the anticipation alone.

I have no idea if I'm ready for whatever comes next. What I do know is that I want it more than I've ever wanted anything in my life.

The floorboards creak behind me.

Steele's steps are steady.

Controlled.

The sound alone makes my entire body tighten. He stops directly behind me, and the sheer presence of him wraps around me like smoke.

When his hand ghosts along my spine, I shudder.

"You're quiet," he says, tone low and dark. "Getting nervous on me?"

I swallow, still facing the chair, knuckles white against the edge of it. "A little."

His fingers trail from the base of my neck down to the small of my back. The sensation is light and teasing.

"Don't be."

He moves around me to sit on the chair with his legs spread. Every inch of him is completely relaxed.

Except for his eyes.

They're dark and filled with hunger.

"Come here," he says, rougher now.

I step toward him, trying not to trip over my own feet.

His eyes never leave mine as he reaches for the button of my jeans. "Let's get these off."

"Here?" Surprise jolts through me.

His mouth curves slightly. "Yes, right here in the dining room."

There's no rush as he flicks the button. The slide of the zipper is deafening in the quiet room before he shoves the denim down my hips and thighs. When it pools around my ankles, I kick off the heels and step free, leaving my legs bare.

He glances at the thin cotton of my panties, and his jaw flexes. There's no way he doesn't notice how the material clings to me.

"You weren't kidding. You're soaked. We should probably take them off as well."

His fingers hook into the delicate fabric before dragging it down my legs so I can step out of the underwear. Heat floods my cheeks as he gently pulls me across his lap. I brace my hands against his thighs, unsure how to position myself. Every part of me is lit up with anticipation.

"Relax," he murmurs. "I've got you. I've always had you."

One hand strokes down the curve of my back, slow and soothing, as his other hand rests on the back of my thighs.

"Do you trust me, Lilah?"

"Yes," I reply without hesitation.

Because I do.

I always have.

And then he lifts his hand.

The first smack is light against my naked flesh.

Barely more than a warning.

I gasp, the sound slipping out before I can stop it. Not from pain. There's almost none. But from the sharp, dizzy rush of pleasure that floods through me. Before the sensation can fully settle, his palm smooths over the same spot, fingers warm and sure.

"Are you okay?" His voice is steady, but there's a roughness to it now. A thread of raw need he's not even trying to hide.

"Yes," I whisper.

"How did that feel?"

A shiver skates down my spine.

"Good," I tell him, my cheeks burning with the admission.

He doesn't pull away. If anything, his touch grows more deliberate, his fingers kneading the soft flesh of my ass. His grip tightens just enough to make me tremble.

"Yeah?" he murmurs. "You liked it?"

There's no teasing now.

Only dark hunger wrapped in every syllable.

I press my lips together before forcing myself to nod. "Yes, I liked it."

A deep, guttural sound rumbles from him as he shifts beneath me, the hard line of him pressing insistently against my hip.

"Maybe I should check for myself," he mutters, more to himself than to me.

His fingers slide between my thighs, stroking over the slick heat waiting for him.

A garbled sound breaks loose from me, my hips instinctively rocking toward his hand.

"Yeah," he rasps, dipping his fingers inside me with a slow, torturous thrust. "You're soaked, baby. Dripping for me."

I bury my face in his legs, mortified and aching all at once.

"You certainly would've made a mess of your panties," he adds. "It's a good thing we took them off."

Heat scorches through me as my entire body tightens under his touch.

His thigh flexes beneath my hands, and it's only then I realize just how aroused he is too.

Not just from touching me.

But from this.

From the way I'm draped over his lap, exposed and trusting and *his*. Even if we haven't said it out loud yet.

And I love it.

I love the way he touches me like I'm precious.

Like I'm his.

"Christ, Lilah," he rasps, his hand sweeping down the back of my thigh before skimming up again, making my heart pound so loud it drowns out everything else. "All I want is to make you feel good," he murmurs. "Over and over, until you forget every asshole who ever made you think you weren't enough."

His words hit harder than any touch, making it impossible to speak or even think.

Because somewhere deep inside, I already have.

When he shifts me slightly, adjusting the angle of my hips over his lap, the evidence of his arousal presses hard against me again, and my whole body clenches with anticipation.

Still, he doesn't rush or lose control.

He keeps me pinned in his lap, his hands roaming as his breath teases my skin, causing a wave of goose bumps to erupt in their wake. His mouth follows, brushing a featherlight kiss along my back, as if he needs to taste every inch of exposed flesh.

The second swat lands harder, igniting a sharper sting that elicits a gasp.

The third follows swiftly, the delicious burn sending a bolt of lust through my entire body, culminating in a moan slipping from my lips. Each strike builds upon the last, a crescendo of sensation that unravels me from the inside out. Yet, after every swat, his hand soothes the skin, a gentle caress that grounds me, reminding me of his unwavering presence.

"You're doing so well, lucky charm," he murmurs, his velvety voice dripping with approval. "You're being such a good girl."

The unexpected praise sends a jolt of warmth through me before pooling low in my belly. I hadn't anticipated how deeply his words would affect me or how much I'd crave his validation. The realization is both shocking and exhilarating.

By the time he pauses, I'm left panting, my body aflame with a need I never knew existed. My core throbs, and I can feel the damp evidence of my arousal against my inner thighs. The combination of his firm hand and tender words has unraveled me completely, leaving me yearning for more.

My body is on fire as my core throbs with desire.

But it's not just arousal pooling in my stomach.

It's something else.

Something deeper.

Something I'm not ready to examine too closely.

"Steele," I whisper.

He shifts me gently in his arms before lifting me like I weigh nothing and carrying me down the hall toward his bedroom. Every step sends a shiver racing across my skin. My ass still stings in the most delicious way. I'm shaking and light-headed. Caught between the hazy afterglow of everything that just happened and the growing anticipation of what's still to come.

Steele nudges open the bedroom door with his foot and then moves toward the bed with a steady, deliberate pace. He lowers me onto the mattress with a gentleness that makes my heart twist.

He leans over, one hand planted beside my head, as he stares down at me. His eyes burn with a dark, hungry intensity that sends a shockwave straight through me.

"That," he murmurs, voice low and rough, "was just a little taste of what I'm going to give you."

His words settle low in my belly, lighting me up from the inside out.

When his mouth finds the curve of my collarbone and brushes over it before nipping the skin lightly, I arch into him without thinking, seeking more.

Needing more.

He grips the hem of my shirt and drags it upward, pulling it over my head and baring me to the cool air and his gaze. He steps back for a beat, gaze sweeping over me like I'm the most captivating thing he's ever seen.

"You're so fucking beautiful."

His hands slide around my back to unclasp my bra, the tension of the fabric easing before he slides it down my arms and tosses it aside. The worshipful way he looks at me makes me ache everywhere.

He reaches out, toying with the little buds, brushing them with his thumbs until they pebble beneath his touch.

"Have I mentioned how much I love your nipples?" he asks, a teasing edge to his tone.

I shake my head. "I don't think so."

The smile he flashes is wicked. "Then I've been remiss."

He tweaks both at once, sending a pulse of heat straight to my core. I arch up into his hands, greedy for more.

"So damn eager," he mutters, trailing his mouth across the curve of one breast. "And so fucking responsive." He palms my chest, kneading gently before pinching both peaks again. "He never understood what he had, did he?"

There's no name mentioned, but we both know who he means.

I can't bring myself to speak. Not when every cell in my body is exploding like fireworks under his touch.

His hands drift down my ribs, leisurely and reverently, like he's savoring every inch he's finally allowed to touch.

The cool air hits the slickness between my thighs, making me shiver, but it's nothing compared to the feel of his hands as they roam lower, his fingers teasing, never quite giving me enough.

"You're soaked for me," he growls against my ear. "Fucking dripping, baby."

I whimper, pressing back against his hand, desperate for more contact, for anything.

"Such a good girl," he murmurs. "Letting me touch you. Letting me feel how badly you need it."

He brushes his fingers along my core, featherlight, teasing me until I'm squirming beneath him.

"You have no idea what you do to me, Lilah," he rasps, dragging his mouth along the curve of my hip. "I think about you spread out for me like this every damn time I close my eyes."

A desperate, broken sound tears from my throat as he finally strokes me where I need him most, until my muscles are tightening with need.

"That's it," he croons. "Let me feel you. Let me make your body sing the way no one else ever has. Let me show you exactly who you belong to."

And God help me, I want it.

I want all of it.

"Turn over," Steele murmurs. "I want to see that gorgeous ass in the air."

For a second, I'm too dazed to move, too wrapped up in the heat of his hands and the low gravel of his command.

Then his fingers slide down to my clit, tapping it once. It's firm yet teasing. "Did you hear me, lucky charm?"

The lazy warning in his tone sends a shiver down my spine

as I shift, rolling onto my stomach. The cool kiss of the sheets meets my flushed skin as I lift my hips obediently into the air, offering myself without a second thought.

And just like that, I'm his again.

Every thought.

Every trembling inch of my body belongs to him.

Steele's palm cups my ass, squeezing, as if he's committing every curve to memory. His hands are everywhere, both grounding and unraveling me with every possessive touch.

I shudder when he parts my flesh, exposing everything without a hint of shame. The air against my damp, aching skin makes me whimper as my heart hammers against my ribs.

I know he can see all of me now.

Every drenched, needy inch.

And the thrill of that knowledge coils tight and hot in my belly, setting me ablaze.

His fingers drift lower, featherlight and unhurried. When the pad of his finger brushes the untouched ring of muscle, my entire body jerks. It's partly shock and a good amount of pure molten heat.

"Has anyone ever taken you here, baby?" he asks casually, like he already knows the answer. Like he's already claimed that part of me too.

I go still, every sense attuned to his voice, his touch, and the low heat blooming deep inside me.

"No," I whisper.

He doesn't move. He just keeps stroking gently, teasing, circling. Absorbing every tiny reaction with razor-sharp focus.

"Is that something you want to explore?" Steele asks.

I steady myself with a ragged inhale.

The question doesn't feel invasive or like a demand.

It feels like an offer. One given with tenderness and layered in care.

And the way he's watching me, the way he tracks every

flutter of my breath, every tremble in my limbs, makes it clear this isn't just about sex for him.

It's about trust.

It's about showing me what it feels like to be cherished while being stripped completely bare.

"Yes," I whisper, heart pounding.

Steele lets out a sound that's raw and guttural.

As if my answer cracked something open deep inside him.

"Good," he rasps, pressing a kiss to the curve of my lower back. "Because the thought of taking you like that drives me out of my mind."

His confession sends a shudder through me.

Something primal twists inside me before trying to claw its way free.

Then his fingers glide back to where I'm already dripping, and he strokes me with a maddening slowness. I tremble beneath him as I bury my face in the sheets, trying to hold on while he pushes me closer to the edge of something that feels overwhelming.

"Mmm," he hums, voice thick with desire. "I love seeing you like this. Spread out and shaking for me."

When he teases that forbidden place again, I whimper, biting down on my lip. The sensation is new and startling.

Too much.

And yet, it's not nearly enough.

I want more.

I want everything.

He leans down until his chest brushes my back, the heat of him a brand against my spine.

The air shifts near my ear as he leans in to whisper, "I'm going to make you feel things you've never felt before, lucky charm. But only if you trust me. Only if you let me."

I trust him more than anyone.

Instead of feeling afraid, I feel seen.

Worshipped.

More than that, I feel like I belong to him.

His fingers trail along my cleft before dipping lower, teasing slow, deliberate circles. My whole body tightens as a desperate ache builds beneath my skin.

Without warning, he pulls back.

"Spread your knees a little wider," Steele murmurs.

I obey instantly, lost in him and the need thrumming through every inch of me.

There's the faint, delicious rustle of clothing being shed from behind me. And then the blunt head of his cock, thick and hard, pressing against my entrance.

"Steele," I choke out as I brace on my elbows, shaking so badly I can barely hold myself up.

"I've got you," he murmurs.

I can feel the tremor in his body too.

He's just as aroused and desperate.

And he's holding it all back for me.

He teasingly drags the head of his cock across my slit, gathering every drop of wetness, as if to savor it. His body quivers as he fights to restrain himself.

"I need you to tell me if it's too much," he rasps against my ear. "If you need me to slow down or stop, just say the word."

His hand sweeps down my back in a soothing caress that grounds me.

"I won't," I say, my voice barely audible over the thundering beat of my heart. "I need you, Steele."

A broken sound, half groan, half something almost like a prayer, rips from him. And then, finally, he pushes inside me.

I gasp, my hands fisting the sheets as he stretches me, fills me inch by careful inch, his body shaking against mine.

"Fuck, baby," he grits out, forehead pressed to my shoulder. "You feel so good. So damn good."

I whimper, arching into him, needing more, needing all of him.

"Do you feel how deep I am inside you?" he murmurs, voice like gravel and sin. "Every stroke designed to worship you. Drown you in pleasure. That's all I want is to give you so much bliss you'll never be able to live without it again. I'm going to ruin you for anyone else. One devastating thrust at a time."

My hips shift instinctively, silently begging him to make good on that promise.

And Steele gives it to me, driving deeper until there's no space left between us.

Until I'm so full of him that it feels like we were made for this.

He builds a rhythm that has my toes curling and moans tumbling out unchecked. Every drag of his cock makes me feel adored, fucked, claimed. He hits something deep inside me that makes my vision blur and my fingers clench in the sheets.

"You're taking me so damn good," he groans. "This pussy was made for me."

I can't argue.

Even more than that, I don't want to.

Because it feels true.

His pace builds.

Faster.

Harder.

My body meets each piston with equal desperation. His grip on my hips tightens as he pounds into me, relentless and perfect. My skin is damp, my thighs shaking, and I know I'm close.

The tension inside me coils tighter with every steady roll of his hips.

Every low groan he presses into my skin.

Every whispered word that falls from his lips.

"So beautiful. So damn perfect."

The pleasure continues to build until it's sharp, sweet, and all-consuming.

Until I'm teetering on the edge.

And when he reaches around, finding my clit with skilled fingers and stroking me in perfect time with his thrusts, I find myself dancing on the brink, barely able to hold it together.

"Steele—"

"I know, baby," he rasps. "Let go. I want to feel you come on my cock."

I shatter with a cry, my muscles clenching around him as my vision goes hazy and stars explode behind my eyelids. My entire body tightens, pulsing with pleasure so intense it makes my knees buckle.

Steele growls before following me over the edge. His hips drive deep one final time as he spills inside me with a hoarse shout of my name.

For a long moment, we cling to each other, unsteady and silent, lost in the aftershocks.

He eases out of me before gathering me up into his arms.

"You're mine now, Lilah," he mutters against my hair, voice rough with emotion.

And nestled against him, heart still racing, body still humming with the echo of him inside me, I know it's true.

For the first time in my life, I understand what it means to be thoroughly fucked.

And nothing has ever felt more incredible.

I lean against the counter as Lilah moves around the kitchen. Her hair is tied in a knot at the top of her head, and a loose sweater slips off one shoulder as she carefully arranges slices of cheese and cured meats on a wooden board.

I've never wanted to devour someone for slicing cheese and arranging almonds in my life. I didn't even think it was a possibility.

"You know it's going to get demolished within ten minutes, right?" I say, grinning as she carefully displays a stack of crackers.

Lilah doesn't bother looking up from what she's doing. "This isn't for you guys. It's for the girls, and we actually appreciate the effort."

She grabs a sprig of rosemary, tucking it between the crackers like she's plating a Michelin-star meal. "Pretty sure Callie, Rina, and Sloane won't care how fancy it looks."

A smile trembles around the corners of her lips. "You just don't understand the art of a good charcuterie board, Sanderson. Presentation matters."

I push off the counter and wander toward her, my movements deliberate. "Oh, is that right?"

She reaches for the olives, completely unfazed when I step in behind her, slide an arm around her waist, and nuzzle the curve of her neck. "Steele," she warns with a laugh.

I nibble at the spot just below her ear. "You smell like vanilla and rosemary."

"You're going to mess up my platter."

"I'd like to mess up way more than that."

With a chuckle, she gently elbows me away. "I have things to do before the girls get here. You, however, need to get ready to go."

I groan dramatically. "Are you kicking me out of my own penthouse?"

"Yup. You and the guys can go bond over beer and bad decisions."

She's right, I should probably get moving, but something about Lilah in my kitchen, at home in my space, makes it almost impossible to walk away.

I fucking love it.

Before I can fire back a response, my cell chimes with a notification that guests are on the way up.

Looks like girls' night has officially begun.

I head to the elevator to greet Callie and Rina. Waffles trails behind me, batting a ball back and forth as I find the two women loaded down with wine and takeout bags.

Callie gives a small smile as she adjusts the strap of her purse. "Hi, Steele."

She's always been a little tentative. Reserved. Especially since her split from Zane.

Rina on the other hand? There's not a shy bone in her body. It's probably because wrangling players as the team's head of PR requires a certain level of confidence.

She lifts a dark brow in greeting. "Thanks for letting us use your place tonight," she says, brushing past me into the entry-way. "We'll try not to get too wild."

"Not making any promises, though?" I ask dryly.

"Obviously not."

Lilah peeks down the hall with a smile. "Looks like you brought enough for a girls' night and a half."

Callie lifts her bags. "I came prepared."

Rina waves a hand. "This week has been hell. I plan on drinking enough to forget I even have a job."

I glance at Callie. "I hope you're driving."

She nods. "Designated mom. Always."

Just as we reach the kitchen, boisterous male voices fill the entryway, and I glance toward the elevator as Knox, River, Oliver, and Jax stroll in.

Knox grins. "Hey, Cap."

My brows furrow. "What are you doing here? I thought the plan was to meet at The Rail Yard."

Knox shrugs, completely unrepentant. "Yeah, but then we heard Lilah was hosting girls' night, and figured we'd crash first."

Oliver smirks, already heading for the wine Rina brought. "Besides, what's a party without me?"

Rina snatches the bottle from his hands. "If you touch my wine, you'll find my size eight lodged up your ass."

"Probably wouldn't be the first thing he's enjoyed up his ass," Jax says with a snort.

Oliver gives him a finger before turning back to Rina, blue eyes dancing with mischief. "Didn't know you were so possessive."

She glares. "Alcohol is what helps me forget about all my interactions with you."

"As if that's possible. I'm the highlight of your week, baby. And we both know it."

"Please, keep telling yourself that," she grumbles.

"We tried to guilt Laiken into some team bonding, but he

was a no go. You know how much he hates leaving Elodie alone," River says.

I snort. "Did you really think he'd want to spend free time with us if he can be with his daughter?"

"Smart man. I'd choose Elodie over you jokers anytime," Knox adds.

River's gaze flicks to Callie and lingers. "Hey, Callie. How's Nora?"

Callie stiffens as she grips the edge of the counter, her expression carefully blank. "She's fine."

River moves closer, undeterred by the cold shoulder she's giving him. "I wanted to talk to you about the other—"

Her tone turns frosty as she cuts him off. "Don't bother. And you don't have to keep checking in on me. If Zane wants an update about his daughter, he knows how to reach me."

River's jaw clenches. "What? No, that's not—"

Before he can finish, Callie turns away, effectively ending the conversation.

Knox mutters, "Well, that was certainly awkward. I have a feeling that's the way most of your interactions with the ladies go."

Before anyone else can comment, the elevator opens. I glance up, expecting the last of Lilah's friends.

"Damn. Who's that?" Jax mutters, attention locked on her.

I follow his gaze to the petite brunette with sharp eyes. "That's Sloane. She works at Lakeshore Sweets with Callie."

Jax nods absently, still staring like she's the first woman he's ever seen in real life.

Before Sloane can greet everyone, Jax beelines in her direction. His lips curve into an easy smile. "So you work at the bakery everyone's always raving about, huh? Maybe I'll have to stop by sometime."

"Really?" Sloane looks him up and down. "You don't strike me as the sweets type."

Jax flashes his signature grin in response. "Not usually, but I'm excellent at taste-testing."

Sloane lifts a brow. "What a coincidence, so is Nora."

Knox chokes on his beer as Jax steps closer, his boyish charm cranked up to full volume.

"Then she and I have something in common."

Sloane exhales through her nose before shaking her head. "Would that be zero self-control and a penchant for throwing tantrums?"

Knox wheezes as River smothers a laugh.

"She's got you there, Jax," Knox says with a chuckle.

Our teammate ignores the jab. "Maybe I can take you out sometime and you can find out for yourself."

Sloane barely glances his way, her tone cool and unreadable. "No, thanks. Some of us don't have time for games."

Jax's smirk wavers for a split second before snapping back into place. "Well, if you change your mind, the offer stands."

"I won't," Sloane says with a roll of her eyes before finally dismissing him.

Knox is full-on losing it as I exchange a glance with River. I don't know Sloane well, but her prickly demeanor doesn't seem to be deterring Jax in the least.

Knox claps me on the shoulder. "Come on, Cap. We should probably head out and leave the girls to it."

I look over at Lilah, who's lounging on the couch and laughing with Callie.

In all honesty, I'd much rather stay here.

Rina glares at Oliver. "Do me a favor and try not to end up on TMZ again."

He winks. "No promises, baby."

Rina grabs a throw pillow and hurls it at him. With a grin, Oliver sidesteps the projectile.

As the elevator doors close, Knox shakes his head with a

laugh. "So, tell me, Cap. Does she even realize how far gone you are for her?"

I shoot him a look. "Not yet. But she will."

Knox grins before clapping me on the back. "I can't wait to see how this turns out. It's way better than the K-dramas my sister watches."

Oliver smirks. "Just your sister, huh?"

"Fuck off, Van Doren." He nods toward me with a smirk. "I'm just hoping Cap finally breaks the dry spell. I'd hate for him to forget how it's done."

They have no idea that the streak is already over.

And I have no plans of ever looking back.

35
LILAH

We're all stretched out in Steele's living room, surrounded by fuzzy blankets, half-eaten charcuterie, and a few empty bottles. The view outside the massive windows is nothing short of stunning.

It feels like the perfect backdrop for a cozy night in.

"So," Rina says, sipping her cabernet and narrowing her eyes at me over the rim of her glass, "I think we're all due for an update."

I arch a brow, playing innocent. "About what?"

Callie snorts. "Um, hello? The friends-with-benefits offer Steele oh-so-casually tossed out. I'm dying to know what you decided. The sparks flying between you two at the Railers event last week were enough to singe our eyebrows."

"I'm still recovering," Rina adds dryly, swirling her wine. "You could cut the tension with a butter knife."

I laugh, but the moment my gaze flicks to the coffee table—the very one I'd been sprawled across not that long ago—heat floods my cheeks.

"I decided to take him up on the offer," I murmur, taking a long sip of wine to hide the rising flush in my cheeks.

There's a collective inhale from around me.

Callie leans in, her eyes wide with curiosity. "As in... you two are sleeping together now?"

I shake my head. "I'm not giving details, but yeah, we are."

Rina lets out a satisfied hum as she sinks deeper into the couch, looking entirely too smug. "I knew it. That man looks at you like you're the only woman on the planet."

"He does," Callie agrees, nudging my knee with hers. "And he always has."

I offer a small, slightly dazed smile. "The difference between him and Devon is like night and day. There's no comparison."

That earns a chorus of nods and a few muttered "obviouslys" from around the room.

Sloane, who's been sipping her wine, sets her glass down with a decisive clink. "Okay, real talk. Friends with benefits can certainly work. But only if both people are clear about what they want."

"And really honest," Rina adds, tapping her nails against her wine glass. "Because otherwise? It gets messy fast."

Callie's brows knit together. "But this is Steele. He's not some random hookup. He's your best friend. That makes it even riskier."

I chew my bottom lip, feeling their eyes on me. "I know. Trust me, I know. It's just being with him feels different. It's not just about sex. It's easy. Comfortable. Almost like our friendship has always been leading to this place."

"Maybe it has been," Callie says gently.

"You deserve easy," Sloane adds firmly. "You deserve to be worshipped and adored."

"Desired," Rina chimes in. "And don't even try to deny it. That man desires you. You can see it every time he looks at you."

Warmth blooms in my chest at their words, at how fiercely they rally around me without hesitation.

"It's scary, though," I admit. "What if I screw it up and lose him?"

"You won't," Callie says, reaching for my hand and giving it a reassuring squeeze. "If it's real, and it looks pretty damn real from where I'm sitting, you're not going to lose him."

"And if you do," Sloane says, shrugging with a mischievous glint, "we'll key his Lamborghini."

I laugh as the knot of fear inside me loosens just a little.

"Whatever happens," Rina says, raising her drink, "you're not alone. You have us."

I clink my glass against theirs, feeling lighter, steadier than I have in weeks.

The conversation dips for a moment, all of us lost in our own thoughts. I shift on the couch and glance at Sloane, who's stretched out in the armchair with her wine glass balanced on one knee.

"Sooo…" I begin, drawing out the word with a teasing lilt. "What did you think of Jax?"

Her reaction is immediate. She lets out a snort and then takes a long sip of her wine, like she needs the strength before answering.

"Not much."

I laugh. "Seriously?"

She raises one unimpressed brow. "He strikes me as your typical hockey player. All swagger and charm, like he's never heard the word 'no' in his life."

Callie grins. "Well, your assessment isn't wrong."

Sloane continues dryly, "From what I've read on the Railers gossip site, he's a headline waiting to happen." She glances at Rina. "Someone she'll have to clean up after."

Callie leans in, a mischievous glint in her eyes. "He wanted to take you out, though. No interest?"

"Absolutely none." Sloane shakes her head without hesitation. "I have way too much going on to throw in the complication of a man. Especially one who collects women like trading cards."

Rina chuckles from her spot across the room. "Remind me never to let you near my dating app profile. You'd murder half my matches."

Sloane lifts her glass. "Probably. But only out of love."

We all laugh, the easy rhythm returning as the conversation drifts from the boys to the gala, to wine preferences, to the worst dates we've ever been on.

But somewhere beneath all of it, I can't stop thinking about Steele. About the way he looked at me last night, like I was the only thing that had ever made sense to him.

And the way I felt when he stared at me.

Seen.

Wanted.

Cherished.

There's a piece of me that knows this friends-with-benefits thing is temporary. That the clock is ticking on whatever it is we've become. But there's another part, one that's growing louder, that wonders what would happen if I stopped fighting the truth and let myself fall completely.

Rina nudges me gently with her foot. "You're quiet."

I blink, realizing everyone's watching me. "Just thinking."

Callie gives me a knowing smile. "About a certain protective center with broad shoulders and golden retriever vibes?"

With a groan, I toss a pillow at her. "Maybe."

They crack up. It feels amazing to be surrounded by people who really know me, and still choose to stay.

No matter what happens with Steele, I'm grateful for that.

Callie shifts in her seat, trailing her finger along the rim of her wine glass. The easy mood evaporates in an instant.

I frown. "Are you okay?"

She exhales and stares down at her drink. "Yeah. Have you seen the latest about Zane?"

Rina's face twists in disgust. "Unfortunately. That man's a walking PR nightmare. And I should know since I'm the one who always has to deal with the fallout."

Callie's mouth presses into a tight line. "He and his new girlfriend were all over each other at the gala last week. They couldn't keep their hands to themselves. She's barely twenty-one and already chasing every camera she can find."

Sloane leans forward, her expression sharp. "You and Nora deserve so much better than to be dragged into his circus."

Callie swallows hard, her fingers tightening around her glass. "It's not about who he dates. I don't care about that. It's just..." Her voice falters, and for the first time tonight, real fear leaps to life in her eyes. "What if he gets serious? What if he marries her and decides he wants to play the family man? What if he tries to take Nora?"

Silence falls over us.

Rina is the first to shake her head. "No way. Not a chance."

Sloane's eyes flash. "Zane's not interested in being a father. He's interested in being famous. That's it."

"But people change," Callie whispers. "What if he decides he wants custody just to look good for the cameras? What if he uses her as a prop to clean up his image?"

I reach for her hand and squeeze it tightly. "You are Nora's home, Callie. Her safe place. Anyone with eyes can see that."

"She's right," Rina says fiercely. "Judges don't just hand over custody to absentee fathers with reality TV dreams. Zane's record speaks for itself."

"And if he even tries to come after you," Sloane says darkly, "he'll have to go through all of us first."

Callie lets out a choked laugh before swiping at her eyes. "You all are the best."

"What we are is loyal to you," Rina says, lifting her glass in a mock toast.

Callie gives a watery smile, her shoulders relaxing slightly.

"Thank you. I guess I'm just scared about what the future holds."

"You're allowed to be scared," I tell her gently. "But you're not alone in this. We've got you."

"All the way," Sloane says firmly.

Callie nods, a little steadier now. "Thank you. That really means everything."

We exchange a look that says it all.

Whatever happens, we'll face it together.

Rina shakes her head, leaning back against the couch as she lifts her wine glass. "I swear, Zane must be on a mission to get mentioned on Railers Rumors more than anyone else on the team. He and his girlfriend are practically staging their own damn PR campaign. Every time I check, there's another ridiculous headline about him."

Callie groans, rubbing her temples. "I know. My phone is constantly blowing up with texts asking if I've seen them. Like I need a reminder that he's making a fool of himself."

Rina takes a sip of wine, her expression darkening. "I've tried to get that site shut down. Or, at the very least, force them to take down some of the more invasive posts. But it's impossible. They're protected under some bullshit free speech loophole, and as long as they're not publishing outright lies, it's all fair game."

Callie snorts. "Yeah, because taking candid photos of guys at a bar or speculating about their sex lives is totally fair game."

"Right?" Rina huffs. "I've had to deal with so many PR disasters because of that site. And Oliver doesn't need any help in that department. Half the time, he leans into the stories like it's a game."

I raise a brow, smirking. "Sounds like someone's taking their job a little personally."

Rina glares at me over the rim of her glass. "I swear to God, Lilah, if you say one more word about me and Oliver, I'm leaving. You know how much I can't stand that guy. I'd be more than thrilled if he got traded to another team. Preferably across the country."

I arch a brow and lift my wine glass to my lips. "Are you sure about that? You two seem to have a lot of chemistry."

Rina snaps her head toward me so fast, I'm surprised she doesn't get whiplash. "Are you out of your mind? How can you even say that?"

Callie smirks. "Because you bicker like an old married couple."

"Please," Rina scoffs. "He's a typical hockey player. All he cares about is scoring. And we're talking both on and off the ice."

I tilt my head. "So you've noticed, huh?"

Her glare is immediate. "It would be hard not to. It's also part of my job. Until he straightens up and stops getting into trouble, I'm stuck with the guy."

Callie shrugs. "I don't know, it could be worse."

"I really don't see how."

"You could have a thing for him."

Rina practically chokes on her drink. "God, no. First off, he's Oliver Van Doren." She pops a brow. "You know, *the big O.* Second, there's no way I'd ever date a hockey player. I'm pretty sure there's a strict no-fraternization rule in place. My entire job is making sure his latest bad decision doesn't end up as a headline."

Callie hums, clearly unconvinced. "You sure about that?"

"Positive." Rina takes a long sip of wine, then sets her glass down with a smirk. "Besides, he's about to have bigger things to worry about."

I narrow my eyes. "Uh-oh. What did you do?"

Rina's grin turns downright wicked. "Let's just say Oliver Van Doren is about to be one of the lucky bachelors auctioned off at next month's charity gala. He just doesn't know it yet."

Callie gasps, looking both amused and horrified. "Oh my God. He's going to lose his mind."

I burst out laughing. "You're so evil. I like it."

Rina shrugs, entirely unapologetic. "I prefer to think of it as a heavy dose of karma."

Sloane raises a brow. "You put him in a bachelor auction without telling him?"

"Correct."

Sloane considers this before nodding. "That's fair."

Callie wipes tears of laughter from her eyes. "I can't wait to hear about his reaction."

Rina sighs dramatically. "And I can't wait to remind him that he really should read his emails before blindly agreeing to things."

I shake my head, still grinning. "You really are his worst nightmare."

Rina smirks. "And yet, he keeps giving me more reasons to torture him."

The room dissolves into laughter as the seriousness from our earlier conversation melts away. I lean back against the couch, wine glass in hand, and let myself soak in the warmth of good friends, good gossip, and the comforting hum of the city just beyond the windows.

Still, in the back of my mind, I can't help but wonder what Steele is up to right now. And if he's thinking about me too.

The penthouse is quiet when I let myself in after midnight, the city lights spilling through the windows in streaks of gold and silver. Everything feels hushed in the way it always does when I'm the only one home.

Except, I'm no longer alone.

The moment I step out of the elevator, I feel her. Lilah's presence wraps around me, weaving through the air, subtle but undeniable.

And all I want—

No, all I fucking *need* is to find her.

Touch her.

Claim her.

What I expect is to find Lilah asleep in my bed. Naked. Sprawled across my sheets, her blonde hair a tangle against my pillow, her skin still carrying the imprint of my hands from earlier. I haven't stopped thinking about her all damn night.

About the way she feels wrapped around me.

Tight.

Wet.

And mine.

It's fucking nirvana.

There's no other way to describe it.

I didn't think it was possible to become addicted to a person.

I was wrong.

Instead of finding my sweet girl asleep in my bed, she's cuddled up on the couch in the living room. She's wearing one of my old Railers tees, and her legs are bare, tucked beneath her. Her hair is piled in a messy twist on top of her head, and Waffles is snuggled on a chair, sacked out.

For just a moment, I take in the sight. It's a cozy, domestic scene that has played out in my head hundreds of times since I bought the place. She looks up at me with a smile that punches through every layer of control I thought I had left.

"Hey," she murmurs.

"Hey, lucky charm." I kick off my shoes, roll up the sleeves of my shirt, and close the distance between us. It's like there's an invisible thread that tethers me to her. I have to wonder if it will always be that way. "I didn't think you'd still be up."

A sleepy smile curves her lips. "Girls' night ran late. Rina got tipsy off two glasses of wine, and we finished all the pastries Callie brought. We talked and laughed a lot. It was exactly what we all needed."

I sink onto the couch beside her, letting the cushion dip and tilt us toward each other. Unable to help myself, my hand settles on her thigh. Her skin is warm beneath my palm. "I'm glad. You deserve it."

She tips her head, her eyes filled with curiosity. "How was your night?"

I shrug. "Fine."

The truth?

I spent the entire evening half-listening to Knox and River, pretending to give a damn about the game replayed on the TVs at The Rail Yard. All while counting the minutes until I could come home and wrap myself around this woman.

"I missed you," I say, letting my hand glide a little higher along her silken thigh.

She shifts closer before swinging one leg over my lap until she straddles me. The T-shirt she's wearing slides higher on her hips, and that's the exact moment I realize she's not wearing panties.

My cock reacts before my brain can catch up, pressing hard against my jeans.

She smirks, her lips curving into a devilish smile. "See something you like?"

"Yeah," I rasp. "Been thinking about it all fucking night."

She leans in and brushes a kiss to the corner of my mouth. "I missed you too."

That's all it takes for my restraint to break. My hands slide up her thighs, caressing the swell of her ass, squeezing gently as I guide her closer.

"How the hell did I go ten years without having you?" I whisper, more to myself than to her.

She rocks her hips against me. "Not sure. Maybe you should focus on making up for lost time."

My lips curve. "Oh, trust me. I plan to."

I draw her T-shirt over her head, baring her to the moonlight. Her skin glows under its silver kiss, so beautiful it nearly drops me to my knees.

She undoes the buttons of my shirt with quick, sure fingers, shoving the fabric off my shoulders before dragging her lips across my pec. The feel of her makes me want to lay her out and worship every inch of her body.

"Seems like my baby's been horny all night long," I murmur, loving the idea of it.

She blushes but doesn't look away. "I couldn't stop thinking about what you'd do to me when you got home," she whispers.

"Every time I looked at the coffee table, I thought about the way you made me come with your cigar."

A low, ragged groan rips from my chest as I palm her breasts. "I love this side of you," I rasp, brushing my thumbs over her nipples until she gasps. "The one who likes to be played with. Spanked. Tasted. Owned."

By me.

And only me.

"And before I'm done," I promise against her mouth, "I'll have every inch of you. Every moan. Every last tremble. I'm going to satisfy you in ways no one else ever has."

She shudders in my lap, already slick and needy.

"You make me feel so good," she admits.

"Prepare for more, baby," I grit out. "Because I'm nowhere near finished with you."

In one smooth motion, I lift her into my arms. Her legs lock around my waist and her drenched heat presses against my abs as I carry her across the room and pin her against the window. The cool glass draws a gasp from her lips as it kisses her spine.

I take her in, haloed by the skyline behind her, and I know in this moment, I'll never get enough.

Not in this lifetime.

And not in the next.

"Do you understand that you belong to me now?" I whisper against her lips.

She nods, silent and wide-eyed.

But that's not enough.

Not even close.

"Say it," I demand.

"I belong to you," she whispers, voice shaking but sure. "Just you."

"That's right."

I grind my cock against her, making her whimper as her nails dig into my shoulders.

I kiss her like a man starved.

Because that's exactly what I am.

In one swift movement, I unzip my jeans, freeing my cock before sliding into her with one deep, claiming thrust.

Her body arches against the window, clenching tight around me.

"Fuck, you're so damn perfect," I groan, bracing her as I begin to move.

Slowly at first.

Then harder.

Deeper.

I drive into her with the need to brand myself on her skin and carve my name into her soul.

Her moans echo in the night air until she shatters in my arms, all the while crying out my name like a prayer. That's all it takes for me to follow her over the precipice, spilling inside her with a groan that sounds more like a vow.

Afterward, I hold her close, her head tucked beneath my chin, our bodies tangled, exhausted and still.

I press a kiss to her damp forehead and whisper, "Now that's how you end a night, lucky charm."

She doesn't answer.

But the way she melts against me says everything I need to know.

37
LILAH

I wake up to the smell of coffee and the feel of warm lips drifting across my shoulder.

A low murmur follows, deep and gravelly. "Morning, lucky charm."

With a smile, I blink open my eyes and turn toward him just in time for another kiss. This one to the tip of my nose.

"You're up early," I murmur, my voice scratchy with sleep.

"I've got practice in an hour," Steele says, already half-dressed in team-issued gear. "I just wanted another look at you before I left."

I snort. "Pretty sure you saw all of me last night pressed against the window."

"Exactly." His grin is playful. "Why do you think I'm leaving in such a good mood?"

I swat at his arm, but he catches my wrist before pressing one last kiss to my lips. It's slow and sweet enough to make me consider begging him to skip practice altogether.

He pulls back with a low groan, his eyes dark with want. "Don't look at me like that. I can't afford another fine."

The last thing I want is to risk Steele's career.

"Then go," I whisper, nudging him toward the door, even

though every part of me aches to keep him here. "Before I do something I can't take back."

With a smirk, he grabs his keys. "Waffles is in the kitchen, glaring at her bowl. Pretty sure she's demanding a tuna breakfast."

I laugh as her faint meow echoes down the hall. "She's so dramatic. Wonder who she gets that from."

Steele winks on his way to the door. "Text me if you get bored. Or lonely. Or hungry. Or if you need a refill on that wine you like."

"I'll see you when you get back."

He's halfway out when he tosses a grin over his shoulder. "Damn right you will."

The elevator doors close, and just like that, the penthouse is quiet again. It's me and Waffles. The kitten hops onto the bed and settles beside me for a catnap.

An hour later, I'm dressed and looking through Steele's upcoming schedule when my phone buzzes with a message from Ashley, my old assistant from the law firm.

ASHLEY:

> Hey! Sorry for the short notice, but we have a box of your stuff here. Any chance you could swing by to pick it up?

My heart flip-flops. I haven't been back since walking in on Devon and Marissa.

ME:

> Yeah, sure. I can come by this morning.

There's a pause before the typing dots reappear.

ASHLEY:

> It'll be waiting for you at the front desk.

I stare at the screen for a second as a little sting hits me.

Ouch.

Guess I'm no longer welcome upstairs.

After feeding Waffles a little bit of tuna and then pulling myself together, I grab my keys and head down to the garage. My Audi has been parked here at Steele's building ever since I left Devon's apartment, and it's weird how quickly I've started thinking of this place as home.

The drive to my old office is short, but my thoughts are loud.

By the time I park and walk through the front doors, my stomach is churning. It's strange being back here. Strange knowing this part of my life is officially behind me.

Ashley steps out of the elevator, a small cardboard box cradled in her arms. Her eyes widen when she spots me.

"Lilah," she says, hurrying over and giving me a slightly awkward one-armed hug. "I'm so sorry about everything. I didn't know what to say."

"It's okay," I tell her gently. "Really."

She hands over the box. It's the last of my things. A few books, some pens, a paperweight shaped like a gavel. The kind of stuff that feels heavier than it should.

"So," Ashley says, biting her lip. "What firms have you applied to?"

I shift my weight. "Actually... I don't think I'm going back. Not to law. At least, not right now."

Her brows rise. "Really?"

"Yeah." I glance down at the box in my hands. "I think I want to do something different. Something that makes me excited to get out of bed in the morning."

As the words leave my mouth, I realize just how true they are. And for the first time in a while, they *feel* right.

Ashley nods. "Good for you. Keep in touch, okay?"

"I will," I promise.

With nothing more to say, I walk out with my box. My

shoulders feel a little lighter than when I arrived. On a whim, I detour a few blocks and pull into a metered space outside a small coffee shop I used to haunt back when I still thought my corner office dreams would make me happy.

The moment I push through the door, I'm hit with the warm scent of espresso and toasted almond. It's like a hug I didn't know I needed.

"Hey, stranger." One of the baristas I used to chat with smiles wide. "Long time no see."

"Yeah," I say, smiling back. "Life's been busy."

"Want your usual?"

I nod. "That would be amazing, thanks."

She gestures toward the pastry case. "Croissant?"

I eye the chocolate-filled one like it's flirting with me. "You twisted my arm. I'll take one."

"Coming right up."

My phone buzzes just as I pull it from my pocket.

STEELE:

I'm having withdrawals. Any chance of a repeat performance tonight?

ME:

I don't know… depends. What's in it for me?

STEELE:

Me. Naked and grateful while worshipping every inch of you.

My lips twitch. I can practically hear his cajoling tone.

ME:

Tempting. But I'm gonna need a better sales pitch.

STEELE:

I'll even feed you after. You like blueberry
pancakes, right?

ME:

Are you trying to seduce me with carbs?

STEELE:

I'm trying to seduce you, period. Where
are you?

ME:

How do you know I'm not at the penthouse?

STEELE:

Because I may or may not be tracking your
location.

My heart skips a beat at that admittance as I type out a response.

ME:

Umm, excuse me?

STEELE:

Relax. It's purely protective. You're everything
to me, lucky charm.

My fingers hover over the keyboard for a beat too long. This man.

ME:

Okay.

STEELE:

So... you didn't answer my question. Where
are you?

I hesitate for half a second.

ME:

Out getting coffee.

Technically, it's not a lie.

STEELE:

You do know there's coffee at the penthouse, right? Like, a whole bag of your favorite beans?

ME:

Sometimes a girl needs a change of scenery.

STEELE:

You sure it's not that you're already missing me?

ME:

Don't start, Sanderson.

STEELE:

Too late. We both know you're my favorite person to mess with.

ME:

What an honor.

STEELE:

You should feel honored. So… are you alone?

ME:

Yes, Dad. Just grabbing a latte. No strange men have abducted me. Yet.

STEELE:

Mmm. I don't know. I might need proof of life. Selfie?

ME:

Hard pass.

STEELE:

One little pic. Humor me.

ME:

You're ridiculous.

STEELE:

Still waiting…

ME:

Not happening.

STEELE:

Fine. But if you're not back in 20 minutes, I'm
sending out a search party.

ME:

You're at practice. Maybe you should focus on
that.

STEELE:

Doesn't mean I can't multitask. Also doesn't
mean I'm not thinking about you with your legs
over my shoulders.

My entire body heats as I press my thighs together and shoot him a glare he can't see.

ME:

Steele.

STEELE:

What? You started it with the "what's in it for
me" comment.

ME:

You're the worst.

STEELE:

Liar. I'm the best.

ME:

Keep dreaming.

STEELE:

Only about you.

I inhale as my heart rate kicks up. His words are always half a joke, half a dare, but there's something about them that slides under my skin and stays there.

> **STEELE:**
>
> Anyway. Repeat of last night is still on the table. And maybe dinner too.

> **ME:**
>
> Free food?

> **STEELE:**
>
> The way to your heart, I know. That's my girl.

I swallow.

Hard.

His girl.

Is that what I am now?

The barista slides my latte and croissant onto the counter with a smile. "Chocolate's still warm. Want a bag?"

"That would be great. Thanks."

"That'll be thirteen dollars," she says.

I slip my phone into my purse and start digging for my wallet when a voice cuts through the air, familiar enough to stop me cold.

"I've got it."

My entire body locks up as I lift my head and turn to find Devon behind me. He looks the same as ever. Polished. Perfect. Not a hair out of place. What strikes me most is how relaxed he seems. Lighter. The lines that used to crease his forehead have eased, and there's a glow to his skin along with a glint in his eyes.

He looks... happy.

And for some reason, that lands like a sucker punch straight to my gut.

I clutch the strap of my bag. "That's not necessary."

"Come on, Lilah. Let me buy you a cup of coffee."

Before I can argue, he passes a twenty across the counter.

The barista smiles as she rings it up. "You two were always one of my favorite couples. Nice to see you're still going strong."

I force a tight smile as Devon mirrors it.

Neither of us correct her.

I take a step back, coffee in hand, hoping to escape the awkwardness. "Well. Thanks again."

"I assume Ashley reached out to you?"

I nod. "Yes, she did."

His mouth tightens. "I told her to just mail your stuff. It would've been easier."

Of course he did.

"I didn't mind," I say. "It was on my way."

He studies me for a beat, head tilted like he's trying to figure me out all over again. "You look good, Lilah."

I stiffen. "So do you. You look happy."

He hesitates. And then, with the kind of ease that still manages to sting, he says, "I am."

The words settle heavy in my heart.

I could walk away right now and let that be the end of this conversation.

But I don't. If I'm going to fully close this chapter, I need to understand how it ended in the first place.

"Why?"

Devon frowns. "Why what?"

"Why weren't you content with me?" I step closer, trying to keep my voice steady. "Why did you say you didn't want kids for five years and now you're having one with someone else?"

His jaw works as he shoves his hands into the pockets of his slacks. "I don't know," he says finally. "Being with you... It always felt like something I *should* do. Not something I actually *wanted* to do."

My stomach twists. "Because of our parents?"

He shrugs. "I'm sure they played a part in it. You know how

they were. Always asking when we were getting married and what our future looked like. It felt more like an obligation. One I didn't know how to get out of."

My mouth opens and then closes again. It's like being hit with a truth I wasn't ready for.

"I wish you would've said something," I murmur. "I never wanted you to feel like that."

"In hindsight, I should have," he admits. "I should've ended things sooner. I should've been honest, but I didn't want to hurt you."

"You did hurt me," I say quietly.

He nods. "I know."

There's still one thing I haven't let go of. One image burned so deeply into my brain it resurfaces every time I think I'm past it.

"When I walked in on you and Marissa..." My voice wavers. "I-I'd never seen you like that before. You looked... I don't even know. Uninhibited. Alive."

His cheeks darken as he glances away. "Do we really need to go there?"

"Yes," I say, firmer now. "I need to understand how you could be one person with me and someone completely different with her."

Devon's gaze drifts toward the windows and the busy street beyond it. "With Marissa... I don't know. I feel freer. Like I can just be myself without thinking about what I'm supposed to be." He shrugs, as if that explains everything. "It made me realize we were never right for each other, Lilah. I didn't understand it at the time, but now I do."

"And yet, you stayed, instead of just ending it," I whisper.

"Yeah, well. I guess I didn't want to be the bad guy. You were always so put together. Smart. Driven. It felt like you had a five-year plan, and I didn't want to be the one to derail it."

The words land like a punch.

They're not meant to be cruel, but they're careless enough to leave a bruise.

"So, you thought you'd coast until something better came along?"

Devon winces. "That's not what I meant."

But he doesn't deny it.

And maybe that's worse.

He glances down at the floor. "Anyway, I'm glad you're okay. Wherever you go or whatever you do, I'm sure you'll land on your feet."

Like I'm a cat who tripped, not a woman who was blindsided and left to rebuild.

I nod tightly. "Take care of yourself."

He opens his mouth to respond, but I'm already turning away. The door chimes as I step into the crisp October air and exhale slowly.

Whatever Devon was supposed to be in my life, that story is over.

And this time, I'm the one closing the book.

38
STEELE

I step off the elevator and into the penthouse, the door gliding shut behind me with a muted thud.

It's quiet.

But it's the kind of quiet I like now.

The kind that makes me smile.

Home used to be just a place to crash between games. A high-rise with sleek finishes, cold surfaces, and a view of Lake Michigan that didn't mean anything to me.

But since Lilah moved in?

Now it feels different.

Full.

Alive.

Bursting with energy.

More than that, it feels like *home*.

The way it was always meant to.

I toss my keys onto the credenza and shrug out of my jacket, glancing toward the kitchen out of habit. Half-expecting to see her barefoot, humming off-key to whatever moody indie playlist she's fallen in love with this week, dancing around while she stirs something that smells like heaven and tastes even better.

But the kitchen's empty.

No music. No movement. No scent of garlic or butter or whatever magic she usually brews up.

A frown tugs at my lips as my muscles tense.

It's ridiculous how quickly the unease sets in.

"Lilah?" I call out, my voice echoing in the stillness as I move through the space.

No answer.

My stomach churns.

Then, a little gray blur shoots out from under the coffee table, meowing as she skids across the hardwood.

"Hey, Waffles." I crouch, reaching out as she trots over, tail held high like a tiny, fuzzy antenna.

She lets out another chirpy meow as I scoop her up and scratch behind her ears.

"Where's your mama, huh?" I murmur, holding her up to eye level. She blinks at me like she's keeping secrets. "You gonna tell me?"

Waffles responds with a dramatic yawn before flopping against my torso, purring like a tiny engine.

I chuckle and rub a hand down her back.

"Guess that's a no."

Her presence eases something in me. The place feels a little less empty with her snug in my arms. But it still doesn't explain where Lilah is.

I carry Waffles with me as I check the bedroom, my heart ticking faster than it should. The door is open, and the first thing I spot is a pile of clothes on the floor near the foot of the bed.

That's a good sign.

She's here.

But something still feels off.

I set Waffles on the bed and give her a final scratch behind the ears before rounding the corner.

Lilah is huddled in the bathtub, knees pulled to her chin, arms wrapped around them as steam rises from the water. Her eyes are red-rimmed and her skin is blotchy. Not from the heat but from something much deeper.

The sight of her stops me cold.

"Lilah," I say gently as I step into the bathroom.

Instead of glancing my way, she continues to stare at the surface of the water, her lashes heavy and wet.

I lower myself to the edge of the tub, close enough that our knees almost touch. "Talk to me, baby. Did something happen?"

Silence.

It's the kind that makes my stomach twist and my jaw grind. My girl never goes quiet unless she's hurting in a way that words can't touch.

"Lucky charm," I murmur, trying for lightness. "Do I really need to threaten to spank your ass, or is that even a deterrent anymore?"

A watery laugh escapes her lips. "Probably not."

That tiny sound hits me harder than it should. But it's something. A sign she's still in there.

I reach out and graze her cheek with my knuckles. Her skin is damp and warm. "Come on, Lilah. Whatever it is, you can tell me."

She takes a moment to compose herself. "Ashley texted this morning and said there was a box of my stuff at the front desk."

"You should've told me. I would've come with you."

She lifts one shoulder in a shrug. "I figured it'd be quick. We had a brief conversation, and it was fine." Her voice wavers on the last word. "And then..." She swallows hard. "I stopped at that little coffee shop I used to love. The one near the office."

There's a pause, and I brace myself for whatever's coming.

"And I ran into Devon."

My hand stills on her cheek, but I don't say a damn word. I just wait, wanting her to get it all out.

"I didn't expect to see him there." She blinks, her lashes trembling. "He looked good. Content. It's not a version of him I recognized."

My jaw clenches until it aches.

"I asked him why he hadn't told me the truth sooner. About how he felt and wanting something different. You know what he said?" Her gaze lifts to mine. "That being with me felt like an obligation. Because our parents expected it. And he didn't know how to get out of it."

Fucking hell.

I close my eyes for a beat and count to three. The only thing keeping me from punching something is the fact that she needs me right now. Not some pissed-off caveman ready to throw hands.

With a ragged tone, she says, "I gave him nearly two years of my life. I kept trying to make it work. Trying to be the version of myself he needed. And all this time... he was just waiting for a way out."

I can't fucking stand hearing her talk like this.

Like she was disposable.

She laughs, but there's no humor in it. "I didn't even see it. How messed up is that? I thought we were solid and that he loved me. And now I don't know if I was ignoring the truth or just holding on to the version of it I wanted to believe in."

She wraps her arms around herself, like she's trying to hold the pieces together.

"He said it never felt right. That with Marissa, it's just easier." She closes her eyes for a moment. "He made me feel like I was the problem," she whispers. "Like loving me was just too much."

I don't realize I've risen to my feet until I'm peeling off my shirt and tossing it aside. My pants and boxers follow. I step into the tub without a word and then settle behind her before pulling her into my arms. In this moment, all I want to do is absorb every ounce of her pain.

Instead of resisting, she melts into me. Her back curves into my chest and her head fits under my chin like it was made for that spot. My legs cage hers as I kiss the bare skin of her shoulder, anchoring her in place.

"He's a coward," I tell her. "And a real asshole for saying any of that."

She doesn't argue as my hold tightens.

"He never really saw you, Lilah. Not the way I do. He didn't *want* to. And that's his loss."

She lets out a broken laugh, as if she doesn't believe me.

"Devon never understood what he had," I murmur, my hand stroking up her side. "You're not someone who fits into a neat little box. You're fire. You're softness. You're strength wrapped in the prettiest fucking package I've ever seen. And he couldn't rise to meet that."

"Then why does it hurt so much to hear it?"

I press my lips to the side of her neck. "Because you gave him the best of you and he didn't know what to do with it."

She shifts, just enough to face me. Her cheek rests against me, and her fingers skim along my ribs, as if memorizing the way I feel.

"I hate that he made you doubt yourself," I say. "But that guy? He doesn't get to define what love looks like for you."

"Then who does?" she asks.

"You do, baby," I say without hesitation.

Her fingers clutch my chest, securing herself to me like I'm the only steady thing in her world.

"Promise that we'll always be friends?" she asks, the question barely audible.

I press a kiss to her damp hair. "I promise."

Even though the word is too small for what I feel for her.

Even though friendship is the least of what I want. But she's fragile right now, and I won't risk breaking that trust. So, I hold the rest of it back. The weight of how long I've loved her.

The ache of not being able to say it yet.

The truth will come out when she's ready.

And when it does, I'll be right here, waiting to catch her.

We sit in the quiet as the water cools around us, our skin wet and our hearts beating in sync.

And I know, no matter how long it takes for her to believe it, no matter how many broken pieces we have to gather, I'll be here through all of it.

Because she's not just my lucky charm.

She's my whole damn heart.

And I'll never let her go.

39
LILAH

The scent in the kitchen wraps around me like an embrace.

There's the smell of spinach and garlic in the air, something warm and buttery from the granola oat cookies cooling on the counter, as the low sound of my playlist drifts from my phone. I pull the muffin tin out of the oven and smile as the protein-packed egg cups sizzle, the tops golden and puffed up just the way I like them.

Waffles is nestled at the end of the rug, paws tucked under her fuzzy little body, her tail flicking lazily. I glance down at her as I slide the tin onto the stovetop.

"I know," I murmur to her with a grin. "I'm already becoming that person who talks to her cat. Just wait, I'll be showing you TikToks next."

The fridge hums in the background, the smoothie I blended earlier already chilling inside, and the cookies are perfectly crisp at the edges.

For once, everything feels right.

I pad barefoot around Steele's kitchen, wearing one of his old Western U hockey sweatshirts that hits mid-thigh. The hem brushes my skin as I move, warm and familiar. My hair's a mess, and I'm makeup free. And I'm happier than I've been in years.

The run in with Devon was painful, but it allowed me to close the door on that chapter. Now I can focus on other things.

Things that make me happy.

Like cooking.

There's something about the rhythm of chopping, stirring, and tasting that brings me peace.

And the idea that I'm feeding someone I care about?

Someone who's become the center of my whole world?

It means everything.

I'm plating the egg cups when Steele's footsteps echo through the hallway, and my heart stutters in that annoying way it always does now when he's near.

It's difficult to remember there was a time when that didn't happen.

He walks into the kitchen, damp from his shower, smelling like fresh soap and clean skin. His dark hair is pushed back from his face. He's wearing joggers and a sleeveless Railers tee that shows off his arms.

The way he's so easily able to command my attention now is seriously unfair.

A grin spreads across his face. "Why'd you sneak out of bed so early?"

He slides his arms around my waist from behind before pulling me into him and pressing a kiss against the side of my neck just below my ear.

"Mmm," I say, tilting my head as goose bumps rise along my skin. "Twice wasn't enough for you last night?"

"Nope." He nips my neck lightly. "Might need a third this morning to tide me over until after practice."

With a laugh, I wiggle out of his arms, handing him a plate with an egg cup. "You're insatiable. Here, try this and tell me what you think."

He raises an eyebrow and bites into the muffin. "Holy shit," he says around a mouthful. "This is incredible."

My smile stretches wider. "Really?"

"Absolutely." He grabs another before I can stop him, already chewing. "You're gonna ruin me, you know that?"

I tuck a strand of stray hair behind my ear and lean back against the counter. Nerves flutter in my belly as I blurt, "So, I had an idea. That's why I got up early."

His gaze flicks to mine. It's steady and attentive. "Yeah? What kind of idea?"

I bite my lip. "What would you think if I started making healthy meals and snacks? You know, for people who are health-conscious, athletes, or busy professionals. Like meal prep, protein treats, baked goods with macros in mind."

He watches me without interrupting, which only makes me more nervous.

"I've always loved to cook. And after everything with the law firm... I just don't think I want to go back. I don't know if I ever really wanted it in the first place." I steady myself and say what I've been holding in. "But this? Cooking? It makes me feel like *me*. And I think I could be really good at it."

Steele doesn't say anything for a second, just keeps chewing as his gaze stays locked on mine.

And then he smiles. "I think it's a great idea, Lilah."

"You do?"

"Of course. You light up in this kitchen." He glances around the room and gestures to the counter, the food, and Waffles, who's still snoozing in the corner. "I've never seen you more in your element. Now's the perfect time to take a leap and go after something that makes you happy."

Emotion swells inside me. Before I can stop myself, I launch forward and wrap my arms around him, hugging him tight.

His arms lock around my waist and his chin drops to rest on my head.

"You're always so damn supportive," I mumble into his shirt. "How did I get so lucky?"

"I'm the lucky one," he says, dropping a kiss on the top of my head.

When I finally pull back, he grins. "You should make a batch of whatever you're planning next, and I'll bring it to the arena. We can let the guys try it."

"You'd do that?"

"Hell yeah. If they like it, you've got yourself an early focus group."

I beam. "Okay. I can do that."

"Of course you can." He taps my nose. "Now, how long do I have before the timer for your next batch goes off?"

"About twenty minutes."

"Perfect." He reaches for a granola cookie and gives me a mischievous look. "That's enough time to drag you back to bed."

I laugh. "Steele..."

"You'll be my dessert," he teases.

Waffles meows from the corner.

"Even Waffles is judging you right now," I say with a grin.

"Whatever," he replies, picking me up bridal-style. "She can be in charge of the kitchen while you're gone."

And with that, we disappear down the hall in a tangle of laughter, kisses, and egg muffin crumbs.

After Steele leaves for practice, I clean the counters, pack up a few muffins for his teammates, and am elbow-deep in a different recipe when my phone rings.

I hit answer on speaker. "Hey, Rina! What's up?"

"Have you been online at all this morning?"

"Nope, I got up early to start breakfast and bake. Why? What's going on?" I pause, narrowing my eyes. "What did Oliver do now? Or is it Zane and his barely-legal girlfriend?

Please tell me they're not plastered all over Railers Rumors again."

Instead of laughing, she remains strangely quiet.

"Rina?" I drop the spoon into the mixing bowl and wipe my hands as unease skitters down my spine.

"It's Steele."

My stomach pinches. "What about him?"

She exhales. "Railers Rumors posted a photo of you two, and it's going viral."

"Okay, so what? Why is that a big deal?"

"It was taken at Gold Coast Table. You're standing in front of him, and his hand is wrapped around your throat."

The image slams into me like a flashbang. I remember the moment. It's when he asked if I'd made a decision yet.

"I don't understand."

"The angle makes it look like he's choking you," Rina says, tone uncharacteristically low. "Like he's hurting you."

"H-he wasn't. He didn't." My voice trembles. "That's n-not what it was."

"I know. I *know*, Lilah. But the internet doesn't care about that. Comments are already flooding in. People are calling him abusive."

My stomach flips. I press a hand to it, trying not to throw up. "This can't be happening."

"Just... don't look at it. I'm working on it. I've already contacted the site to try to get it taken down, but it's spreading fast. I'm so sorry."

"Thanks, Rina," I whisper.

We hang up, and despite her warning, I open the browser and type in Steele's name.

It's the first image that pops up.

They zoomed in, cropped out the world, and left only a story they wanted to tell.

My expression is caught in a moment of raw need that looks reckless without context.

His hand, always steady and worshipful, becomes something darker through a lens hungry for scandal.

Something sharp twists in my gut as I scroll through the comments.

I'm not surprised. He's always been aggressive on the ice.

He's clearly controlling her.

Disgusting.

She needs help.

That's all it takes for the room to spin. My legs give out, and I drop onto the stool beside Waffles, who meows in alarm and jumps down.

I can't believe this.

One moment taken out of context.

A second of affection turned into something ugly.

And Steele has no idea.

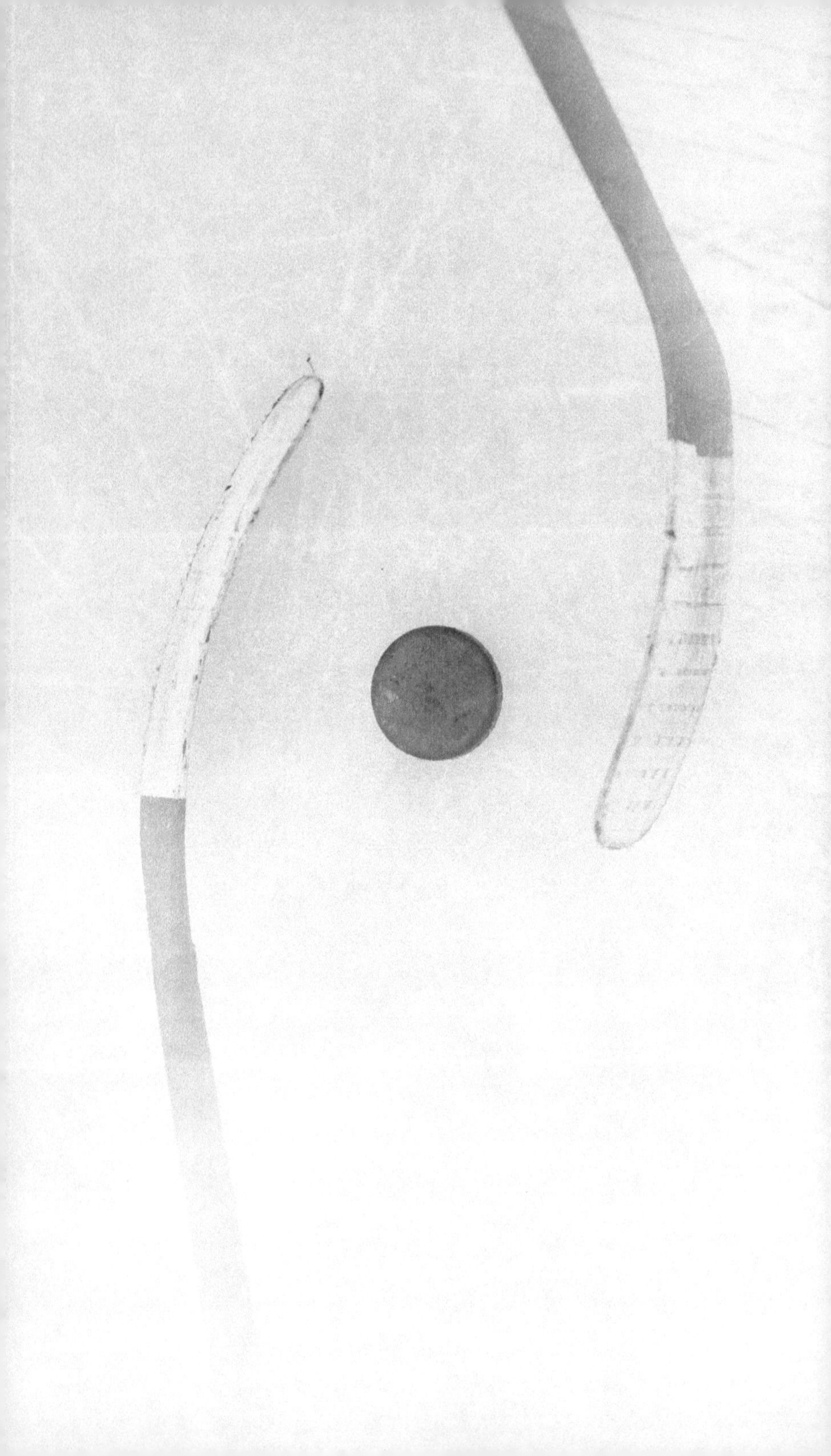

STEELE

I'm still smiling when I walk into the locker room thirty minutes later.

There's a lightness in me I haven't felt in a long time. Probably because I just left Lilah standing in my kitchen, hair messy and cheeks flushed, whipping up something healthy and delicious after being thoroughly fucked.

The best part?

She was happy.

Relaxed.

And damn if that doesn't do something to me.

I toss my bag into my stall and stretch my arms overhead. "Morning," I say, uncapping my water bottle.

"Hey, Cap." Jax gives me a chin lift in greeting.

"What's up, Cap?" Oliver says.

A few of the guys greet me as I make my way through the locker room, but something's off in their tone and the way they stare before glancing away.

With a frown, I slow my steps.

Knox looks up from lacing his skates, his jaw working like he's chewing on something he doesn't want to say.

"Don't worry about it," he mutters, eyes avoiding mine. "It'll blow over."

My brows pull together. "What, exactly, will blow over?"

Before anyone can answer, the locker room door opens and Coach steps in.

"Sanderson," he calls out, his tone clipped. "Landry wants to see you in his office."

I freeze. That's all it takes for the warmth from earlier this morning to fade.

The owner of the team wants to see me?

Well, shit.

That's never a good sign.

My mind starts to spin.

Did I miss something?

Blow off an appearance?

Screw up a PR commitment?

No one's offering any answers, and a low buzz of unease starts working its way through me.

I give him a curt nod and follow him out. By the time I reach Hugh Landry's office, the smile I came in with is long gone. I can barely remember what it felt like. Once at his door, I rap my knuckles on the thick wood.

"It's open," he calls out.

As soon as I step inside, I realize he's not the only one in the room. Evelyn is seated near the window, her expression solemn, and Rina is standing next to her. The spark that usually fills her eyes along with her fiery disposition is nowhere to be found.

Fuck.

Whatever is going on is even worse than I imagined.

Hugh is seated behind his desk with his hands clasped like he's prepping for battle.

My stomach knots. "What's up?" I ask, lowering myself into the chair across from him.

No one says a word at first.

Rina avoids my gaze, just like some of the guys in the locker room.

Hugh shifts slightly, the movement enough to draw my attention back to him. "Just know that this situation is uncomfortable for everyone."

"What situation? Someone needs to tell me what's going on," I demand.

Rina pulls out her phone, hesitating for a second before finally handing it over.

I take it.

The screen lights up with the Railers Rumors site.

There's a photo.

Grainy but clear enough.

It's of me.

I'm standing behind Lilah at Gold Coast Table.

And my hand is wrapped around her throat.

It looks wrong.

Really fucking wrong.

Rage and disbelief crash into me all at once.

"What the fuck," I mutter. "This isn't what it looks like."

I look up, meeting Hugh's eyes before glancing at Evelyn and Rina. "Both of you know that Lilah is my best friend."

Evelyn arches a brow. "From the looks of it, she's way more than that."

My face heats. "She is," I admit. "But I wasn't hurting her. It was a private moment. Something intimate that's been twisted."

"You're a public figure, Steele," Hugh says. "Perception is everything. That photo, stripped of context, paints you as aggressive, even abusive."

I grit my teeth and cross my arms. "My private life is my business. Not theirs."

"You know how this works," Rina says quietly. "You've been in the league long enough to understand that people love to fill in the blanks. And right now, the narrative they're building is getting ugly."

I shake my head as frustration bubbles up inside me. "What am I supposed to do? Let the media paint me as a fucking monster? I didn't hurt her. I would *never* hurt her."

"We know that," Evelyn says gently. "But the world doesn't."

Hugh leans forward. "We need to do some damage control before this mess gains more traction."

"It might help if Lilah addressed it," Rina says with a sigh.

My gaze snaps to her. "Absolutely not."

She tries again. "Steele—"

"No." My jaw tightens. "I'm not dragging her into this any more than she already is. This isn't her mess to clean up."

Evelyn's gaze holds steady. "But right now, she's the only one who can shape the narrative."

My fists clench as a thousand images of Lilah flash through my mind. Her face when she sees that photo, the hurt in her eyes, the backlash she never asked for. The helplessness curdles into something sharp.

"I'll handle it," I say, pushing to my feet.

I don't wait for any of them to argue. I'm already out the door, every step driven by one thought and one thought only.

I need to get to Lilah before this story does.

41
LILAH

The sky outside is a blanket of gray, heavy with clouds that haven't quite committed to rain. Lake Michigan stretches out in front of me through Steele's wall of windows, but even the water looks dull and colorless today. It matches the knot in my stomach. The tight, uncomfortable weight of dread that's been sitting with me since I saw the photograph.

My phone is pressed to my ear as my mother's sharp voice cuts through the quiet.

"I've had a dozen people send me that photo, Lilah. *A dozen.* Do you have any idea how embarrassing that is for me? For *us*?"

I close my eyes and rest my forehead against the glass. "I didn't ask for the picture to be taken."

"That's hardly the point. You put yourself in that position and let him wrap his hand around your throat in public. What kind of message do you think that sends?"

I don't answer right away. Mostly because I'm unsure what to say.

It wasn't what it looked like.

At all.

But it doesn't matter to the gossip sites or to the people who only see what they want to. Who have painted it as something dark and ugly.

Her tone creeps up a notch. "How do you expect to get another job at a reputable law firm after this? Who will hire someone involved in such an ugly scandal?"

"I don't want another job practicing law," I blurt out before I can stop myself.

The silence that follows is brutal. "I'm sorry, what did you just say?"

"I said that I don't want to be a lawyer." My voice is quiet but steady. "I don't think that world is for me anymore. If it ever was."

There's a stunned beat before she says, "After we spent over a hundred thousand dollars on your degree, you're just going to throw it all away?"

Tears sting the backs of my eyes. "It's not about the money."

"I have no idea who you are right now, Lilah. I really don't. Are you having some kind of mental breakdown? Is this a cry for help? Do you want me to book you a stay at Miraval so you can relax and get your head on straight again?"

"I'm not having a breakdown, Mom."

"I don't understand what's happening with your life. First the breakup, then you get fired, and now this... *photo*. I've never been so disappointed."

The words are like a slap across the face. I press my lips together, so I don't say something I'll end up regretting, before blinking up at the ceiling. I've always tried to make my parents proud. Sometimes to my own detriment.

And I refuse to do it any longer.

"Did you cheat on Devon with him?" she demands. "Is that what really happened?"

"No," I say. "Of course not."

"Then what are you doing with Steele Sanderson? Are you

in a relationship now? I always knew that hockey player was trouble. It's such a violent sport."

I squeeze my eyes shut. "We're friends," I whisper. "We've always been friends."

It's not entirely a lie, but it doesn't quite feel like the truth either.

"I need to go," I say, cutting her off before she can ask anything else.

"I—"

"Bye." I hit the end button before I lose my nerve.

I'm still standing near the window when I feel Steele's presence behind me. Moments later, his arms slip around my waist and his lips brush the side of my face.

"I take it that was your mom?" he asks quietly.

I nod, not trusting my voice. After a moment, I say, "They saw the photo. Let's just say they're not happy about it. Their friends have been completely scandalized."

He presses his lips against my temple. "I don't give a shit about your parents' friends. But I do care about you. Are *you* okay?"

"Honestly? I don't know," I admit before twisting in his arms to face him. "Wait... Why are you home so early? Did something happen?"

He hesitates for a beat. "I got pulled into a meeting with Hugh. Evelyn and Rina were there too."

My stomach drops. "Because of the photo?"

"Yeah."

"I'm so sorry," I whisper, the guilt hitting me all over again. "I never thought... I mean, we were having a private moment. It didn't even cross my mind that someone might take a picture of us."

"That's on me," he admits. "I should've known better. I should've realized people are always watching. Especially when it comes to professional athletes."

"Are you in trouble?"

When he remains quiet, my heart clenches.

"It'll blow over," he finally says. "I'm not worried."

The way he avoids direct eye contact tells me everything I need to know.

Everything he refuses to say out loud.

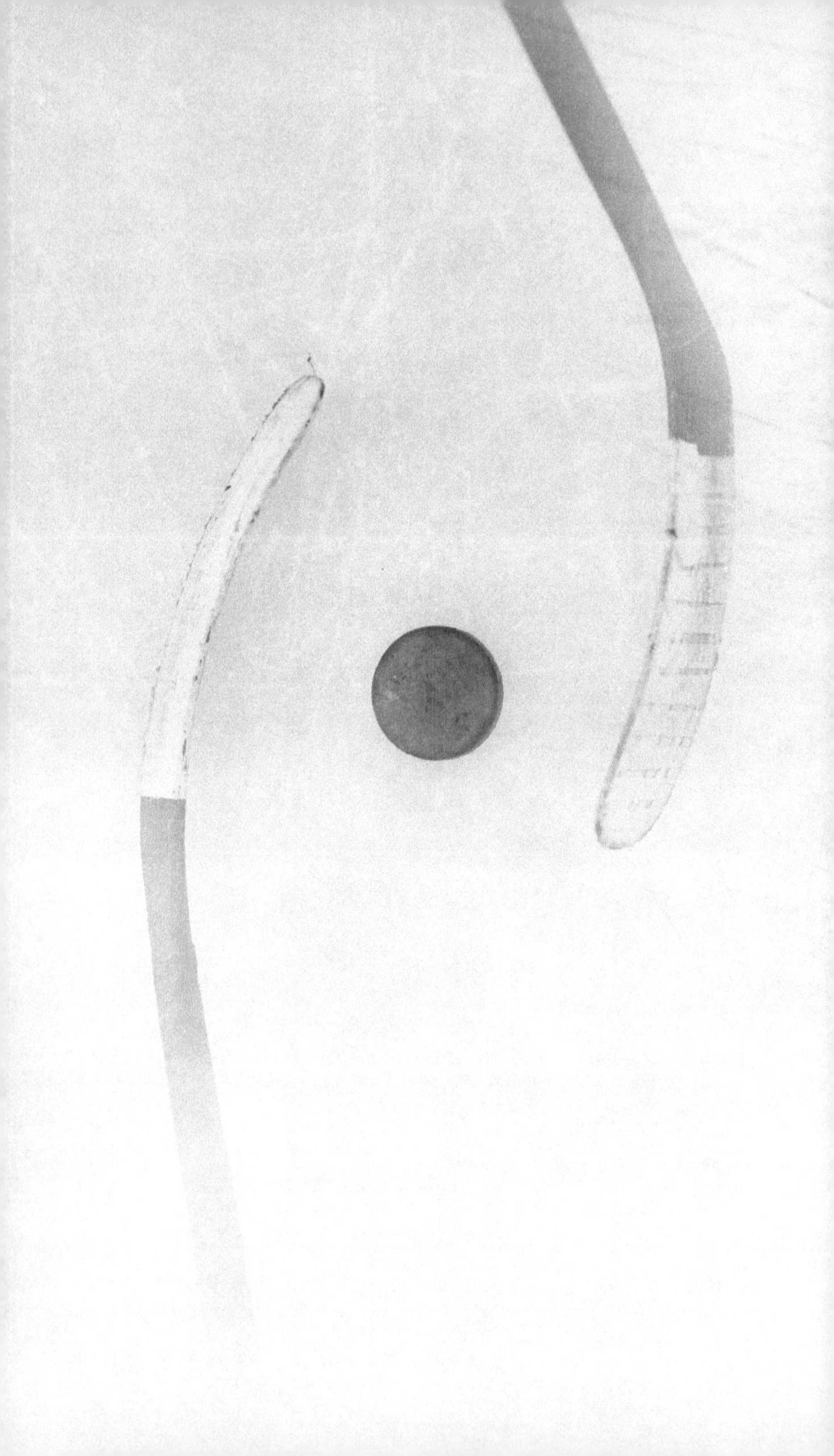

42

STEELE

ow that Lilah's in my arms, everything finally settles. I tighten my hold, wishing I could absorb some of the weight she's carrying and make it my own.

"I'm worried this will damage your career," she whispers.

I pull back just enough to look at her before tucking an errant lock of hair behind her ear. "You think I give a damn about hockey right now?"

She tries to smile, but it doesn't quite land.

She's concerned.

All the positivity and excitement from earlier this morning has vanished.

I'll be damned if I allow anyone, including her mother, the media, or some faceless internet troll to steal her sunshine.

Especially when she was just starting to turn a corner.

Fuck that.

I press my lips to the top of her head. Her body fits against mine like she was made to be there as we stand in the quiet of the living room. The city beyond the glass is gray and cold, a reflection of the storm brewing inside her.

I wrap my arms tighter around her before whispering against her temple, "I think you need a distraction."

She huffs out a dry laugh. "From what, exactly? The internet branding me a victim or my mother disowning me for not wanting to be a lawyer?"

"From all of it," I murmur, tightening my hold. There's a part of me that's afraid she'll slip right through my fingers if I'm not careful. "Let them talk, baby. While they're busy judging, I'm the one who gets to be here with you."

She stiffens slightly. "Steele..."

Instead of letting her finish, I scoop her up into my arms.

Waffles stirs from her spot on the couch before lifting her head lazily and glancing our way. Then she curls back up like she knows what's coming next and refuses to be part of it.

Smart cat.

Lilah stares up at me. "What are you doing?"

"I'm taking care of you," I say simply. "That's all I've ever wanted to do."

I carry her through the penthouse to my bedroom, not stopping until we're in the bathroom. Only then do I set her down gently and step away just long enough to turn on the shower, adjusting the temperature until steam rises in the air.

When I turn back around, she's watching me with wide, questioning eyes.

I reach for the hem of her shirt, lifting it slowly and giving her every chance to stop me if it's not what she wants. My hands are careful as I peel the fabric over her head and let it fall to the floor. I take my time with the rest of her clothing, touching every inch of bared skin that gets revealed. There's no rush or roughness. Only patient, steady devotion. I want her to feel it every second and in every part of her.

The way she deserves.

By the time her clothes have been removed, she's trembling. Not from anguish but from the kind of anticipation that leaves your entire body buzzing with need.

"You're so damn beautiful," I murmur, letting my thumb graze her hip bone.

Then I strip off my own clothes and lead her into the shower until the warm spray cascades over us. Lilah releases a sigh as the water hits her.

I reach for the shampoo and lather it into my hands before moving behind her. She tilts her head back, allowing me to massage it gently into her scalp. After rinsing it out, I repeat the process with the conditioner. My fingers comb through her hair until the strands are silky soft to the touch.

Lilah leans back against me when I finish, her muscles loosening, as if she's finally letting go. I press a kiss to her shoulder and then another before trailing my mouth along the side of her neck until she turns her face toward mine.

"I hate seeing you like this," I murmur. "Tense and sad. Questioning yourself and the decisions you've made."

"I'm okay," she whispers.

"No, you're not. But I'm going to do everything in my power to make sure you will be."

I run my hands down her arms, over her ribs, and across her stomach. She stills, tension rippling through her when my palm slips between her thighs. She moans as I touch her the way I know she needs. Slow, skilled, and focused entirely on her. I worship every inch of her like it's the only thing I've ever wanted to do.

And when she starts to unravel in my arms, I catch her.

She lets out a moan when I press her against the wall, caged in between my bigger body and the tiles. Her fingers bite into my shoulders as she wraps her legs around my waist.

"Please don't hold back," she pleads.

That's the last thing I'm going to do.

Because this isn't just about pleasure.

It's about reminding her she's wanted.

Loved.

Cherished.

Not for what she does.

Or who people expect her to be.

But for exactly who she is.

After we've both found our release, I hold her close, my hands gentle as I rinse her clean.

She leans her forehead against mine with her eyes closed. "Thank you. Somehow, you always know exactly what I need."

I press a kiss to her lips. "And don't you ever forget it, lucky charm."

If I have my way, I'll spend the rest of my days making sure she never questions where she belongs.

Or the man she belongs to.

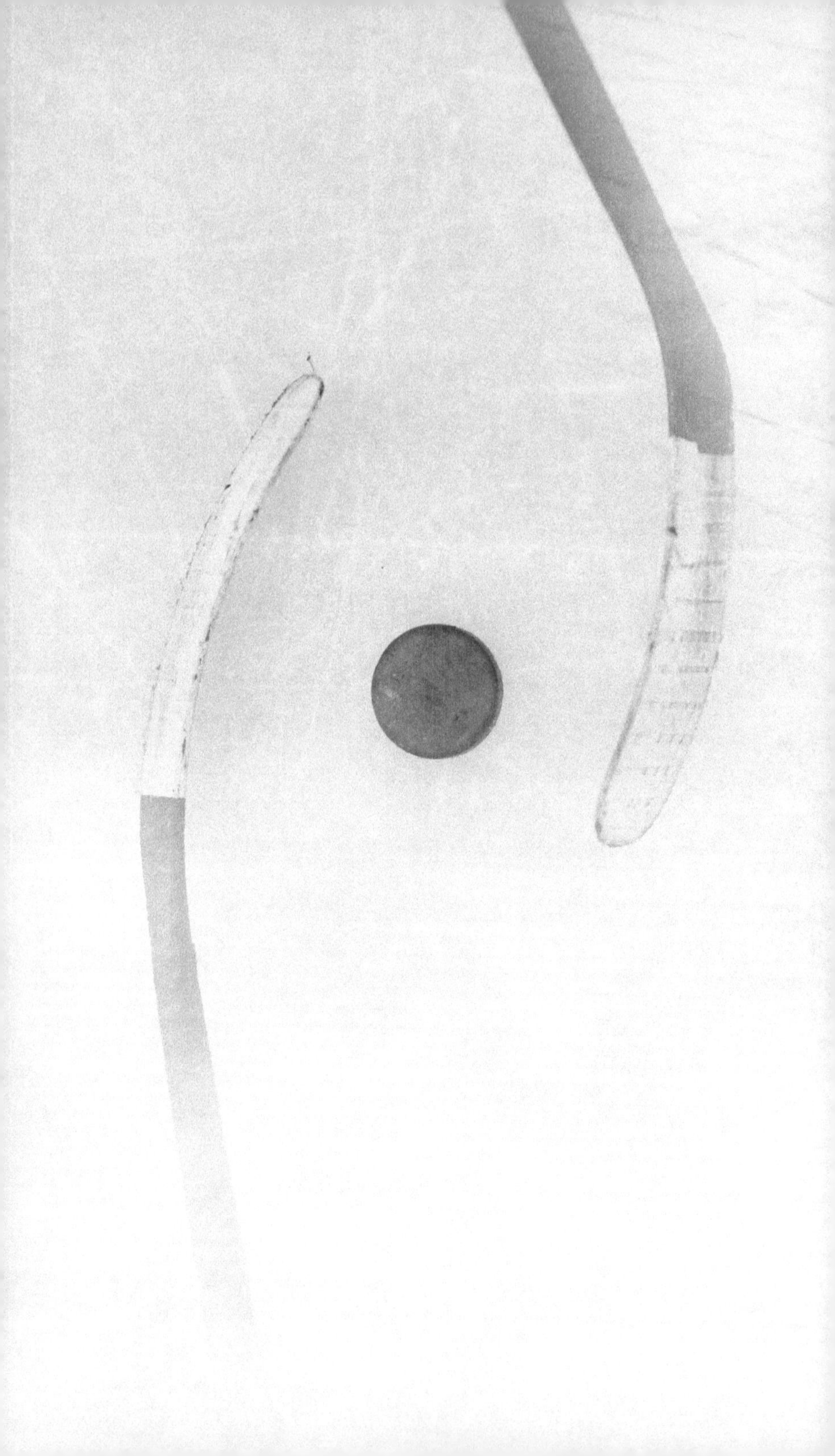

With my elbows braced on my knees and eyes locked on the stretch of fresh ice in front of me, I sit alone in the empty arena. The air inside the rink is cool, crisp, and silent. It feels like the calm before the storm.

This place has always been my sanctuary.

Even before I turned pro, the rink was where everything made sense. No noise, no headlines, no bullshit. Just the scrape of skates, the sharp cut of blades, and the rhythm of the game.

Today, it feels different.

Heavier.

I drag a hand down my face just as my phone buzzes in my pocket.

Bridger's name lights up the screen.

Although, if you want to get technical, "fuckface" is the name that flashes on the device.

I swipe to answer.

"Hey," I say.

His voice crackles through the line. "You at the arena?"

"Yup. Practice in forty."

There's a slight delay before he asks, "You doing okay?"

I scrub a hand through my hair. "Yeah. I'm fine."

"I saw the story," Bridger says tightly. "The photo. No one who knows you believes any of that garbage. It's nothing more than clickbait."

"Some people do," I murmur. "But they're not the ones who matter."

"It still pisses me off," he mutters. "You've always kept your head down and your nose clean. And now they're acting like you're some violent asshole? It's total bullshit."

There's a beat of silence between us before he asks, gentler this time, "How's Lilah?"

I exhale. "About as well as you'd imagine."

"That bad?"

"She's holding it together," I say. "But, yeah. It's eating her up inside."

"Give her our love," Bridger says. "Seriously. Holland's been fuming since she saw the post."

I nod, even though he can't see me do it. "Tell her we appreciate the support."

Movement from my periphery catches my eye, and I glance up to see Rina entering the lower bowl of the arena. Her gaze sweeps the stands, and when it locks on me, she heads in my direction with a purposeful stride.

"I appreciate you checking in," I tell my cousin, shifting on the chair. "But I gotta go."

"Love you, man. Take care of yourself."

"You too."

I hang up just as Rina climbs the last step and settles beside me in the front row. She doesn't speak right away, just stares out over the empty ice.

"I thought you'd be in the locker room by now."

"I needed a minute," I say, leaning back in the seat beside her. "What's up?"

She hesitates, then sighs. "I heard about Peak Sportswear pulling out. I'm sorry."

I drag a hand through my hair. "Yeah. My agent called this morning with the news. They gave the usual 'optics' line—said I'm a PR liability and they're reevaluating the direction of their brand. Translation? A grainy photo and a bunch of internet warriors with too much time on their hands were enough to make them run scared."

She glances sideways at me. "Does Lilah know?"

I shake my head.

"Have you talked to her yet about making a statement?"

The anger that rises within me is sharp and immediate. "No."

"Steele—"

"I'm not dragging her into this," I snap before making a conscious effort to lower my voice. "She's already in the middle of a firestorm. I'm not adding more fuel to it."

Rina folds her arms as her jaw tightens. "She wouldn't want you to lose sponsorships over this. You know that."

"I don't give a damn about the money. I've invested well over the years. I'm not hurting."

She blinks, startled. "Then what—"

"I care about *her*," I say flatly. "I care about protecting her and the way she looks at me. What I don't give a shit about is how the media spins their narrative. She doesn't owe anyone an explanation about what happens between us. Period. End of story."

Rina exhales. "Okay. Then we deal with it the best we can. Quietly."

"Yeah," I say in agreement. "Quiet works."

We sit for a moment, both of us staring at the smooth sheet of ice.

"She's lucky to have someone so loyal," Rina says eventually.

"No." I shake my head. "I'm the lucky one."

And I'll fight anyone who tries to destroy what we've built.

44
LILAH

I'm already sitting at the corner table in Lakeshore Sweets, nursing the mocha latte Callie made special just for me, when she and Sloane slide into the seats around me.

"How are you holding up?" Callie asks, her expression gentle as she unwraps a muffin and pushes it in my direction.

"I don't even know," I admit. "I feel like I'm caught in the middle of a tornado, and no matter what I do, the wind just keeps picking up."

Sloane frowns. "It's disgusting, honestly. The way that picture was taken completely out of context? I mean, it's you and Steele. Anyone with eyes can see how much he adores you."

Callie nods, her jaw tight. "And don't even get me started on how they're spinning it. I know exactly what it's like when people think they're entitled to your life. Between Zane's bullshit and the media circus, I've had more than my fill. I won't ever let myself or my daughter get dragged through that again."

Before I can respond, the bell above the door jingles, and Rina hurries in, tugging off her scarf, cheeks pink from the wind.

"You're late," I say. As grateful as I am to see her, I can't help but eye her with caution. I'm almost afraid of the news she'll bring.

She hesitates, her hands tucked into the pockets of her coat. "I had to talk to one of the players."

I tilt my head as everything inside me stills. "One of the players?"

Rina shifts, her gaze darting away before returning.

"Was it Steele? You can tell me."

Rina opens her mouth, closes it, and then groans. "I knew I shouldn't have come here right after my conversation with him."

"I'll get you a coffee," Callie says, already rising. "Extra large."

Rina sinks into the seat beside me and mutters, "Thanks, babe."

My stomach clenches. "Rina, just tell me what's going on. You know how Steele is. He wants to shield me from everything."

"He's going to be so pissed if I mention any of it to you," she states, unbuttoning her coat.

I lean in, my voice low. "Please. Just tell me what's going on. I need to know."

She glances around before her shoulders wilt. "One of Steele's longtime sponsors pulled out this morning. Said the optics of the photo didn't align with their brand, and they've withdrawn all advertising from the arena."

For a moment, I just blink, unable to form a single thought. "What?"

Sloane places a hand over mine while Callie returns and sets the coffee in front of Rina.

"He lost a sponsor?" I whisper, barely able to get the words out.

"He didn't want you to know," Rina says gently. "He just wants to protect you as much as he can."

My stomach bottoms out. "What can I do to fix this?"

Rina hesitates. "I don't think there's a magic fix, Lilah. But… What if we did a quiet interview? One-on-one with someone we trust. A female journalist with integrity. Someone who won't twist your words."

It's not even something I need to think about. As much as he wants to look out for me, I want to stand up for him just as fiercely. "I'll do it."

Callie squeezes my arm while Sloane passes me a napkin for the tears I didn't realize had gathered in my eyes.

"Let's take control of the story," Rina says firmly. "We'll write the ending ourselves."

For the first time in days, I feel the smallest spark of hope.

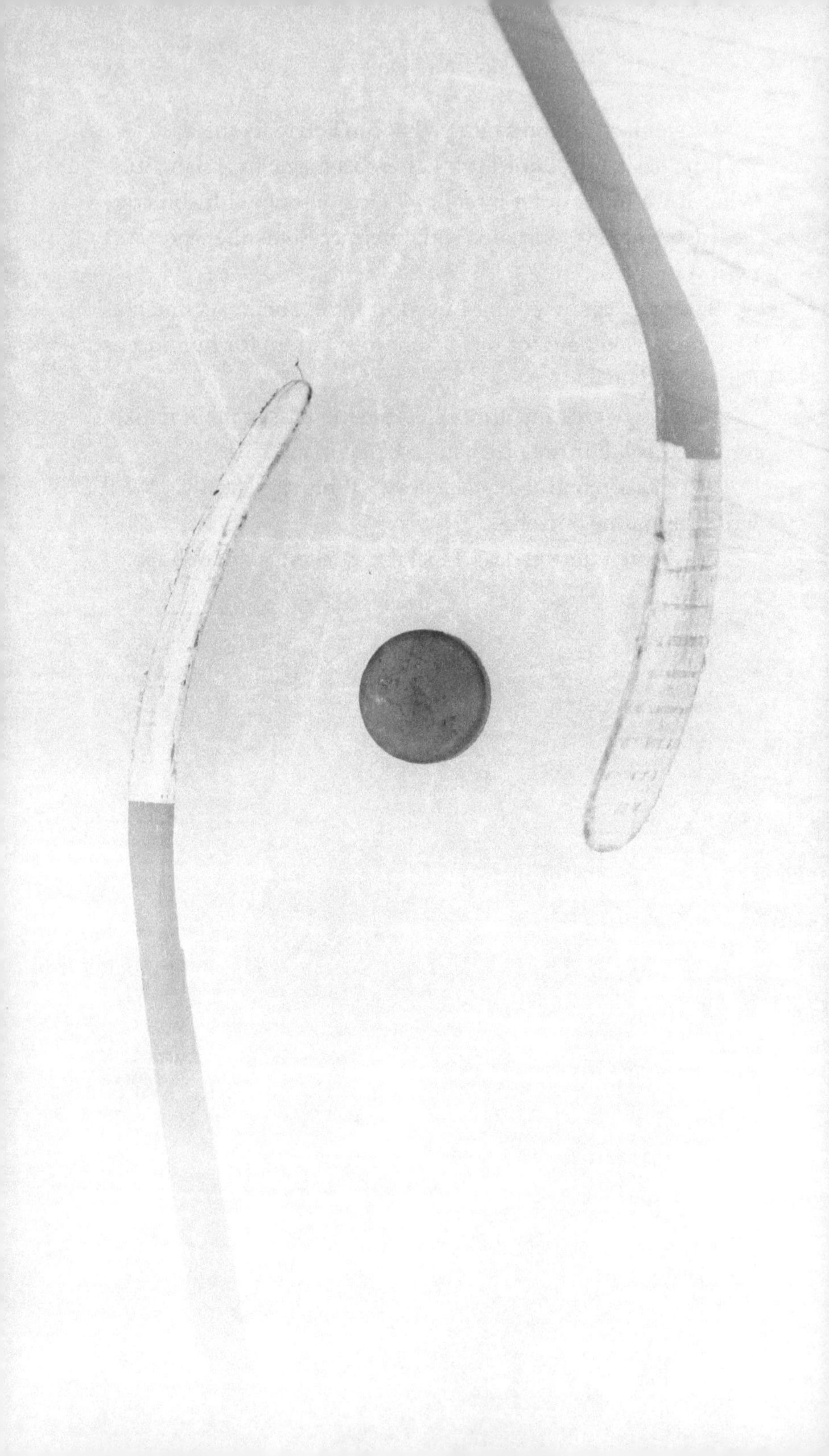

STEELE

The locker room hums with post-practice energy. Guys are peeling off gear, towels are being snapped, and someone's speaker is blasting a mix of throwback rap and classic rock. The smell of sweat and wintergreen fills the air, and the laughter that bounces off the walls feels more like a relief than routine.

For the first time all week, my mind feels calm.

Not because the noise has died down, but because I left it all on the ice.

I tug off my sweat-soaked jersey, the fabric sticking to my back like a second skin, and toss it into my locker. My muscles are fatigued in the best way.

Wrung out, sore, and spent.

But my head?

Clear.

What helps more than the adrenaline rush is the support, unspoken but solid, from the guys around me.

Earlier, Knox clapped me on the shoulder as he passed by and said, "Don't sweat it, Cap. People love the drama. It'll blow over in no time."

Laiken, in his usual stoic way, stood in the corner, taping his stick. When I walked by, he looked up just long enough to say, "You're good. We know what kind of man you are. Let the bull-shit run its course."

Their quiet confidence in me hit harder than I expected.

This team and these guys have my back.

And that means everything.

I nod at Oliver and Jaxon, who are mid-argument about whether a protein shake qualifies as lunch. River's got his feet up, already chugging one, as if that settles it.

I sling my bag over my shoulder and push out into the hall. My phone buzzes in my pocket just as a familiar voice calls out from behind me.

"Sanderson."

I glance up and find Hugh striding my way. The team owner is dressed to kill in a tailored navy suit that probably cost more than my first car. He's all smooth edges and sharp confidence, but today, he looks almost pleased, which is a far cry from his expression the other morning in his office.

He claps a hand on my shoulder. "Glad you came around and talked to her. I knew that was the route to take."

My brows pull together. "Talked to who?"

"Lilah," he says, glancing at his silver Rolex. "The interview should be starting any minute. And doing it here at the arena was a smart PR move."

My stomach plummets. "What interview?"

Hugh's eyes narrow. "The one Rina scheduled a couple hours ago. You didn't talk to her about it?"

No. No, I fucking didn't.

And I had no intention of bringing it up either.

Because she shouldn't have to go on record to explain what's between us to the world. Not after everything she's already been through.

Not after I swore I wouldn't put her in that position.

With my jaw locked tight, I drop my bag to the floor and

pivot without so much as a goodbye. My feet move quickly, eating up the distance to the conference room where all the media crap usually takes place.

I shoot Rina a text.

Then another.

But there's no response.

Fuck.

As soon as I round the final corner, I hear the calm and polished voice of a woman and then Lilah's. Instead of hesitating, I shove open the doors, and the room goes silent as heads snap in my direction. The cameraman freezes, his lens still mid-adjustment. The reporter blinks like she's just been caught red-handed. And my sweet girl sits in the chair, looking wide-eyed and nervous.

What pisses me off the most is that she's alone.

"If someone's going to speak for us," I say, striding into the room, "then it's going to be both of us. As a couple."

Lilah's lips part slightly, as if she can't believe I just busted in here. The last thing I'm going to do is leave her to face this mess alone. I grab a chair from the side of the room and carry it over, placing it directly next to hers before dropping down and slipping her hand into mine.

"You good, lucky charm?" I ask quietly.

She nods, eyes glassy with emotion. "Yes."

Unable to help myself, I lift her hand and press a kiss against her knuckles. "We'll get through this together. Understand?"

Her lips tremble into a smile. "Thank you for being here."

"There's nowhere else I'd rather be. And no one else I'd rather be with."

And that's the truth.

The reporter clears her throat, trying to gather her bearings. "Mr. Sanderson, I didn't realize you were—"

"Hi, Chandra," I cut in smoothly. "Thanks for making time. We're ready to talk."

She glances between us, then gives a signal to the cameraman, and the red light glows to life.

One at a time, she asks the hard questions.

Are we in a relationship?

What happened in the photo?

Was there consent?

I let Lilah speak first because her voice matters and she deserves to be heard in her own words. It's only when she's finished that I lean forward and look straight into the lens.

My voice is steady.

Controlled.

But every syllable is wrapped in truth.

"What people saw in that photo wasn't violence. It was intimacy. It was private. And it was real." I pause, squeezing Lilah's hand. "This woman isn't just my best friend, she's the one I love. The same person I've loved since college. Whether she realized it or not, it was always her. And no matter what happens in the future, it will always be her."

Lilah lets out a shaky exhale beside me, and her grip tightens in mine.

The camera keeps rolling, but all I see is her.

And all I feel is the truth of my words. Raw and out in the open, no longer hiding between stolen glances and half-finished sentences.

It's us against the noise.

Us against the narrative.

Us against the world.

And after a decade of friendship, it finally feels like we're exactly where we're supposed to be.

46
LILAH

The silence in the car is thick but not uncomfortable.

Well, not exactly.

I sit with my hands folded neatly in my lap, my jacket wrapped tightly around me like armor. My mind continues to replay the interview on a constant loop, stuck on one moment.

One statement.

"This woman isn't just my best friend, she's the one I love."

He said it so plainly.

As if it had always been obvious.

And maybe to him, it was.

But not to me.

The city blurs past the window as we drive toward the penthouse. The lights, the traffic, the noise all fade to the background. Inside the car, it's just me and the echo of his words.

Steele doesn't try to fill the silence. One hand rests on the wheel while the other is draped casually over the gearshift. Every so often, I catch his gaze flicking to me.

Checking in.

Watching.

Waiting.

But he doesn't push.

He never does.

Maybe that's why it took me so long to see what was right in front of my face all these years.

When we pull into the underground garage, I blink, as if finally waking from a dream. Steele cuts the engine and turns toward me. His face might be the epitome of calm, but his eyes are filled with concern.

He reaches over, gently brushing a few loose strands of hair from my cheek. "Are you okay?"

"I am," I say automatically, even though it's only half true.

"Good." He studies me for a beat. "I wish you would have told me what you were doing."

I bite my bottom lip and hesitate. "I was afraid you'd try to stop me."

"You're right." His jaw flexes. "I would've."

The warmth of his fingers seeps into the side of my face as he cups my cheek, and I can't help but lean into the touch, grounding myself in it. This man has always been a steadying presence in my life.

"All I've ever wanted is to protect you."

"I know," I whisper. "But you don't have to. Not always. I'm strong enough to handle what life throws my way."

He gives a small smile. "I know you are, baby. You're the strongest woman I know. Strong enough to walk away from a career that didn't make you happy. Strong enough to start over. Strong enough to fight for what you want."

I study his face, every line of it carved with sincerity. "Can I ask you something?"

"Anything."

"When you told Chandra that you've loved me since college... did you mean it? Or was that just for the camera?"

He doesn't blink. "I meant every damn word, Lilah. I've always loved you. I've always been *in* love with you."

My world tilts sideways at the declaration. "Then why didn't you ever say something?"

He exhales, the sound weary and full of regret. "You were always with someone else. And when you weren't... I was too afraid to ruin what we had. If friendship was all you could give me, I'd take it. Because any version of you was better than none."

Tears prick my eyes. "I love you, Steele," I whisper. "More than I ever thought I could love anyone."

"I love you too, lucky charm." He reaches for my hand. "Ready to go upstairs to our home?"

I nod, the weight of the day giving way to something warmer. Lighter. As we walk hand in hand to the elevator, a bubble of joy builds inside me. It's bright and full of promise. Everything is finally falling into place. And that has everything to do with the man at my side.

The one who's been there through every heartbreak.

Every misstep.

Every storm.

Steele has been the one constant through it all.

Inside the elevator, he wraps his arm around me, and I press against his side, inhaling the warm, woodsy scent that's always had the power to calm me. Only now do I understand why.

Because he's my home.

This man has *always* been my home.

We step inside the penthouse and find Waffles nestled on the couch. She lifts her head just long enough to acknowledge us before flopping back down with a sleepy meow.

The lingering aroma of dark roast and baked vanilla hangs in the air from this morning, but everything feels different now.

Settled.

Whole.

I set my bag down by the elevator and drift toward the

windows. The lake stretches out in the distance, a dark blue canvas sparkling under the sun.

I press a hand to the glass. It's not the skyline that draws me in but the life I finally see waiting for me. The one I get to live with Steele.

He steps behind me and slips his arms around my waist. His body is solid against my back as his warmth seeps into my bones.

"You always get quiet when you're thinking deep thoughts," he murmurs, his mouth grazing the curve of my neck just under my ear.

I smile. "Just taking it all in."

"And?"

"And for the first time, I feel like I'm exactly where I'm supposed to be."

His arms tighten. "Good. Because you're not going anywhere."

I turn to face him. "I don't want to."

He searches my eyes. "You sure about that? Because once you say the word, I'm all in. No more friends with benefits. No more lines. Just us. All of it."

And he means it.

Every word.

"I've never been more certain of anything," I tell him.

The brush of his lips is slow and reverent, a promise written in silence. I kiss him back with everything I have. Every scar, every hope, every ounce of love I've been too afraid to say out loud until now.

When we finally pull apart, his thumb brushes over my cheek. "So... we're really doing this?"

"We're doing this," I whisper.

And just like that, the ache I've been living with for years dissipates.

The man I've always loved as a friend?

He's mine now.
And I'm his.
Not just for tonight.
Not just until the spark fades.
But for all the days ahead.
This isn't the end of our story.
It's just the beginning.
And I wouldn't change a single page.

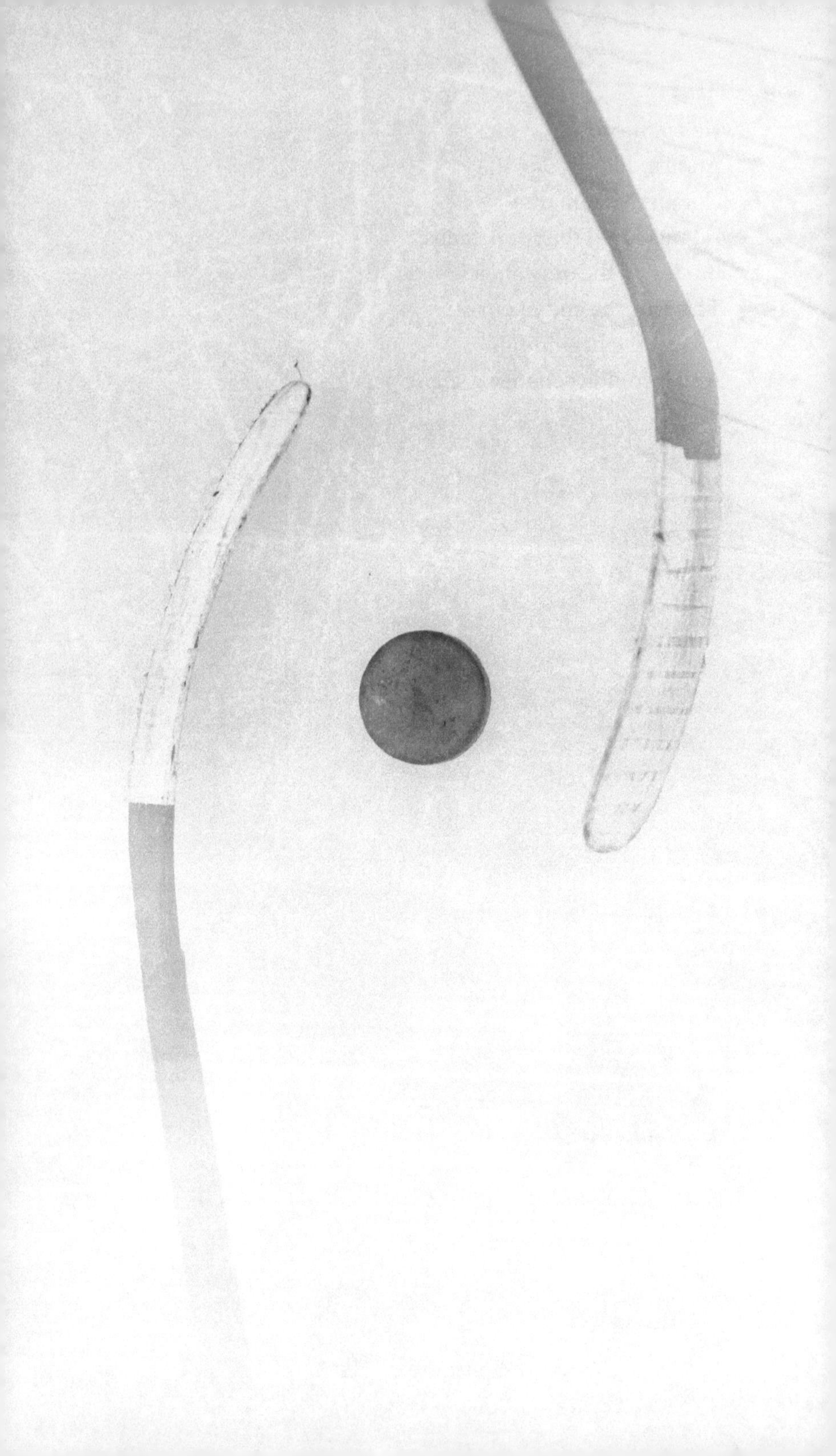

STEELE

The elevator dings, and I glance toward the doors just as they slide open. The first wave of my teammates spills into the penthouse. Knox, River, and Laiken leading the way, followed by Jax and Oliver bringing up the rear. They're already talking shit and laughing like we're in the middle of the locker room.

I look back to find Lilah standing near the kitchen island, nervously smoothing her apron. Her shoulders are a little too stiff, her eyes wide as she tracks every movement.

Only wanting to offer comfort, I step behind her and slide my hand along her waist before leaning in close to press a kiss against her neck. "It's going to be fine."

She glances up at me with uncertainty. "What if it's not?"

"There's no way they won't love everything you made," I tell her.

"I really hope so," she says. "This just... It matters. What if they hate it and they tell me they love it only to be polite?"

"I'm sorry, have you actually met these guys before?" I ask without hesitation. "The only one who has a polite bone in his body is Laiken. The rest of them? Total cavemen."

That earns me a reluctant laugh. Barely a huff, but I'll take it.

"You've worked your ass off on this," I continue, brushing my thumb along her side. "You're talented as hell, Lilah. This is going to go way better than you think. Trust me."

The elevator dings again, and more footsteps echo through the penthouse. There's another chorus of greetings that fills the air as the guys descend like hungry bears waking from hibernation.

Oliver beelines straight to the display, swiping one of the protein balls before Lilah can say a word.

"Holy hell, what is this?" he asks with his mouth full.

Rina, who arrived a few minutes earlier and is standing beside the fridge with a wine glass, sighs like her soul just left her body. "You eat like a feral animal."

He gives her a wink. "I do other things like an animal as well. Any interest in finding out firsthand?"

Her face scrunches. "You're the last person I would ever sleep with."

"So, what you're telling me is that I'm on the list? Good to know."

"There isn't a list, but if there were, you would definitely not be on it."

"Keep telling yourself that, sweetheart. Methinks the lady doth protest too much."

Rina lifts her hand to massage her temple before glancing at us. "Do you see what I have to deal with on a daily basis? Is it any wonder I drink too much?"

I decide now is probably a good time to cut in before Rina chooses violence. "Lilah made all of it. Everything is clean, high-protein, and low sugar."

"You mean all this is actually healthy?" Knox picks up one of the oat and almond cookies and inspects it.

"It is," Lilah says, stepping forward. "There's no refined sugar. Just honey, chia, flax, and oats."

One by one, the guys sample the spread. There's a quiet beat before the reactions roll in.

"This is good," Laiken mutters. Which, coming from him, is high praise.

"Are these egg muffins?" River grabs one. "Wow, delicious. What's in them?"

"Spinach, turkey sausage, and sweet potato," Lilah answers, more confidently now as she steps away from me and toward the counter.

Jax lifts a jar of overnight oats closer to his face for scrutiny. "And this?"

"Almond butter, oats, vanilla protein, chia, and blueberries," she rattles off.

Jax takes a bite and groans. "This is really good."

The tension in Lilah's shoulders loosens. A smile blooms across her face like sunlight after a storm, and it crashes into me like a wave I didn't see coming.

It's one thing to believe in someone and another to watch the world finally catch up.

My teammates go back for seconds and then thirds. There's talk about game-day fuel, meal prep help, and requests for recipes. The whole vibe shifts to one that's filled with genuine interest and enthusiasm.

Once the tasting is over, the guys file out one by one. Laiken nods his approval, Jax offers to pay her in cold brew if she makes him a batch every week, Oliver tries to get her number again and gets smacked by Rina in the process. With everyone gone, the penthouse finally settles into a comfortable hush.

I walk over and wrap an arm around Lilah's waist, pulling her against me. Her cheeks are still flushed and her eyes are bright from the high of the night.

"You did it," I murmur against her temple.

"I did," she says, still a little dazed. "So... yeah. We'll consider that a win."

I tuck a strand of hair behind her ear. "You did more than win. You crushed it. I'm so fucking proud of you, lucky charm."

She swallows, the movement small but telling. I can feel the emotion vibrating within her. All the joy, disbelief, and pride.

She turns more fully to face me before sliding her arms around me. "Thank you," she says quietly. "For everything. For believing in me even when I didn't believe in myself. And for always being there."

I brush my knuckles along her cheek. "I will always be there for you, no matter what," I murmur. "It's not even a question."

She leans into the touch. "You've been my constant through everything. The one thing I could always count on. And I don't say it enough, but I'm grateful for that. I'm grateful for *you*."

I rest my forehead against hers. "You never have to thank me for loving you, Lilah."

Her breath catches, and I feel her smile.

"Still," she says, voice barely above a whisper, "thank you."

That's all it takes for something inside me to settle.

She's mine.

And she knows it now.

Whatever comes next, whatever dreams she chases, I'll be standing right beside her.

Just like I always have.

48
LILAH

Perched on one of the stools near the front counter of Lakeshore Sweets, the scents of cinnamon, espresso, and vanilla fill the air as I cradle my mug between both hands.

Callie's bakery is quiet now that the morning rush has come and gone. For the moment, there's a lull. No customers, no deliveries, no distractions. Just the four of us girls, a tray of pastries, and enough gossip to fuel a reality TV series.

Rina moans around a bite of chocolate-filled croissant, dark eyelashes fluttering closed. "Oh my God, Callie. This is seriously indecent."

Sloane snorts, kicking her feet up on the empty stool beside her. "You sound like you're having sex."

"Please." Rina waves a hand, not even a little embarrassed by the pronouncement. "I'm much louder than that. Sometimes I like to throw in a little extra for dramatic effect. You know... for the plot."

I sputter into my coffee, choking on a laugh. With a cough, I swipe a napkin across my mouth as Sloane pats me on the back.

"You okay over there?" she teases, amusement dancing in her green eyes.

"Fine," I wheeze. "Just wasn't expecting that level of honesty with my caffeine."

Callie gives Rina a pointed look as her lips twitch. "Can't say I remember what any of that sounds like."

Rina lifts a brow. "What do you mean?"

Callie shrugs, suddenly interested in the swirl of her latte. "Let's just say that it's been a while."

Rina's eyes narrow. "Exactly how long are we talking about?"

There's a beat of silence before Callie admits, "Since Nora."

That was over two years ago. Judging by the way her voice quiets, she's embarrassed by the confession.

"Ugh," she mutters. "I hate talking about this."

"Hey." I nudge her gently with my elbow. "If you can't talk about it with us, who can you talk to?"

"She's right," Sloane adds. "We're your people. We're not judging you. Unless you put raisins in cookies. Then I have a serious problem."

Callie lets out a little laugh, but before she can respond, the bell above the front door chimes. All four of us turn toward the entrance, and my eyes widen as River Thompson walks in.

Rina's brows shoot up. "Well, this is an unexpected surprise."

He's wearing jeans and a black Railers hoodie, his blond hair is still damp, as if he just got out of the shower. He nods politely in our direction. When his gaze lands on Callie, it fills with something raw and aching.

"Hey," he says, softly. "I didn't know you'd be working."

Callie's expression turns guarded. "I own the bakery, River. I pretty much live here."

Ouch.

Sloane, sensing the tension, rises and grabs a cup. "Did you want your usual?"

Usual?

I glance at Rina with a raised brow, and she returns the look.

River's attention remains on Callie before flicking to Sloane. He gives her a small polite smile. "Yeah, that'd be great. Thanks."

As Sloane gets his coffee and a bagel, River shifts, as if he's trying to decide whether to say more.

"How's Nora?" he finally asks.

Callie barely spares him a glance. "She's good."

He nods, accepting the limited info. "I'm glad."

Even after Sloane hands over his bag and drink, River lingers a beat longer than necessary.

"Bye, Callie." His voice is gentle. "I'll see you around."

There's a beat of silence before she says, "Bye."

He gives the rest of us a nod before reluctantly heading to the door.

Silence hangs for a full five seconds after it closes.

"I'm sorry, that man comes here often enough to have a regular order?" Rina hisses, spinning toward Callie. "Um, excuse me? Why didn't we know about this?"

Callie sighs. "He likes the coffee. And, apparently, the bagels."

Rina snorts. "Oh, honey. He likes something all right. Spoiler alert. It's not the carbs."

Callie gives her a look. "It doesn't matter. I'm not interested."

I tilt my head, not even trying to hide my curiosity. "Really? He's such a sweetheart."

Callie's expression hardens. "Are you forgetting that he's part of Zane's inner circle?"

And there it is.

That bitter knot of history tied too tight to unravel.

"But he's not Zane," I say gently.

Her gaze flicks to mine, pain tucked behind her eyes. "No. But he stood by him. Through everything. Even when Zane didn't deserve it."

I reach over and squeeze her hand, only wanting to offer comfort and support.

Rina frowns. "I get it. But maybe it's not that simple. Sometimes people stand by the ones they love because they're trying to hold on to the good they remember. It doesn't mean they agree with all the choices being made."

"I don't know," Callie whispers. "It's hard not to see him as part of that world. The one that hurt me."

Sloane nods. "Okay. That's fair. But he looked at you like you were the only person in this room."

Rina hums her agreement. "If I were you, I might give him my number just to make a point to Zane."

Callie finally cracks a smile. "You're ridiculous."

"But we're your kind of ridiculous," I say. "That's why we're all such good friends."

Rina steals another bite of her pastry before adding, "But seriously, you have to realize that if the man is here often enough to have a usual, it has nothing to do with the coffee."

Callie releases a heavy sigh as she glances toward the front of the bakery. "He's just always been around. At first, I thought it was a coincidence since we're so close to the arena. But lately, I don't know. Maybe it's not. But come on, he's Zane's friend. They used to be partners in crime."

Rina tilts her head, her gaze sharpening. "You don't owe Zane a damn thing. And you have every right to protect your peace. But also? You deserve someone who looks at you like you're their entire universe."

Callie exhales, her voice barely above a whisper. "The last thing I want is more drama. Or to get pulled back into that spotlight. That world doesn't feel like mine anymore."

"You've been through hell and back these last few years," Sloane says, topping off her mug. "But if River really isn't like Zane, maybe it's okay to stop bracing for impact and just see what's there."

"I'm not saying fall into bed with him," Rina adds. "But if he's trying to prove he's not like his teammate, maybe give him a little room to do it."

Callie gives us all a long look, her gaze moving around the table. "You're kind of ganging up on me right now."

"You're right, we are," I admit, grinning. "But it's only because we love you."

"And we want more for you," Sloane adds. "Someone who treats you like a queen."

Rina leans back in her chair and swirls her coffee. "Also, someone who could maybe serve as a visual distraction when Zane and his twenty-one-year-old reality-starlet-of-the-week show up at the next Railers event."

Callie rolls her eyes. "I can't believe you just said that."

"Oh, I'm not above a little petty justice," Rina says cheerfully. "Just imagine the look on Zane's face if River walked in with you on his arm."

"You're terrible," Callie says with a laugh.

Rina shrugs. "I'm just saying. Maybe he deserves to squirm a little."

We all fall quiet for a beat, the scent of fresh coffee filling the space around us. Outside, golden leaves swirl in the crisp October breeze, dancing past the bakery window like confetti.

Callie lifts her cup with a sigh. "Okay, fine. If he comes back again... maybe I'll say more than one word to him."

Sloane claps her hands. "Progress!"

Rina beams like she just won a gold medal. "That's definitely a start."

I sit back and watch my friends laugh, tease, and sip their coffee as the comforting hum of the bakery envelops us. Callie's smiling now, and for the first time in a while, she looks a little lighter. She deserves someone who sees all of that. Her strength, her softness, and everything in between.

As I glance toward the door where River stood just moments ago, I can't help but wonder if maybe someone already does.

49

EVELYN

The view from my office never gets old.

The floor-to-ceiling windows overlook the rink where practice is in full swing. Skates carve across the ice, jerseys blur in motion, and the dull thud of pucks slamming into the glass reverberates through the arena like a heartbeat.

I cradle a cup of Earl Grey between my hands, its warmth grounding me as I lean slightly against the window frame.

Steele Sanderson is back in top form. Dominant, focused, and unstoppable. The scandal that once loomed over him like a storm cloud has lifted, replaced by highlight reels of him tearing down the ice and flashing a smile meant for one woman alone.

The interview worked, and the narrative has shifted. The jackals have retreated, at least for now.

Even better than that?

Peak Sportswear came crawling back yesterday with a revised contract in hand.

"Redemption looks good on him," Rina says from her seat across the room, tapping through emails on her iPad.

I hum in agreement. "He deserves it. And so does Lilah.

They've handled themselves with more grace than most people twice their age."

Rina grins. "It doesn't hurt that their story is straight-up catnip for the media. You should see all the TikToks with engagement theories and baby countdowns. There's even a fan page dedicated to her wearing his jersey."

"Oh, please," I say, smiling despite myself. "Let them live a little first."

I'm just setting my tea down when I feel the shift in the air. That unmistakable charge that always comes before he enters a room.

I don't need to turn around to realize who it is.

Hugh Landry.

The scent of his cologne hits me next. Warm amber with undertones of something richer. Something darker. Once upon a time, it was the scent that clung to my sheets after he slipped out of them—setting my pulse racing and my better judgment faltering.

I straighten and glance over my shoulder.

That was a long time ago.

Another lifetime.

He leans against the doorframe, his charcoal suit perfectly tailored to a body that somehow hasn't aged a day in all the ways that matter. His black hair, streaked now with silver at the temples, is slicked back, and that insufferable glint in his blue eyes is as cocky as ever.

He's too confident.

Too at ease.

Like he didn't leave my world in ruins twenty-five years ago.

"Rina," he says smoothly. "Always a pleasure."

"Hello, Hugh," she replies, her tone polite.

Even if she doesn't know the full story, she senses it. The undercurrent and tension that flows between us. The history that never quite settled into dust.

"Would you mind if I speak to Evelyn alone?" he asks, his gaze pinned to mine.

I arch a brow. "Oh, I don't think that's really necessary, do you?"

His reply is immediate. "Yes. It is."

When Rina glances at me, I nod and offer her a practiced smile. I've had twenty-five years to perfect it. "It's fine. We'll talk more tomorrow."

Once she slips out, Hugh closes the door behind her without being asked.

Typical.

"There's no need to shut the door," I say coolly. "You won't be here long enough to make it worth the trouble."

"Actually," he replies, stepping farther into the room, "there's quite a bit for us to discuss."

It would be impossible not to notice how the space shrinks around him.

I pick up my cup and take another sip of tea just to avoid snapping something I'll regret. This man has always had the ability to rattle me. And I hate that after all these years, it still holds true.

There was a time when all he had to do was look at me and my knees weakened. I would have done anything he asked without question. For just a second, my mind tumbles back almost thirty years to the man he was when we first fell in love.

As soon as that thought pops into my head, I shove it away. It took years for me to get over our broken engagement and move on with my life. It wasn't the same for Hugh. He married my best friend less than twelve months later.

"Well, now that you chased Rina away, don't keep me in suspense. Just get it over with." I pretend to glance at my watch. "I have dinner plans this evening."

He raises a brow. "Cancel them."

I straighten and blink. "Excuse me?"

When he steps closer, it becomes necessary to lift my chin in order to hold his steady gaze. "I said cancel them. I've made reservations at your favorite restaurant."

Disconcerted by his proximity, I force out a laugh. "As if you would know what that is."

"Gold Coast Table," he says without hesitation.

"That's... right." I shake my head and set the tea back down. "What's this about? Never mind. Get out. I'm not interested in anything you have to say."

"Peter Michaelson agreed to sell me his four percent."

The words hit like a lightning strike. Sudden, jarring, and nearly impossible to process. "You're lying."

"I'm not. The paperwork will be finalized by the end of the week, which means that I'll own fifty-two percent of the Railers."

Pressure builds inside me until it feels like I might explode. "He said he would never sell to either of us."

"I made him an offer he couldn't refuse."

Of course he did.

Bastard.

It might have taken him two decades, but Hugh Landry always finds a way.

I step back, needing space.

Needing air.

It feels like I'm suffocating. It's tempting to claw at my throat.

"So, what happens now?" I whisper.

Even with a little distance between us, the scent of his cologne drifts toward me, dragging me back to memories I have no desire to revisit.

"We talk over dinner and figure out what's next for the team. And, more importantly, for us."

I shake my head and glance away, unable to hold his steady gaze. "There is no us, Hugh. There hasn't been for a long time."

His hand rises slowly, and before I can move, his fingers brush beneath my chin, tipping it upward until I'm forced to look at him.

"There could be."

My heart trips.

The worst part?

A small, treacherous piece of me wants to believe him.

But I've already survived his promises and the ruins he left behind.

I have no desire to do it again.

"You want to talk business?" I manage. "Fine. But keep your hands to yourself."

The smile he flashes is knowing. "I'll be ready in thirty minutes."

Without waiting for a reply, he turns and walks out, like he didn't just rearrange the ground beneath my feet.

And I hate him a little for it.

But not as much as I hate the part of me that wants to follow.

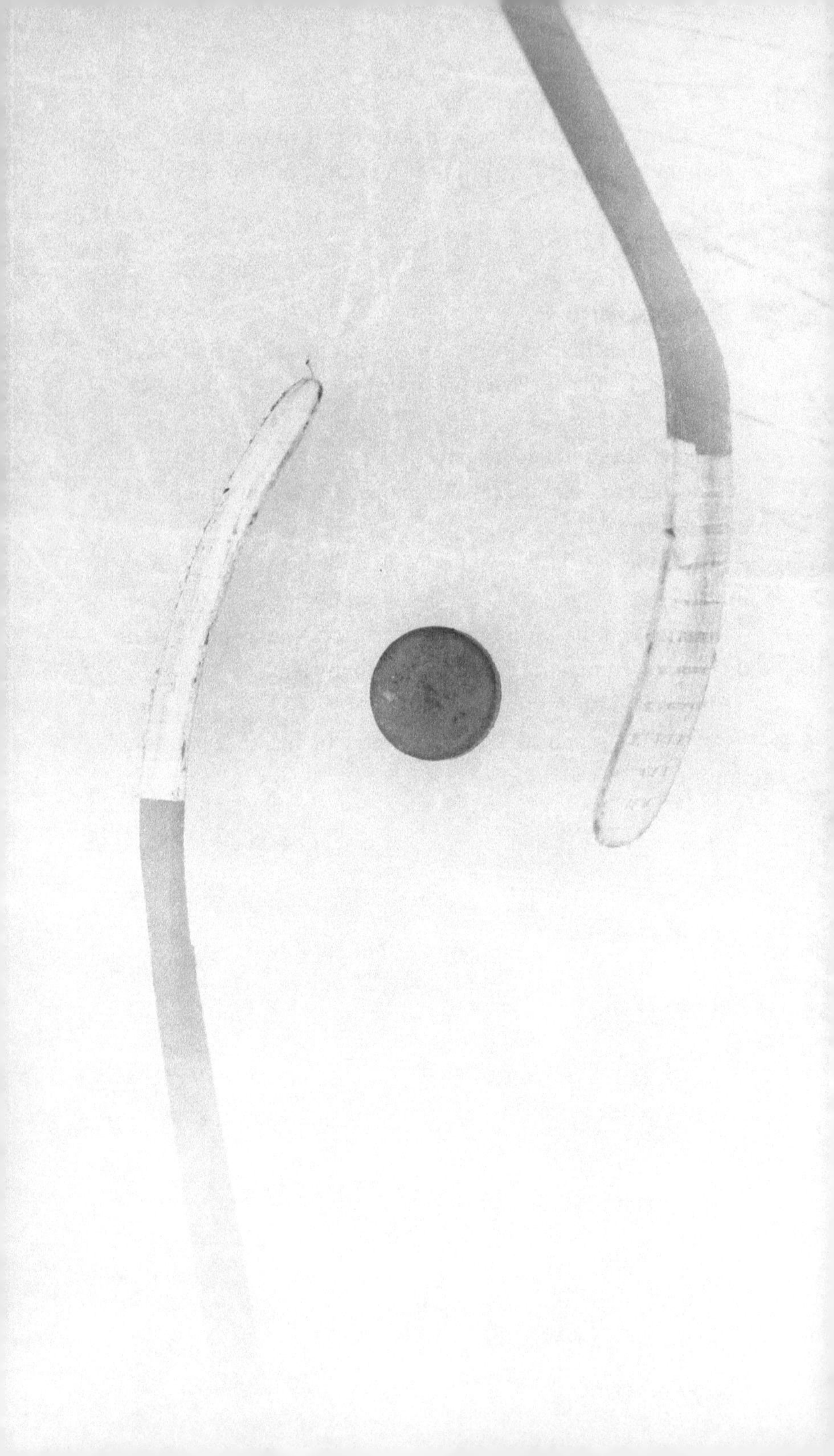

EPILOGUE

STEELE

I step off the elevator into the penthouse, duffel slung over my shoulder from practice.

"Lilah?" I call out, already unzipping my hoodie and toeing off my sneakers by the door. "Are you home?"

The scent is what hits me first.

The air is thick with the aroma of garlic, rosemary, and something mouthwatering. My stomach grumbles in appreciation as I follow it to the kitchen. I toss my bag onto the bench, expecting to find Lilah humming along to some playlist in leggings and a sweater.

What I find instead makes my brain short-circuit.

She's standing at the stove wearing nothing but an apron. Her hair is pinned up in a messy twist and her bare legs are on full display. I get an eyeful of her naked backside as she stirs something in a skillet.

I lean against the doorway, arms crossed, all the while fighting back a grin.

This woman is fucking adorable.

"Well, well," I murmur. "What's a guy gotta do to get more dinner prep like this?"

With a glance over her shoulder, she grins. "Tip well."

I push off the wall, closing the distance with deliberate steps. My fingers twitch with the urge to touch her, but I keep them to myself.

For now.

"Keep talking about tips, lucky charm, and I'm gonna end up sinking every damn inch into you right here against the counter." I circle around her, letting my eyes drink her in before raising a brow. "And what exactly is under that apron?"

She winks. "Absolutely nothing."

A low growl rumbles from me as I step behind her and press in close. My hands slide along her waist, fingers teasing at the edge of the apron's bow tied at the small of her back.

"I think you might be trying to kill me."

Even though her laugh is light and easy, there's heat in it too. "Go sit down. I'm spoiling you tonight."

I press a kiss to the curve of her neck. "Is that so?"

"Yup," she says, nudging me with her hip. "Dining room. Now."

With a groan, I obey, giving her ass one quick smack before retreating.

As soon as I round the corner into the other room, I stop short. The table is set, and there are candles flickering low, casting shadows across the white linen. There's a bottle of wine and two glasses. Not to mention, cloth napkins. It's the whole nine yards.

"Damn," I mutter. "Fancy."

"Nothing but the best for my baby."

She saunters in, carrying two plates before setting them down with a flourish. Then she unties the apron and shrugs it off, tossing it onto the back of a chair.

That's all it takes for air to clog my lungs and everything else to fall away.

"How do you expect me to eat when you're completely naked?"

Instead of letting her sit across from me where she set her plate, I reach out and snag her hand before towing her toward me and onto my lap.

"Right here," I say, adjusting her until she's straddling me, my hands splayed across her bare ass. "This is where I want you."

She laughs, brushing her fingers through my damp hair. "You're not going to be able to focus on food if I sit on your lap like this."

"Oh, I'm aware," I say, picking up a fork. "But I still want you here."

I cut into the chicken and bring a piece to her lips. "Open."

She raises a brow but obeys, her lips brushing the tines as she takes the bite. I bring the next one to my mouth, but my other hand is already stroking a path along her thigh, tracing idle circles that make her shiver.

"You like feeding me now?" she teases.

"I think we both know how much I like taking care of you." My fingers drift higher. "And I enjoy touching you. So, yeah, this feels like a win-win in my book."

Her laugh is low as she tilts her head back just a bit.

And that's exactly how we eat. Slowly feeding each other between kisses and caresses. She hums when I drag my mouth along her jaw.

"You're dangerous like this," she whispers.

"Dangerous?" I echo, bathing her pulse point with my tongue.

Her hands fist in my shirt. "Yeah. You make me forget that anything exists beyond these walls."

I press a kiss against her shoulder. "That's the point, baby. You and me? It's all I've ever wanted."

The way she easily melts into my body tells me she feels the same way.

She rests her forehead against mine, the softness of her

exhale brushing my skin as her fingers trace lazy patterns on my chest. "If I'm not careful, you're going to make me fall harder, you know that?"

I smile, tucking a strand of hair behind her ear. "Good. All you have to do is trust me, and I'll be there to catch you every single time."

For a moment, neither of us moves. The candles flicker as the city hums outside the windows. The scent of dinner lingers in the air, but food is the last thing on my mind.

She shifts on my lap, pressing in just enough to make me hiss through my teeth. "This was supposed to be a sweet little dinner," she murmurs, her lips grazing the shell of my ear.

"And it was," I tell her, my hands gripping her hips. "Until you decided to make it a test of my fucking restraint."

Her lips tilt in a wicked little smile. "Restraint? You're not exactly known for that where I'm concerned."

"No," I admit, my thumb skimming over the top of her pussy, "but I'm trying to be good."

"You sure about that?" she teases, reaching for my wine glass and taking a small sip before offering it to me. I take the drink from her hand. My eyes stay locked on hers as I set the glass down on the table.

"Pretty sure I'm about to fail," I say, my voice a low rumble. "Miserably."

Before she can respond, I scoop her up and rise from the chair in one smooth movement.

"Steele," she gasps, arms twining around my neck.

"Dinner was perfect," I say, already carrying her toward the bedroom. "But I'm more than ready to have my dessert. In our bed."

She bites her lip, trying to fight back a grin. "What if I want cake?"

"You're getting something much sweeter, baby."

"Is that right?"

I lower her to the mattress like she's something precious. "Yes. And if you're a good girl and drink down all my cum, I'll feed you cake in bed. Maybe I'll eat it off those pretty little titties."

Her laughter fades as I hover above her, brushing my nose along hers. "Deal."

"I meant what I said earlier," I whisper, searching her eyes. "All of it. This—us—it's everything."

Her eyes fill with warmth as her palm cradles my cheek. "I know."

And just before I kiss her, she says the words that send my heart straight into overdrive.

"I love you, Steele Sanderson."

I smile against her mouth. "You're my everything, lucky charm. Everything and always."

Then I kiss her gently.

Thoroughly.

It's not just a kiss. It's a confession, a promise, and a plea, all wrapped into one.

She arches into me, her hands threading into my hair, her legs wrapping around my waist like she never wants to let go.

And I hope she never does.

"Tell me what you want," I murmur against her mouth.

"You. Just you."

That's all I need to hear.

My gaze stays fastened to hers as I rise to my knees and strip off my clothes. She looks at me as if I'm something she wants to savor. And when I'm finally as bare as she is, all I see in her expression is desire.

The kind that burns slow and deep, meant to last a lifetime, not just a night.

I take my time with her because that's exactly what she deserves. I kiss the slender column of her neck, across her collarbone, tasting every inch of skin that's mine to touch. She shivers when my mouth finds the spot beneath her ear, and I smile.

Her fingers tremble as she skims them down my chest, tracing the lines she's already memorized. I shift lower, lips dragging across the swell of her breast, savoring her sigh when I take her nipple into my mouth. She arches beneath me, needy and open, her breath coming in fast, broken gasps.

"Steele," she whispers, nails digging into my shoulders.

"I've got you, baby." I press a kiss to her sternum, then lower, worshipping every part of her.

By the time I finally slide inside her heat, we're both shaking. Two heartbeats pounding in sync, two people who've been circling this moment for years. Her eyes lock on mine, glassy and full of emotion.

This isn't just sex.

It's love.

Every thrust, every whispered word between kisses, every brush of her fingers across my jaw tells me so. When she falls apart beneath me, her cry muffled against my mouth, I follow right after, groaning her name like it's a vow.

Because it is.

And when it's over, I stay exactly where I am, our bodies tangled, her hand resting over my heart.

"I don't want to move," she murmurs.

"You don't have to." I kiss her temple, then her jaw. "I'm not going anywhere."

Not tonight.

Not ever.

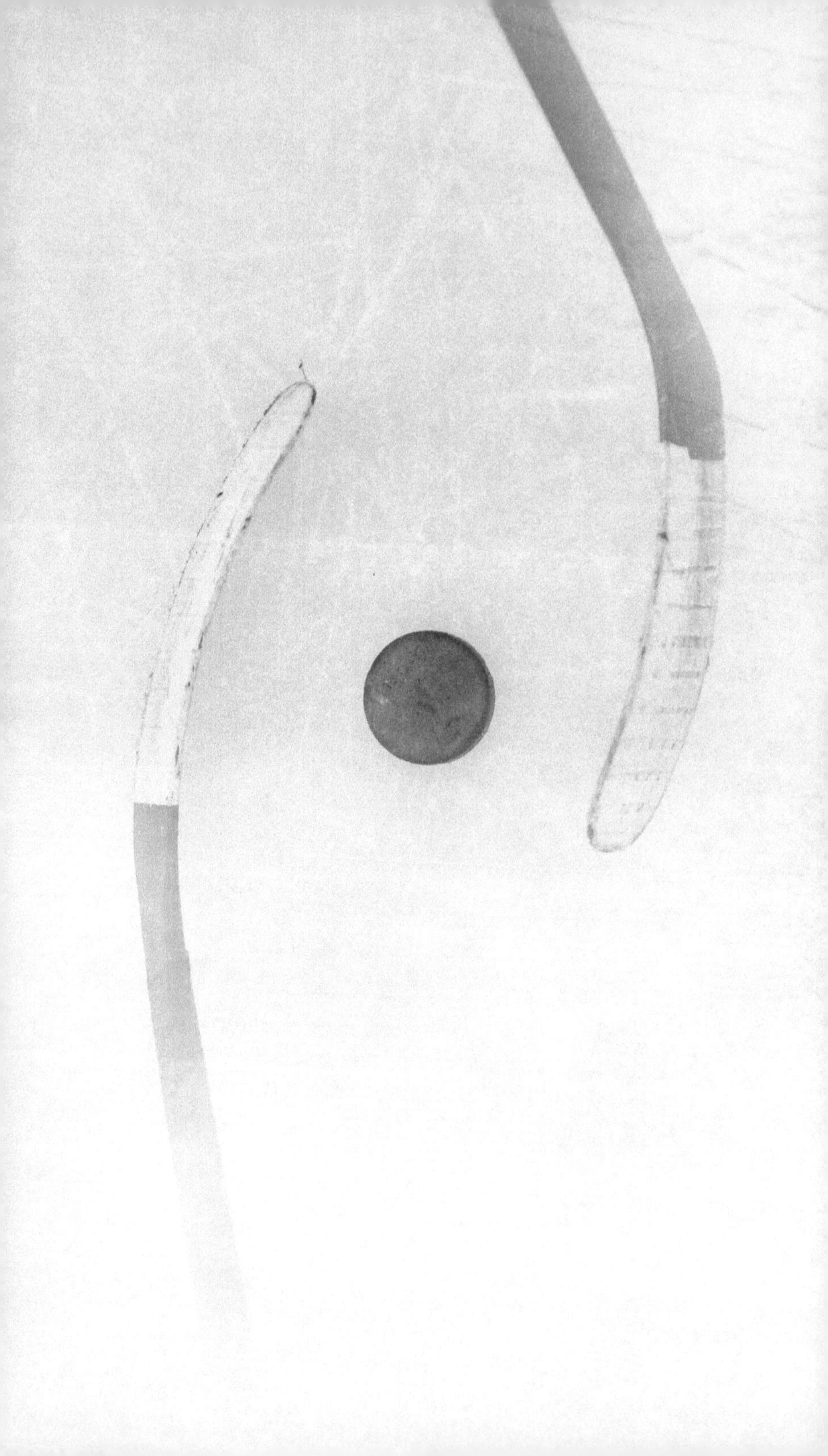

BONUS EPILOGUE
STEELE

The Rail Yard is packed, and the entire place buzzes with the high of our win. Music thumps overhead, glasses clink, and laughter echoes off the exposed brick walls. The giant neon sign that reads "Da Bar" glows electric blue in the far corner, casting a cool hue over everything. It's exactly the kind of over-the-top charm the bar is known for.

Someone's perched a Railers hat on the head of the massive wooden bear statue that stands guard near the dartboards, and River is trying to throw a ring onto its ear.

My gaze meanders to Knox, who's holding court at the far end of the bar, already halfway through a Jack and Coke. Oliver and Jax are doing shots while Laiken shakes his head in mock disapproval.

Zane's also here. He's pressed against his girlfriend, who is currently filming herself kissing him for her followers. They're obnoxious and loud, putting on a show for whoever's watching.

Callie's sitting with Rina and Sloane, sipping a cocktail and pretending like Zane doesn't exist. Rina's the one who dragged her out tonight, claiming that just because her ex is a media whore doesn't mean she shouldn't have fun with her friends.

It's hard to pay attention to any of it when my girl is tucked against me, her body molded to mine like it's where she's always belonged.

Because it is.

And now, she finally understands it too.

It might have taken her a decade to find her way home, but she's here now.

And she's not going anywhere.

Lilah leans into me, her laughter brushing against my jaw. I press a kiss to her temple as my arms tighten around her waist. I can't seem to stop touching her tonight.

Or ever.

A waitress swings by with a notepad in hand. "Another round?"

The guys rattle off their drinks. Beers, bourbon, tequila. Rina orders a margarita on the rocks.

Lilah smiles at the waitress. "Just water for me."

I glance down at her in surprise. "Are you sure, babe? They've got that wine you like. I made sure they stocked it."

She shakes her head. "Nope, water's good. Thanks."

Rina narrows her eyes. "I'm sorry, what's going on here? Are you dying? Detoxing? Or wait—" She gasps dramatically and points her straw at Lilah. "You're pregnant, aren't you?"

Lilah freezes.

The entire table goes silent, heads turning in our direction.

Her gaze flicks around nervously before she nibbles her lower lip. "Actually, yeah. I am."

It takes a second or two for her words to penetrate.

"What?" I turn toward her as my pulse pounds. "Wait a minute. You're pregnant?"

She nods again, more firmly this time. "I just found out."

A grin breaks out across my face as I lift her off her feet and spin her in my arms before gently setting her back down. "Sorry. Shit. I didn't hurt you, did I?"

She laughs, eyes shining bright. "Of course not."

I touch her face, overwhelmed by the swell of emotion rising inside me. "You're really pregnant, baby?"

"I really am," she says.

Laiken claps me on the back. "Welcome to the club, Sanderson."

Knox slams his glass down on the table. "You heard the man! The new dad-to-be is buying a round of drinks!"

The entire bar erupts in cheers.

Unable to help myself, I press my lips to hers.

"Hey!" Oliver calls out. "Isn't that how you two ended up with a baby on board in the first place?"

I just smile against her lips and kiss her again.

Because yeah, that's exactly how it started.

One kiss.

One touch.

One moment that changed everything.

And if I'm lucky, it's only the beginning of forever.

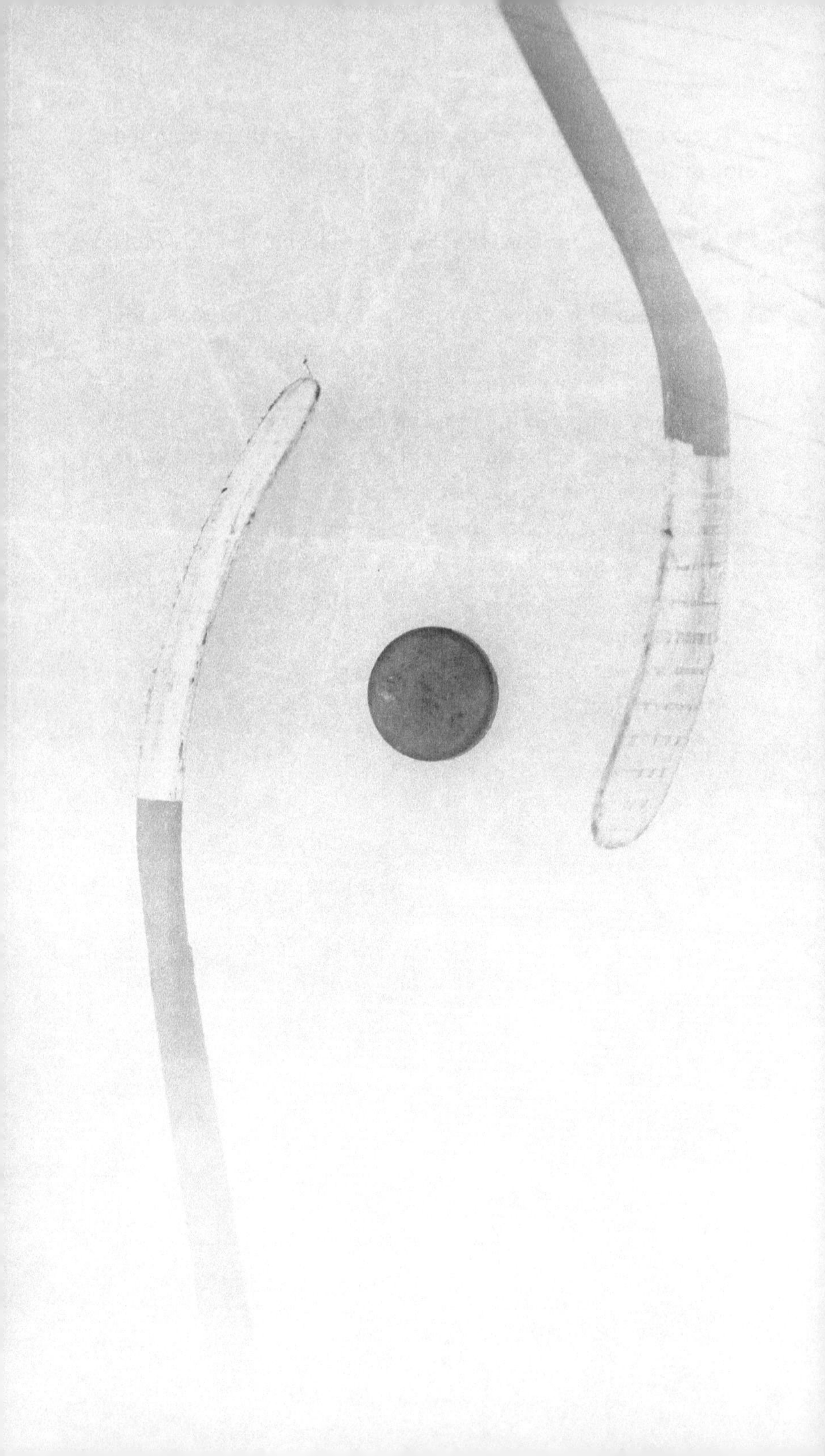

SECOND BONUS EPILOGUE HUGH

I guide Evelyn with a hand pressed lightly to the small of her back through the rooftop terrace at Gold Coast Table.

She mutters, "I still don't understand why I couldn't have taken my own car."

I lean in, letting my lips brush just behind her ear. "Because we're going to be spending a lot more time together. You should get used to it."

She stiffens beneath my touch, her spine drawn tight like a bowstring as she seethes quietly. Evelyn Kingston has fire stitched into her bones. It's one of the things I love about her. Even when I was too damn young and stupid to appreciate it properly.

The hostess leads us to a private corner table with a sweeping view of the lake and skyline. I slide Evelyn's chair out for her, and earn a glare for the effort.

After settling in across from her, I order without bothering to glance at the menu.

"A glass of cabernet for the lady," I tell the waitress, "and a bourbon for me. Neat."

As soon as the server walks away, Evelyn pins me with a look sharp enough to draw blood.

"And what if I wanted something else?"

The smile I give her is slow and deliberate. "Did you?"

She opens her mouth before slamming it shut again.

"I just figured cabernet was your usual. Every time we're at a function, it's what you order. You might not realize it, but I do pay attention."

And have been for years.

Decades.

Her gaze slices to mine, and there's a flicker of emotion in it.

Surprise, maybe.

Or a distant memory?

She drops her gaze to the menu. "Can we just get to the reason you forced me into this dinner, please?" she asks, voice clipped. "I'm not interested in playing games."

When the waitress returns with our drinks, Evelyn takes a long sip of her wine. I match her, watching her carefully over the rim of my crystal tumbler.

She hasn't changed.

Not where it counts.

Her posture is regal. Her composure, flawless. But I know her well enough to see the tension in her narrow shoulders and in the way her fingers are wrapped too tightly around the stem of her glass. She's bracing for a fight. The woman always did like to walk into battle with her chin held high.

"I want to propose a deal," I say, setting down my bourbon.

Her brow arches. "What kind of deal are we talking about?"

"I give you two percent of the shares so you'll own fifty, making us even. Just like it was always supposed to be."

Her eyes narrow. "Just like that? You're going to hand them over?"

A smile tugs at the corners of my mouth. "Not quite." I take another sip of bourbon, savoring it before delivering the blow. "There's a caveat. You'll move in with me until the end of the season."

The laugh she lets loose is sharp and filled with disbelief. "You've got to be kidding me."

"Do I look like I'm joking?"

She blinks, and that's all it takes for the amusement to drain from her face.

"I'm not talking about separate rooms and polite small talk over breakfast," I continue. "You'll live in my space. Sleep in my bed. No pretending."

She stares at me like I've lost my mind.

And maybe I have.

I've spent more than two decades wanting her, wishing I could go back and change everything I did wrong. This isn't about power. It's about proximity. About finally having the woman I never stopped thinking about, close enough to reach again.

She throws back the rest of her wine and sets the glass down with a decisive thud.

As the waitress passes by, she lifts the empty glass without glancing her way. "Another, please." Then she mutters, "I'm going to need it."

She turns her attention back to me with eyes that are sharp and full of fury. "Why are you doing this? If you remember correctly, you're the one who left me. Not the other way around."

I lean forward, elbows on the table, voice low. "I'm not trying to punish you, Evie."

She exhales, the sound unsteady. "Don't you dare call me that."

"It's what I always called you."

"That was over twenty-five years ago."

"I know exactly how long it's been."

The silence swells between us.

"Don't do this," she whispers. "What we had is over. It has been for a long time."

I study her.

The slope of her cheekbones.

The hurt that flickers behind her anger.

The stubborn hope she keeps trying to kill inside herself.

"I don't believe that," I say quietly. "And I don't think you do either."

She lowers her gaze. "If I say no?"

I take a drink of my bourbon. "Then I force you out."

She flinches, as if I've struck her. "You're a real bastard, you know that?"

"Yes, I do."

The waitress returns and sets down her fresh glass of wine. Evelyn wraps her fingers around it like it's a lifeline.

I settle back in my chair. "You've got twenty-four hours to make a decision."

She doesn't look at me.

But she doesn't immediately say no either.

And for the time being, that's more than enough.

Thank you so much for reading Make Me Yours! I hope you enjoyed Lilah and Steele's story as much as I loved writing it!

Did you miss the free prequel for Make Me Yours? Scan the code to get it delivered straight to your inbox!

Ready for the next book in the Chicago Railers Hockey series?
Check out Callie and River's story in Hold Me Tight

Did you know that Bridger and Holland have their own book?
Plus... you can catch a glimpse of Lila and Steele in it!

CAN you really blame me for loving the scandalous texts exposing Bridger Sanderson for the jerk he is? As far as I'm concerned, it's sweet karma for ghosting me after we hooked up two years ago. Cocky, infuriating, and way too gorgeous for his own good, Bridger thinks he's untouchable.

The best part?

He's convinced *I'm* behind the messages.

Ha! I wish.

Unfortunately, my life takes a turn for the worst when Bridger uncovers my secret side hustle. Now he's blackmailing me, forcing me to stick close—we're talking 24/7—until he figures out who's airing his dirty laundry on campus.

I should hate him for dragging me into his mess.

And I do...

Mostly.

Except... the more time we spend together, the harder it becomes to ignore how he looks at me. It's almost like he can see straight through the walls I've built to protect myself. Or how his own guard slips, revealing the cracks in his armor when he thinks I'm not paying attention.

The only person who's ever gotten this close is *ColdAsIce17*, my anonymous confidant on the school chat app. With him, I can totally be myself.

But what happens when the lines blur between the guy I hate and the one I can't stop thinking about?

What happens when I realize... they might be the same person?

TURN THE PAGE FOR AN EXCERPT...

NEVER YOUR GIRL

HOLLAND

A digital chorus of beeps and dings sweeps through Slap Shotz like a wave as the buzzing of my phone coincides with dozens of others. In the split second before I read the message, I catch the shift in the room. The way conversations die mid-sentence, the collective intake of breath, the sudden tension that crackles through the air like static before a storm.

Damn.

Shots fired.

I shouldn't smile.

I really shouldn't.

But there's something darkly satisfying about watching the mighty fall, especially when that fall involves Bridger Sanderson. The same type of texts have been terrorizing him for months now, and no one has been able to trace their source.

Not the tech department.

Not campus security

Not even the chancellor himself.

As far as I'm concerned, Bridger deserves it.

If I didn't believe in karma before, I certainly do now.

"Oh boy," my bestie, Willow, mutters from where she's sitting across from me. "That's not good."

"Says who?" I arch a brow, not bothering to hide my amusement.

Willow tips her head in Bridger's direction. "Probably him."

Near the bar, I can feel Bridger's presence like a physical weight. He's been brooding in the same spot all night, radiating the kind of darkness that makes people give him a wide berth.

Not that I've been watching.

Much.

Our eyes meet across the dim space, and that familiar jolt of awareness hits me like a sucker punch. His gray eyes narrow, and I respond with my middle finger, a gesture that feels childish even as I do it.

"Real mature," Willow says dryly.

"What can I say? I have my moments."

She flicks a glance at him before refocusing her attention on me. Questions and curiosity swim in her blue depths. "Are you ever going to tell me what happened between you two?"

I take a long sip of my root beer to buy time.

Not deterred in the least by my silence, she lifts a brow, prodding me for an answer. Only then do I grudgingly say, "Nope."

"Ahhh. Now we're finally getting somewhere." She holds her hand up. "Stop. We're bordering on information overload. Why must you be so dang chatty? It's *such* a personality defect."

I roll my eyes as a smile trembles around the corners of my lips.

I love Willow to pieces, but she doesn't need to know the

gory details of what happened between Bridger and me. Most of the time, I wish I could scrub them from my memory.

I'm saved from further interrogation when my phone chimes with a work reminder. Thirty minutes until my shift starts at a job my best friend doesn't even know I have.

"I need to head out," I say, already gathering my things.

"Already?" Willow frowns. "We've only been here for an hour."

"Yeah." I tuck an errant strand of hair behind my ear. "You know I can only handle being around these guys in small doses. Unfortunately for you, I've reached my quota of hockey players and drama for one night."

"Want company? We could watch a horror movie like we used to. I'll let you pick the goriest one, even though we both know I'll have nightmares for weeks."

The offer makes my chest ache with nostalgia.

I miss those days.

Now that Willow has a boyfriend, everything has changed.

"Nah, you stay here and celebrate with your man." I force lightness into my tone that I don't feel. "This week has been exhausting. I probably wouldn't make it through the first murder. And that's my favorite part."

"I'm sorry, did you just say murder?" Maverick McKinnon's eyebrows shoot up. "Should someone warn Bridger?"

"Please." I grab my bag, glad for the excuse to shield my expression. "If I were going to murder Bridger Sanderson, I wouldn't be foolish enough to incriminate myself by talking about it. And you'd never find the body. No body, no murder. Isn't that how it works?"

"That's…" Maverick glances at Willow. "Concerning."

"Don't worry," my bestie says, tipping her face toward him with a softness that brings a small, wistful smile to my lips. "We were talking about movies."

He brushes his lips across hers, whispering something that

makes her giggle, and just like that, they're in their own little world. I watch them for a moment, torn between genuine happiness for my best friend and a loneliness that cuts bone-deep. Willow deserves this—deserves *him*—after everything she's been through. But sometimes I miss when it was just us against the world.

My phone buzzes again.

Twenty-five minutes until my shift starts. Randi's face flashes through my mind. My boss could make a drill sergeant cry with one perfectly arched eyebrow.

"I'll see you tomorrow," I say, already backing away.

Willow surfaces from her Maverick-induced haze. "Let me know if you change your mind about that movie."

"I won't." The words come out softer than intended as I turn away to weave through the crowd, dodging familiar faces and wondering, not for the first time, what Willow would say if she knew where I was really going.

Everyone has secrets, but mine feel heavier lately.

"Taking off already?" Garret Akeman materializes in front of me, all cocky grin and practiced charm. "The night's just getting started."

"Yeah." I shift my weight, uncomfortably aware of Bridger's gaze burning into my back from the bar. "I think we both know Slap Shotz isn't my scene."

He glances around with disinterest. "Maybe I'll come with you. We can chill for a while."

I shake my head. "Sorry, not tonight."

"Why not?" His jaw tightens as his eyes sharpen. "You have better plans?"

"As a matter of fact, I do. With my pillow," I tack on to soften the blow. My gaze strays to the bar, only to find the tall defenseman watching us. "I'll catch you later."

"Yeah, sure," Garret mumbles as I slip past him into the night air, sucking in a deep breath that tastes like freedom.

Being around Bridger does this to me. It sets everything inside me spinning until I can barely breathe. Two years later and I still can't shake him, no matter how hard I try.

My ancient Toyota grumbles to life on the third attempt, and I pat the dashboard like a faithful pet. "Just a little longer, baby. Keep it together."

The drive to the Envy Room feels like crossing a border between worlds. Here, I'm not Holland Tate, college student just trying to scrape by. I become someone else entirely.

The club's exterior is understated elegance. It's nothing like the neon-soaked dives people imagine. Inside, Rocco mans the door in his usual suit and ever-present aviators, gold chains glinting around his neck.

"You're cutting it close, Tate," he says with a flash of a smile.

"Yet still technically on time." I glance toward the bar where Randi sits with her laptop, looking like a CEO who took a wrong turn and ended up running a strip club. Her raised eyebrow speaks volumes.

After she took a chance and gave me this opportunity, she's the last person I want to disappoint.

Once inside the club, the dim lighting and thumping music are familiar, almost comforting. A few of the girls wave as I head to the dressing room.

Two years ago, I could never have imagined this place and the people in it would feel like family, but that's exactly what they've become. These girls are more like older sisters. They've given me the necessary skills to not only survive but thrive in this world.

Along with the one that lies outside these walls.

The dressing room is where I shed one identity before slipping into another. Each piece of Lavender Smoke's costume feels like armor, from the black, lacy bustier, the barely-there bottoms, and the silky purple wig that turns me into someone else.

Someone who's untouchable.

Heavy, smoky makeup follows. Since I've never been a girl to wear eyeshadow, blush, or lipstick, it took months of practice to perfect. Thankfully, Jade and Megan were patient teachers. The most fascinating part is watching Holland Tate fade with every stroke of the brush, replaced by the persona I've grown to love over the past year.

It's what allows me to step out of my comfort zone and onto the stage three nights a week. Holland Tate wouldn't be caught dead strutting around and taking off her clothes for a bunch of horny men.

Lavender Smoke, on the other hand, has zero issues with that.

For a price.

One that pays my tuition, rent, and groceries in full every single month.

"Looking good," Megan says, adjusting her own wig beside me.

My phone buzzes with a message from *ColdAsIce17*, and something in my chest loosens. It's ironic that the person who knows me best is someone I've never met.

COLDASICE17

Just wanted to check in and see how you're doing.

A smile tugs at my lips as I type back.

ME

I'm good. Just hustling for a living. How about you?

COLDASICE17

The usual. Ready to run away from it all yet?

My fingers hover over the keys. With him, I don't have to pretend.

ME

> Every day. But someone's gotta make sure the
> bills get paid, right?

The banter is easy, our messages laced with sarcasm, but there's a warmth that lies beneath the surface that keeps me coming back for more.

"Holland!" Jade's voice cuts through my thoughts. "You're up in five."

I shove my phone in my bag, taking one last look in the mirror. Holland Tate stares back at me for a moment before disappearing completely, replaced by someone stronger, someone who doesn't flinch when the music starts.

Time to give them a show.

Check out Never Your Girl now!

HATE TO LOVE YOU

"**D**ude, I thought you'd be back earlier." Cooper, one of my roommates, grins as I walk through the front door. There's a half-naked chick straddling his lap. "We had to get this party started without you." He shrugs as if he's just taken one for the team. "It couldn't be helped."

I snort as my gaze travels around the living room of the house we rent a few blocks off campus. Even though there are only four of us on the lease, our place seems to be a crash pad for half the team. By the looks of the beer bottles strewn around, they've been at it for a while. I'm seriously thinking about charging some of these assholes rent.

Although, I guess if I were stuck in a shoebox of a dorm, I'd be desperate for a way out, too. I played juniors straight out of high school for two years before coming in as a freshman at twenty. I skipped dorm living and went straight to renting a place nearby. There was no way I was bunking down with a bunch of random eighteen-year-olds who'd never lived away from home. Not to mention, having an RA up my ass telling me what I could and couldn't do.

That sounds about as much fun as ripping duct tape off my balls.

Which is, I might add, the complete opposite of fun. Hazing sucks. And for future reference, you don't rip duct tape off your balls, you carefully cut it away with a steady hand while mother-fucking the entire team.

My other two roommates, Luke Anderson and Sawyer Stevens, are hunched at the edge of the couch, battling it out in an intense game of NHL. Their thumbs are jerking the controllers in lightning-quick movements, and their eyeballs are fastened to the seventy-inch HD screen hanging across the room.

I can only shake my head. Every time they play, it's like a freaking National Championship is at stake.

I arch a brow as the girl on Cooper's lap reaches around and unhooks her bra, dropping it to the floor. Apparently, she doesn't mind if there's an audience. Cooper's lazy grin stretches as his fingers zero in on her nips.

I'd love to say this scene isn't typical for a Sunday night, but I'd be lying through my teeth. Usually, it's much worse.

Deking out Luke with some impressive video game puck handling skills, Sawyer says, "Grab a beer, bro. You can take over for Luke after I make him cry again like a little bitch."

"Fuck you," Luke grumbles.

I glance at the score. Luke is getting his ass handed to him on a silver platter, and he knows it.

"Sure." Sawyer smirks. "Maybe later. But I should warn you, you're not really my type. I like a dude who's packing a little more meat than you."

My lips twitch as I drop my duffle to the floor.

"Hey, you see that bullshit text from Coach?" Cooper asks from between the girl's tits.

I groan, hoping I didn't miss anything important while I was out of town for the weekend. I'm already under contract with the Milwaukee Mavericks. My dad and I flew there to meet with the coaching staff. I also got to hang with a few of the defensive players. Saturday night was freaking crazy. Next season is going to rock.

"Nah, didn't see it," I say. "What's going on?"

"Practice times have changed," Cooper continues, all the while playing with the girl's body. "We're now at six o'clock in the morning and seven in the evening."

Fuck me. He's starting two-a-days already?

"You think he's just screwing around with us?" I wouldn't put it past Coach Lang. I don't think he has anything better to do than lie awake at night, dreaming up new ways to torture us. The guy is a real hard-ass.

Then again, that's why we're here.

But six in the morning...that sucks. Between school and hockey practice, I already feel like I don't get enough sleep. And it's only September. That means I'll need to be up and out the door by five to make it to the rink, get dressed, and be on the ice by six. By the time eleven o'clock at night rolls around, I'll fall into bed an exhausted heap.

Sawyer shrugs, not looking particularly put out by the time change.

Cooper pops the nipple out of his mouth and fixes his glassy-eyed gaze on me. "Can't you have your dad talk some freaking sense into the guy?"

Luke grumbles under his breath, "I can barely make it to the seven o'clock practice on time."

"Nope." I shake my head. I'd do just about anything for these guys, except run to my father with anything related to hockey. Coach and my dad go way back. They both played for the Detroit Redwings. I've known the man my entire life. He helped me lace up my first pair of Bauers. So, you'd think he'd have a soft spot for me. Maybe take it easy on me.

Yeah...fat chance of that happening.

If anything, he comes down on me like a ton of bricks *because* of our personal relationship. I think Lang doesn't want any of the guys to feel like he's playing favorites.

Mission accomplished, dude.

No one would ever accuse him of that.

"Then prepare to haul ass at the butt crack of dawn, my friend." With that, Cooper turns his attention elsewhere, attacking the girl's mouth.

Luke eyes them for a moment before yelling, "Hey, you gonna take that shit to the bedroom or are we all being treated to a free show?"

Not bothering to come up for air, Cooper ignores the question.

Luke shakes his head and focuses his attention on making a comeback. Or at least knocking Sawyer's avatar on its ass. "Guess that means we should make some popcorn."

I pick up my duffel and hoist it over my shoulder, deciding to head upstairs for a while. I love hanging with these guys, but I'm not feeling it at the moment.

"Hi, Brody." A lush blonde slips her arms around me and presses her ample cleavage against my chest. "I was hoping you'd show up."

Given the fact that this is my house, the chances of that happening were extremely high.

I stare down into her big green eyes.

"Hey." She looks familiar. I do a quick mental search, trying to produce a name, but only come up with blanks.

Which probably means I haven't slept with her recently.

When it comes to the ladies, I've come up with an algorithm that I've perfected over the last three years. It's simple, yet foolproof. I never screw the same girl more than three times in a six-month period. If you do, you run the risk of entering into the murky territory of a quasi-relationship or a friends-with-benefits situation. I'm not looking for any attachments at this point.

Even casual ones.

I'm at Whitmore to earn a degree and prepare for the pros. I'm focused on getting bigger, faster, and stronger. The NHL is no place for pussies. If you can't hack it, the league will chew you up and spit you out before you can blink your eyes. I have no intention of allowing that to happen. I've worked too hard to crash and burn at this point.

Or get distracted.

In a surprisingly bold move, Blondie slides her hand from my chest to my package and gives it a firm squeeze to let me know she means business.

I have no doubts that if I asked her to drop to her knees and suck me off in front of all these people, she would do it in a heartbeat. Other than a thong, the girl grinding away on Cooper's lap is naked.

My first year playing juniors, when a girl offered to have no-strings-attached-sex, I'd thought I'd hit the flipping jackpot. Less than five minutes later, I'd blown my load and was ready for round two. Fast forward five years, and I don't even blink at a chick who's willing to drop her panties within minutes of me walking through the door. It happens far too often for it to be considered a novelty.

Which is just plain sad.

When I was in high school, I jumped at the chance to dip my wick.

Now?

Not so much.

It's like being fed a steady diet of steak and lobster. Sure, it's delicious the first couple of days. Maybe even a full week. You can't help but greedily devour every single bite and then lick your fingertips afterward. But, believe it or not, even steak and lobster become mundane.

Most guys, no matter what their age, would give their left nut to be in my skates.

To have their pick of any girl. Or, more often than not, *girls*.

And here I am...limp dick in hand.

Actually, limp dick in *her* hand.

Sex has become something I do to take the edge off when I'm feeling stressed. It's my version of a relaxation technique. For fuck's sake, I'm twenty-three years old. I'm in the sexual prime of my life. I should be ecstatic when any girl wants to spread her legs for me. What I shouldn't be is bored. And I sure as hell shouldn't be mentally running through the drills we'll be doing when I lead a captain's practice.

I pry her fingers from my junk and shake my head. "Sorry, I've got some shit to take care of."

And that shit would be school. I have forty pages of reading that needs to be finished up by tomorrow morning.

Blondie pouts and bats her mascara-laden lashes.

"Maybe later?" she coos in a baby voice.

Fuck. That is such a turnoff.

Why do chicks do that?

No, seriously. It's a legitimate question. Why do they do that? It's like nails on a chalkboard. I'm tempted to answer back in a ridiculous, lispy-sounding voice.

But I don't.

I'm not that big of an asshole.

Plus, she might be into it.

Then I'd be screwed. I envision us cooing at each other in baby voices for the rest of the night and almost shudder.

"Maybe," I say noncommittally. Although I'm not going to lie, that toddler voice has killed any chance for a later hookup. But I'm smart enough not to tell her that. Chances are high that she'll end up finding another hockey player to latch on to and forget all about me. Because let's face it, that's what she's here for.

A little dick from a guy who skates with a stick.

Just to be sure, I run my eyes over the length of her again.

Toddler voice aside, she's got it going on.

And yet, that banging body is doing absolutely nothing for me.

Which is troublesome. I almost want to take her upstairs just to prove to myself that everything is in proper working order. But I won't.

As I hit the first step, Cooper breaks away from his girl. "WTF, McKinnon? Where you going?" He waves a hand around the room. "Can't you see we're in the middle of entertaining?"

"I'll leave you to take care of our guests," I say, trudging up the staircase.

"Well, if you insist," he slurs happily.

My bedroom is at the end of the hall, away from the noise of the first floor. As a general rule, no one is allowed on the second floor except for the guys who live here. I pull out my key and unlock the door before stepping inside.

My duffel gets tossed in the corner before I open my Managerial Finance book. I thought I'd have a chance to plow through some of the reading over the weekend, but my dad and I were on the go the entire time. Meeting people from the Milwaukee organization, hitting a team party, checking out a few condos near the lakefront. Just getting the general lay of the land. On the plane ride home, I had every intention of being productive, but ended up sacking out once we hit cruising altitude.

Three hours later, there's a knock on the door. Normally an interruption would piss me off, but after slogging through thirty pages, my eyes have glazed over, and I'm fighting to stay awake. This material is mind-numbingly boring, and that's not helping matters.

"It's open," I call out, expecting Cooper to try cajoling me back downstairs.

When that guy's shitfaced, he wants everyone else to be just as hammered as he is. I've never seen anyone put away alcohol the way he does. It's almost as impressive as it is scary. And yet, he's somehow able to wake up for morning practice bright-eyed and bushy-tailed like he wasn't just wasted six hours ago. Someone from the biology department really needs to do a case study on him, 'cause that shit just ain't normal.

When I suck down alcohol like that, the next morning I'm like a newborn colt on the ice who can't keep his legs under him.

It's not a pretty sight. Which is why I don't do it. Been there, done that. Moving on.

The door swings open to reveal Blondie-With-The-Toddler-Voice. And she's not alone. She's brought a friend.

I raise my brows in interest as they step inside the room.

In the three hours since I've seen her, Blondie has managed to lose most of her clothing. The brunette she's with appears to be in the same predicament. They stand in lacy bras and barely-there thongs with their hands entwined.

My gaze roves over them appreciatively.

How could it not?

Their tummies are flat and toned. Hips are nicely rounded. Tits jiggle enticingly as they saunter toward the bed where I'm currently sprawled.

I should be a man of steel over here. I haven't gotten laid in three weeks. Which is almost unheard of. I haven't gone that long without sex since I first started having it.

But there's nothing.

Not even a twitch.

Which begs the question—What the hell is wrong with me?

It must be the stress of school and the skating regimen I'm on. Even though I'm already under contract with Milwaukee and don't have to worry about the NHL draft later this year, I'm still under a lot of pressure to perform this season.

National Championships don't bring themselves home.

I'd be concerned that I have some serious erectile dysfunction issues happening except there's one chick who gets me hard every time I lay eyes on her. Rather ironically, she wants nothing to do with me. I think she'd claw my eyes out if I laid one solitary finger on her.

Actually, all I have to do is stare in her direction, and she bares her teeth at me.

Maybe these girls are exactly what I need to relieve some of my pent-up stress. It certainly can't hurt.

Decision made, I slam my finance book closed and toss it to the floor where it lands with a loud thud. I fold my arms behind my head and smile at the girls in silent invitation.

And the rest, shall we say, is history.

Check out Hate to Love You now!

MORE BOOKS BY JENNIFER SUCEVIC

<u>Chicago Railers Hockey</u>

Make Me Yours

Hold Me Tight

Show Me Forever

<u>The Campus Series</u> (football)

Campus Player (Demi & Rowan)

Campus Heartthrob (Sydney & Brayden)

Campus Flirt (Sasha & Easton)

Campus Hottie (Elle & Carson)

Campus God (Brooke & Crosby)

Campus Legend (Lola & Asher)

<u>Western Wildcats Hockey</u>

Hate You Always (Juliette & Ryder)

Love You Never (Carina & Ford)

Always My Girl (Viola & Madden)

Dare You to Love Me (Stella & Riggs)

Never Mine to Hold (Fallyn & Wolf)

Never Say Never (Britt & Colby)

Mine to Take (Willow & Maverick)

Break my Heart (Ava & Hayes)

Never Your Girl (Holland & Bridger)

<u>Parent Books for the Western Wildcats</u>

Hate to Love You (Hockey) (Natalie & Brody)

Just Friends (Hockey) (Emerson & Reed)

The Breakup Plan (Hockey) (Whitney & Gray)

<u>The Barnett Bulldogs</u> (football)

King of Campus (Ivy & Roan)

Friend Zoned (Violet & Sam)

One Night Stand (Gia & Liam)

If You Were Mine (Claire & JT)

<u>The Claremont Cougars</u> (football)

Heartless Summer (Skye & Hunter)

Heartless (Skye & Hunter)

Shameless (Poppy & Mason)

<u>Hawthorne Prep Series</u> (bully/football)

King of Hawthorne Prep (Summer & Kingsley)

Queen of Hawthorne Prep (Summer & Kingsley)

Prince of Hawthorne Prep (Delilah & Austin)

Princess of Hawthorne Prep (Delilah & Austin)

<u>The Next Door Duet</u> (football)

The Girl Next Door (Mia & Beck)

The Boy Next Door (Alyssa & Colton)

<u>What's Mine Duet</u> (Suspense)

Protecting What's Mine (Grace & Matteo)

Claiming What's Mine (Sofia & Roman)

<u>Stay Duet</u> (hockey)

Stay (Cassidy & Cole)

Don't Leave (Cassidy & Cole)

<u>**Standalone Football**</u>

Love to Hate You (Daisy & Carter)

<u>Collections</u>

Claremont Cougars

The Barnett Bulldogs

The Football Hotties Collection

The Hockey Hotties Collection

The Next Door Duet

ABOUT THE AUTHOR

Jennifer Sucevic is a USA Today bestselling author who has captivated readers worldwide with her sizzling new adult romances. With over thirty novels to her name, her stories of love, heartbreak, and swoon-worthy heroes have been translated into six languages, including German, Italian, and Portuguese, making her a truly global voice in the genre. Armed with a bachelor's degree in history and a master's in educational psychology from the University of Wisconsin-Milwaukee, Jen initially worked as a high school counselor before embracing her passion for writing full-time. Her background in psychology lends a depth to her characters that resonates with fans everywhere.

When she's not crafting irresistible love stories, Jen enjoys biking along scenic trails and soaking up the sun at the beach. She currently resides in Michigan with her family, where she continues to dream up heroes and heroines you'll want to fall in love with again and again.

If you would like to receive regular updates regarding new releases, please subscribe to her newsletter here-
Jennifer Sucevic Newsletter

Or contact Jen through email, at her website, or on Facebook.
sucevicjennifer@gmail.com

Want to join her reader group? Do it here -)
J Sucevic's Book Boyfriends | Facebook

Social media links-
https://www.tiktok.com/@jennifersucevicauthor
www.jennifersucevic.com
https://www.instagram.com/jennifersucevicauthor
https://www.facebook.com/jennifer.sucevic
Amazon.com: Jennifer Sucevic: Books, Biography, Blog,
Audiobooks, Kindle
Jennifer Sucevic Books - BookBub

www.ingramcontent.com/pod-product-compliance
Lightning Source LLC
Chambersburg PA
CBHW061044310726
48969CB00004B/1079